BREACH OF
ETHICS

Previously published Worldwide Mystery titles by
SHARON ST. GEORGE

DUE FOR DISCARD
CHECKED OUT

BREACH OF ETHICS

SHARON ST. GEORGE

W RLDWIDE®

TORONTO • NEW YORK • LONDON
AMSTERDAM • PARIS • SYDNEY • HAMBURG
STOCKHOLM • ATHENS • TOKYO • MILAN
MADRID • WARSAW • BUDAPEST • AUCKLAND

This book is dedicated to my wonderful sons, Kenneth and Scott Redden, with a mother's pride and all of my love.

Recycling programs
for this product may
not exist in your area.

Breach of Ethics

A Worldwide Mystery/January 2019

First published by Camel Press, an imprint of Epicenter Press, Inc.

ISBN-13: 978-1-335-45524-6

Printed in U.S.A.

ACKNOWLEDGMENTS

Heartfelt thanks to my multi-talented assistant, Jennifer Michelle, who proofreads early drafts, listens while I brainstorm plots, rides shotgun on road trips, and even helps me train my llamas. To George Souza, who once again offered his expertise with police matters, and to Scott Redden, who keeps me straight about jujitsu. Both of them also contributed critical advice about construction that was essential to the story. My gratitude goes to members of Sisters in Crime who work in the medical profession for offering their expertise in post-surgical care of a fragile young patient. Thanks to all of my talented and savvy critique partners: Chloe Winston, Laura Hernandez, Ellen Jellison, and Vickie Linnet. And, of course, my wholehearted gratitude to Jennifer McCord and Catherine Treadgold at Camel Press for the finest editing any writer could hope for, and for their belief in the Aimee Machado Mysteries.

ONE

THE LAST THING I expected to be doing at a Monday morning meeting of the Timbergate Medical Center's Ethics Committee was breaking up a fist fight.

Setting up the meeting was my responsibility, thanks to a recent promotion. Originally hired as TMC's health sciences librarian, I now had an ID badge that read: *Aimee Machado, Director of Library, Continuing Education, and Ethical Affairs*. Nowhere did my job description say *Referee*.

Dr. Gavin Lowe threw the first punch, but my boss, Hospital Administrator Jared Quinn, countered with a left hook. It connected with Lowe's chin and knocked his lanky frame backward across the conference table, scattering agendas and sloshing coffee cups.

Lowe regained his footing and started to swing again, but I caught his arm and took him to the floor with a wristlock. With his free hand, he tried to loosen my grip, so I applied more pressure. He wouldn't be able to hold a scalpel for quite a while if I had to break his wrist. At that point he quit struggling. Meanwhile, Committee Chair Sybil Snyder called for a motion to adjourn. After a hasty vote, Dr. Snyder and the rest of the physicians bolted from the room.

Moments later two husky security guards arrived, registering dual expressions of surprise at the sight of a man as big as Lowe restrained by a petite Eurasian woman. Understandable, since they didn't know about my black belt in jujitsu. The guards took Dr. Lowe off my hands, secured his arms behind his back, and waited for Quinn's orders.

I waited too, watching blood trickle from the side of Quinn's mouth down onto his white shirt collar. Even bloody and disheveled, he was easy on the eyes, with dark hair, a strong jaw and a smile that could make a nun blush. I resisted the urge to clean the blood off his face. Instead, I handed him a paper napkin.

"Mr. Quinn," one of the guards said, "what would you like us to do here?"

Quinn worked his jaw, winced, and addressed Dr. Lowe. "Well, Gavin, do we call the police?"

"That's up to you," Lowe said, "but I'd prefer to settle this privately. Neither of us needs that kind of publicity."

Quinn turned to the guards. "Thanks, fellas. You can go." The guards shrugged and left the room. I offered to leave, but Quinn told me to stay. He pushed the conference room door closed.

Lowe glared at Quinn. "I'm still pissed as hell, Jared. How dare you imply that I was bribed?"

"Gavin, I didn't imply anything of the sort. I simply asked you to tell the committee why you ordered a blood transfusion for Hector Korba's granddaughter against her mother's clearly expressed wishes."

"Because she would have died without it," Lowe said. "For God's sake, Jared, I wasn't bending to pressure from Korba, and I sure as hell wasn't expecting anything in return for saving his granddaughter's life. The girl's mother is a gullible dupe, and the stepfather with his trumped-up pseudo-vegan religion is a dangerous charlatan. The diet they were imposing on that child nearly killed her."

"Then your reasons for the transfusion need to be documented in the committee's minutes. Everyone knows Hector Korba is president of the TMC Governing Board, not to mention he's rich as Croesus. It won't look good for you or TMC if the mother files a complaint."

"Let her. I had her kid in the OR with a burst appendix. I did what I had to do."

"And this committee probably would have agreed, but I wish you'd tried to consult at least one of us before you went ahead with that transfusion."

"There wasn't time. She was bleeding and chronically anemic. I was doing my damned job."

"And I'm doing mine." Quinn dabbed at his bloody mouth with the napkin. "Trying to keep all of us out of court."

"Not by throwing me under the bus. If you can't back up your medical staff, you might want to look for another job."

"Let's take this down a notch, Gavin. I'm employed at the discretion of the governing board, not the medical staff. If you have a complaint about me, take it there."

"Ideal, since that's Hector Korba's bailiwick and I just saved his granddaughter's life. You think you can trump that?" Lowe smoothed his graying brown hair and squared his shoulders.

"I'll take my chances." Quinn picked up his briefcase, signaling he'd had enough. Witnessing their hostile exchange made me squirm. I raised an eyebrow at Quinn.

Quinn looked at Lowe. "Well, Gavin? What's it going to be? Do you want to have me fired, or shall we get back to work?"

"Aw, hell." Lowe looked down at his hand, wiggling his fingers, and then glanced up at Quinn. "You didn't break my hand with your damned jaw, so if it's okay with you, I'll perform the surgery I have scheduled for this afternoon."

"Fine, but first have someone in the ER evaluate your hand. Make sure they check that wrist, too." Quinn glanced at me with a hint of amusement, earning him a malevolent glare from Lowe.

"You'd better hope your little bodyguard didn't injure my wrist."

"I don't want to hear anything from you that sounds like a threat," Quinn said. "If you're cleared to operate, we'll forget this happened and we'll all get back to work."

Lowe suddenly seemed bewildered. He sank into a chair and shook his head. "Jared, I'm sorry. I feel like an ass for losing it like that. It just pissed the hell out of me. I shouldn't have to explain why I saved that little girl. She's not just a rich man's granddaughter, she's a piano prodigy with an incredible future. Have you heard her play?"

"I have. It's an amazing experience."

"Then you know why I couldn't let her die. I wouldn't let any child die if it's within my power to save her, but Natasha Korba's gift is nothing short of miraculous."

"I know, Gavin. That's why I'm not pressing this. But if there's something more going on with you, something causing enough stress to make you act out this way, we should talk about it."

"Thanks, but it's nothing I can't handle." Lowe frowned at the coffee-drenched agendas on the conference table and turned to me. "Sorry about the mess." He left the room.

Quinn closed the door behind him and said, "Aimee, you handled this situation far beyond anything in your job description. If Lowe gives you any trouble, I want to hear about it. Understood?"

"Understood." I sighed and stared out the window at the overcast February sky.

TWO

UNTIL MY PROMOTION, I had been in charge of the hospital's library and the medical staff's continuing education programs, working under the supervision of Dr. Vane Beardsley, the former chief of staff. His retirement resulted in my being designated head of a new department. The new title combined my former duties with the added responsibility of "facilitating all medical staff business related to ethics issues." Although I conferred as needed with the doctors who chaired the Continuing Medical Education Committee and the Ethics Committee, I no longer reported to a medical staff supervisor. I answered directly to Jared Quinn, which was reason enough to step in with a jujitsu hold when Dr. Lowe tried to clean Quinn's clock.

After I gathered up the soggy agendas and apologized to the Dietary Department staff for the mess, I stopped by the Medical Affairs Office to ask Cleo Cominoli for her take on the dust-up in the conference room. As Director of Medical Staff Services, she'd spent several years leading the bulk of TMC's monthly medical staff meetings.

Pushing fifty, but still a curvy and glamorous brunette, Cleo was an invaluable mentor but also a good friend. The vivacious Italian had finally walked down the aisle with her darling Sig Modaresi a month after he recovered from prostate surgery with a clean bill of health. Everyone at work was relieved that she kept her maiden name. To her colleagues, she would always be the ageless and lively Cleo Cominoli.

I sat in the chair opposite her desk and gave her the nutshell version of the incident.

When I was finished, she dropped her half-moon glasses on her desk and grinned. "Wow, your first Ethics Committee and you took down Gavin Lowe? Wish I'd seen that."

I squirmed in my chair. "It wasn't pretty—it was awkward and embarrassing—but that's not why I stopped by. What I wanted to know is whether you've ever seen blows exchanged in one of your meetings."

Folding her arms, she gave it a moment's thought. "Only the verbal kind," she said finally, "but believe me, when you work in a room filled with colossal egos revved up on caffeine, anything can happen."

I leaned forward. "Has Lowe ever acted out in one of your committees?"

She replied quickly, "No! In fact, he was one of my favorite docs until about a year ago when he started missing mandatory committee meetings. And he's hard on the OR nurses these days, swearing and throwing things during surgeries." She hesitated for a moment. "The truth is, he's become a real horse's patootie."

Curious, I prompted Cleo for more. "Are you saying a physical attack on Jared Quinn takes it to a new level?"

She nodded vigorously. "You bet. I've never heard of him losing it like that. Sounds like being asked to justify his actions in the Korba girl's case really set him off." She cocked her head. "You've heard about her, haven't you? How she began playing piano when she was only three years old? She's ten now, and being compared to Mozart." Cleo stood and put her coffee in the microwave.

"I knew *of* her," I said, "but until I came to work here, I didn't realize her grandfather was on TMC's governing board."

"*President* of the board," Cleo said, sipping her coffee and leaning against the desk. "Anyone who has ever met Hector Korba knows he's devoted to Natasha, and to guiding her career. Korba's already booking regional appearances for her. She played a guest solo with the Sawyer County Symphony last month." She took her seat again.

"I attended that one with my grandmother. Isn't Korba a member of that orchestra?"

"Korba plays bass clarinet. Sig says he's been with them for about two years." Cleo's husband, Sig, played tuba with the orchestra.

"Imagine how devastated Dr. Lowe would be if he'd lost that girl on his operating table," I said. "I can almost understand his lashing out at the meeting."

Cleo put her half-moon glasses back on and gave me a pointed look over the rims. "Lowe's medical career would have been finished. Korba would have seen to it."

"So how do you think I should handle the minutes? Do I document the incident in vivid detail?"

She shrugged. "Let your committee chair decide. Isn't that Dr. Snyder?" Cleo's mind was an encyclopedia of every doctor on the medical staff and which ones served on what committees.

"That's right, but she adjourned the meeting and left the room before Quinn and Lowe made peace."

"Doesn't matter." Cleo said. "All that goes in the

minutes is what happened before the meeting was adjourned."

"That doesn't seem fair to either Quinn or Lowe."

She tapped her pen on the desk for emphasis. "Maybe not, but you have to stick to your guns when it comes to committee minutes. Let all of them know they can't manipulate you. Remember that when you talk to Snyder."

I couldn't leave without asking her about married life.

With a glowing smile, she said, "It's been two months, and the honeymoon isn't over. I can't believe I waited so long. If you ever decide to tie the knot with that hottie of yours, you'll see what I mean. It's different when you're married."

"Nick and I are still a long way from taking that step."

Cleo got up and walked around her desk to pull me into a hug. "Life is short, sweetie. Don't wait too long."

I walked back to the library thinking about Nick Alexander. Everyone assumed that all I had to do was say the word and he'd supply the ring. It wasn't that simple.

Nick's job as a private pilot for billionaire philanthropist Buck Sawyer required him to spend a lot of time with his co-pilot, Rella Olstad, who was almost as different from me as night is from day. Despite the lack of height in my gene pool, I had managed to grow to five feet and four inches and had jet-black hair and deep brown eyes, inherited from my Portuguese father and Chinese mother. In contrast, the Nordic beauty was not only blue-eyed and blond like Nick, she was a former fighter pilot who also happened to be Nick's former girlfriend.

When she was hired, I'd tried to take the high road, but an incident six months ago in Paris had sorely tested my trust in Nick and caused a near-fatal rupture in our relationship. Eventually we had talked it out and agreed to start over as friends with options. Reminding myself that everyone has a dating history, I'd almost succeeded in putting Nick and Rella's former relationship into perspective when Buck decided to spend December and January exploring investment opportunities in Europe and Asia. Buck hadn't needed both pilots while he was abroad, so only Nick had to stay overseas, not only to fly Buck from one appointment to another, but also to act as his personal assistant.

Nick's sporadic phone calls and texts from foreign locations were brief and cryptic, which he explained by saying Buck's investment deals involved a need for secrecy. Whatever the reason, they were a poor substitute for the kind of communication we needed to get back on solid ground as a couple.

I set aside thoughts about my personal life and put in a call to Dr. Snyder's office. She came on the line almost immediately.

"Aimee? Sybil Snyder, here. Are you calling about this morning's meeting?"

"Yes. I have a question about the minutes."

"I understand." There was a slight pause. "Here's the thing. I'm backed up with patients—this stomach bug that's going around. Why don't you draft the minutes and I'll stop by later? What time are you off?"

"Around five, if nothing comes up."

"Then I'll see you at four thirty. Does that work for you?"

I told her it did. She went back to her patients and I tackled a draft of the minutes, weighing how to document the drama over Natasha Korba's transfusion. I decided on an abbreviated version of the truth and avoided mention of the altercation.

Dr. Gavin Lowe and Administrator Jared Quinn entered into a vigorous discussion regarding the blood transfusion of patient Natasha Korba. No conclusions were reached by committee and no actions were taken. The meeting was adjourned at 7:40 a.m. by Dr. Sybil Snyder, Ethics Committee Chair. I saved the draft, and for the rest of the morning tackled the day's busywork in the library.

My regular volunteer, Lola Rampley, was celebrating her eighty-second birthday, so I had arranged a little lunchtime party for her in the library, inviting the other volunteers on duty. Jared Quinn stopped in, always an enthusiastic supporter of our auxiliary members. I had to admire the man. Even after taking a punch to the chin four hours earlier, he wore a blood-free shirt and a bandage on his face, which he explained away as a slip while shaving.

We had chipped in to get Lola two tickets to Marty Stockwell's upcoming hometown concert. My invaluable snowy-haired helper was a die-hard fan of our resident country music icon. Quinn did the honors, presenting her with the tickets and Marty's latest CD. I saw Lola's eyes well up with tears for just a moment, but she caught herself before they spilled, and hurried to cut generous slices of her cake.

I noticed Quinn didn't try to eat cake. He was having enough trouble talking without wincing, and I suspected his jaw was hurting like a son-of-a-gun. I gestured toward my desk and mouthed, *pain pills?* He shook his head, pointed to his mouth and held up four fingers. He was already loaded up.

The cake disappeared down to the last crumb, and the volunteers left, including Lola, whose shift was over. She walked out of the library on the arm of Oslo Swanson, an elderly gentleman volunteer. I suspected he might be her date to the Stockwell concert. From the crestfallen face of one of the other male volunteers, I could see that someone else had hoped to be Lola's chosen escort. *Love triangles can be problematic at any age*, I thought.

Quinn and I were left alone in the library with the specter of the morning meeting hanging over us. I waited for him to either bring it up or be on his way.

"So, have you had time to write up this morning's minutes?" He got the words out, but the way he moved his jaw reminded me of a ventriloquist.

"I have a draft," I said. "Dr. Snyder is coming by later to have a look."

"Want to let me see what you have so far?" The slurring got worse each time he spoke.

His request posed a problem. There was a fine line between my loyalty to Quinn, who signed my paycheck, and my loyalty to the doctors who served on the medical staff committees. Quinn was an ex-officio member of the Ethics Committee, and I wasn't sure he had the same rights as full members. I knew for sure that it wasn't his place to dictate what went into the minutes. That was Dr. Snyder's job. I hesitated for an awkward moment.

"Well?" Quinn said.

"I'd rather wait until Dr. Snyder comes by."

"She left before Lowe and I made peace. She doesn't know the whole story."

"But that happened after she adjourned the meeting. It won't be in the minutes."

Quinn formed a word on his lips that looked like

it started with an F, but it must have hurt, because he winced. Instead he said one that started with an S, making me wonder if I would ever get up the nerve to start a swear jar.

"I'm sorry," I said, "I asked Cleo about the minutes, and she said I was to include only what happened up until the adjournment."

"You told Cleo?"

"I sort of had to. When you promoted me, you said to use Cleo as a mentor, and I needed her advice. She's not going to spread it around."

"I know. And you stepped in just in time, but it's still damned embarrassing. Those security guards probably had a good laugh later. What do you suppose they thought when they saw you sitting on Lowe with his arm twisted behind his back?"

"They probably thought you were rescued by a woman, but so what? Someone had to do something. Everyone else sat there like they'd been turned to stone."

"True, but they don't have your trained reflexes, and I'm pretty damned sure none of them hold black belts in any form of martial arts."

My phone rang, the noise jarring both of us. Quinn waited while I answered. It was Dr. Snyder's appointment clerk letting me know the doctor couldn't meet with me after all. She had a patient who needed to be worked in at four thirty. I said we could reschedule and hung up without explaining to Quinn.

"Was there anything else you wanted?" I asked.

Quinn cautiously touched his hand to his cheek. "Yes. I wanted to thank you."

"You're welcome, but you know he caught you with a sucker punch."

Quinn smiled. "No need to protect my male ego, but I happen to agree. If he tries a stunt like that again, I'll be ready for him."

His comment was not like the even-tempered Quinn I had come to know, but under the circumstances, it was understandable. I made a mental note to check the bylaws and to ask Cleo about ex-officio members. The issue had never come up in CME Committee, but clearly, Ethics Committee was a whole different ball game.

QUINN'S LAST WORDS to me came back to haunt him the next morning. It was Cleo who broke the news as soon as I opened my email.

CALL ASAP. URGENT.

That message jump-started my pulse. I called.

"Jeez, Aimee, have you heard?"

"Heard what?"

"Oh, God. It's so…you should come over to my office."

"Cleo, just tell me. How bad can it be?"

"Gavin Lowe's dead. Shot. When Varsha unlocked Quinn's office this morning for the woman from House-keeping, they discovered Lowe's body."

I gripped the edge of my desk for a moment to keep my balance. After managing my initial shock, I closed the library and ran across the hospital complex through the windy, overcast morning to Cleo's office in the main tower.

"The whole fourth floor is off-limits," she said. "A forensic unit is already up there. Lowe is still… I mean, his body is still in Quinn's office where they found him. It. Damn."

"Where's Quinn?"

"It's only seven thirty. He hasn't come in yet. Varsha says he has a Kiwanis Club meeting this morning."

"Quinn *must* know about it. Varsha would have called him right away." Quinn relied heavily on Varsha Singh, his executive assistant. If anyone knew where to find him, she would.

"She tried. Couldn't reach him on his cell or home phone, so she told Security to call the police. Then she called me to see if I'd heard from Quinn. I hadn't, so we had no choice but to let Sanjay take charge."

Sanjay D'Costa, TMC's assistant administrator, was a recent hire fresh from grad school and still wet behind the ears.

"Is Sanjay up there with the crime scene people?"

"Yes." Cleo got up from her desk and put her arm around my shoulder. "Don't worry about Quinn. The police will get to the bottom of this."

Worry about Quinn? It was Lowe who was dead. Then I realized what she meant. Someone must have mistaken Lowe for Quinn. Someone who wanted Quinn dead. Why else would Lowe be shot in Quinn's office? But why would Lowe be *in* Quinn's office after hours? Finally my brain stopped spinning, and like the ball that drops in a pocket on a roulette wheel, I landed on the truth of what Cleo meant.

"My God, Cleo. Quinn's going to be a suspect. We have to do something."

Cleo's phone rang. She glanced at the caller ID. "It's him." She grabbed it up.

"Jared, where are you?" She maintained eye contact

with me while she listened to him, then said, "Sanjay's in your office with the investigators." She listened again, said, "Okay," and hung up.

"What did he say?"

"He's at the police station, but he hasn't been arrested or charged. He didn't know about Lowe until he checked his calls after the Kiwanis meeting. He said he volunteered to be questioned."

"What should we do?"

"Our jobs." Cleo sat at her desk, picked up a pen, then put it back down. "He said do our jobs and try not to worry."

I hurried back to the library and found the door unlocked, which was wrong. It was Tuesday. Lola had recently gone back to working only on Monday, Wednesday, and Friday mornings. No one should be in there. I was sure I had locked the library when I left. Spooked by Lowe's death and by the police presence, I stepped inside cautiously, wondering who my intruder might be.

Dr. Sybil Snyder stood by my desk, leafing through my appointment calendar. She looked up at me, seemingly untroubled by being caught snooping. She had to be at least fifty, but her forehead was unwrinkled by surprise or any other emotion. There was no flush of embarrassment on her cheeks. Every hair on her head held its proper place in a smooth, champagne-blond cap. I couldn't help thinking she looked expensive.

"Aimee, there you are. I took the liberty of asking Security to let me in." She walked toward me and reached out to touch my arm. "I'm sure you're as upset as I am about what happened at yesterday morning's meeting."

"Of course." When she didn't mention Dr. Lowe's death, I wondered if she had heard. If not, I wasn't eager to give her the news. I decided to wait. "Let's sit down." I took the chair behind my desk, leaving her to use a visitor's chair. After the liberties she had taken in my domain, I wanted the power position. She pursed her lips for a moment, but she sat and leaned forward, drumming her fingers on my desk.

"I've come by to review your draft of yesterday's minutes."

I opened the locked file cabinet where I stored confidential committee minutes and pulled the file. Back at my desk, I slid the single sheet across to Dr. Snyder, who leaned in and read it.

"This won't do." She pushed it back to me. The diamond ring on her hand looked expensive, too.

"It's just a draft, Dr. Snyder. I wasn't sure how much detail you would want. This is my first time taking minutes for this committee."

"You think an assault on the hospital administrator is an insignificant detail? That meeting lasted all of ten minutes. I'd say it was the only thing worth mentioning." She stood up and jabbed at the page with her finger. "Get that abysmal scene recorded in the minutes and let me know when they're ready to sign." She headed for the exit, but I couldn't let her leave.

"Please wait, Dr. Snyder." I followed her to the door. "Did you know they made up after you left? Have you talked to Mr. Quinn since the meeting?"

"No, and that's not relevant. I haven't talked to either of them, and they certainly didn't make up before I adjourned the meeting, did they?"

"No, but after that they did agree to forget about it. I thought we might be able to leave it out of the official record."

"Look, your job is to prepare agendas and see that minutes are recorded at the discretion of the committee chairs. My signature will be on the bottom line, so I'd better see what I want to see on that page."

It occurred to me that she hadn't said a word about the drama unfolding in Quinn's office at that moment. I had to ask if she knew.

"Dr. Snyder, I wonder…have you heard the news about Dr. Lowe?"

"No. What news is that?"

"Varsha Singh and one of the staff from House-keeping found Dr. Lowe's body in Mr. Quinn's office early this morning. He'd been shot. I'm afraid that's all I know."

She blinked rapidly several times. "Did you say Dr. Lowe is dead?"

"I'm sorry. I thought you might already know."

The pitch of her voice rose. "How on earth would I know about that?" A shaky hand flew to her chest.

"Word got out right away. It's being talked about all over the hospital."

"Well, this is quite a shock." Snyder stiffened her spine and took a deep breath. "Under the circumstances, it's all the more important that we document the alter-cation that took place in the Ethics Committee meet-ing." She checked her watch. "I'm going over to the main tower to check on a patient. I'll be back in half an hour. Please have the minutes rewritten and ready for me to sign."

I did as she asked, including the blows that followed the verbal argument between Quinn and Dr. Lowe. When Dr. Snyder returned, she quickly signed the revised minutes, offered a curt "Thank you," and hurried away.

The rest of the day was spent answering phone calls and emails from curious employees. A rumor had started about what happened at the Ethics Committee meeting. In the aftermath of Lowe's shocking death in Quinn's office, speculation was running wild. I didn't dare say a word about the events in the meeting. The medical staff's committee business was legally protected, unless someone spoke about it outside committee. If that happened, the minutes could be subpoenaed and anyone present could be required to testify in court.

My last call of the day was from Quinn, who had not appeared at the hospital all day. I wondered if he'd been released after being interviewed by the police. He asked if I could meet him that evening. *Good. He wasn't in jail.*

"Where?" I said.

"Someplace where we won't be noticed."

"How about my apartment? Do you remember how to get there?"

"I do if you're still in Coyote Creek. The llama barn, right?"

"Right. I'm going home now. What time?"

"I can be there by eight. Will that work?"

"That's fine. When you pull into my grandparents' driveway, come down the lane to the barn. I'll leave a light on for you."

"Do I need to check in with your grandparents?"

"No. I'll let them know you're coming."

On a better day, Quinn would have teased me about living in a studio apartment above my grandparents' llama barn. He had been there a couple of times in the past. Once when I needed a ride home, and again when a murder suspect attacked me. This time, it looked like he was the one in trouble. I wasn't sure why he was asking to meet me, but I couldn't refuse.

THREE

WHEN I PULLED into my grandparents' driveway to take the access lane to the barn, Amah stepped out her front door and waved at me from the porch. I stopped and rolled down the window. A few drops of light February rain sprinkled the passenger seat of my car. My brother, Harry, called the green hand-me-down Buick coupe my old lady car, but not in front of Amah, who had given it to me when she bought her Prius. Until I managed to pay down my grad school loans and credit card debt, it was all I could afford.

"Jack made sweet and sour venison," Amah called. "Do you want to have dinner with us?"

"Sounds wonderful. What time?"

"See you at six." She blew me a kiss and stepped back inside. Now in her early seventies, Amah had silver threads in her short, dark hair, but she was still as petite and energetic as a hummingbird.

I drove down the lane alongside an empty llama pasture. The rain had driven the woolly herd into the shelter of the barn. After parking in the barnyard, I ran up the outdoor steps to the covered deck that surrounded my little apartment. Inside, I checked the time. Five thirty. I considered texting Harry to see if he was invited to dinner but decided against it. Instead, I changed into jeans and a turtleneck sweater, poured a glass of Merlot, and turned on the TV. The last half of the local news reported

Gavin Lowe's body being found in the administrative offices of Timbergate Medical Center. Police were calling it an apparent homicide. No mention of anyone being questioned or charged.

It hadn't occurred to me that the murder would be on the news so soon. Amah and Jack would pepper me with questions. So would Harry, if he showed up.

I turned off the TV and looked out my window. The rain had intensified from a sprinkle to a fairly ambitious shower. In waterproof boots and a rain slicker, I sprinted to the main house. Amah met me at the back door.

"I was watching for you." She took my slicker and hung it on a peg in the mud room. "You can leave your boots here, too."

I slipped them off and set them on the floor. "Is anyone else coming to dinner?"

"No, it's just the three of us." She looked down at my stocking feet. "Are you going to be warm enough? I have a pair of slippers you can borrow."

"No thanks, I'm good." I followed her into the kitchen, where Jack stood at the stove, tall and straight in boot-cut Levis and a blue-plaid shirt. His close-cropped sandy gray hair, parted on the side and slicked back, always reminded me of pictures I'd seen of forties movie idols. I helped Amah with salad and cornbread, while the tantalizing aroma of the venison dish filled the room.

We traded news over dinner about my parents' latest Skypes from the Azores, where they had been living for the past year. When Dad inherited property on the island of Faial from one of his elderly relatives, he and Mom felt the time was right to turn the reins of their construction business over to Harry. They missed us, of course, but they were still happy about their decision to retire.

"They're coming for a visit in early summer," Amah said, "but they'll stop in New York first to visit your Grandpa Machado and Tanya." Amah and Grandpa Machado had divorced amicably before I was born when they realized their goals and ambitions were at odds. Grandpa longed for city life. Amah loved nature and animals and trekking in the wilderness. They remained good friends, but each had found a more compatible spouse.

Grandpa Machado had worked as a doorman in a luxury condo building in Manhattan, where he met his second wife, a character actress named Tanya Tremont. She was a widow when they met, and only a few years younger than Grandpa. A comfortable-looking woman, she used minimal makeup and wore her light-brown hair in a simple shoulder-length cut. When Grandpa brought her to California for a visit a few years ago, the whole family took to her. Especially Amah. She seemed to feel no awkwardness at meeting the woman who had married her ex. Instead, she and Tanya seemed to have an instant rapport and got along like BFFs.

When Grandpa retired, Tanya talked him into auditioning for a few off-Broadway plays. With his dark brown eyes, silver hair, and handsome Portuguese features, he had been cast in several roles calling for a distinguished character actor.

"Are Mom and Dad going to stop in Virginia to visit Auntie Maria?" I asked.

"I think so. She said they had to check Maria's concert schedule."

My mother and her sister were born in India, daughters of a Chinese merchant. Their parents died very young, and the girls were adopted by an American family from Sacramento. Dad and Mom met in college at UC Davis. Auntie Maria attended a music conservatory in Baltimore, became a concert violinist, and married a dentist from Roanoke.

The conversation about concerts brought me around to the drama playing out at Timbergate Medical Center. Little Natasha Korba, a piano virtuoso at the age of ten, was in the Pediatric Intensive Care Unit, while the doctor who saved her life might still be lying in the TMC holding morgue. And my boss, Jared Quinn, could very well be facing a murder charge.

The three of us sat down at the glass-topped wrought-iron table in their dining room. Jack served the sweet and sour venison over a bed of rice. Amah's green salad and cornbread muffins rounded out the menu. I was about to bring up my news about Dr. Lowe's death when their doorbell rang. Amah looked across the table at Jack, whose mouth was already full. He put his napkin on the table and started to stand.

"You two sit," I said. "I'll go."

I walked through the house to the living room and opened the front door to find Harry and Nick standing on the porch, smelling like they'd just come from a locker room. It took a shocked moment to register that Nick was here in the flesh. While they both stood there grinning, I found my voice.

"Nick, when did you get home?"

"A few hours ago. I should have called, but I wanted to surprise you. I was planning to go home and clean up first, but then—"

"My fault," Harry said. "I picked him up at the airport and dragged him to black belt class."

Amah came up behind me. "For heaven's sake,

Aimee. Let them in." I stepped aside. She caught a whiff and said, "Oh, my. You'll probably want to wash up while I set more places."

"We're not staying, Amah." Harry glanced at Nick. "We were working out at the dojo when we heard some-one talking about the murder at TMC. We came by to learn the details firsthand from Aimee."

A puzzled look crossed Amah's face. "Murder? What do you mean? And what's it got to do with Aimee?" Obviously, she and Jack hadn't watched the news.

"I was about to explain when the doorbell rang."

"Rosa, what's going on out there?" Jack yelled from the family room.

Amah insisted on filling plates for Harry and Nick, who had managed to clean up well enough to sit with the rest of us. After Nick fielded several questions from Amah and Jack about his time overseas with Buck, the conversation turned to the murder at the hospital.

I told what I could about Lowe's death, which wasn't a whole lot. I was careful not to divulge anything that had happened between Lowe and Quinn during the com-mittee meeting.

"I get that you can't spill everything you know," Nick said, "but the man's body was found in your boss's of-fice. Will that have an impact on your job?"

"No more than anyone else's."

Not quite true, since I was a witness to Lowe's as-sault on Quinn at the Ethics Committee meeting. But I wasn't the only witness. The half a dozen doctors in the room had all seen the blows exchanged. What they hadn't seen was the aftermath. Not even the two secu-rity guards witnessed that. Both of them had left before Quinn and Lowe's dialogue about Natasha's transfusion and before Lowe's apology. I was the only other person who heard that, and the only person to hear Quinn ask Gavin Lowe about stress in his life. Only Quinn and I heard Lowe's answer when he said, *"It's nothing I can't handle."*

Amah broke into my thoughts. "Your hospital is certainly getting its share of negative publicity lately." She looked to Jack. "Remember, honey? There was something else just last night on the news. It was about that little girl prodigy who plays piano. She was a patient and her parents were raising a fuss about something. Do you know what that was about, Aimee? Is that child going to be okay?"

"I'm sorry. I can't talk about that, either."

"Let the girl eat, Rosa." Jack picked up my plate of cold food and headed to the kitchen. "I'll nuke this for you, kiddo." He came back to the table and placed one hand on Harry's shoulder and the other on Nick's. "If you gentlemen are finished, maybe you should go home and hit the showers." Jack wasn't known for subtlety. With him, blunt usually got the job done.

Harry excused himself and headed toward the bathroom. Nick tossed a look at me that said he wanted to talk. I followed him to the front door where he leaned in for a quick kiss. I backed up and pressed my hand to his chest.

He covered my hand with his. "When can we get together?"

Before I could answer, Harry appeared and clapped Nick on his shoulder. "Let's go, buddy, I have to get home and clean up for a late date."

"Right." Nick turned to me. "He's my ride, unless… any chance?"

"I'm afraid not. Someone's coming by in a little while to talk about what's going on at work." I didn't mention that it was Jared Quinn. In spite of my protests, Nick still thought my boss had a thing for me.

I recognized Nick's look as the one he gets when he's thinking something he doesn't want to say. "Okay, then, I'll call you later."

After Harry and Nick left, Jack retreated to his den to work on an article about bass fishing. A professional outdoor writer, he contributed articles to a variety of magazines for outdoor sportsmen and women. I helped Amah clean up the kitchen, and while we worked she asked if I was excited to have Nick home.

"I'm happy he's back, but we hadn't ironed out all the wrinkles in our relationship before he left. While he was gone, it was easy. We didn't have to deal with them." I couldn't give Amah the answer she wanted to hear just yet. "I'm still making the mental transition from Nick thousands of miles away to Nick as near as a ten-minute drive from Coyote Creek to Timbergate."

"You know I'm always here for you if you want to talk about it."

"Thanks, I know."

After we worked in silence for a few minutes, she brought the subject around to Harry.

"Do you know if he's seeing anyone special?" Her question surprised me. She seems to think my love life is fair game, especially where Nick is concerned, but she doesn't usually show a lot of interest in who Harry's dating.

Two years younger than me, Harry is a busy architect and commercial builder, and that hasn't left a lot of time for a long-term relationship, especially with a lucrative contract to construct a three-story shopping mall in the heart of Timbergate. Along with his income and professional status, he has dark good looks and plenty of interested women. Although he's played the field for years, I've never believed the role of playboy was a good fit. I hoped Amah's suspicions were on target.

"You know Harry," I said. "He's always seeing someone, but none of them ever last. I gave up and stopped trying to keep track a long time ago."

"Hmm." Amah scrubbed at a pot for a long moment. Now I was curious.

"Why are you asking?"

"It's probably nothing," she said, "or just wishful thinking. He's dropped a few hints."

"Well, if he is getting serious about someone, it's news to me." I loaded the last pot in the dishwasher. "You think I should ask him?"

"Oh, no. If I'm right, he'll let us know in his own good time." She gave me a hug. "Let's go have dessert. I made pecan pie." She didn't have to twist my arm.

Before I left I mentioned that Quinn would be arriving in about an hour. "I told him I'd alert you and Jack so you wouldn't wonder who was driving down the lane to the barn."

"Wasn't it his office where the body was found?" I saw the concern in her eyes. I assured her he wasn't a danger to me, and apologized for being so stingy with information.

"Just promise to stay safe," Amah said, "and tell us what you can."

I promised and made my exit, jogging down the muddy lane to the barn. I looked forward to having some alone time before Quinn arrived. I wanted to sort out my thoughts about Lowe and Quinn and whether the murder *would* have an impact on my job. Several people had seen me take Lowe down in that conference room. And the two security guards had been surprised and probably amused when they saw me restraining him.

Quinn's headlights flashed through my kitchen window at eight o'clock. By then I had brewed a fresh pot of coffee and tidied up most of the signs of my casual approach to housekeeping. I emptied a bag of pretzel twists into a bowl just as he knocked on my door. I checked my peephole and opened the door.

"You remembered how to find me," I said. "Come in."

"Animal Farm. How could I forget?"

He stepped inside, trying for a smile, but thanks to his sore jaw, it wasn't his best effort. As we sat at my little table, I realized I'd put out the wrong snack.

"Sorry about the pretzels. Would you like some ice cream? I have marble fudge."

"No thanks, just coffee's fine."

I poured coffee and we sat at my little dinette table with the bowl of pretzels between us. I waited while Quinn managed a careful sip. He avoided my eyes and fiddled with the handle of his cup.

"I'm sorry you're mixed up in this, Aimee."

"But I'm not really, am I?" Then I guessed where he was headed. I thought about his interest in the minutes, and about Dr. Snyder's reaction when she heard Dr. Lowe was dead. "Does this have something to do with the Ethics Committee minutes?"

"Not directly. It's what happened after the meeting was adjourned that's important."

"Why?" But I knew why. Because I was the only wit-

ness in the room when Lowe and Quinn made peace.
Or was it a truce?

"Did Cleo tell you I volunteered to be interviewed by
a police investigator?"

"I was in her office this morning when she talked to
you on the phone. How did that go?"

"For something that was supposed to be voluntary, it
felt more like an interrogation than an interview." Quinn
worked his shoulders. "The two detectives didn't slap me
around or play good cop, bad cop, but it wasn't pleas-
ant. I answered every question, then they asked them
all again and I answered them again, and again until I
began to wonder if they were hard of hearing." He took
a pretzel from the bowl. Held it up and stared at it. "This
is what I felt like by the time it was over."

"If you volunteered to be questioned, you could have
left at any time, couldn't you?"

"I could have, but that would have given the wrong
impression, and besides, I want to do what I can to help
get this thing resolved."

I paused, reluctant to ask the obvious question, but
there wouldn't be a better time. "I heard a rumor that
Lowe was shot with your gun."

"That's true." He spoke so softly I barely heard him.
"It was the twenty-two semi-automatic pistol I keep in
a drawer in my office desk."

"Wait. You're telling me you keep a gun at work? In
the *hospital*?"

"It's legal. And contrary to what most employees assume, TMC has no anti-gun policy. I told you months
ago why I always keep a weapon with me."

"I remember." His wife's murder in Ethiopia. And the

attempt on his life. "But we work in a hospital in California. We're not in a third-world country."

"Tell that to ISIS and Al Qaeda. Or to our homegrown terrorists and local loonies." Quinn rubbed a finger along the scar running through his eyebrow. "Hospitals are supposed to be safe, civilized places, but so are elementary schools, movie theaters, and shopping malls. It only takes one shooter to blow that notion to bits. It happened in an Alabama hospital a few years ago and again in Reno. There was another one in the news just the other day. Boston."

"I heard about it," I said, "and I get it. Hospitals are filled with ill and injured patients. The most vulnerable of potential victims."

"So you see my point."

"Was the gun found in your office? That should be enough to prove you didn't do it. There's no way you would have left your own gun there if you shot Lowe."

"But it wasn't found there. It was found by the Housekeeping staff this morning shortly after Lowe's body was discovered. The gun was wrapped in soiled linens and stuffed in the bottom of a Housekeeping cart. The woman who used that cart said she'd returned it to the Housekeeping Department around eleven thirty. The gun was wiped clean of prints, of course."

"Had the woman been working on the fourth floor during her shift last night?"

"She says not. She only worked the third floor. She has no idea when the gun was hidden in her cart, but she does leave it unattended while she's changing beds or taking a bathroom break. Apparently the killer wanted to hide the gun someplace in the hospital, but not in a place that would look like a too obvious attempt to frame me."

"But knowing it was your gun, and knowing about your fight with Lowe, the police didn't arrest you?"

"I've been cooperating. I told them it was my gun. I told them I kept it in my desk. I couldn't explain how it got out of my desk when I wasn't there, but they can't place me at the crime scene and there were no prints on the gun."

"Still, I'm surprised. His body was in your office. It seems like they'd almost have to—"

"Damn, Aimee, whose side are you on?" Quinn rose up in his chair, then caught himself and sat back down. "Look, I know you're trying to help, and I'm not off the hook, but the security cameras show me leaving the office at eight o'clock last night. I haven't been allowed in there at all today."

My pulse quickened in reaction to Quinn's tension level. "Obviously this is none of my business, but were you with anyone through the night who could verify that you didn't go back to the hospital?"

"I wish that were the case." Quinn splayed his fingers wide, then made them into fists. "Unfortunately, I slept alone." I didn't know if that was unusual for him, and didn't ask. His body stiffened, and I saw him make a conscious effort to relax his shoulders as he sipped his coffee.

"Were there signs of a break-in?"

"I asked both Varsha and Sanjay about that. Apparently there were no signs of forced entry. The door from the corridor to the administrative suite opens into Varsha's reception area. It was untouched, and so was the door from her reception area into my office."

Interesting. "Then someone from Housekeeping or

Security must have unlocked both those doors to let Lowe in."

"They all claim they didn't. The cameras didn't record me or anyone else going through the doors to the administrative suite during the night, and the third floor cameras didn't capture anyone tampering with the laundry cart."

"Did you view the camera footage yourself?"

He stared into his coffee and sighed. "No. I only know what Sanjay told me. He was present when the police viewed the footage."

I hoped there was still an avenue he hadn't investigated. "What about elevator cameras? I've never noticed whether we have them."

"We don't, and I've been harping about it to the board ever since I was hired. They've always balked at the expense, but once this mess is resolved, you can bet that's going to happen."

I didn't know what else to suggest. "I hope the police get it solved soon."

"So do I." He worked his sore jaw, reminding me it still hurt him to talk. "The police are still analyzing the camera footage, looking for evidence it was tampered with."

"Will you be back at work tomorrow?"

He raised his eyes to mine, and I saw profound weariness in his expression. "Doubtful. I don't think I'll have access to my office yet." He broke the pretzel into pieces and dropped them on a napkin. After a long pause, he said, "There are a couple of things you need to know."

My stomach did an odd kind of twitch. "What kind of things?"

"You'll most likely be questioned to corroborate my

story about the incident with Lowe and how we resolved it."

I answered too quickly. "That shouldn't be a problem. I'll just tell the truth." I remembered how they had both backed off while the three of us were alone in the conference room, but I also remembered what Quinn had said later in my office. *If he tries a stunt like that again, I'll be ready for him.*

"There's something else." Quinn toyed with another pretzel. "The police know you were the one who subdued Lowe at the meeting."

My neck stiffened. "How do they know about that?"

"One of the security guards thought it was too funny to keep to himself."

"But that's just hospital gossip." I sounded whiney, even to myself. "I don't see what it's got to do with Lowe's being shot."

"I'm afraid there's more."

"What do you mean?" I heard the strain in my voice.

"Lowe noticed some tenderness in his wrist during his surgery that afternoon and had to let the assistant surgeon finish the case. As soon as he left the surgery suite, he started mouthing off to anyone who would listen that he was going to get both of us fired."

Now I was really angry. "That's ridiculous. Everyone at that meeting saw Lowe throw the first punch. He even apologized to us."

He raised a finger to stop my protests. "But no one witnessed his apology except you and me. And your black belt gave Lowe just enough ammunition to go to Hector Korba with an ultimatum. Either fire the two of us or Lowe would sue TMC for bodily injury and loss of income."

I couldn't believe what I was hearing. "Did he actually go to Korba?"

"Unclear," Quinn said, "but I doubt it. I think Hector would have told me, but as you can imagine, I'm not about to ask him." He dropped the second pretzel on his napkin. "Sorry to break the news, but you needed to know. I'm sure the police will ask you where you were the night Lowe was killed."

The odd feeling in my stomach became a sharp cramp. "But this is the first I've heard about Lowe wanting either of us fired. I had no idea he wasn't able to complete his surgery. When did you hear about it?"

"Not until this morning, but I can't prove that and neither can you."

I was fully on the defensive. "Even so, the security cameras won't show either of us near your office that night."

"In spite of the cameras, they're going to suspect everyone, Aimee, until they find the killer. It would be good if you had someone who could verify your whereabouts."

I raced through my memory. I had come home, fixed a meal of crab salad and French bread in my apartment. I checked email from a few friends, watched the eleven o'clock news, and went to bed. *Alone.*

Amah and Jack were the only people who could vouch for me, but they couldn't swear I hadn't left the ranch while they were asleep. I hoped they wouldn't be asked.

Nick called just as Quinn and I were finishing up. I told him I'd have to call him back. When I did, I sensed he was waiting for me to tell him who my company had been, so I did.

"I assume it had to do with the dead doctor," Nick said. "Want to fill me in?"

"It did, but I'm pretty tired. I'd rather not get into it tonight. How about tomorrow?"

"Maybe, if I'm home in time. My sister just had her first baby and they're all going nuts over it. It's my parents' first grandchild, and apparently I'm its godfather. I promised my folks I'd visit, so I'm driving down first thing in the morning."

Nick's family lived in a small town in the hills above Placerville. His parents were retired schoolteachers, and his only sibling, a younger sister, was an oral surgeon in a busy practice with her husband.

"Okay then, have a good visit." I'd only met his family once, back before Nick and I hit a snag in our relationship. They seemed like good people, and Nick was fond of them.

"I'll call when I get back tomorrow evening," he said. "I'm guessing I'll be showing off photos of the little tyke. Sis named him Bradley Nicholas Brooks." Nick sounded so proud, I couldn't help wondering how he'd react when he had a little tyke of his own.

FOUR

WEDNESDAY MORNING AT work my email was clogged with messages. Most were questions about Lowe's death that I couldn't answer. There were several more on my voicemail. I ignored them all and went to work filling routine requests for articles and interlibrary loans.

An hour into the morning, I called Cleo to see if she had heard anything about Natasha Korba's condition and whether she was still in the Pediatric Intensive Care Unit.

"She's still in the PICU, and from what I hear, she could be in for a long stay. She's on antibiotics and cardiac monitoring, among other things. But at least she's alive, thanks to poor Dr. Lowe. I feel bad that the last thing I said about him was so negative."

I remembered. *Horse's patootie.*

"You were being honest. He did have a reputation for being volatile."

"I know, but he wasn't always like that." I heard her sniffle. "He used to be easygoing and caring. His temperament seemed to change in the past year or so."

"Do you know who's taking over as Natasha's primary physician?"

"I heard it was Dr. Snyder."

That was odd. *Dr. Snyder?* "Curious. I didn't know she treated children."

"She doesn't usually, but she does have pediatric privileges, and Hector Korba asked for her, specifically. Apparently Natasha's mother agreed." Cleo's information pipeline was obviously working. "I guess you don't refuse the president of the governing board."

We ended the call and I searched my memory for what little I knew about Dr. Snyder. She and her husband, Glen Capshaw, were internists who had practiced together in Timbergate for ten years. No one seemed to know much about them, except that they were childless and guarded about their private lives.

Later in the morning I spotted Sanjay D'Costa coming through the library's entrance door. That was a first. He had never visited the library in the three months since he had been hired. The ink was barely dry on his degree in health services administration, but Quinn appeared to be satisfied with his work.

Still, I had trouble thinking of Sanjay as my superior. He looked like a skinny teenager and wore thick glasses with dark frames that made his eyes seem perpetually wide with surprise. Watching him approach my desk, I thought twenty years and thirty pounds would look good on him. And contact lenses.

"Hello, Sanjay," I said. "What brings you to the library?"

"Official business." He pushed his glasses up on his nose. "I'm letting everyone know that Mr. Quinn will not be present today. It is uncertain when he will return. If you have needs, you will want to address them to me."

His speech was so correct and formal that when he referred to my having "needs," I had trouble keeping a straight face.

I waited until I was sure I was in control before replying, "Thank you for letting me know." After my conversation with Quinn the previous night, I wasn't surprised to hear he was taking the day off. I wondered if Sanjay would explain, but he stood staring down at me as if I were some sort of puzzle he wanted to solve. "Was there something else?" I asked.

"Not really. It's just… I was told you may have relatives in India, but that's too personal. I shouldn't pry into your family background."

"I don't mind, but I don't know anyone in India. My mother came here from Calcutta as a child. There may be some distant cousins there, but she doesn't have contact with anyone."

"I am from Kolkata, myself."

"Kolkata? Is that near Calcutta?"

Sanjay smiled. "No, not *near*. Kolkata *is* Calcutta. That is, it used to be, but it has been Kolkata since 2001. And its state changed from West Bengal to Bangla as well. In recent years, many of India's cities have undergone name changes. Bombay is Mumbai; Madras is Chennai." He adjusted his glasses again then beamed at me with a flash of brilliant white teeth. "But I'm boring you. I must let you work. Remember to address me if you have needs." With that, he turned on his heel and hurried toward the exit.

Needs. I had lots of needs but none that Sanjay could help me with. Although he did stimulate my overactive curiosity gene with his lesson on place names in India. Why hadn't I known that? Rather than let myself spend the day distracted by his geography lesson, I went online and discovered the reasoning behind many of the changes. Most were meant to eliminate place names associated with Portuguese or British colonies.

With those questions answered, my attention shifted

back to Lowe's murder. How to prove that neither Jared Quinn nor I had shot Dr. Gavin Lowe in cold blood? And how should I react if Quinn was right about the police wanting to interview me? I could honestly say I knew nothing about the crime, but I would have to admit to being home alone the night it was committed.

I had enough trouble wrapping my mind around the idea of Quinn as a murder suspect, but the idea that I could be suspected was a waking nightmare.

I tend to murmur an apology every time I have to kill a fly or an ant. I can't imagine taking a human life, unless it was done to save to myself or someone I love.

Surely the police didn't suspect that Quinn and I together had cooked up some kind of murder plot. Nevertheless, I'd breathe easier when the killer was caught.

I walked over to the shelves that held the library's forensic collection, reading the titles on the spines and hoping for inspiration. What evidence did the police have so far? A body and Quinn's gun. Quinn said they were still analyzing the security footage. I wondered what information they were keeping to themselves.

I thought about motive. Money, love, hate, revenge? The only two people I could think of who might want revenge were Natasha's parents, Abel and Melissa Gailworth. Dr. Lowe had ordered the girl's life-saving transfusion in spite of their objections. In the news reports on television, the husband had seemed most adamantly opposed to giving the girl blood. But even so, murdering the doctor who saved their child seemed like a dreadful overreaction. I went back to my desk to look up the online versions of those newscasts. Because of Natasha's fame as a piano prodigy, her story was bound to remain newsworthy, even beyond the local media.

Sources reported that Natasha's mother, the former Melissa Korba, had been widowed five years earlier when her husband, Natasha's father, died fighting in Afghanistan. Almost three years ago she had married a man named Abel Gailworth. He was described as a pastor, but no specific church affiliation was mentioned.

My phone interrupted my research. The caller was Sanjay, saying a police investigator had just left his office after asking where to find me. My face grew hot and butterflies swarmed in my midsection while I scanned the library for patrons browsing in the stacks. *No one. Good.* If I was going to be accused of murder, I didn't want an audience. I hurried to the restroom and blotted my burning cheeks with a cold, wet paper towel. I'd barely made it back to my desk before the officer came through the door, holding a badge for me to see.

"Aimee Machado?" He walked toward me with a slight limp, which I pretended not to notice. "Walter Kass, TPD." He put the badge back in his pocket. "May I have a few minutes?"

"Yes." I motioned him toward the visitor's chair next to my desk. "Let me put up my *closed* sign."

I had expected the stereotypical detective type—middle-aged in a rumpled suit—but this guy was in his early forties, with a body that indicated time in a gym. Rather than a uniform, he wore khakis and a plaid shirt, and his buzz-cut left the color of his hair hard to determine.

I offered him coffee, which he declined. He looked around the room, satisfied we were alone. I sat and leaned back slightly in my chair, hoping to appear relaxed and willing to help. He took a small notebook from his pocket, opened it and tapped a page with his pen. I felt my mouth go dry.

"Ms. Machado, I'm interviewing a number of people here at the hospital regarding the circumstances surrounding the death of Dr. Gavin Lowe. Please don't infer that you're being singled out for any particular reason."

"I won't. I'll be happy to answer any questions."

"Good enough. When did you first hear of Lowe's death?"

"It was only minutes after I arrived at work yesterday morning, around seven thirty. I checked my email and saw a message from a coworker, Cleo Cominoli, telling me to call her. When I did, she told me what had happened."

"And what did she tell you?" His pen was poised.

"That Dr. Lowe had been found dead in Mr. Quinn's office, apparently the victim of a gunshot." I waited, figuring it was best to answer only what was asked and not to elaborate.

"What was your reaction?" He still hadn't used his pen.

"Disbelief, of course. Then I was confused about how it could have happened."

"What part confused you?" This time he did jot down something.

"It didn't make sense that Dr. Lowe would have been in Mr. Quinn's office after hours."

"And why do you assume he was there after hours?"

"Well, if he was shot in Mr. Quinn's office during working hours, surely someone would have noticed."

He wrote again, then looked up and studied my face for what seemed like much too long before posing his next question.

"I understand you were involved in a physical altercation with Dr. Lowe the day before he died. Would you describe that for me? Include as much detail as you can remember."

And there it was. The question hung in the air between us.

FIVE

"IT WASN'T AN ALTERCATION. I simply used a wrist hold to restrain Dr. Lowe."

Kass looked up from his notepad and maintained eye contact with me. A trickle of sweat slid down my spine.

"Why did you believe he needed to be restrained?"

"He became agitated, and I was concerned for the safety of others in the room."

"What caused him to become agitated?"

"I'm sorry. I can't answer that without violating the confidentiality of medical staff peer review."

Kass frowned. I hoped he'd been briefed on that legal roadblock. "Yes, your Mr. D'Costa explained that to me." He frowned at his notepad. "The Peer Review Protection Act. Is that it?"

"Yes. That's right."

"Then explain why the security guards were willing to talk."

"Because they only witnessed what happened after the committee meeting was adjourned. You're asking me to divulge something that happened during the meeting's peer review process."

My response resulted in Kass taking a moment to clear his throat, but then he went on with his questioning.

"The guards observed Dr. Lowe on the floor with you restraining him, and Mr. Quinn standing nearby with blood on his face. They assumed you broke up a physical altercation between Quinn and Lowe. Is that correct?"

"Again, I can't divulge anything that happened in that room except what happened after the meeting was adjourned. You'll have to draw your own conclusions based on what the guards observed."

"My conclusion is that you intervened to break up a fight between your boss and the deceased doctor. Humor me. If that scenario is indeed correct, why would you take it upon yourself to step in?"

"I'm not confirming that your scenario is correct. All I can say is that I'm trained in jujitsu. If a situation calls for intervention, my reaction is pretty much instinctive. I do what needs to be done."

"And you can verify your martial arts training?"

"Of course. I have an ID card from the dojo where I'm a member. It's in my purse. Would you like to see it?"

"I'd better have a look." I gave him points for maintaining an objective demeanor. I removed my purse from my desk drawer slowly, hoping he wouldn't think I was going for a weapon. He examined the card I handed him.

"Third degree black belt." He gave me an appraising glance. "I'm impressed."

"I'm surprised you didn't ask about my name. Most of the TPD officers know my brother, Harry Machado. He teaches at the dojo on weekends."

"I transferred up from Fresno a month ago. I haven't been to the Timbergate dojo since I got here." Kass handed the card back to me. "When I was assigned to this case, I did a search of the TPD database. Your name came up four different times. Always as a victim. That's a little unusual, especially for a librarian. Any theories about why trouble seems to follow you?"

"I'm afraid not." I tried to bring the interview to a close. "Is there anything else? If not, I really should open the library. The health care providers at TMC depend on our services." A shameless exaggeration, but it worked.

"That's all for now, but we may need to talk again." If he'd gotten wind of Lowe's threats to have Quinn and me fired, he was keeping it to himself. I couldn't prove I hadn't known about the threats until after Lowe was killed, so I wasn't about to bring the matter up myself.

I went to the exit door with him and watched as he walked toward the main tower. Which other employees would he be questioning? I hoped no one who was present during the Ethics Committee meeting had broken the confidentiality protection.

But there were other possibilities. Which security guards had been on duty at the time Lowe was killed? Had they been interviewed? Had one of them let someone into Quinn's office after hours? Quinn had already told me that both Security and Housekeeping personnel denied unlocking the doors to the administrative suite and to Quinn's office. Maybe someone had lied.

I might get some answers from Sanjay, if the police were keeping him informed. I was impressed that he had warned Kass about peer review protection. Maybe our fledgling assistant administrator was more on the ball than I'd given him credit for.

Though I managed to keep my mind on my job for the rest of the morning, my focus was disrupted when Cleo called to tell me she'd been interviewed by Kass. I told her he had questioned me, too. We agreed to meet for lunch and compare notes at Margie's Bean Pot, a small restaurant a block from the hospital.

I closed the library at noon and walked the short distance through a chilly drizzle that did nothing to improve my mood.

"Aimee, wait up." I turned to see Jared Quinn hurrying toward me. *Now what?* Cleo was probably waiting for me at Margie's, and my boss, the murder suspect, was hailing me on the sidewalk.

"Quinn? What are you doing here?" Fatigue had etched lines around his eyes, and his cheeks were unshaven and dark.

"I'm going nuts sitting around my house." He opened an umbrella and held it over the two of us. "Are you headed to Margie's?"

"Yes, I'm meeting Cleo."

"Good, I'll come along."

"It's okay with me, if Cleo doesn't mind." We were only a few steps from Margie's door.

"Trust me. She won't." Quinn closed the umbrella and opened the door for me. My stomach rumbled when I breathed in the tantalizing aromas filling the room.

Cleo spotted us from her table against the back wall. When she waved us over, it was clear that she'd been expecting both Quinn and me. We made our way through the buffet line where I chose the special, a delicious combination of fava beans and artichoke hearts. Quinn opted for chickpea soup.

Cleo had already finished most of her bowl of minestrone when we reached the table. She put her spoon aside. "There are no TMC employees in here right now. Let's talk while we have a chance."

"Want to bring me up to speed?" I said. "Looks like you and Quinn are a few steps ahead of me."

"I thought the three of us should compare notes, since we've all been interviewed by the police." Cleo cast Quinn a sympathetic glance. "I asked Jared to meet us here."

Quinn spoke, his voice soft. "Aimee, if you're uncomfortable helping us try to sort this out, you don't have to get involved."

"I'm already involved. You were right that I might be a person of interest. Detective Kass has already told me we may need to talk again."

"He was one of the two who interviewed me," said Quinn, scraping a hand across his stubble. I saw a trace of bruising and realized that was why he hadn't shaved. "How did it go?"

"I'm not sure," I said. "Kass stressed the fact that I was seen restraining Lowe in the conference room that morning. I didn't disclose anything that happened during the meeting, but he assumed you and Lowe got physical and that I had stepped in. *Intervened*, was how he put it."

"Anything else?" Cleo asked. "Did he ask if you knew of anyone who might want Lowe dead? That was one of the questions he asked me."

"No, but he did ask me about my previous troubles involving the law. He seemed to imply that I somehow bring violence upon myself." Remembering his tone brought a shiver.

Quinn looked at Cleo. "So it was Kass who interviewed you?"

"Yes," she said. "And he's too big for his britches, if you ask me. I told him I wasn't at the meeting and even if I had been, I couldn't repeat anything I'd seen or heard."

"But you knew about the fist fight," I said. "I told you about it when I asked you how to write the minutes."

"Huh… I guess I must have forgotten about that."

Her wry smile said otherwise. "Doesn't matter anyway. That's confidential committee stuff, right Jared?"

"It's a gray area, but for now, I'm going with yes."

I asked Cleo if she'd heard the rumor going around about Lowe leaving in the middle of his surgery and making noises about going to Korba to get Quinn and me fired.

"Cripes, no." She darted concerned looks at both of us. "I don't like the sound of that. Gives both of you motive—" she cut off her sentence.

"So Kass didn't bring it up during your interview?" Quinn asked.

"No, and I'm damned glad." She shook her head. "That would have caught me off guard."

I changed the subject, asking Quinn if he'd heard anything more about the security cameras. I was still counting on them to prove he hadn't been in his office after hours.

"Apparently there's nothing. The data is stored digitally on TMC's network servers. Sanjay offered to give the police copies, but they wanted to view the original footage."

"Has Sanjay seen it?" Cleo asked.

"He viewed it with them. He said from the time I left at eight o'clock that night until Varsha arrived at seven in the morning, no one went through the door to the administrative suite."

"That's impossible." Cleo's lips twisted. "There's no other way in or out of your office. Lowe and whoever shot him had to go through the outer door to the administrative suite and then through the reception area to get to the door to your office. Someone must have rigged the cameras."

"Is that possible?" A rush of adrenaline made me queasy. If we couldn't trust the cameras, how could we prove our innocence?

"Anything's possible," Quinn said. "I'm guessing our friend Detective Kass will make that argument." I noticed Quinn's eyelids droop and wondered when he last got any sleep.

"Can you think of anyone who would want to pin Lowe's murder on you?" I asked.

"No." Quinn pushed his bowl away. His soup was untouched. "But I guess the best way to get away with murder is to frame someone else."

The lunch crowd had cleared out, and Margie was eyeing us with a look that said it was time to close. Taking the hint, we went outside and huddled under the entrance canopy.

"When will you be back to work?" Cleo asked Quinn.

"I'm not sure, but I'll keep in touch." He pulled us into a group hug. "With both of you."

LATER WEDNESDAY AFTERNOON I texted Harry and Nick, asking when they would be free for a brainstorming session. They'd already had a teaser the night before at Jack and Amah's house: a body in Quinn's locked office, the victim shot with Quinn's gun, the killer having entered and exited without being captured on security footage. Could they resist a puzzler like that? I upped the stakes by mentioning in my text that I'd been questioned by the police. If the guys thought I was also a person of interest, they would definitely want to know what had happened in that room.

My library patrons helped the rest of the long day pass. A few doctors and nurses needed reliable sources for treating obscure medical conditions. One trainee from the pathology lab who hoped to become a forensic scientist made his daily visit, returning one issue of *Forensic Magazine* and checking out another.

Harry responded via text half an hour before quitting time, asking if I wanted to meet him at the dojo when I got off work. I replied that I could be there by five thirty. Nick checked in a few minutes after, saying he'd be there, too. Missed you, he added. Me, too, I texted.

I took a moment before I locked up to call Cleo, asking how Natasha Korba was doing in the Pediatric ICU.

"Not much change," Cleo said. "That's all they'll say."

"Any idea how long it will be before she's released?"

"Too soon to tell. The nurse I talked to hopes Dr. Snyder will keep her here as long as possible. Best case, she'll be in PICU for at least a week. Could be longer if there are complications." I heard frustration in Cleo's voice. "That little girl's body needs all the help it can get."

"I got that impression from Dr. Lowe, the morning of the Ethics meeting. Apparently her iron-deficiency anemia was close to life-threatening even before the appendix ruptured."

"Not only that. I happened to talk to Edna Roda earlier today. I asked her to give me a hypothetical about kids who eat vegan diets, since she couldn't discuss Natasha's case in particular." Edna was the hospital's chief nursing officer and a good friend of Cleo's.

"What did she tell you?"

"Some troubling facts. Did you know that long-term vitamin B12 deficiency can result in permanent brain damage?"

"No." I was thinking I should have researched it myself. "How is that related to veganism?"

"The primary source of B12 in our diets comes from eating foods from animals. Meat, eggs, and dairy."

"So kids on vegan diets can suffer permanent brain damage if their parents don't do their homework?"

"That's right," Cleo said. "They have to know how to compensate for the lack of foods rich in B12."

"That's a frightening thought," I said. "It explains why everyone involved in Natasha's case is afraid the child will relapse when the parents get her home and start restricting her diet again."

After talking to Cleo, I closed the library and headed for the dojo. On the way, I found myself hoping Dr. Snyder would get Child Protective Services involved in Natasha's case. Iron-deficiency anemia should not be taken lightly, and the possibility of brain damage on top of that was appalling. I recalled Natasha's piano solo with the Sawyer County Symphony. She was a thin, pale child who looked younger than her age. Surely Dr. Snyder would warn Natasha's mother about the danger of organ failure from extreme iron deficiency. And about the prospect of brain damage.

Nick's new pickup was already in the dojo parking lot when I arrived. He had bought the black F150 a few months earlier when we were in Idaho tracking down a missing nurse. It was supposed to be my backup ride when my car was laid up, but so far, I hadn't had a chance to get behind the wheel. Harry's Jag was the only other vehicle in the lot.

Since there were no classes scheduled for the evening, we would have the place to ourselves. I grabbed my gi bag out of the trunk in case they planned to do some sparring.

Inside, I heard voices and laughter in the men's changing room. I called out to let them know I'd arrived.

"Hey, guys, are you changing into your gis?"

The door opened and I had my answer. Both of them were ready to bow onto the mat. Harry outranked Nick by one black-belt degree. He had recently graduated to fourth. Nick was still at third, like me, but only because he was gone so often, flying Buck Sawyer from one state or country to another. He didn't have a lot of time to concentrate on jujitsu.

"Get your gi on and get out here, woman," Nick said. "We have plans for you." The glint in his eye told me they were going to give me a hard time.

SIX

As I SUSPECTED, I took the brunt of the workout. After two hours we called it quits and changed back into street clothes. I filled paper cups from the water cooler and the guys dug around in the sensei's desk, looking for snacks. Harry grabbed a half-full jar of roasted peanuts and Nick found a bag of dried apricots. We sat at a small table in a corner of the dojo's office area with our improvised dinner.

Harry glanced at the wall clock. "Nearly eight thirty, Sis. Let's do this. All we know so far is that someone shot a doctor in your boss's office and you're sure your boss is not the killer."

"Right." I hesitated for a moment. "*Almost* sure."

Nick shook his head. "I don't like this already."

"Hear me out," I said. "I'm not going to get us involved in anything risky just to prove Quinn is innocent."

"I'll believe that when your grandparents' llamas sprout wings and fly," Nick said. "You've had a taste of crime solving and now you're hooked. Admit it, Aimee. You get a high from any adventure that gets you out from behind your desk at the library."

"*Me* high on adventure? What about you? Flying a billionaire all over the world in a corporate jet isn't what I'd call a tame way to make a living."

"That's different. It's my job. Your job is to run a

library, not to play savior to your boss when he's accused—"

"Hold it, you two." Harry flashed a timeout signal. "You're both turning into adventure-seeking adrenaline junkies, so just admit it and we can get back on track. Apparently the police are taking a hard look at Aimee—if not as a killer, at least as an accomplice." Harry gave me a raised eyebrow. "You hinted at it in your text. Want to fill us in?"

"Okay, guys," I brushed a stray lock of hair away from my face, "I hope I don't regret this, but I'm going to tell you everything that happened during that Ethics Committee meeting. Before I do, you need to understand something. There's a *Breach of Workplace Ethics* clause in my contract. I'll lose my job immediately if anyone finds out I violated confidentiality and divulged committee business."

"Understood," they said in unison.

I knew they'd never talk out of turn and put my job in jeopardy, so I filled them in on everything from the fists thrown at the meeting to the police interviews of Quinn, Cleo, and me. I told them about the surveillance cameras that showed no one had entered Quinn's office after hours. And about the gun that shot Dr. Lowe being registered to Quinn.

"So why do the police think Quinn had a motive for wanting this doctor dead?" Harry asked. "You're saying they suspect that Lowe physically attacked Quinn during the meeting, but they have only circumstantial evidence of that."

"Yes, because the security guards saw Quinn's bloody face and me restraining Lowe."

"So you broke up the fight. Sounds like you were completely justified."

"I was, and Lowe seemed to agree right after it happened, but I've just learned that he later changed his mind." I told them what Quinn had heard about Lowe being forced to step away from a surgery because of his tender wrist, and his threats about having Quinn and me fired.

"Come on," Nick said, "even if you had known about it at the time, that's hardly a motive for murder."

"Depends," Harry replied. "Add it to the other evidence. The body in Quinn's office, shot with Quinn's gun."

"That's all on Quinn, not Aimee." Nick turned to me. "Is there anything else we need to know? Anything that puts suspicion on you?"

"Maybe, but it's so minor, I doubt it matters."

"Tell us," Harry said.

"Lowe said something that Quinn took as a possible threat aimed at me." I searched my memory for Lowe's exact words. "He said, 'You'd better hope your little bodyguard didn't injure my wrist.'"

"Hold on," Nick said. "You and Quinn were threatened by the victim face to face?"

"You could put it that way, but he apologized right away."

"Even so, does the detective know about that threat?"

"I'm not sure. Quinn didn't say whether he mentioned it when he was interviewed."

"What about you?" Harry asked. "Did you mention it to the detective?"

"No. I didn't want to volunteer it."

"Anything else?" Nick said.

"I can't think of anything else. I was hoping you two would have a fresh perspective."

The gleam in Harry's eyes told me his brain was in high gear. "The fight broke out over the little girl's transfusion. Something the doctor did to save the girl's life in spite of her parents' objections?"

"Yes." I explained that both Natasha's mother and stepfather objected to the transfusion. "Melissa Korba Gailworth is the widow of Hector Korba's son, who died in Afghanistan. Her husband, Abel Gailworth, is a self-styled pastor of something he calls Abel's Breath Ministry. Apparently he espouses veganism as part of his doctrine."

Nick picked up the thread. "Sounds like it's some kind of cult. And the girl's grandfather is the president of your governing board, so Lowe felt he had clout with the guy if he wanted action taken against you and Quinn?"

"I'm sure he did. He even said so when he and Quinn were arguing. He said saving Natasha's life would give him an edge if he wanted to take a complaint to Hector Korba."

"When the flap came up about the transfusion, was the grandfather on the side of the doctor?"

"Yes. And I've heard he's trying to get custody of the child."

Harry glanced at Nick. "Sounds like there's a family feud to add to the equation."

"Sure does," Nick said. "Aimee, have you heard whether the police are talking to the girl's parents and grandfather?"

"I don't know. I could ask Sanjay if he's being kept informed."

"Who's Sanjay?" Harry asked.

"Our assistant administrator. He's filling in until Quinn comes back to work."

"Sis, is there any chance you could get me into Quinn's office?" Harry asked.

"Maybe. Why?"

"You're saying the doctor was shot dead in there, yet during the time frame when that took place, the cameras show no one going in or coming out. I'd like to have a look at the layout."

"You mean the camera placement?" I asked.

"That, for sure. But I'd also like to look around inside Quinn's office."

"That's asking a lot, but I'll see what I can do."

"And in the meantime," Nick said, "I'll see what I can find out about the girl's parents, in particular what gives with the stepfather and his iffy church."

Nick's offer took me by surprise. "What about your job? Are you going to have time for this?"

"Rella's trying to save up to pay off some debts, so she's taking all the solo flights and I'm on a well-deserved leave. Unless something comes up that requires both of us, I'm pretty much free right now."

While Harry was shutting things down inside, Nick walked me out to the parking lot. "So where are you?" he asked.

"My car's parked next to Harry's."

"I'm not asking about your car," he said. "Where are *you*, Aimee? Where are *we*?"

I stopped and turned to face him. "You've been gone, Nick. We've barely communicated for the past two months. Most of the time I didn't even know where you were. How am I supposed to know where *we* are?"

He took hold of my hand, and I didn't pull away.

"There are times when I can't tell you where Buck's business takes us. You understand confidentiality. We just talked a few minutes ago about how it impacts *your* job. I have to deal with the same restraints in mine."

I gave his hand a squeeze. "I know, but that doesn't make it any easier. Just when we were getting our footing back and had a chance to work things out, to get closer, Buck took you away again."

"I'm back now." He leaned against the side of my car and pulled me against him. "All I'm asking is whether we're still headed in the right direction."

"I hope so," I said. "That's what I want, but—"

He stopped me in mid-sentence with a kiss that wiped everything else from my mind. I felt like a traveler who'd come home at last from a long, lonely voyage.

At that point, Harry came bounding out of the dojo, laughing. "Hey, you two, quit necking out here in the parking lot. You're going to give the dojo a bad name."

Nick and I broke off our embrace. Harry walked over and looked at me, serious again. "Keep us informed if you hear anything more from the police. I don't like knowing you're on their radar." I promised I would.

"All right then," he said. "I'd tell you two to have a good evening, but it looks like you're already headed in that direction." He slipped into his red Jag and pulled away.

But Harry's interruption had caused the momentum from our kiss to slip away. We both stood silent for an awkward moment, watching his taillights disappear into the dark night. Then I recalled the question Amah had asked about him. Was Harry seeing someone special? If anyone knew, it would be Nick.

"I have a question," I said.

"About us?"

"No, about Harry. Amah has a feeling he's seeing someone special. She's hoping she's right, of course. She asked me, but I haven't seen any evidence of it."

"Are you asking me to spill the beans about your brother's love life?" Nick's eyes narrowed, an expression that meant he was amused.

"You guys are so close I wondered if he's said anything to you."

"Sorry. If you want that kind of info, talk to your brother."

"You're invoking the *Guy Code*?"

"Something like that." Nick put his arm around my shoulders. "It's getting late, and my gut tells me we're not going to have the kind of good evening Harry was hinting at, so we should probably call it a night."

I shrugged away from his arm. "You know something, don't you?"

"Aimee, there's only one Machado I have on my mind right now, and it isn't Harry." He opened my car door for me. "My first priority is to untangle you from the murder at your workplace. Then you and I need to make up for lost time." He planted a kiss on my forehead. "Drive safe."

THURSDAY MORNING AT work I considered how I might give Harry access to Quinn's office. It seemed unlikely during the workday. How would I explain it? And without a key, I couldn't possibly get in after hours. I called Cleo for an update. She said the office was no longer off limits as a crime scene, but Quinn was not back at work. Sanjay remained in charge, working from his own office. Varsha Singh, as executive assistant for both men, was forwarding Quinn's calls to Sanjay. I asked Cleo if there had been any change in Natasha's condition.

"I can't get the actual facts on Natasha's case because of patient privacy, but I got a hypothetical from Edna Roda this morning. She said a patient with Natasha's combination of problems would still be on IV meds and fluids. She'd be getting antibiotics for at least three days, and there would be a hematology workup to make sure iron deficiency is what's making her anemic—to rule out other causes. They would also be watching for a possible abscess at the appendectomy site. If that occurred, she would need a drain."

"Sounds like a complicated treatment plan," I said.

"Yes, but the good news is that the hypothetical patient should do well under that treatment regimen. It's just that the gains would be slow because of the combination of problems."

"Getting back to our real patient, have you heard whether Hector is being allowed to visit Natasha?"

"No doubt about that. He's been in and out of PICU several times a day. Imagine the tension around that little girl's bed if her grandfather shows up while her mother and stepfather are visiting... Oops, gotta go. Later."

With that, our call ended. Not unusual. Cleo's office was Timbergate's Grand Central. Any one of the medical staff's twenty committee chairmen might drop in to discuss an agenda or sign minutes, but that was only part of it. Cleo was the gatekeeper when nurses or other department heads needed to propose items for committee agendas. Those same people relied on her sympathetic ear when they wanted to vent frustrations in private.

Privacy in a hospital was scarce, which brought me back to my original problem. How to get Harry into

Quinn's office without being noticed? First, I'd need a key. I didn't want Varsha or Sanjay involved just yet, and I definitely didn't want to ask any of the security staff to open the office. They had already gotten me into enough trouble. I suspected Quinn would be happy to provide his key, since Harry would be looking for evidence that might explain how Lowe had died in there—especially anything to take the heat off Quinn and me.

The police were still focused on Quinn, and who could blame them? I couldn't be sure how high I ranked as a suspect, but I grew uneasy every time I recalled my conversation with Detective Kass. Back then it seemed like a stretch to think I was Quinn's accomplice in a murder just because I had restrained Lowe in the conference room. When Kass interviewed me, had he known about Lowe's threats to have Quinn and me fired? If he did, he probably assumed I knew, too, and wondered why I didn't bring it up. Not a comforting thought, but it was too late to correct misleading impressions.

The only people I could think of who had reason to be angry with Lowe were Natasha's parents. Curious, I decided to have another look at the Abel's Breath Ministry website. Gailworth's verbiage was ambiguous, but he appeared to be operating outside the mainstream, to say the least. With his unconventional alternative religion and dangerous pseudo-veganism, it was hard to tell whether he believed in his doctrine, or whether he was a devious predator preying on an unsuspecting congregation. I wanted to know more.

Nick was already planning to investigate Abel Gailworth. Maybe if he and I showed up on Sunday as a couple looking for a church that suited our lifestyle, we could get a firsthand look at the Abel's Breath Minis-

try. I had never met Gailworth or Melissa, so it was unlikely they would recognize me as a TMC employee.
Unlikely, but not impossible. I decided it was worth the
risk. I texted Nick, asking him to call me at home later.
Convincing him would take more than a few keystrokes,
and I didn't want to deal with it at work.

Cleo's comment about the change in Dr. Lowe's personality nagged at me the rest of the morning. She was
right on about his intermittent flares of temper. First
striking out in the meeting, then apologizing, then flar-
ing up again, wanting Quinn and me fired. I puzzled
over his unpredictable behavior as I filled emailed requests for medical literature searches. I found myself
longing for a flesh and blood patron to walk through
my doors. When one finally did, it took me by surprise.

"You are Miss Machado, aren't you?" Hector Korba
said. The distance of twenty feet from the library entrance to my desk seemed to shrink under his long
strides.

"Yes, Mr. Korba. What can I do for you?" I stood up,
which only put me at eye level with his chest and brought
to mind David and Goliath. Some powerful men don't
look the part, but that was not the case with Korba.

"You know about my granddaughter?" His voice, a
deep bass, rumbled from low in his chest.

"Yes, I'm so sorry Natasha is ill." I gestured toward
the visitor's chair next to my desk. "Would you like to
sit?"

He gave the chair an appraising look, probably wondering if it would support his weight, and said, "I prefer
to stand, thank you. But please be seated if you wish."

I didn't wish. I was already looking up at the man.
Any higher and I'd develop a kink in my neck. Curios-

ity about his visit burned deep. He didn't take long to get to the point.

"You are the keeper of Ethics Committee files. Is that right?"

"That's right." Where was he going with this? No place I wanted to go. I had already gone rounds with Quinn and Dr. Snyder about the minutes; now I had to refuse to discuss them with the president of TMC's governing board.

"I want to read your minutes. I want to see what they say about my Natasha." *His Natasha*. No beating around the bush. Natasha belonged to him. In his mind, she was not her mother's child, and certainly not her stepfather's.

Korba's demand forced me into a gray area. Like Quinn, Korba was an ex-officio member of the Ethics Committee, and I wasn't sure his status allowed him access to the minutes. This situation was even more problematic. Protocol had dictated that he be excluded from the meeting because of his relationship to the patient whose case was being discussed. Until I could get an opinion from Cleo—or failing that, from our legal counsel—I was not going to let him see the minutes.

I hesitated, praying silently for a convenient interruption—a phone call, another patron walking in, a slight stroke. His, not mine. But he loomed over me as if his wish were my command.

"There's a problem," I said. "I'm still learning the protocols involved in meetings and their minutes, particularly as they apply to a situation like yours."

"Situation? What situation?" He folded his arms across his broad chest.

"You were absent from that meeting due to a conflict of interest. I'm afraid I can't give you access to the minutes just yet." He glowered at me. I tried not to flinch. "Mr. Korba, I'll have to contact the committee chair. If she gives me an okay, I'll let you know right away."

"Miss Machado, you do realize I will hear them read at the next Ethics Committee meeting, so what is the problem?"

"But Ethics Committee meets only as needed. It could be a few months before we have another meeting. In the meantime, this situation is still ongoing and very sensitive because of Dr. Lowe's death, and I don't want to—"

"All right, enough. I understand." Korba surprised me by smiling. The smile was a little creepy on a face as large as his, with bold features that seemed carved from granite, but apparently he intended to back off, at least temporarily.

"You know Natasha's father is dead. My Darius gave his life to protect others."

"Yes, I'm so sorry for your loss."

"My wife is gone, too. Her heart was weak. A year ago, it stopped. Natasha is all I have now. Her mother, my former daughter-in-law, is under the spell of that huckster, Gailworth." He worked his mouth as if the name left a foul taste.

"I'll call Dr. Snyder about the minutes, Mr. Korba. If she tells me you may see them, I will let you know." I maintained eye contact, hoping to convince him that was my best offer.

"Do as you must," he said, "but take a word of advice. If you wish to succeed in life, you must learn your job well enough to make your own decisions." With that, he strode out of the library. I felt the floor shake with each of his Goliath steps. I called Dr. Snyder's office immediately, leaving a request for a callback with her office manager.

SEVEN

THAT NIGHT NICK sat at my dinette table rolling his empty beer bottle between his palms while I rinsed our dinner bowls. Amah had given me her leftover kale and linguiça soup the night before, and all day I had looked forward to having it for dinner. It was barely enough to share, but it was Nick's favorite too. I had invited him to dinner so I could pitch my idea about attending Abel Gailworth's Sunday service under the guise of wanting to join his congregation.

"I don't like it," Nick said.

"Why not?" I sat at the table across from him. "Have you dug up something alarming about Gailworth?"

"You mean since yesterday?" Nick asked. "I get that you're in a hurry, but it can take a while to do that kind of digging. It requires the help of unusually talented folks."

"You've recruited Buck's geeks?"

"They're the best. You want this done right, don't you?"

"Of course, but, let's speed things up by attending one of the Reverend Gailworth's services. In the meantime, the geeks can keep digging."

Nick's silent stare told me he was calculating the odds of talking me out of the idea. Not good, and I was pretty sure he knew it. Plus, the prospect of pulling off an undercover visit appealed to his sense of adventure as much as it did mine. Harry had called us adrenaline junkies, making us sound like addicts who couldn't resist poking around in a mystery. I wasn't sure about Nick, but I only poked around in mysteries if they involved me or someone I cared about.

Finally, he said, "I assume you already know where and when Gailworth's church meets."

"They've converted the old Cartwright meat-packing building south of town."

"No kidding?" Nick gave me a puzzled look. "Didn't you say they're vegans?"

"They are. And I don't know if they chose that building to make some sort of statement, or if they just got a good deal on the rent."

"Either way, it's pretty damned ironic. Talk about leading lambs to slaughter. If we go, we'll need a cover story. Any ideas?"

I shrugged. "I thought we'd just show up as a couple. Isn't that enough?"

"Not if Gailworth starts asking questions. Why do we want to join his congregation? Are we looking for like-minded vegans? And if we're a couple, we need to decide if we're married or maybe engaged—at least committed to each other."

I couldn't quite meet his eyes. "I see your point. The vegan part is an easy yes." But his questions about our status as a couple were hitting too close to home. "Since this is Thursday, we still have two days to figure out our relationship. We don't have to do it tonight. It's getting late."

Nick reached across the table for my hand and turned it palm up. "Maybe the answer is here." He traced my heart line with his finger, sending an electric tingle up my arm. "We have to figure it out soon, Aimee." I knew he wasn't talking about our cover story.

"I know." I eased my hand away, feeling dizzy and wondering if the level of desire I felt could actually make me swoon. I got up on slightly wobbly legs and walked across the kitchen toward my door. "Why don't we talk again on Saturday?"

With that, Nick came to me, pulled me into his arms and lifted my chin. "Are you okay? You look a little flushed."

I leaned into him, taking comfort in his warmth and familiar scent. "Just tired. It's been rough at work the past four days. Lowe's unsolved murder is keeping everyone on edge. I haven't slept much since it happened."

"Shall I kiss you goodnight and let you get some rest?"

"Probably."

He did a thorough job with the kiss, then left as promised. I watched his taillights until he reached the road in front of Jack and Amah's house. My empty apartment seemed to mock me, leaving me to wonder if I would have slept better if he stayed.

I crawled into bed and listened to the tick of my wall clock as the weight of the lonely night settled over me.

MY CELL PHONE jerked me awake at five thirty Friday morning.

"What?" I croaked.

"Any luck getting me into Quinn's office?" *Harry.*

"Not yet. I'm still working on it. Why are you calling so early?"

"I don't get to sleep in. I have a mall to build." Harry's three-story mall project was quite a feather in his cap, and I didn't blame him for being protective of it. According to the latest estimate, it would be almost three years before it was finished. The City of Timbergate had placed a lot of faith in him as the architect and general contractor, and knowing my brother, he would get the job done in time and on budget.

"Let me see what's going on today," I said. "I'll get back to you."

I checked my email as soon as I got to the library. A message from Cleo told me Quinn was back at work. She made a point of mentioning that he was working out of his own office. Apparently the crime scene people had finished that part of their investigation. I still needed to get Harry into that office, and I wasn't sure if Quinn's presence would be a plus or a problem.

My second message was an automatic reminder sent out from Quinn once a month. Due to the increased incidence of shootings at hospitals in the past few years, employees of TMC were required to wear their name badges at all times while on the hospital premises and to be on the lookout for anyone seen in the building without an employee name tag or a visitor's badge. The shooting death in Quinn's office gave the reminder a new sense of urgency.

I read through another dozen messages, answered what I could, and made notes to follow up on the rest. Then I called Varsha Singh and asked for a few minutes with Quinn. When Lola Rampley arrived at nine o'clock to begin her volunteer chores, I left her in the library and walked to the main tower, hugging my light sweater close against a brisk breeze hinting at rain. The warmth of Quinn's office chased away the chill.

"How are you, Aimee?" Sitting at his desk, he held himself rigid, as if prepared to ward off a blow.

"I'm all right, under the circumstances." I sat across from him. "What about you? It must seem surreal, working in here." I stopped to clear my throat. "I mean, right here where it happened."

"It's bloody hell. Worse than a nightmare, because I'm not going to wake up, and it's not going to go away. And I can't think of a damn thing I can do to prove I didn't do it."

"But you haven't been arrested. And you're back at work, so that must mean the home office isn't too freaked out."

"That's not quite true. I'm only working part-time. Monday, Wednesday, and Friday. And that's because they think Sanjay is too green to run the place by himself. He'll be acting administrator on Tuesday, Thursday, and weekends."

"Still, they haven't suspended you."

"Not yet, but they've warned me an administrative leave of absence could be the next step. It all depends on how the investigation goes."

Suddenly chilled again, I sat down and hugged my sweater close around me. "That's what I wanted to see you about. I don't know if it would help, but I was hoping you'd let my brother have a look at your office."

"Why?" Quinn pushed back in his chair, looking surprised and unhappy.

"I'm not sure, but I told him the cameras didn't show anyone entering or leaving the administrative suite that night, and he said he'd like to take a look. Maybe his architect's eye would notice something."

"That's not going to happen. This is none of your brother's business."

Like a fist to the solar plexus, Quinn's harsh rebuke took my breath away. Never had he used that tone with me. Not long after I was hired, a work-related crisis had caused us to confide in each other on a deeply personal level. When the crisis passed, we had settled into a bond of loyalty and friendship that had remained constant over the past six months.

"I'm sorry, I thought it might help."

"I want to show you something." He walked over to a large Persian rug in the center of the floor. I stood next to him as he pulled it back to reveal a dark stain on the beige wall-to-wall carpet. It had to be blood.

"See that? They've covered it with this damned rug until the carpet can be replaced. I'm supposed to pretend it isn't there and get back to doing my job while I wait to see if I'm going to be arrested for something I didn't do." He let the rug drop.

"But Harry might notice something the police missed. And it *is* his business, in a way. He's afraid I might be accused along with you."

I watched Quinn calm himself with a deep breath before he spoke. "Aimee, I don't want your brother anywhere near this office, do you understand?" A scowl distorted his attractive features. With a jolt of sadness, I realized there had to be something he was hiding. Could this person I liked and trusted be a murderer? There must be some other explanation.

"But maybe he—"

"No." Quinn stared down at the rug for a moment, then looked up at me. "I almost forgot. Edna Roda called just before you got here. Apparently she was told you were on your way. She asked if you would stop by her office before you go back over to the library."

"I'll do that." I was glad for a change of subject. Edna was our chief nursing officer, and I'd recently worked with her to put together a collection of forensic references for the TMC nursing staff.

Quinn walked to his door and opened it, an obvious invitation for me to leave. "Once again, keep your brother out of this. Do you understand?"

"Yes."

I lied, of course. It would be more difficult without Quinn's permission, but now more than ever I wanted Harry to see that office. What was Quinn hiding?

I took the elevator to the first floor and stopped in at Edna Roda's office. Her secretary said she had left for the ER about ten minutes earlier to handle a scheduling mix-up. The emergency room was nearby, so I headed over to see if I could catch up with her. When I got there, Edna had just left, so I retraced my path back to her office, where her secretary asked me to wait while Edna finished a conference call. When I finally got in to see her, she asked about an online forensic nursing magazine she had heard about. I assured her the TMC library could afford to subscribe to *The Journal of Forensic Nursing*, and that I'd submit a purchase order right away.

With that time-consuming wild goose chase out of the way, I had killed more than thirty minutes since leaving Lola alone in the library. I sent Harry a text as I walked back across the campus. Quinn said no. Call me.

A rain cloud overhead burst open just before I reached the library building. I ran to the entrance, gave the door a shove, and smacked into it, banging my forehead on the heavy glass. I reached in my pocket for my work keys, and then realized I had left them in my desk. I did have my cell phone. I dialed the library number, hoping Lola would pick up. She was a reliable volunteer, but elderly, and her hearing wasn't the best. Especially if she had her ear buds in. She often listened to country music while she worked.

I was about to hang up when she spotted me waving at her through the glass entry door. She removed her ear buds as she hurried over to the door to let me in. I walked to my desk with my shoes squishing, leaving wet prints on the industrial-grade carpet. My library keys were in the top drawer where I had left them. I dropped them into my pocket.

"Lola, why did you lock the door?"

"I witnessed someone behaving suspiciously while you were gone," she said. "I confess I was alarmed." I didn't like the sound of that. Lola was not easily spooked. Like most career librarians, she had seen her share of patrons behaving badly. Teens making out in the study rooms, patrons stealing library materials or sneaking in food and spilling it on valuable textbooks. Even a few oddballs hiding out at closing time and sleeping in the library overnight.

"What kind of suspicious behavior are you talking about?"

"I was opening the door to come out of the restroom when I saw someone standing at your desk. He glanced around as if to see if he was alone in the library, which he was. Then he leaned over and opened one of your drawers. He seemed to be searching for something." Her cheeks colored pink as she continued. "Well, that wouldn't do, but I didn't want to get close in case he was dangerous, so I called out from restroom, 'Sir, may

I help you?' He flinched, closed your desk drawer, and hurried out."

"You saw someone looking through my desk?" I flashed back to the image of Dr. Sybil Snyder snooping at my desk the day she had convinced someone from Security to let her in. "Are you sure it was a man?"

"Almost sure. He was tall and wearing a long coat and a stocking cap." She hesitated. "Of course, everyone looks tall to me."

Lola was four foot ten with a significant dowager's hump. Even I towered over her, and I was only five four.

"Lola, you would recognize any of our usual patrons. Did this man look familiar?"

"I couldn't say. I was across the room and only saw him from behind. I couldn't even see his hair because of the cap."

She seemed to be recovering from her scare, but I didn't want to cause her more stress by grilling her further. I urged her to take the rest of the morning off, asking her to let me know if she recalled anything else.

After I sent Lola home, the library seemed emptier than usual. The wind and rain had picked up velocity, and the storm-darkened day had undoubtedly discouraged any further walk-in patrons. Fine with me. The idea of a mysterious intruder snooping in my desk had me chewing over Lola's story. I could think of no legitimate reason why someone would be searching through my desk. I decided to scour the library for evidence of suspicious activity.

I walked the entire room, looking for anything that might have been disturbed on the shelves. The rows of books and magazines were lined up evenly, precisely one inch from the edges of the shelves as Lola insisted they should be. No gaps suggested anything had been shelved carelessly by someone without a librarian's sense of neatness and order. I made another pass through the room, this time examining the floor, but saw nothing foreign. No dropped pen or pencil, no stray bit of tissue.

Trace evidence came to mind. The favorite forensic topic on television and in mystery novels. I pulled a forensic reference book off the shelf and turned to that section. The list was long: dirt, fibers, glass, hair, paint, tape, wood, scratches, metal shavings. I stopped there and hurried over to my metal file cabinets. Of the three people who had asked me about the Ethics Committee minutes, only Sybil Snyder knew what they contained. That left Quinn and Hector Korba still wondering. Feeling more than a little silly, I pulled a small, hand-held magnifying glass from my desk and scrutinized the front of each cabinet, looking for scratches near the keyholes. *Nothing.*

When I opened the drawer to put the magnifying glass back, I remembered that I had left my office keys in that same unlocked drawer while I was gone. Someone with knowledge of the hospital could have easily used my own keys to open the file cabinets and look for the minutes. I opened the cabinet and found the printed and signed copy in the Ethics Committee folder just as I had left it. But there was another way to get to the minutes. They were stored in my computer. My computer files were password-protected, which would keep most people out, but not necessarily the hospital administrator. Had Quinn come to the library knowing I was tied up meeting with Edna Roda? Looking for the password to my computer? But Lola knew Jared Quinn well. Surely she would have recognized him.

A howling surge of wind slammed against the library's double doors, rattling the glass and my nerves. I forced myself to push the mysterious visitor to the back of my mind and concentrate on my accumulating workload.

I checked the few phone messages Lola had left for me. Two were insignificant; the third captured my attention. *Call Mrs. Lowe.* Lola had written the caller's number with a clear, steady hand. Unfortunately for me, Lola was gone, so I couldn't ask for details.

Only one possibility came to mind. Dr. Lowe had a wife. Or he'd *had* a wife. Now he had a widow. I didn't relish the idea of returning Mrs. Lowe's call. Not when there was a chance that she believed I was an accomplice in the murder of her husband.

I called Cleo to see what she could tell me about Mrs. Lowe. I caught her with a few minutes to spare before she had to facilitate a luncheon meeting of one of TMC's many medical staff committees. She checked Lowe's credentials file and confirmed the phone number.

"Rita Lowe called you?" Cleo sounded puzzled. "I have no idea why she would do that."

"What do you know about her?"

"I've been around her off and on at hospital functions," Cleo said. "She isn't exactly unattractive, but she looks her age, and as a couple, she and Gavin Lowe always reminded me of a showy peacock and his nondescript peahen. Sometimes Rita's gracious and friendly, and other times she's somber and depressed."

"Do you think she's bipolar?"

"Not really. I've always thought her moods had more to do with her marriage than her brain chemistry."

"How so?" I asked.

"It's the old cliché. Lowe was ten years her junior. In return for a wedding ring, she put him through med school. Her reward was the MRS degree and the big house, but putting up with his affairs for almost twenty years must have taken a toll."

The *Mrs. Doctor* degree. I wondered how many women still considered that the ultimate achievement.

"So you're saying Gavin Lowe cheated on her? Was that common knowledge?"

"Pretty much," Cleo said. "He was good-looking and charming ten years ago when I first came to work here, but I've been told that when he first joined the staff ten years before that, he was so hot that a lot of women were throwing themselves at him. Even married women."

"Interesting. I didn't see him that way."

"No, you're too young or too smart. Probably both, but Lowe was still getting some action, from what I've heard."

"One other thing. Has Mrs. Lowe called you since her husband died?"

"No, I haven't heard from her. Oops, look at the time! Almost noon. I'd better get to my meeting. Let's catch up later."

I locked the door and put up the library's *Out to Lunch* sign. I didn't want to be interrupted or overheard by a patron while I spoke to Mrs. Lowe. She answered on the second ring. I identified myself and explained that I was returning her call.

"Oh, Miss Machado, thank you for calling. I'm sorry to impose on you at your work, but I felt compelled to speak to you about Gavin."

It must have been one of her gracious and friendly

days. She sounded perfectly stable and reasonable in spite of her husband's murder only five days earlier.

"How may I help you, Mrs. Lowe?"

"Please, call me Rita. I wanted to speak to you because the day before Gavin's death, he told me about a scuffle between himself and Jared Quinn. I understand it took place in a committee meeting and that you were present."

"I'm afraid I can't talk about that, Mrs. Lowe. I'm bound by a confidentiality clause in my employment contract."

"No matter. I already know all about it. Gavin described the entire incident. He was pleased that you stepped in when you did. He said you had done him a favor."

"Then what is it that you want from me?"

"First, you may already know that Gavin hasn't always been a faithful husband. I know that sort of gossip travels quickly in hospitals and throughout the medical community." She paused to clear her throat. "I've come to terms with that, but the police have already come knocking, so it wouldn't surprise me if I was on their radar as the long-suffering and resentful wife of a philanderer."

"I'm sorry to hear that," I said, "and I'm sorry for your loss."

"Thank you. Now I understand you've been questioned as well, so you see, it behooves both of us to see that the real killer is identified. Regardless of the circumstances, I'm unwilling to believe it was Jared Quinn." I wondered how she knew I'd been questioned, but I let it go.

"Is there someone else you suspect?"

"Miss Machado, my husband was a good person and I loved him. He treated me well in every respect but one: he cheated on me with other women. I know he had affairs, but he was careful to keep me in the dark about the women's identities."

"How is this pertinent? Do you suspect one of those women killed him?"

"I think it's possible. I know I didn't kill him, and based on what Gavin told me about Jared Quinn and you, I'm sure neither of you would kill to avenge a silly squabble. I'm more inclined to suspect jealousy. It's a powerful emotion. I learned to deal with it a long time ago, but there are people who let it fester and rule their lives."

"Are you thinking one of Dr. Lowe's women friends decided that if she couldn't have him, no one could?"

"Precisely. Gavin never once came close to asking me for a divorce so he could be free to be with someone else. I'm sure he never would have. If that's why he died, I suspect you're in a better position than I am to find out who's responsible. He had very little opportunity to meet women outside the hospital or the medical community."

"I'm not sure about that. I'll keep it in mind, but I can't make any promises."

"Nor do I want promises. I'll contact you again if I come across any helpful information, and I hope you will do the same for me. In the meantime, do what you can. And stay safe. You and I are not only vulnerable to the police, but in attempting to clear our own names and Mr. Quinn's, we could also be perceived as dangerous to Gavin's killer." That had already occurred to me, but it was unsettling to hear it from Rita Lowe.

LATER FRIDAY AFTERNOON I was filling out a requisition form for the journal Edna Roda had requested when Harry called. I asked if he had seen my text about Quinn.

"Yeah. Kinda odd he reacted that way, isn't it? You think he's guilty?" Harry had met Quinn but had never really gotten to know him. Still, his blunt question threw me.

"I doubt he's guilty, but something's going on with him. We need to know what it is."

"Hey, you know the guy better than I do, but now that he knows you're curious about the crime scene, you should watch your back."

I didn't like what Harry implied. I still couldn't buy Quinn as a killer, but his determination to keep Harry out of his office was suspicious. I was more determined than ever to find out what Quinn was hiding.

EIGHT

FOR THE REST of the afternoon my attention to library business was diverted by the mystery surrounding Gavin Lowe's death. The rainstorm dwindled down to an occasional sprinkle by quitting time, and a solitary Friday night loomed ahead, making me wonder if Nick might call. The only date we had made for the weekend was our Sunday morning visit to the Abel's Breath Ministry's nine o'clock service. But we had agreed to meet again before that to get our stories straight.

Driving home I struggled with a jumble of thoughts stemming from one central fact: someone shot Dr. Gavin Lowe dead in Jared Quinn's office. So far, it looked like Quinn and I were the two prime suspects. I knew it wasn't me, and I had been sure it wasn't Quinn either, until he refused to let Harry look at his office.

Harry called just as I was sitting down to a lonely dinner of clam chowder from a can. He was at loose ends and asked if I had any plans for the night.

"Not unless you count watching a couple of old episodes of *Monk* with Amah."

"I like those old shows," Harry said. "Especially that part where Monk says, 'He's the guy.'"

"Of course you do. You and Monk think a lot alike." It was true, but only the part about figuring out how to piece the puzzles of a mystery together. Harry wasn't OCD—he was the opposite, if there is such a thing. I envied how he usually went with the flow while I was the one obsessing over trivia. "Why are you asking about my evening?"

"I've been thinking about Quinn's office and the security cameras that show no one going in or coming out. If we can't access the office, I'd at least like to get some idea of the floor plan and the camera placement. We can't go there without being caught on the cameras, so I have another idea."

"Why don't you just go to the city building department? I thought all building plans were available to the public."

"Most are," Harry said, "but hospital construction is under the jurisdiction of the state. The plans aren't accessible online, so I'd have to travel to Sacramento to see them. And if my hunch is right, what I'm looking for would have been done without a permit or inspections, so it wouldn't show up in any case."

"You want to do this tonight?"

"Why not? Tell Amah I want you to go to a movie with me. She won't mind watching her TV show without you."

"Of course not. If I told her you wanted me to walk on hot coals, she'd help me get my shoes off. But why can't you come out here?"

"Trust me. I'll explain when you get here."

"All right, I'll be there in half an hour."

HARRY'S LUXURY CONDO sat on a bluff overlooking the Sacramento River. His living room windows faced west, and the nighttime view was a panorama of Timbergate's city lights. He let me in and led me to his home office, where he explained his plan.

"I pulled up my drafting program. If you can give me some rough sketches of the fourth-floor layout, I can create a blueprint that might be helpful."

"You can draw blueprints on your computer?"

"Of course. That's how it's done these days, except by the old-timers who don't trust the CAD system."

"What's CAD?"

"Computer-aided design. Here, take these." He handed me a pencil and a ruler. "Let's start with you making a sketch of the public part of that floor. It doesn't have to be perfect, just start with the corridor and the elevator and stairwell placement."

I took the pencil and ruler and sketched. Harry entered what I gave him into the blueprint program. "How does that look?"

"Amazing," I said, "very close."

"Now let's get specific. Think about the part of the fourth floor where Quinn's office is located. I need to see where his door is in relation to the cameras. Do you know where they're mounted?"

I tried to visualize his office. I had only begun to pay special attention since Gavin Lowe's death. "I looked for them the day after the shooting. One is focused on the entrance door to the administrative suite, and the other is mounted at the opposite end, showing the length of the corridor."

"Do you know if there are cameras in the elevators?"

"I asked Quinn. He said no."

Harry squinted at his blueprint on the screen. "Okay, go ahead."

I sketched a floor plan of the administrative suite at the east end of the corridor, showing Quinn's office on the north side and Sanjay's on the south side with Varsha

Singh's reception area between them. I told Harry that visitors had to enter through the outer door to the administrative suite and check in with Varsha, who acted as receptionist and executive assistant to both men. The only access to Quinn's office, or Sanjay's, was through the inner doors in the reception area.

"Is there anything behind the reception area?" Harry asked.

"No, only the outside of the building."

Next I sketched in a little alcove on Quinn's side of the corridor a few feet from the administrative suite's entrance door.

"What's that?" Harry asked.

"Nothing, really. It's a small dead space left after an elevator was removed several years ago. There's nothing there except a little sofa and a magazine rack. It's used occasionally for people waiting outside the administrative suite."

Harry drew in a graphic of a sofa. "Now draw the floor plan of Quinn's office. Try to remember everything you can."

I drew a rectangle and sketched in the position of the door and a large window in the wall facing the mountains to the east. "That's about it."

"You're sure? You've been in that office any number of times, but you were focused on Quinn and whatever business brought you there. Close your eyes for a moment and tell me what you see."

I closed my eyes. "I don't think this is going to help. There's nothing…wait." My eyes popped open. "There's an interior door toward the back of the room. I think I remember Cleo saying Quinn's office has a private bathroom."

"Good, that's excellent." Harry pointed to his blueprint. "Which wall is it on?"

I had to orient myself. Quinn's window faced east, and the bathroom door was on the opposite wall. "It's on the west wall, near the back corner."

Harry clicked a few keys and pointed at the screen. "Would Quinn's bathroom be behind that alcove waiting area in the corridor?"

I nodded slowly. "You know, I think it would. I guess you really are the genius in the family."

"No, that was actually pretty obvious. You said they removed an elevator there. That's probably where they got the space for Quinn's bathroom."

"Maybe a real genius could tell us how someone tampered with the cameras in a way that couldn't be detected."

"Maybe," Harry said, "but I'm going to save this blueprint. If you think of anything to add or change, let me know."

SATURDAY MORNING IN Coyote Creek started early. Jack's turkeys flew down from their roost at dawn. Then the llamas started foraging in the manger attached to the back of the barn, hoping to find leftover hay from their evening meal. The barnyard activity woke Amah's cat, Fanny, who had done me the honor of sleeping on my bed. She wanted to be let outside, and when her insistent meowing didn't rouse me, she poked at my face none too gently with her paw.

If I didn't get up and let her out, she would start grabbing mouthfuls of my hair and yanking hard enough to cause serious pain. I often wondered how someone as sweet and gentle as Amah ended up with such an intractable feline.

Once Fanny was dispatched and coffee was brewing, my thoughts drifted back to the fist fight in the Ethics Committee meeting. It seemed to have kicked off a chain reaction, starting with the killing of Dr. Lowe. Then there was the intruder Lola Rampley had spotted looking through my desk in the library. My guess was that someone had been searching for keys to the locked file cabinet that held minutes to the ill-fated meeting. Quinn and Hector Korba had both asked about them, but it didn't make sense that either would resort to something so sneaky when they could have gone over my head to Dr. Snyder. It occurred to me that she had not returned my Thursday morning call. I made myself a note to follow up with her on Monday. I didn't want to go another round with Hector Korba about those minutes.

More puzzling than the library intruder was Quinn throwing up a roadblock when asked if Harry could look around in his office. I couldn't stop thinking about Lowe's dead body lying in there and the security cameras showing no one had entered the administrative suite. I decided there might be something to do with a long, empty Saturday after all. I called Harry.

"I'll be teaching classes at the dojo from nine until noon." Harry's voice raised over background noise that sounded like a blender. "What's up?"

"What are you doing this afternoon?"

"No special plans." The blending stopped. "Why, what do you have in mind?"

"Want to come with me to TMC?" I asked.

"The boss's office? You want to risk that?"

"No, I have another idea. I'll see you at the dojo. I could use a workout."

With a couple of hours to kill, I put a load of laundry in Amah's washing machine. While I waited, she and I volunteered to be Jack's preview audience for a Power-Point presentation he was preparing on wild turkey hunting. Back in my apartment, I gathered a few items I'd need if Harry agreed with my plan. By then, it was time to head to the dojo.

As I drove into town, what kept nagging at me was Quinn's gun. Why would the killer go down one floor and then hide the gun in a Housekeeping cart? Why hide it in the hospital at all? It would have been so easy to drive away from TMC and toss the gun into the river. I could think of only one reason. The killer wanted to frame Quinn.

I helped Harry teach his brown-belt class, enjoying the workout. Afterward, we fixed salami sandwiches and tomato soup at Harry's condo and sat down to eat in his kitchen.

"Okay, tell me your idea," Harry said. "Are we going to get you fired?"

"I hope not." I opened my tote bag and took out a case that held my blue contact lenses.

He gave me a skeptical frown. "Since when do you wear contacts?"

"They're not real contacts. I wore these to a Hallow-een party back in New Haven a couple of years ago."

"Wait," Harry said. "Librarians at a Halloween party? How does that work?"

"We all dressed as literary characters we admired. I was Katniss Everdeen."

"*The Hunger Games*. Figures she'd be your hero. Or

heroine. Back to our stealth mission at your hospital. Do you really think you need a disguise?"

"Probably not. I'm rarely on the patient care floors in the main tower. The personnel who work there almost never come into the library. They email their requests and I send the articles back by return email. If they want something in print, I send it by the hospital's in-house courier service."

Harry went to the stove and refilled his bowl with more soup. "Then why the disguise?"

"Just playing it safe. After the way Quinn reacted when I asked if you could look at his office, I'd rather not be recognized snooping around the hospital with you." I took a blond wig from my tote bag and pulled it on. I had used it a time or two before when I didn't want to be recognized.

"So what's my disguise?" Harry asked. "Quinn knows what I look like."

"True, but the nurses don't, and Quinn isn't supposed to be there today. Now that he's a murder suspect, the home office is only letting him work Monday, Wednesday, and Friday. Sanjay's acting administrator on Tuesday, Thursday, and weekends, and he's never met you. There shouldn't be anyone around who would recognize you."

"Good thing, 'cause I tossed my Batman costume about twenty years ago."

I stood and took my bowl and plate to Harry's sink. "Just wear a baseball cap and keep the brim pulled low while we're in the building."

"Won't I have to check in as a visitor?"

With mixed emotions I thought about the recent reminder Quinn had circulated about checking for ID badges. Just this one day, I hoped no one looked too carefully.

"Under normal circumstances, yes," I said, "but I don't want to call attention to our visit. We'll use my master key to get into the building through a back entrance. With luck, we can get in and out without being seen."

Harry gave me a dubious look. "Do you have an excuse prepared in case we're confronted?"

"I do, but I don't like it." I handed him a fake visitor's badge. "Put this in your pocket. It's a dummy I rigged up in case we need it, but I'd feel guilty as the devil if we have to use it. Not to mention I could get fired."

"Damn." Harry pushed his empty bowl aside. "Any kind of criminal could dummy up something like this and have the run of the hospital. That's pretty scary."

"Tell me about it! I work there. Which reminds me, Quinn asked me to research some pretty sophisticated visitor management systems. As soon as this case is solved and he's back to work fulltime, he wants to recommend that the board approve putting a system in place."

"If you don't find something you like, let me know. I read up on them recently in a trade journal. He should consider metal detectors, too. Seems like a no-brainer for a hospital."

"It is, but Quinn and the board have to convince home office to foot the bill."

I went back to struggling with the blue contacts.

Harry picked up the fake ID badge, studying it for a moment. "Now tell me what you hope to accomplish on this covert mission."

I explained my theory that Quinn's gun had been

left hidden in the hospital to cast suspicion on him. I wanted to know how someone might have navigated from Quinn's office on the fourth floor down to the third floor without being seen on any of the security cameras.

"We keep coming back to those cameras," Harry said.

"I know. And Sanjay swears no one tampered with them."

He put the badge in his pocket. "So who's to say he isn't mixed up in this somehow?"

"Ouch. Darn." His question startled me and I poked myself in the eye. I blinked away the stinging tear. "Sanjay's as innocent as a newborn calf."

"Hmm." Harry's face got what I call The Look, an expression of extreme cynicism. "You're sure about that?"

"I suppose anything's possible, but you're the one who wanted to check the floor plans and have a look in Quinn's office." I gave him a significant look of my own. "You must have an idea that doesn't involve the cameras."

"I might, Harry said, but I don't want to get your hopes up. Let's do this reconnaissance mission and see if it pans out."

NINE

HARRY ADJUSTED THE bill of his baseball cap while I made sure my blond wig was on straight. Leaving his car in the TMC parking garage, we walked to a seldom-used employee's entrance that opened near the hospital's holding morgue. I wore a raincoat and bundled a scarf around my neck to hide the lower part of my face. Harry's navy-blue down jacket had a puffy rolled collar at the neckline.

I led Harry halfway down the first floor corridor until we reached the elevators. I wanted to get up to the penthouse without using them, so we took the adjacent stairwell to the third floor landing.

"I'd rather we didn't go out onto the floor unless you think it's necessary," I said. "I just wanted you to see for yourself that other than elevators, this stairwell is the only access between the fourth-floor administrative suite and the third floor where the woman with the laundry cart was working."

"Does anyone know where that Housekeeping cart was located when the gun was hidden in it?"

"Not exactly. From what I heard, the woman had only worked the east end of the third floor before she had a full load of dirty linens. She didn't spot the gun until she got all the way back to the Housekeeping Department and started emptying her cart. Housekeeping is in the building that shares space with the library and the Security Department."

"That's all the way across the hospital complex, right?"

"Right."

Harry gave the stairwell door a slight push, opening it a few inches so he could look up and down the third floor corridor.

"What's on this floor?" he whispered.

"Pre- and post-op patient rooms are on the east end, and the surgery suites are on the west end."

He stepped back and let the door close softly. "Let's go on up to the fourth floor."

We had just climbed the stairs to the landing halfway between the third and fourth floors when a rasping male voice echoed up the stairwell. I recognized it immediately as belonging to Dr. Sybil Snyder's husband, Glen Capshaw.

"Bullshit, Sybil. You're not as good a liar as you think you are with your fictional committee meetings."

I shushed Harry with a finger to my lips and gestured him to follow me up the remaining stairs.

"Glen, you're imagining things as usual. And your incessant jealousy is not only boring, it's extremely unattractive."

I heard no sound of footsteps coming up toward us. Apparently they had stepped into the stairwell down on the second floor to argue in private.

"You must think I'm blind *and* stupid. You're my wife, dammit, and you were making me look like a fool. I saw you and that bastard exchanging lovesick glances."

"There's nothing going on, dear husband, except what's happening in your overactive imagination."

"It's a good thing, sweetheart, because if you were

thinking of leaving me, you have no idea what kind of price you'd pay."

There was a moment of silence, then Snyder said, "I've had enough of this. We both have patients to see. Natasha Korba is far from out of the woods, and I should be in the Pediatric ICU right now, not standing here defending myself against your ridiculous accusations."

A door opened and closed. Snyder and Capshaw had apparently headed into the second floor corridor. Harry and I stood in the stairwell just inside the door to the fourth floor.

"Do you know those people?" Harry whispered.

"They're doctors. A husband and wife who work together in an Internal Medicine practice."

"Not exactly a loving couple, are they?"

"Doesn't sound like it. Up until now, I didn't know anything about their personal life. He doesn't do much in the way of committee work. From what I've heard, he's pretty much stopped admitting patients here. Snyder's the opposite. Admits here regularly and chairs the Ethics Committee."

"Isn't that the committee where the fight broke out?" Harry asked.

"It is."

"Is she hot?"

"What?"

"Her husband thinks she's having an affair. She must be hot, or why would he think she's cheating?"

"She's got to be over fifty. Would you call Diane Sawyer or Meryl Streep hot? Seems kind of insulting."

"So she's classy-looking?"

"I guess. I never really thought about it."

"What does her husband look like?"

"What difference does that make?"

"He thinks she's cheating. Maybe he's insecure. His voice sounded kind of scratchy, like an older man's. Is he a lot older than his wife?"

"Not really. They seem about the same age. He's pretty average-looking except for red hair and a ruddy complexion. And a bushy red moustache."

"What about her body?"

"She seems fit, but I don't spend a lot of time checking out women's bodies. Now can we drop this and get back to what we came for?" I pointed to the door that opened onto the fourth floor. "If you peek out, you'll see the entrance to the administrative suite to your right. The rest of the floor to the left houses the boardroom, two more conference rooms and the IT Department."

Harry pushed the door open and looked both ways, as he had on the floor below. "This isn't helping me much more than the floor plan we worked up in my condo." He let the door close. "Can you think of any other way to gain access to the fourth floor?"

"No. Just elevators and this stairwell."

We stood there listening for a moment to be sure there was no foot traffic in the stairwell.

Harry looked around and shook his head. "Then unless there's something we don't know about your administrator's office, it looks like the security cameras lied."

"The only people who've seen them are Sanjay D'Costa and the police."

"Maybe we should find out who saw them first and whether there was tampering."

I had a hard time wrapping my mind around Sanjay as a suspect, but Harry had a point. Either the camera data was rigged, or a ghost had shot and killed Gavin Lowe.

"How would we go about that?"

"Let me think about it. For now, let's get out of this cave. I don't want to get stuck in here if that unhappy couple decides to start round two of their domestic dispute."

We made our way out to the parking garage and headed back to Harry's place in his Jag. I pulled off the wig and heavy scarf. "Whew, much better. That wig is hot."

"Looks like you didn't need the disguise after all. We didn't see anyone the whole time we were there," Harry said. "And I didn't need the badge, so your conscience is clear."

"Thank God. Quinn was so adamant about keeping you out of his office that I didn't want to risk being caught with you anywhere near there."

Harry looked doubtful. "You really think he'd fire you over something like that?"

"I wouldn't have thought so until yesterday when I saw a side of him I never would have expected."

Harry parked in the single car garage at his condo. "Are you coming in or going home?"

"In, but just for a few minutes. I have a couple of questions." We went inside to his kitchen, where he nuked two mugs filled with chocolate milk and dumped a few assorted cookies on a plate. We sat at his dinette table fortifying ourselves with the sugary snacks.

"What are your questions?" Harry asked.

"What did you mean back there about there being something we don't know about Quinn's office? We've already looked at the floor plan. I described it as well as I could."

"You did fine. But I can't be sure what's really there

unless I can see the physical space and inspect every inch of it."

"Could you tell me what to look for?"

"It's not that simple. And even if I could, you don't want Quinn to get suspicious. If he thought you were casing his office, your job could well be in jeopardy, but if he's hiding something criminal, being unemployed might be the least of your problems."

"I can't believe Quinn's a killer, but you're right. His reaction when I asked about his office was so unreasonable it bordered on paranoia. We'll have to let it go for now."

"For now." Harry picked up an Oreo and stared at it. "Keep it in mind, though. You said Quinn's only there three days a week. Does that mean his office is empty the other four days?"

I shrugged. "As far as I know. Sanjay works out of his own office. But there are the cameras, and other people working on the fourth floor."

"Just keep it in mind. Maybe an opportunity will come up." He took out his phone and checked his messages, reminding me that we had both turned off our phones while we were at the hospital. "Looks like you and Nick are getting together tonight. Check your messages. You'll probably want to get home and do something about your hair. That wig didn't do you any favors."

I turned on my phone and saw a message from Nick wanting to meet that evening to get our stories straight for our visit to Gailworth's phony church the next morning.

At home I saw what Harry meant about my hair. It was plastered to my head like black seaweed. I sent a message to Nick asking him to show up at seven. That gave me time to shower, dry my hair, and apply a little makeup. I slipped on a pair of washed-denim jeans and a stretchy black turtleneck, then added silver hoop earrings and my favorite black suede boots.

Harry's cookies and hot chocolate had taken the edge off my appetite, but by the time Nick tapped on my door, my stomach felt hollow and I wished I had stopped for groceries on the way home. I let him in.

"You look hot," Nick said.

"Thanks." He did, too. In jeans and a Chamois shirt the color of warm wheat, he looked so touchable that I had to shove my hands in my pockets.

"Hungry? I brought enough for two." He held up a takeout bag from Wu's Palace. The food was already filling my little apartment with the promising aroma of a Chinese dinner and making my salivary glands tingle.

"I'll set the table," I said.

"I'll pour the wine. Let's eat, then we'll talk."

We ate quickly, finishing all the moo shu pork and Maureen Wu's special shrimp chow mein. I disposed of the cartons and paper plates and started a pot of coffee. This wasn't a night to drink more than one glass of wine.

Rain started up again, pattering on the barn roof over our heads. I had stoked my little wood stove earlier, but Nick went out on the deck to bring in more wood. The weather outside and the cozy warmth inside worked against our resolve. We were supposed to be plotting and planning to pull the wool over Abel Gailworth's eyes, but instead we were lulled into a setting that suggested intimacy and romance. I broke the spell by pouring us each a cup of coffee.

"Guess it's time to talk about the Gailworths," Nick said. "You first."

"The problem for Natasha is that they claim to be vegans, but apparently don't follow appropriate nutritional guidelines. They've allowed Melissa's daughter to become dangerously malnourished."

"Let's see if we can get a handle on what Gailworth is up to with his so-called church." Nick sipped from his cup. "Is he just another con in it for money, or does he really believe his own dogma?"

"Speaking of dogma, I visited his Abel's Breath Ministry website and saw almost nothing concerning traditional religious beliefs based on the Bible or any other holy book."

"Let me have a look."

I pulled up the site on my laptop while Nick watched over my shoulder.

"Look at the column of topics on the left." I pointed at the screen. "See the link all the way down at the bottom? It says, 'Is food optional?' Do you suppose Gailworth is espousing some sort of breatharian philosophy?"

Nick concentrated on the paragraphs on the screen. "His writing on the subject is convoluted, but he seems to be using the air-breather concept to make the point that the whole world is being brainwashed about food." Nick pointed to a specific sentence. "He implies that nutritional guidelines are a government conspiracy designed to keep the economy stable."

I was horrified. "God, Nick. I'm afraid for Natasha. We can't let her go back under his control. His philosophy could be a gateway into something even more dangerous. How can he possibly draw people into his congregation?"

Nick was scowling, as grimly determined as I'd ever seen him. "By preying on desperate people seeking meaning or miracles. We need to hear Gailworth preach and see how effective he is."

"We need to observe Natasha's mother, too, if she's there. Melissa Gailworth plays the key role in her daughter's life." I paused and shook my head. "I wish I knew more about her. I don't even know what she looks like. If her husband has won her over and she's devoted to his cause, that little girl of hers could be in a lot of trouble."

Nick went to the counter and refilled his cup. "You're right. We need to learn a lot more about Melissa Korba Gailworth. You wouldn't happen to know her maiden name, would you?"

I watched him standing at the counter, so cool and confident, and I realized how much I had missed him. "No idea, but I'll see if I can find out."

"Good. On another topic, I gather you and Harry did a bit of legwork this afternoon."

"If you've talked to him, you probably know the whole story." I held out my cup. As I watched Nick fill it, I realized how much I loved looking at his hands, even when he did something as simple as pouring coffee. His palms were broad, hinting at masculine strength, but the shape of his fingers had a sensuous quality that made me want to reach out and entwine them with mine. He put the pot back on the coffee maker and sat down again.

If he'd noticed any longing in my eyes as I'd observed him, he didn't let on. "Harry told me what he was able to observe about the layout of the third and fourth floors, which wasn't much, but he said you should be the one to fill me in on the husband and wife argument you heard in the stairwell."

I thought for a moment. "I had no idea their relationship was in that kind of trouble. I know her better than I do him, because she chairs the Ethics Committee, but I don't think I've ever been around them when they were together."

"So she was there at the meeting when the doctor threw the punch at your boss?"

"Yes, but not for long. She adjourned the meeting and bolted, along with all of the other doctors on the committee."

"You think she had a dog in that fight?" Nick asked.

"I hadn't thought about it, but now that you mention it, she was pretty shaken when I broke the news to her about Lowe's death."

He raised an eyebrow. "Shaken the way she'd be if someone told her that her secret lover had just been murdered?"

"Damn." I got up and walked into my little living room. "I can't believe I didn't make that connection." Nick followed behind me and put his hands on my shoulders.

"Don't be too hard on yourself. You and Harry were following another train of thought this afternoon." He steered me to my daybed and we sat side by side. He took my hand and held it. I loved the feeling.

"What a complicated twist this is. Nick, you're right. Snyder could have been having an affair with Lowe. What if her husband knew? What if Lowe's wife knew?" I told him about my phone conversation with Rita Lowe.

"Looks like you have a brand new inventory of potential suspects to consider." Nick let go of my hand and yawned, stretching his arms wide. Always a sign in the past that he was in the mood for more than hand holding.

A glance at my wall clock told me it was time to either send him away or ask him to stay.

"I guess we'd better call it a night," I said.

"You're sure you can get to sleep with all this on your mind?" He stood and pulled me up, folding his arms around me.

"It might take a while, but I have to try. It's almost midnight." I stepped back just enough to leave the circle of his arms.

"Okay, then. I'll be back tomorrow morning at eight thirty to pick you up. Let's see what we can find out about the Abel's Breath Ministry."

"Wait…" I followed him to the door. "We didn't decide about our cover story. Are we engaged or married?"

Nick's eyes held mine. "Let's just say we haven't set a date."

I watched as he drove slowly up the lane. His signal light blinked as he reached the road fronting Jack and Amah's house. *It's like our relationship*, I thought, *proceeding slowly, but heading in the right direction.*

TEN

THE SUNDAY MORNING service at Abel's Breath Ministry started at nine o'clock, but I was awake at five, so I put coffee on to brew and went to my computer. Curious about the name of Gailworth's church, I entered *Abel's Breath* in my search engine and found several links right away. I discovered that one of the translations of the Biblical Abel's name was *breath*. I realized that must be where Gailworth came up with the name. It could also explain why his website had a link to a breatharian site. Did he really believe life could be sustained by breath alone? More likely it was just a gimmick he'd come up with.

Another translation of the name Abel was *vanity*. I decided to keep that in mind while Nick and I listened to Gailworth's sermon. Vanity is an easy trait to spot in most people, but it's usually harmless. Vain or narcissistic people are annoying to be around, but Gailworth, if he was a full-blown megalomaniac with some sort of religious delusion, could be something different. Megalomania could explain his interest in breatharianism. He might be delusional enough to think that faithful followers of his ministry could exist without food.

It was time to close my laptop and search my closet for clothing that would attract the least notice possible. I didn't want the Gailworths to have any reason to remember me if we crossed paths at the hospital. I found an outfit I'd borrowed from Amah to wear to a memorial service for one of the TMC volunteers. It was a two-piece navy dress, one size too large, with a matching pillbox hat. The hat's veil, probably designed to hide the ravages of weeping for a lost loved one, would easily mask the upper half of my face.

Nick arrived, wearing jeans and a heather-green corduroy blazer over a pristine white dress shirt open at the collar. I caught the scent of his cologne, a combination of lime and exotic spices that traveled straight to my reptilian brain and evoked a quick slide show of erotic memories. I stood there breathing him in, wearing the drab navy dress with my hair pulled up into a bun.

"Nice outfit." Nick grinned. "Did you borrow that dress from your grandmother?"

"As a matter of fact, I did. It's part of our strategy."

I told him I thought we should arrive at the last minute, sit in the back, and leave immediately when Gailworth's Sunday morning service ended. Then I told him my theory about the definitions of Abel's name. I said we should keep the two words in mind during our reconnaissance visit.

"Breath and vanity," Nick said. "I don't know any living person who doesn't breathe." He grinned at me. "And everyone I know has at least a trace of vanity."

"True, but we've already seen the disastrous result of his approach to veganism, and if he's charismatic enough to be convincing, the breath thing could endanger the health or lives of his congregation."

"How do we know the breath believers aren't for real?" Nick asked.

"I don't. And I suppose anything's possible. There are documented cases of people who remain perfectly healthy on one hour of sleep a day. But it's a genetic mutation that only works for those who have that particular gene. It wouldn't work for the rest of us." I paused for a moment. "There's always a chance this breatharian thing could be something similar. And a breatharian website I visited did make it clear that it takes years to work up to existing on only air and water."

"Still, that's pretty far out."

"I know. But I'm not after the breatharian believers. Practicing their beliefs will prove them right or wrong. I just want to make sure Gailworth's dogma isn't putting members of his congregation in jeopardy."

"Including his own stepdaughter," Nick said.

"Especially his own stepdaughter."

We located the former meat-packing building a few miles south of Timbergate near the railroad tracks. Definitely the low-rent district. Nick parked his hybrid SUV on the opposite side of the street to avoid getting blocked in by other cars in the parking lot. We waited in the car until it looked like everyone else had gone inside. A makeshift banner hung from the eaves, proclaiming the name of the place of worship. I counted only fifteen vehicles in the parking lot, so our chances of going unnoticed were dicey at best.

"Ready to do this?" Nick asked.

"I don't know. Maybe it's a mistake."

"Maybe, but it's now or never. Let's take a peek. We can always turn tail if our instincts tell us not to go inside."

We crossed the street and made our way to the entry door. Nick pulled it open a few inches and we both peeked inside. Abel Gailworth stood at a lectern at the front of the room, coaxing his audience with a persuasive voice coated in honey. He looked like the guy every woman dreams of—or dreams her daughter will marry. Plenty of height—about six feet—and an impressive, well-proportioned physique, dressed in a suit that his congregation couldn't afford if they pooled their paychecks for a year.

He was handsome in an innocent, clean-cut way that inspired trust. His smile lit up the room, and he used it often in just the few minutes I observed him. The only off note was the color of his hair. It was a thick and wavy medium brown, but the sheen of it under the lights seemed unnatural, as if it might be dyed. He couldn't be more than forty, but many people go gray at an early age. Maybe he wasn't ready to accept that. *Vanity, is thy name Abel?*

The congregation, seated on folding chairs near the front of the large interior space, consisted of about twenty adults and a few children. They filled only a fourth of the room. The back row of chairs was empty. Nick gave me a questioning look. Should we go inside? I shook my head. There was no way to get lost in that small crowd. I motioned him to close the door. We walked around the building and stood near a back door, where we could hear Gailworth's preaching. Even muffled by the outside wall, I could appreciate the cadence and strength of his oratory. I tried to follow his message. It seemed to be offering solace to the unhappy, lonely, and depressed.

"Do you need a friend?" Gailworth called out.

"Yes," the voices shouted.

"Do you need a bridge over troubled water?" I heard Simon and Garfunkel's signature song playing in the background.

"Yes." This time the chorus of responses was mingled with sobs. What he said didn't matter; it was the delivery that seemed to mesmerize his followers. Each time he paused for a response, we heard the voices of his congregation calling out, "Praise Abel."

"I will lay me down," Gailworth said. "I will be your bridge. Let us breathe together."

"Let us breathe," they replied.

As the volume went up on the final verse of "Bridge Over Troubled Water," Nick very gently turned the handle of the back door and slipped it open just enough to peek inside. He immediately pulled back and quietly closed the door.

"Let's go," he whispered. I followed him back across the street where his car was parked. As he pulled away from the curb, I asked why he was in a hurry to leave after looking in the back door.

"What did you see? You acted like something spooked you."

"I saw what looked like two bodyguards. They were standing in the wings on each side of Gailworth's stage."

"Did they see you?"

"No. They both had their backs to me, but anyone in the congregation who took his eyes off Gailworth could have noticed the door open."

"That's why you're in a hurry to get us away from there?"

"Right. I didn't want those goons to come out and find us."

"But why bodyguards for such a tiny congregation? Maybe they were a couple of guys waiting to pass around the collection plates?"

"Maybe, but I wasn't going to stick around to find out."

NICK PULLED INTO the driveway at Amah and Jack's house and drove down the lane to the llama barn. We went up the steps to the deck and paused to look out at the pasture. The day had warmed into the high fifties. The past two weeks of intermittent rain and sunshine had encouraged tender green grass to spring up. Jack's grazing llamas were busy mowing it down as fast as it appeared, leaving the field as smooth and flat as a putting green. We inhaled a few breaths of freshly washed, sweet-smelling air before going inside. No matter how sweet the air, I wasn't ready to give up eating.

I started coffee and told Nick I wanted to change out of my church-lady outfit.

"Need help?" He grinned and started toward me. "I could lead you into temptation."

I *was* tempted, but I poked a finger at his chest. "No thanks, I'll manage. Go ahead and raid the kitchen if you're hungry." I grabbed jeans and a sweatshirt from my closet, did a quick change in my bathroom and brushed out my hair, letting it hang loose. Back in the kitchen, Nick had two cups poured. He had taken me at my word. There were two bowls on the table, one filled with my stash of dark chocolate kisses and the other with my incredibly expensive macadamia nuts.

"Ah," he said, "Aimee's back. What did you do with that other woman?"

"She's in the closet. I see you've discovered my two favorite health foods."

"Yup, we could live forever on this stuff." He popped a few macadamia nuts in his mouth.

I unwrapped a kiss and bit off the tip. "Now let's decide whether we accomplished anything by spying on Abel's Breath."

"I'll go first," Nick said. "It's either some sort of two-bit scam Gailworth has going, or a front for something he's tied into that's bigger."

"You got all that from seeing those two men standing in the wings?"

"Trust me. They had a certain 'look.' I've seen that look a time or two."

"What can we do with that?" I asked. "We're trying to decide whether Natasha is safe in this guy's custody. What you're saying doesn't seem to bode well for her or her mother."

"That reminds me...did you see her mother when you glanced inside the front door?"

"I don't know. I haven't any idea what Melissa Gailworth looks like. I was hoping if she was there, she'd be on the stage with him, or at least he would acknowledge her presence."

"Nothing like that happened." Nick frowned. "You've never seen her at the hospital?"

"No, and remember, there were no photos of Gailworth or his wife on the Abel's Breath website—just lots of artists' renderings of meadows and snowy mountains, and rays of sunshine slanting through clouds. And a bridge over a foaming river, of course."

We went silent for a few minutes, munching our snacks and sipping coffee until my cell phone rang. It was Harry, asking for a report. I filled him in on the scant intelligence we had gathered and asked if he had any ideas.

"You know my idea, Sis. Get me into your boss's office."

"I'm working on it."

"Work harder. You'll think of something."

Nick motioned for the phone, so I passed it over to him. He made arrangements to meet Harry later at the dojo, then rang off and put the phone on the table. After a minute it rang again. Cleo's ring tone. Alarmed, I picked up right away. Cleo almost never called me on weekends.

"Aimee, I thought you'd want to know. Natasha Korba's taken a turn for the worse."

"Oh, no! What is it?" I had a sinking feeling I wasn't going to like her answer.

"Peritonitis."

"Damn and double damn."

Cleo had been called by a nurse who was having trouble getting through to Dr. Snyder. It seemed Snyder had decided to treat herself to a spa day, leaving her husband on call for all their mutual patients. Melissa Gailworth panicked when she saw Glen Capshaw arrive in his wife's place and insisted that Sybil Snyder be called in to deal with her daughter's worsening condition.

Capshaw claimed to have no idea where his wife was. Cleo had followed a hunch and called the spa, because she and Snyder were both members there. It turned out that Snyder wasn't answering her cell phone because she had left it in a locker, along with her purse and clothes.

"Are you at the hospital now?" I asked.

"No, I didn't have to go in," Cleo said. "I called the spa from home, and they put Sybil on the phone. When she heard 'peritonitis,' she was all over it. I wouldn't be surprised if she showed up in Pediatric ICU with an avocado mask on her face and cotton between her toes."

Cleo went back to her Sunday afternoon with Sig, and I told Nick the grim news about Natasha. Peritonitis is an inflammation of the tissue that lines the inner wall of the abdomen. If it spread into Natasha's blood and other organs, she would need extensive antibiotic treatment to prevent multiple organ failure and death. Her blood chemistry would have to be checked daily, and if her hemoglobin dropped to a critical level, she would require another blood transfusion. Ironic, since her mother and stepfather had objected so strongly to the one Gavin Lowe had ordered just one week ago.

Nick's eyes were wide by the time I finished explaining. "You do know you sometimes sound like a medical dictionary, don't you? Did you ever want to be a nurse? Or a doctor?"

"Nope. I'm only good with rounding up information and passing it around. I'd be terrified to lay hands on a patient."

"Speaking of laying on hands…" Nick walked over and put his hands on my waist. I closed my eyes and raised my face for a kiss, feeling vulnerable and wanting him. After a moment, when nothing happened, I opened my eyes. He stood there looking down into my face with a puzzled expression.

"You're not going to pull away or tell me you're not ready for this?" His voice was husky and urgent, but his question had broken the spell. I stepped back.

"What is it, Aimee?"

"Are you sure *you're* ready? You seemed to have doubts last night."

"What do you mean?" His brows rose as he remembered. "That business about saying we haven't set a date? That was for our cover story."

"Are you sure? We were stuck in neutral the two months you were away. We might not be ready… I don't know, Nick. Somehow I think we're both holding back."

"You're right." He stepped away from me and leaned

against my kitchen counter, crossing his arms in front of him. "I've been patient because of Paris, and because no matter how many times I tell you nothing happened the week I was there with Rella, you'll always have doubts. I want to be with you, but I won't make that commitment unless you believe that I would never cheat on you or lie to you."

"And do you believe the same about me?"

"Absolutely, and that's the problem, as I see it. I believe in your integrity one hundred percent." As he walked to the door, he shook his head again. "I keep hoping you'll eventually feel the same way about me, but I'm running out of ways to convince you."

This was my chance to make him understand. "You don't have to *convince* me of anything. I've finally realized that whatever is going on with me goes deeper than Paris."

"Want to explain?"

"I'm not sure I can. Did you ever want something terribly, wait for it, then get it, only to fear that it might be snatched away?"

"Not really. I've always been of the school that says cut your losses and move on."

"You make that sound so easy."

"It was, until you came along." He pulled me into a hug. "I'm not ready to cut my losses yet."

"Neither am I."

"Then we're still in this together. That's enough for now."

After he left, I realized Nick and I had learned nothing concrete about Abel Gailworth. On the other hand, we at least had defined the problem holding back our relationship. *Trust.*

Thinking it through, I realized what was holding me back. I had never felt insecure or vulnerable with other men I dated because I'd never cared about them the way I cared about Nick. I wanted to be with him for the rest of my life, and a few months ago, I'd almost thrown that chance away. Since then I'd learned a hard lesson. I wanted no part of an emotion as negative as jealousy to come between Nick and me.

That reminded me of the conversation Harry and I had overheard in the TMC stairwell the day before. Sybil Snyder was right when she told her husband his jealousy was boring and unattractive. His tirade was downright ugly.

Harry had been struck by Capshaw's jealousy, too. He had asked me then if Sybil Snyder was hot. I thought I knew why he asked. Some men can't deal with a pretty wife. Snyder *was* attractive, but lately her hair was a lighter shade of blond and its style more glamorous. Was she grooming herself to please a man other than Glen Capshaw, her suspicious husband? An interesting question, one I had told Harry had nothing to do with Lowe's death.

Now I wasn't so sure. Was there a chance she and Lowe had been stealing moments together? She had seemed shaken when I told her he was dead, but so was I when I first heard the news. I thought back to the Ethics Committee meeting. Had Snyder and Lowe been giving off signals? I recalled the seating arrangement. Snyder had sat at the head of the table, and I had been on her right, facilitating and taking minutes. Gavin Lowe had sat on her left. Quinn was next to Lowe. Could I make any inferences from Lowe sitting close to Snyder at that meeting?

I couldn't recall any telling glances exchanged between them that morning, although I did flash on a moment before Snyder called the meeting to order. She realized she didn't have a pen and asked me if I had an extra. Before I could answer, Lowe had taken one from his inside jacket pocket and held it out to her. She hesitated, then took the pen without thanking him and proceeded to call the meeting to order. She wasn't a warm fuzzy type, but I'd never known her to be rude to her colleagues.

The pen exchange didn't prove anything was going on between Lowe and Snyder, but the more I thought about it, the more I was convinced it struck an odd note. The quarrel Harry and I overheard in the stairwell proved Glen Capshaw was jealous of someone he referred to as *that bastard*. He had not mentioned a name, and he hadn't referred to Lowe's murder, but I had a feeling Capshaw belonged on the list of people who might have wanted Lowe dead.

ELEVEN

FIRST THING ON Monday morning I spotted an email reminder of TMC's Department Head meeting scheduled for ten o'clock. Quinn was still working on Mondays, Wednesdays, and Fridays, so I assumed he would chair the meeting, as usual. There was no agenda attached, which was often the case if last-minute items were being added on the day of the meeting.

Department Head meetings were mostly routine, with each person giving an oral report. I rarely had any exciting information to share, so my turn usually came toward the end when my colleagues were sneaking peeks at their watches or phones and hoping I'd be brief.

I pulled my report from the previous month and updated a few minor points about subscriptions to new databases and medical journals. I added a reminder that many popular medical texts, such as *Gray's Anatomy* and *Harrison's Principles of Internal Medicine*, were available for download into e-readers like Kindle and Nook.

With that out of the way, I called Cleo to see if she had any new word on Natasha Korba's condition.

"She's improving," Cleo said. "But I hear her stepfather is questioning every minute detail of Natasha's care."

"That's going to be a problem if Natasha needs more blood."

I heard Cleo sigh. "No doubt, unless Sybil Snyder

can win over Melissa Gailworth. That husband of hers seems to have a powerful hold on her."

"What about Hector Korba? Have you heard how he's reacting to all this?"

"Not well. He's in the unit demanding to be kept informed almost hourly. The nurses know he's president of the governing board, so they're complying, but you can imagine their stress level."

"It's so unfair—their job is already so demanding."

"I have to get off," Cleo said. "I'll see you at the Department Head meeting."

I thought about Gailworth's dangerous hold over his wife and what it meant for her daughter and found myself hoping Korba could convince the courts to give him custody. He might be gruff and intimidating, but I guessed he was a softy where his granddaughter was concerned.

A while later Sanjay D'Costa walked into the library along with a slightly familiar elderly man wearing the orange blazer of a hospital volunteer. He was shorter than my five foot four, and the sleeves of his jacket almost hid his hands. His blue eyes twinkled behind wire-rimmed glasses, and he sported an impressive crest of thick white hair.

"Good morning, Aimee." Sanjay flashed a brilliant white smile. "This is Mr. Bernard Kluckert, here to become your Tuesday and Thursday auxiliary helper."

Before I could ask why I was getting another volunteer, and why he was here on Monday if he was supposed to work Tuesday and Thursday, Mr. Kluckert put out his hand.

"Bernie's my name. Put 'er there, miss." I shook his leathery hand. He was one of those men who don't want to let go, but I managed to pull my hand away.

"Nice to meet you. I'm Aimee Machado. Thank you for volunteering." I gave Sanjay a questioning look, which he didn't seem to notice.

Bernie looked around the room. "I'll be here tomorrow morning, Miss Machado, ready to work, don't you see?" I heard clicking noises when he spoke and guessed his denture adhesive wasn't getting the job done. Apparently my fate was sealed. I had a new volunteer, whether I wanted him or not.

"Mr. Kluckert made a special request to be transferred to the library," Sanjay said. "I know you no longer have help on Tuesday and Thursday, so it occurred to me that this is the perfect arrangement." He seemed so proud of himself I decided to let it go. If Bernie had any skills at all, I could probably find something for him to do.

"Is Lola Rampley working today?" Bernie asked.

I glanced at the wall clock. "She'll be arriving soon. Do you know her?"

"Oh, yes." His eyes lit up and I began to suspect where his interest in the library was really focused. Lola, a widow for more than a decade, had put herself back on the market, and she was in demand. I thought back to the day a week ago that I had organized a birthday party for Lola. She'd left with another volunteer, Oslo Swanson. Now I recognized Bernie Kluckert as the man who had seemed disappointed to see Lola on Swanson's arm.

"You know, Bernie, you won't be working with Lola. She's here only on Mondays, Wednesdays, and Fridays."

Bernie seemed unfazed. "I'm aware of that, but working here will give us something in common to chat about, don't you see." The clicking sounded again, and he used his thumb to push up on his two front teeth. "When Lola said you needed help, I jumped at the chance. Beat out that kid, Swanson, don't you see?"

Just what I needed. Another love triangle. I knew Oslo Swanson was no kid. Lola had confided to me that he was seven years her junior, which put him at seventy-five. I suspected that Bernie Kluckert was closing in on ninety. I'd have to remember not to do anything on his work days that might startle him.

Sanjay and Bernie left, missing Lola's arrival by five minutes. When I told her the news about my new volunteer, she blushed and fluffed her snowy cap of hair with delicately manicured pink fingertips. "He's a very nice man. I'm sure he'll be helpful."

I waited for more, but Lola kept any other thoughts about Bernie to herself and went about shelving the newly arrived journals. Requests for online resources kept me busy until it was time for the Department Head meeting.

I reached the conference room in the main tower in time to save a seat for Cleo. She blew in and sat down next to me as Sanjay called the meeting to order. Varsha Singh sat at his right, taking minutes. Cleo and I exchanged sidelong looks. Where was Quinn? Sanjay had never chaired a Department Head meeting. We soon learned why Quinn was absent.

Sanjay stood. "First order of business. I should like to explain that Mr. Quinn will no longer be working on Mondays, Wednesdays, and Fridays." He cleared his throat and continued. "Nor will he be on the premises of Timbergate Medical Center any other day. Although his administrative leave of absence is probably temporary, you must understand that I now hold complete responsibility for every facet of this medical center until he is permitted to return." Varsha looked up from her note taking, her expression grim.

"Crap on a cracker," Cleo whispered.

Murmurs filled the room, and several hands were raised. Sanjay held up both of his hands, palms out. "Please do not ask for details. This is a home office decision and I have been instructed that no explanations are forthcoming at this time. Now let us get on with the usual business of routine reports." He sat down and nodded at Edna Roda, chief nursing officer, whose face was beet red. She'd been blindsided just like everyone else, but she managed to get through her report.

The meeting dragged on for an hour and a half, ending with my yawn-inducing report on the business of the Health Sciences Library. As soon as we were out of the room, Cleo headed across the street to Margie's Bean Pot to save a table, and I hurried to the library to tell Lola I was going to lunch. I asked her to leave early so I could lock up, then sprinted over to Margie's so Cleo and I could hash over the news about Quinn.

Cleo had picked a table in the back corner, where we could avoid being overheard. I ordered the special, navy bean and bacon soup.

"Good choice," Cleo said. "That's what I'm having."

I unfolded a napkin. "Did Sanjay warn you about Quinn?"

"Not a word. And I haven't heard from Quinn, either. You?"

"Nothing. What do you think it means?"

Cleo took a sip of water and said, "I'd ask Sanjay, but he's been inaccessible lately. I'm starting to think his newfound responsibility is going to his head."

"No kidding. Besides, he's already warned all of us that it was a home office decision."

"'No explanations are forthcoming,'" Cleo said. "What kind of BS is that?" She thought for a moment. "I've met TMC's legal counsel in L.A. a time or two, and we confer by phone fairly often about medico-legal stuff. I'll give Loren Davidson a call."

Knowing Cleo's winning way with men, I guessed that was our best shot. Any man who had met her would remember her voluptuous figure, and most of them would probably tell her more than they should.

"That's a good idea. Do you think one of us should call Quinn?"

"Definitely." Cleo grinned. "Why don't you do that? He seems to think a lot of you."

"I thought he did, until I asked him if Harry could have a look at his office." I hadn't told Cleo about Quinn's adamant refusal, so I filled her in.

"My God, Aimee, that sounds so unlike him." Cleo's obvious distress made me I wish I'd kept the news to myself. I knew what she was thinking, because I had thought the same thing. If he's innocent, why be so protective of his office? *The crime scene.* "I'd better call him myself," she said. "I'll play dumb if anything comes up about you wanting Harry to have access to his office."

"Good. You'll probably have a better chance getting through to him, but he might not be taking calls."

"Can't hurt to try," Cleo said. "We need to get back to work. With Sanjay in charge, I'm afraid we're going to be busy keeping him out of trouble. He's awfully green."

"Speaking of that, do you think Varsha Singh knows why Quinn was put on leave? Executive assistants are usually privy to almost everything that involves their supervisors."

"She might, but she's bound by a confidentiality clause just like we are, and her loyalties are divided between Quinn and Sanjay. She's paid well to keep what she knows to herself. I'd rather not approach her until we've consulted our other sources. She can't afford to risk her job; I happen to know she's a single mom."

"Wow, I didn't know that."

With her four kids at home and Sanjay at work, Varsha wasn't someone to envy, no matter how well she was paid. I remembered her somber expression at the Department Head meeting. She clearly had her doubts about Sanjay's ability to fill Quinn's shoes.

Cleo and I were finishing our soup when Margie strapped on her accordion and perched on a stool across the room from us. The remaining Bean Pot diners were in for a treat. Margie's spot-on renditions of tunes heard in Parisian cafés and bistros in the first half of the twentieth century delighted her loyal patrons.

We left reluctantly and walked back across the street together. When we got to the library, Cleo said she needed to come inside and use the restroom. While she took care of business, I went to my desk and found a message Lola had written earlier while I was at the Department Head meeting.

Call Mr. Korba.

I thought back to my unpleasant confrontation with Hector Korba about the Ethics Committee minutes. Was he calling about that, or was something else on his mind?

I had forgotten to ask Cleo if Korba was allowed to see the minutes, but this would be the perfect time. If she wasn't sure about the status of ex-officio members

of TMC's medical staff committees, she could ask for
a legal opinion when she called Loren Davidson. She
came out of the restroom and started toward the exit
with a wave in my direction.

"Wait, Cleo, I just remembered a legal detail I've been
meaning to ask you."

She turned and came up to my desk. "You can try
me, but I'm no lawyer."

"I'm sure this is something you know, but it came
up for the first time for me last week, and I wasn't sure
how to handle it." I told her about the day Korba had
come by asking about the content of the Ethics Committee minutes.

She raised her eyebrows. "Did you let him see them?"

"No, and I meant to ask you then, but Korba never
approached me about it again, and it slipped my mind."

She nodded. "You did right. He's an ex-officio member of the Ethics Committee. He doesn't have the same
rights as the physician members of the committee."

"Is that also true for Quinn?"

"Yes, and he and Korba are both peeved about it. They
sit on the governing board, where they're full members with equal rights, and it rubs them the wrong way
when the medical staff committees make them feel like
second-class citizens."

"Do ex-officio members of committees always have
restricted rights?"

"No." She smiled. "Remind me, do you have a copy
of *Robert's Rules of Order* in your library?"

I blushed. "Of course. I never thought—"

"Don't be embarrassed. It's helpful in general terms,
but it wouldn't have answered your question. *Roberts*
clarifies that ex-officio is a method of sitting on a committee, not a class of membership." She raised a finger,

"But—and this is the stickler—the bylaws covering the committee in question can restrain their rights, and that's our situation. TMC's Medical Staff Bylaws do not allow any ex-officio members the same rights as our physician members."

After Cleo left, I returned Korba's call with a sense of dread. Sybil Snyder had not returned my call, so I assumed the answer was still *no*. I didn't look forward to refusing him again. I wondered if he had gone to Snyder himself to request access to the minutes. Korba was out, so I left a message and went back to my routine tasks with snippets of Margie's mellow accordion serenade playing in the back of my mind.

Harry called as I was shutting down the computers at quitting time. As I picked up, I remembered that there was one plus to Quinn's being banished from the TMC campus. His office would be empty until he was allowed to return.

"I have news," Harry said.

"So do I, but you go first."

"Not now. Do you want to come to the dojo tonight?"

"Why? Aren't you teaching a class?"

"I am, but it's peewees, so I'll finished at six thirty. Why don't you come and help? We can compare notes after."

"Sounds like fun. I like working with the kids." Harry's peewee class started at five thirty. The children were ages three to six, so an hour was a challenge to their energy and attention spans. My gi bag was in my car, so I drove straight from work to the dojo.

THE PEEWEE CLASS was made up of half boys and half girls—sixteen in all. They wore their little gis with pride and took their instruction from Sensei Harry with dignity beyond their years. It was a source of pride to watch him work with the youngest kids and a special treat when I had a chance to help out. After we put them through their basic holds and throws, they played the sumo game where they were matched with an opponent and put inside a circle. Whichever opponent caused the other to step outside the circle was declared the winner. The kids looked forward to the game as a treat at the end of their hour.

They bowed off the mat and went to their respective changing rooms, where I heard happy laughter coming from the boys and giggles and squeals from the girls. The final ritual was collecting their treats from the candy jar, and then the peewees headed home with their parents.

Harry and I changed out of our gis, locked the dojo, and headed to his condo. His place was warm, clean, and cozy. As usual, I took a moment to look through the wall of windows overlooking the Sacramento River at the panorama of Timbergate's city lights. While he poured two glasses of Merlot, I shrugged out of my jacket and shoes. Then I took my glass to his living room and sat on the couch with my feet curled under me.

"Long day." Harry came out of the kitchen carrying a plate of crackers and cheese. He put it on the coffee table and sank into his easy chair. "Let's trade intel and see if we have anything to work with. You first."

"Okay. As of today, Quinn is no longer working three days a week. He'll be on leave for an unspecified period of time. Sanjay announced it at our Department Head meeting."

Harry lifted his glass. "A toast to serendipity."

"What?"

"My news and your news might bring us the chance we've been looking for. I heard a couple of guys talking at the gym this morning about a fire drill scheduled at TMC."

"We have them every month. Why?" Then my brain clicked into gear. "Oh, I get it. A fire drill might be our best chance to sneak you into Quinn's office."

"I was hoping you'd say that." Harry left his easy chair to come over and sit next to me on the couch. "Tell me about the drills. The fire department doesn't show up, does it?"

"No. The staff in the area of the drill activates the nearest fire alarm box, so the alarm sounds throughout the hospital during the drills. When the drill is scheduled, the hospital alerts the company monitoring the fire alarm system in advance, so the fire department won't be dispatched."

"The guys I overheard must work for the fire alarm company that TMC uses."

"Sounds likely. After the drill, the hospital administrator contacts them to verify the time that an alarm signal was received and to let them know when the drill is completed."

He gave me a little punch in the arm. "You have this down, don't you? I'm impressed."

I smiled and shrugged. "I had to memorize the whole fire drill procedure. I'm a department head, so I have specific duties if there's a drill in my building. I'm responsible for guiding any patrons or employees to safety. Then I wait outside with them until an all-clear is announced."

He tapped his chin thoughtfully. "You said the administrator follows up. That will be your acting admin-istrator?"

"Right. Sanjay should be physically present in which-ever location the drill takes place. Did they say anything about which area or which shift?"

"They were talking about middle of the night," Harry said. "I heard them mention the emergency room."

"Oh, boy." I set my glass down and turned to Harry. "That's the worst. They could be handling any variety or number of critical patient situations when that alarm sounds, but when their turn comes up, they have to do the drill just like everyone else."

"If it's in the middle of the night, would anyone be up on the fourth floor?"

I thought for a moment. "Sanjay would have to be in the building, but he'd be supervising the drill. Emer-gency's on the first floor."

"Anyone else work on the fourth floor at night?"

"Varsha Singh—Quinn and Sanjay's executive assis-tant—wouldn't need to come in after hours for the drill, so no, that floor would be empty."

"Any chance of us getting in and out of the adminis-trative suite while no one's in there?"

"During the drill? A good chance, but only if I had keys, which I don't, and even if no one's around, there's still the problem of the security cameras."

He punched his hand with his fist. "Damn the cam-eras! I have an idea, but we'll need Cleo's help. Does she have keys?"

"As far as I know, she has keys to everything *except* the administrative suite."

He reached for his glass again, then realized it was

empty. "She has a lot of clout there, doesn't she? Is there any way she could get her hands on those?"

"I don't know, but that reminds me, she was going to call legal counsel at the home office to ask about Quinn's abrupt leave of absence." I picked up my phone. "Let's see what she found out." I reached Cleo at home and asked if she had talked to Loren Davidson.

"I did, but it was just before I left work. I was going to fill you in tomorrow morning. What's up?"

I explained Harry's idea about the fire drill and asked about her keys.

Cleo sighed. "This must be your lucky day…or my unlucky one."

"Why?"

"I wasn't supposed to tell anyone, but Davidson is uneasy with Sanjay at the helm, so he's already ordered Security to issue me a set of keys to the administrative suite. I picked them up this morning, but I'm supposed to use them only if there's a catastrophic emergency." I heard the wariness in her voice. "He mentioned an earthquake or a shooter, God forbid."

"Or a fire?" I asked.

"Of course, but not a fire *drill*."

I smiled at Harry and gave him a thumbs up. I was pretty sure I could convince her. "This is a special case. I think you should tell Sanjay that home office wants us to assist him with the drill. He's never been in charge of one. He'd probably appreciate our help."

"Is this plan of Harry's supposed to save Quinn's neck?"

"That's the idea, but I think Harry's more concerned about my neck than Quinn's."

"Why? Have the police contacted you again?"

"Not so far, but I get uneasy every time my phone rings."

After a silent moment, Cleo said, "Okay, come by my office tomorrow and tell me what we have to do."

"I will. Don't forget to approach Sanjay about the fire drill. As soon as we know for sure what time it's scheduled, we need to let my brother know." Harry heard that and broke into a grin.

Cleo sighed again. "I'll take care of it. Anything else?"

"One more question. Have you tried calling Quinn?"

"Didn't need to after I talked to Loren at home office. Remind me to tell you about that tomorrow morning."

I filled Harry in on Cleo's half of our conversation. "I guess that's all we can do for now. I'd better get home."

"Not yet. I just refilled your glass." Harry, who'd been pacing during the phone call, plopped down in his easy chair. "I want to hear about that lip lock I saw the other night in the dojo parking lot."

His quip about the kiss Nick and I shared triggered a reminder. I'd asked Nick if he knew who Harry was dating, and he'd replied that I should ask my brother. If I was going to do that, now was the time.

"Only if you agree to a *quid pro quo*," I said. "And you go first."

Harry set his glass on a marble-topped side table next to his chair. "What makes you think I have anything to tell?"

"Call it woman's intuition. Not mine—Amah's. She thinks there's a woman in your life. She's always had a sixth sense when it comes to us. Remember? We used to think she could read our minds."

"Amah wants to know who I'm dating? Since when?"

"Since she thinks it might be serious, even exclusive. I asked Nick, but he invoked the *Guy Code*. He said to ask you, so I'm asking."

"You might not like the answer." Harry gave me an apprehensive look.

"Come on, that doesn't make sense. I'm always on your side. If you're seeing someone who makes you happy, how could I object to that?" I did have some *no-nos*. Married women were off-limits. So was any woman who might get cold feet about dating a man with our Eurasian parentage, especially if her family objected. That had already happened to Harry once. I'd seen my brother's heart break a little back then, and I wasn't about to see it happen again.

While I was waiting for his answer, Harry's cell phone rang. He reached for it, looked at the screen and answered. "Hi. Aimee's here, I'll call you back." He put the phone back on the table next to his chair. "Speak of the devil," he said.

"That was her? You told her I'm here. That means she and I know each other, doesn't it?"

Harry glanced at the phone in his hand. "It means she knows I have a sister named Aimee."

"No, it was the way you said it…like she knows me." I was more curious than ever. "Come on, if you're going to keep seeing her, you can't hide her forever."

"You're right. But first, finish that glass of wine."

"Better not. I have to drive home."

"Then here goes," Harry said. "I've been seeing Rella Olstad for about two months."

"Rella? Nick's ex?" I sprang to my feet.

Harry yelled, "Sit." I forced myself back onto the couch, took a deep breath and let it out before I spoke.

"You've been…*what*? How?"

"We started dating not long after she helped you out of that scrape a while back."

"And Nick knows?"

"Of course. He's my best friend and Rella's his co-worker. It would have been pretty difficult to keep him in the dark."

"Then why have you waited so long to tell me?"

"Because you and Nick split over that mix-up with Rella in Paris. The three of us realize it threw you, hurt you, and we weren't sure how you'd feel about my dating her. We could have kept it quiet if she and I had one or two dates and hadn't clicked. Now we're pretty much exclusive, so I guess it's time to bring it out in the open."

"Nick's okay with it? You're sure?"

"Of course. You might not know him as well as you think you do. I think you've underestimated both of them, Aimee. Especially Rella. It's time you got to know her a little better."

His words humbled me, made me feel a little like a child who's been scolded, knowing it's deserved and saddened for having disappointed the person doing the scolding.

"You're asking me to do something very difficult, you know."

"I know." Harry rose and pulled me up from the couch, wrapping me in a bear hug. "But you're my Big Sis. We've always had each other's backs. However this turns out, we'll get it right."

The late hour and the heavy conversation had drained the last of my energy. I told Harry I needed to get home.

"Not fair," he said. "The deal was *quid pro quo,* and I didn't get any juicy tidbits about you and Nick."

"I don't have anything to tell you that tops what you've come up with tonight…except that this news adds a whole new twist to my own relationship. Give me time to process it."

"Whatever you want." He picked up his phone. "Now scram. I have a call to make."

TWELVE

I'D HAD A nearly sleepless night after my visit with Harry and our conversation about Rella, but I managed to push that diversion aside and got on with my Tuesday morning. Library business took a back seat for the first hour. I called Natasha Korba's nurse in the Pediatric ICU and got the standard answer offered to callers who are not relatives: "Doing as well as can be expected."

Hector Korba had not called back, and I'd had no word from Sybil Snyder giving him permission to read the Ethics Committee minutes. The phone sat on my desk like a coiled snake. It would ring eventually. When it did, I hoped it would be Snyder and that the answer would be yes. If it was, Korba would read about the altercation between Lowe and Quinn, but that couldn't be helped. At least he'd stop hounding me about the minutes.

My close ties to my own grandparents made me sympathetic to Korba's concern for his little granddaughter. Amah once told me that Harry and I were her greatest happiness. I suspected Natasha was the greatest source of happiness in her grandfather's life. Maybe the only source.

I also wondered about Cleo's call to home office to ask about Quinn's leave of absence. I planned to walk over to the main tower to get her report, but I couldn't leave until my new volunteer arrived.

Bernie Kluckert strolled in at nine sharp wearing the auxiliary members' bright orange blazer. I had wondered about the color when I first began working at TMC, but eventually I was told it was important that the volunteers be easy to spot. Over the years there had been a few who wandered off course.

"Top of the morning to ya, miss." Bernie greeted me with a salute. He held it, standing at attention until I realized he was waiting for me to respond somehow.

"At ease," I said. I felt silly, but it worked. He lowered his arm. "It isn't necessary to be so formal, Mr. Kluckert."

"Navy man," he said. "Korea. Old habits die hard, don't you see?"

The clicking of his false teeth reminded me of our introduction the day before and of his interest in Lola Rampley. Lola was so efficient on her three mornings a week that there was very little for Bernie to do. How would I keep him busy for three hours every Tuesday and Thursday? Bernie solved the problem for me.

"Looks like your plants are thirsty, miss." He touched the drooping leaves of a philodendron in a pot on the corner of my desk. "Are they being fed regular?"

I had inherited dozens of potted plants from a former volunteer. She had made it her mission to rescue any left behind by discharged or deceased patients. An unfortunate medical situation had forced the volunteer with the green thumb to leave town, and neither Lola nor I had been diligent about caring for the plants. When they looked near death, either or both of us would douse them with water, but that was about the extent of our horticultural commitment. Bernie might be their savior.

Bernie and I worked out a schedule for his two mornings a week. He protested that he would need more to do than care for the plants. I noticed that he frequently ran a finger along any flat surface within reach to check for dust, so I added light housekeeping to his routine. I hoped he wouldn't feel the chore was too menial, but instead of being disappointed, he seemed pleased.

"Good on me." He beamed and pulled a little white dust mask from his pocket. "I tend to get to sneezing if I'm around a lot of dust. We'll get this place cleaned up right smart. Lola will be impressed, don't you see?"

I took out the can of furniture polish I kept in my desk and handed it over as if giving him the keys to the city.

With Bernie's three hours mapped out, I turned to the details of the Lowe mystery that were grappling for my attention. I had planned to walk over to the main tower to hear what Loren Davidson had told Cleo about Quinn's mandatory leave of absence. Then we had to iron out the details of how to slip Harry into Quinn's office during the fire drill. I warred with my conscience about leaving Bernie alone in the library on his first day, but I decided to risk it. I gave him specific instructions about how to answer the phone and take messages and asked him to tell any walk-in patrons I'd be back within the hour. With some misgivings, I headed to the main tower to meet Cleo.

"Close the door." Cleo got right to the point. "The fire drill in ER is scheduled for tomorrow night—or to be precise, one o'clock Thursday morning. I've convinced Sanjay that home office wants you and me to be there to act as his backup."

I sat across from her. "Excellent. I'll let Harry know."

"All right," Cleo leaned toward me, "now tell me how this is going to work."

"I will, but first I want to hear what Loren Davidson had to say about Quinn."

"Not much." Cleo glanced at a notepad on her desk. "Home office doesn't like the idea of a murder suspect roaming the hospital. Admission numbers have dropped substantially in the week since Lowe's death was reported in the media. A lot of doctors are refusing to admit their patients here until the grisly matter is resolved."

"So Quinn is banished, even though he hasn't been charged? What about me…am I going to be next?"

"I doubt it," Cleo said. "You're so low profile, home office is barely aware of your existence." She reached across her desk and patted my arm. "Sorry if that sounds insulting, but in this situation it's a blessing, so let's get back to the fire drill and the plan you and your brother concocted."

"Okay. It's pretty simple. You and I will tell Sanjay that during the drill, the fire alarm agency wants one of its employees to check something in Quinn's office called an annunciator panel."

"Are you sure there's a panel like that in his office?"

"Yes. Harry showed me some photos of different models and I recognized one of them as that rectangular red box on the inside wall of Quinn's office next to his bathroom door. Harry says it has groups of lights that show the status of all sorts of systems in the building. If it picks up anything abnormal, an audible signal goes off to alert the person in the office."

"Abnormal like a fire?" Cleo asked.

"Right. Harry tried to explain more about how it works, but all I needed to know is that we can tell Sanjay it must be checked during the drill."

"So the person doing the checking is going to be your brother? Won't he be recognized on the security cameras?"

"I doubt it. No one at the hospital knows him except Quinn, and he's not going to be around. We'll rig him up a fake uniform, complete with a billed cap to obstruct the view of his face."

"This seems like a boatload of trouble." Cleo looked up from her notepad where she'd been jotting. "Tell me again why Harry needs to get in there?"

"Because no one has found any evidence of tampering with the data on the security cameras, yet somehow Lowe and his killer ended up in Quinn's office. Harry thinks that room holds the key to finding the killer. I know it wasn't me, and I'm almost certain it wasn't Quinn."

Cleo blanched. "*Almost?* How can you say that? Of course Jared didn't do it."

"So let's see if we can figure out how Lowe and his killer got in there."

Cleo took a deep breath, and the color returned to her face. "Let's. What time shall we show up for the fire drill tomorrow night?"

"How about midnight in the parking garage? That'll give the three of us plenty of time to go over our plan. Maybe we can get into the administrative suite a little ahead of time before the drill starts at one o'clock." I glanced at my watch. "I'd better go. I left a new volunteer in the library by himself."

"Before you go, I thought you'd want to know the word is out that Natasha's gaining ground. According to Hector Korba, she's making remarkable progress."

I smiled with relief. "That's great news. Have you

heard any more about her mother and stepfather? Or about Hector's efforts to get custody?"

"Hector's pushing it pretty hard right now. I guess he thinks Natasha's hospitalization is going to make his case for him. It's obvious that the girl was malnourished and in poor health even before the emergency appy."

"That appendectomy might have been a blessing in disguise," I said, "if her restricted diet had set her up for brain damage and heart problems."

"Exactly." Cleo nodded, dropping her pen on her desk. "Her condition might not have been discovered in time. I suspect all that's been recorded in her chart where Hector has doubtless seen it."

It occurred to me, not for the first time, how lucky I was to have Cleo for an ally. "No wonder he's determined to get her away from the Gailworths," I said. "I wonder if Sybil Snyder will testify for him if he and the Gailworths end up back in court."

"She won't have a choice if Korba's attorneys subpoena her."

"Without a doubt they would have subpoenaed Lowe if he had lived."

"Of course. Gives you something to think about, doesn't it, Aimee?" Cleo picked up her pen and tapped it on her desk, lost in thought. "Who had a stake in making sure Lowe didn't testify at a custody hearing?"

"Only Natasha's parents. But do the police know that?"

She shook her head. "Doubtful. Who would have told them? The subject didn't come up when I was interviewed. How about you?"

I stood, glancing at my watch again. "No. It didn't occur to me. I just answered the questions I was asked.

Maybe Quinn mentioned it when he was interviewed."
I started for her door, nervous about leaving Bernie
Kluckert alone in the library.

"Wait, one more thing." Cleo pulled an envelope out
of her desk drawer. "I have two extra tickets for the Sawyer County Symphony on Saturday night. I wondered if
you could use them."

"I'd love to, but I can't afford to reimburse you."

"Nonsense." She walked over and thrust them in my
hand. "They're yours if you want them. I thought you
might invite Nick. Sig will be playing tuba for the first
time since his surgery, so I'll be by myself in the audience. I'd love to have the two of you sit with me." Cleo
never missed an opportunity to nudge me closer to Nick.

"I should ask my grandmother first. If she can't make
it, I'll try Nick."

I thanked her for the tickets and headed back to the
library. Cool, clean air filled my lungs, and pale winter
sunshine cast a semblance of warmth across the TMC
complex.

Bernie gave me a little wave with his free hand as I
entered the library. He pulled the white mask away from
his face just long enough to greet me with a cheerful,
"Hullo," then went back to work. He had made good
progress with the dusting while I was gone. By the time
he left at noon, the metal bookshelves glistened and the
whole place smelled of furniture polish.

THIRTEEN

I WAS IN my small break room washing down a peanut butter sandwich with coffee when I heard knocking on the library door. The knocking had escalated to pounding by the time I reached the entrance and saw Hector Korba standing outside with his legs spread and fists clenched, fixing me with an impatient glare. I unlocked the door and invited him in.

"Thank you, Miss Machado," he said in a deceptively calm voice. "I'm surprised to find the library locked. Do no other people stop by during their lunch hour?"

"Not really, Mr. Korba. I'm required to take a lunch hour myself, and there being no other staff, I have to lock up."

"Ah, I see." Apparently it hadn't occurred to him that I had the right to inconvenience him by feeding myself.

"What can I do for you?" I asked.

"Read this." With a self-satisfied flourish, he produced a note written on a sheet torn from Dr. Sybil Snyder's prescription pad. It read: *Please allow Mr. Korba to view the minutes of the Monday, February 3 Ethics Committee meeting.* I recognized Dr. Snyder's signature. It had taken him a full week to gain her permission. No wonder he was impatient.

"Give me a moment." I didn't bother to offer him a seat. I remembered from his last visit that he preferred to stand so he could tower over me. I pulled the Ethics Committee binder from its drawer in one of my file cabinets and handed him the page with the minutes. He read the scant description of the meeting and handed the page back to me.

"That's of no use at all, is it?" His face turned dark. "It appears to be a whitewash."

"What do you mean?" I thought the description of the physical altercation was anything but a whitewash.

"I mean that there is nothing specific in there about my Natasha's condition. No record of her dire medical status. Surely Dr. Lowe must have testified to that in this meeting. I don't see that here. Why is that?" His tense fingers creased the paper. I thought he might roll it into a ball and throw it at me.

I took an involuntary step backward. "The minutes record only what happens between the time the meeting is called to order and the time it is adjourned, Mr. Korba. That's all."

He shook the paper at me. "But there is nothing written that will help me to save her from her ridiculous mother and that con artist she married. You were present at that committee meeting. Do you know more than what is recorded?"

I felt a traitorous rush of blood to my cheeks. *Damn*. I did know more, but I certainly wouldn't admit it to him.

"Mr. Korba, I have done what you and Dr. Snyder asked. You have seen the minutes. If you need Natasha's medical details, you'll have to get them from Dr. Snyder."

"Only Lowe could have testified to what he dealt with during Natasha's surgery. Dr. Snyder was not present in the operating room." A vein pulsed at Korba's temple.

I tried to reassure him, with what I hoped was a calming tone. "But Dr. Lowe would have dictated all of that in his operative report. It will be recorded in Natasha's medical record. Dr. Snyder could interpret that in court. She would be the ideal person to do that, since she's taken over the case."

Korba's face flushed purple. He dropped his bulk into one of the chairs across from my desk. "Dr. Lowe's operative report is inconclusive in that regard."

I thrust my hands out in a helpless gesture. "I'm sorry, I don't understand." How did he know what was or wasn't in Natasha's medical record?

"My Natasha has only two blood relatives on this earth, myself and her mother. As such, we are both allowed access to the information in her medical chart. I have made certain of that."

"I see." News to me, but I shouldn't have been surprised, considering Korba's clout with the hospital.

"Since your minutes are not helpful, it appears I must rely entirely on Dr. Snyder to support my bid for custody."

I didn't envy Sybil Snyder and even felt a little guilty about hitting the ball into her court, but I had no other advice to offer the man. At least he would stop breathing down my neck.

"That seems to be your best option," I said. "I'm very sorry your granddaughter is ill, but I've heard that Natasha's condition is rapidly improving. I hope, for her sake and for yours, that she'll be well enough to be discharged soon."

"Discharge her and put her life in the hands of that insane couple?" His flash of anger was followed by signs of fatigue. He reached a hand up to massage the back of his neck. "We'll see about that. I've demanded a new hearing. She must not leave this hospital until her custody has been decided."

As on his first visit, he surprised me with his unattractive rictus of a smile. He thanked me, and just as he stood, preparing to leave, an unfamiliar woman dressed entirely in black came into the library, walking toward my desk. Startled recognition flashed across Korba's face, but he recovered his composure quickly.

"Mrs. Lowe, my condolences." He proffered a solemn nod of his head. The woman had to be Dr. Lowe's widow, Rita. Why was she visiting the library? Thin and nondescript, with short gray hair and wearing no makeup or jewelry, she brought Cleo's assessment to mind: *a peahen to Gavin Lowe's peacock.*

"Thank you, Hector." She turned from him to extend her hand to me. "And you must be Aimee Machado. I apologize for coming by unannounced. I was tending to some affairs in the business office, so I thought I'd drop by to return several items Gavin had borrowed from your library." She placed a soft leather briefcase on my desk. "You'll find two books and a few medical journals in there." Her face had the drawn look of someone in pain.

"Thank you, Mrs. Lowe. I'm so sorry for your loss." I didn't make reference to our previous phone conversation. Neither did she. Hector stood awkwardly by, as if uncertain whether to leave or stay.

"Well, that's another unpleasant task done." Rita gestured toward the briefcase. "You may keep Gavin's attaché case, if you like. Or donate it to a charity. I don't particularly want it back." She seemed eager to leave, so I thanked her and she went on her way. I expected Hector to follow, but he remained at my desk.

"Poor woman." He shook his head. "To think of returning books at such a difficult time."

I zipped the case open. "Yes, but I'm glad to have them back. Some of our medical texts are very expensive." I lifted the books and journals out, noticing that they all had to do with nutrition. Lowe had obviously done his homework with regard to Natasha's case. I didn't recall processing his checkouts. Apparently Lola had handled them at a time when I was away from the library.

Next I checked the various pockets of the briefcase to make sure they were empty. I felt something in one of the interior pockets and extracted a small flash drive. Opening my desk drawer, I dropped the drive inside my purse, thinking I'd call Rita later to see about returning it to her.

Hector still stood at my desk, so I asked if he had any further business for us to discuss.

"Not at this time, Miss Machado. Please carry on." I watched him walk toward the exit. *Carry on* sounded so pompous. I hoped he used less formal language with his granddaughter.

After dual visits from Rita Lowe and Hector Korba, my lunch hour was gone, along with my appetite. Before Rita's unexpected arrival, Korba had seemed to view Lowe's death mainly as a setback in the custody struggle for his precocious granddaughter. That, in spite of the fact that Gavin Lowe had saved little Natasha's life. I was pleased that Korba had shown sympathy for the widow.

Alone in the library, I glanced at the briefcase Rita had left behind, thinking Lola or Bernie might like to have it. That reminded me of the flash drive I'd put in my purse. Curious, I took it out and stared at the innocent-looking inch of plastic, wondering how guilty I would feel if I had a look. Did it hold something important to Gavin Lowe? Or to the hospital? I glanced at the time and checked my medical staff calendar. No committee meetings this lunch hour meant Cleo would be free, so I called her.

I gave Cleo a quick rundown of the last hour, including Hector's visit, Rita Lowe's dropping by, and the flash drive she left behind.

"Do you think I should have a look?"

"I think it would be justified," Cleo said. "If it is related to one of our patients, we'll want to see that it gets to where it belongs. If not, you can return it to Rita."

With a semi-clear conscience, I plugged the little drive into a port on my computer.

Two files appeared. Lowe had named one of them *NKOP*. Natasha Korba's initials? It was dated Sunday, February 2, the date he had operated on Natasha. I opened the file. It was unnerving reading notes written by a man who had died only a week ago.

The first document was obviously Lowe's OP report, following standard format. A list of the events in the order they had taken place during surgery, including the dangerous blood loss and the decision to go ahead with a transfusion in spite of the parents' objections. The second document, separate from the OP note, captured my attention. He'd titled it *Notes to self.*

DISCHARGE WILL BE complicated by pending custody hearing.

Recommend mother and stepfather retain custody, but with two conditions: 1. presiding judge requires parents' participation in nutritional counseling, and

2. regular monitoring of patient's health status on a monthly basis—indefinitely.

WHAT TO DO with this information? In good conscience, I had to offer to return the drive to Rita Lowe, but the information it contained should go to someone involved in Natasha's care. That would be Sybil Snyder, who I was reluctant to approach directly. Normally, I'd have gone to Quinn, but he was on leave. Sanjay? No. That left Cleo. With her depth of experience and knowledge of medical staff issues, she'd know how to handle the situation. I printed a copy of Lowe's notes for her, put the flash drive back in my purse and made a quick trip across campus to her office.

"What do you think? Should we turn the flash drive over to Sybil Snyder?"

"No," Cleo said. "That's not our call. Rita Lowe left it with you. You keep it for now until you can check with her to see if she wants it back. I'll take printed copies of both documents to Health Information and talk this over with Jerrylu. She'll have to decide whether Lowe's note to himself can be considered part of Natasha's official record."

Cleo was right. Jerrylu Stanley was TMC's director of health information. It was her call.

Back in the library, I called Rita Lowe. She told me to do what seemed appropriate with the flash drive. She had no reason to want it back. I devoted the rest of my workday to library business, and then headed for the refuge of my barn-top apartment in Coyote Creek.

On the way I stopped at the Four Corners Market to pick up something for dinner. While I waited for my deli-ordered turkey panini, I decided to pick up staples like bread, milk, and assorted salad veggies. I walked to my car in the nearly dark parking lot, balancing my takeout carton in one hand while I held my grocery bag in my other arm. I had almost reached my car with my keys out when something slammed against me from behind. I felt my arm being jerked as I went crashing to the ground, face first into a puddle. My groceries scattered and my panini popped out of its box, landing next to me in the muddy water.

A motorcycle revved up and screamed out of the parking lot just as a spry senior couple hurried over to ask if I needed help. I pushed myself up on hands and knees. Intense pain told me both knees were banged up. I stood on shaky legs and wiped my face.

"We saw it," the woman said. "He snatched your purse and got away on a motorcycle."

Her husband handed me his cell phone. "Here, I've dialed 911 for you."

A sheriff's deputy arrived within a few minutes to question me and the witnesses about the mugging. After I assured him that I didn't require medical attention, he told me they'd do everything possible to track down my purse. He also said not to count on its return—that random purse snatches usually left law enforcement little to go on. The elderly witnesses weren't able to identify the assailant or the make of motorcycle he rode.

"Looked like the guy was lurking—maybe waiting for *this* young lady."

"Yes," his wife said. "Soon as she came out, he took off after her."

The officer nodded. "Probably *was* lurking, watching for an easy target."

Great. An easy target. I planned to keep the deputy's

remark to myself, or I'd never hear the end of it from Harry and Nick.

At home I made a phone call reporting my stolen credit card. In a stroke of luck, my cell phone had been in my car and not in my purse. After I called the DMV about my driver's license, I showered and applied antibiotic ointment and bandages to the abrasions on my knees. I decided not to worry Amah and Jack about the attack, which I wasn't at all sure was random. There were lots of other people coming and going in that parking lot. Thinking back to what the senior couple said, I suspected I'd been targeted. If so, why me?

Then I recalled the flash drive in my purse. I called Cleo and told her about the incident.

"My God, are you okay?"

"Except for the embarrassment. I'm probably being paranoid, but I'm not positive it was a random thing."

"What do you mean?"

"The witnesses thought the guy was lying in wait for me. The only thing unusual in my purse was that flash drive. I'm wondering what happened when you told Jerrylu about its contents."

"She took the printed copy of the OP report that you gave me and said she'd append it to Natasha's chart. She was glad to get it. All she's had up to now is a handwritten operative progress note from Lowe with just enough information to manage Natasha's post-op care. She's going to leave Lowe's note to himself about Natasha's custody in the chart, at least until Sybil Snyder decides what to do about it."

"What time did you talk to Jerrylu?"

"Early this afternoon. Not long after you gave me the printed notes."

"Did you tell her I had the flash drive?"

"Oh, hell." I heard Cleo take a breath. "I did. You think you were mugged for the flash drive?"

"Maybe."

"But the copy of its contents is already in the chart."

"Unless it isn't." I told her what Korba had said—that both he and Melissa Gailworth had access to the medical record. If Melissa had access, so did her husband.

"I get you," Cleo said. "The Gailworths wouldn't be happy with Lowe's demand for rigid monitoring of Natasha's dietary regimen. But would they go to extremes like accosting you in a parking lot?"

"Maybe not Melissa, but I wouldn't put anything past Abel Gailworth."

"I'll check with Jerrylu first thing tomorrow and let you know if Lowe's note about custody is still in the chart. Be a shame if it's not. Dr. Lowe wanted that little girl protected." Cleo paused. "Did you happen to copy it to your hard drive?"

"No, I wasn't sure I should do that until we heard how Snyder wanted it handled."

"Too bad, but I see your point. I'll let you know if I hear anything more."

My next move was to 'fess up to Nick and Harry about the snatched purse. I called Harry first. He berated me, as I'd expected, for not being aware of my surroundings, then asked if I'd told Nick. I assured him that I would.

FOURTEEN

WITH CRIME STILL on my mind, I put off calling Nick long enough to watch the local six thirty news for any mention of Dr. Lowe's murder. The anchor said that leads were being pursued by the police. I wondered how many of their leads were the same as those Cleo and I wanted to pursue with the help of Harry and Nick.

The police would undoubtedly focus their energy on Jared Quinn, their most obvious suspect. He had to be ruled out or arrested at some point. If the police were keeping Sanjay informed, he wasn't sharing updates with the rest of us. Cleo believed Quinn was innocent, and I was almost sure she was right. With the help of Harry and Nick, we could explore other possibilities, including a jealous mistress or even Mrs. Lowe herself.

Jealousy seemed to be a common theme. First Harry and I had overheard the exchange in the TMC stairwell between Sybil Snyder and her husband.

Then Rita Lowe had implied that one of her husband's jealous lovers might be responsible for his death. Even my masked dust-buster Bernie Kluckert was troubled by jealousy. He had it bad for Lola, who seemed more interested in her younger suitor, Oslo Swanson. Pushing ninety, Bernie was probably old enough to keep his emotions in check even if he was unlucky in love.

But jealousy was only one possible motive. I wasn't ready to discount Abel or Melissa Gailworth. At the time of Lowe's death, they'd probably had no idea Lowe leaned toward recommending they retain custody of Natasha. Most likely they thought the opposite. If anything, it was Korba who would have expected Lowe to recommend in his favor.

I recalled Hector Korba's description of the Gailworths as *that insane couple* who would have Natasha's life in their hands when she was released from the hospital. How crazy were the Gailworths? Crazy enough to kill a doctor who ordered the blood transfusion that saved their child? Maybe, if they assumed he was going to testify against them.

The news ended just as I polished off a bowl of Jack's venison stew. Amah supplied me with an extra container for my freezer whenever Jack made a new batch. On a chilly February evening it was the perfect comfort food.

Considering the aggravation of the day's events and the physical pain of my battered knees, the only comfort I really wanted was Nick. When had I last seen him? We had visited the Abel's Breath church on Sunday morning and after, we'd had an uneasy talk about where our relationship was headed. Only two days ago, but it seemed so much longer.

The days when we had lived together as a couple seemed long ago, too. We'd had five months of closeness, followed by six months of living apart. During that time our feelings for each other drew us near then pulled us away like a tide at the mercy of the moon.

Time to call him. Not only about the purse snatching, but to fill him in. Harry had probably told him all about the fire drill plan we had hatched, but neither Harry nor Nick knew about my visits from Rita Lowe and Hector Korba, or about the parking lot incident. Nick had some of Buck Sawyer's super geeks digging into Abel Gailworth's past. I wondered what they'd found. Korba was so set against seeing his granddaughter released to her mother and stepfather, I felt compelled to know more about them. I reached for my cell phone and it rang in my hand. It was Nick. *Telephone ESP*. A good sign. Maybe he and I were back on the same wavelength.

"Hi," I opted for light and breezy, "I'm glad you called. What's up?"

"I have a bit of news about our preacher boy. What's new on your end? And don't say a butterfly tattoo, because then I'd need to see proof."

"No tattoo, but I do have news. It sounds like yours is more specific though. Why don't you start?" I wasn't in a hurry to get into the purse snatching.

"Do you want to do this on the phone or can we meet? My night is open, how about yours?"

"I'm free. Do you want to come to my place? I'll heat a bowl of Jack's stew if you haven't eaten."

"Do that," he said. "I'll be there in twenty minutes."

I could do a lot of primping in twenty minutes. I freshened my makeup and hair and started to pulled on my favorite skinny jeans, only to realize they weren't going to work over the bandages on my knees. Sweat pants would have to do.

Nick arrived just as I finished dressing. I closed the door behind him, shutting out the cold and the rest of the world.

"That stew smells delicious." He pulled me into a hug. "But you smell even better."

So did he. *Lime and spice*.

I stepped back reluctantly and took his steaming bowl of stew out of my microwave. He sat at my dinette table and dug in while I poured soda crackers into a bowl and popped the caps on two bottles of beer. After polishing off his meal in a matter of minutes, Nick took his bowl to the sink and rinsed it. Back at the table, he said, "Ready to trade intel?"

"I am. I'm dying to hear what you have on Gailworth."

Nick pulled his chair next to mine and dropped a pocket notepad on the table in front of us. "Well, for starters, we have to roll back a few years, before he married Melissa Korba. My guys found evidence of something called the Holy Gail Ministry back in Arkansas. It was founded and run by a Reverend Gailworth."

"Oh. *Holy Gail*. I get it," I said. "What a narcissistic cheese ball. Are you sure it's the same guy?"

"Yep. The photos from back then match up to what I saw of him on Sunday."

"So what happened to that gig? Did he get run out of Arkansas?"

"More or less. Seems there are several churches using forms of the Holy Grail in their names. A few of them weren't too happy with Holy Gail. They thought his play on words was blasphemy, so they got together and threatened to sue the pants off him."

"So he took his business elsewhere. How did he meet Melissa Korba?"

"The way it's done these days. An online dating service. She was lonely and apparently gullible. He proposed before they ever met in person and she accepted."

Nick had draped a casual arm over the back of my chair, playing havoc with my concentration. I forced myself to stop thinking about the scent of his aftershave and to focus on the matter at hand.

"Do you think Gailworth already knew about Natasha's musical gift when he proposed to Melissa?"

"No doubt about it. He's a hustler and an opportunist. He must have thought he'd found the goose that laid the golden eggs."

"Then why the veganism and the Abel's Breath church? Why not just take over managing Natasha's career?"

"Hector Korba is why not. Korba's been managing his granddaughter's musical career since she was three years old, and I can't see him relinquishing that position. He's shrewd enough to sniff out a phony when he sees one. He's been fighting for custody of Natasha since the day Melissa Korba married Gailworth."

"How long ago did they marry?"

"Almost three years now. And I'm guessing veganism is a ploy Gailworth has been using to try and lure upper class, upper income types into his congregation."

"From what we saw at his church, that isn't working."

"He doesn't seem to care. At this point, the church seems to be little more than a front to keep him occupied until he can wrest control of Natasha Korba from her grandfather."

"What I don't understand is, if Melissa was vegan before she married Gailworth, why wouldn't she know about her daughter's dietary needs?"

"Apparently she wasn't vegan, but converted after she remarried."

Did anything Nick was telling me shed light on Lowe's murder? Gailworth might not hesitate to commit a variety of cons and frauds, but he seemed too concerned with his own survival to resort to homicide.

"Is there anything else? Was there any record of violence in Gailworth's past?"

"Nothing but some traffic tickets." Nick flipped through a few pages of his notebook. "Apparently he's never been arrested. Not the bar brawl type." Nick laughed. "You must have noticed that he's a good-lookin' dude. That's probably his greatest asset. He'd shy away from any altercation that might mess up his pretty face."

"He's a little too pretty for my taste, but I did notice he dyes his hair, so you're probably right about his preoccupation with his looks."

Nick's looks were my standard. Hair the color of summer wheat, blue eyes that crinkled at the corners when he smiled. I loved the planes of his cheekbones and the angle of his jaw.

"Aimee? Did you hear me?" Nick waved his hand in front of my face.

"Sorry. What did you say?"

"I said Gailworth must be doing something more than preaching his gospel. His congregation is miniscule, and mostly low-income. There's no way his church is supporting him."

"Have Buck's cyber sleuths nosed out any other sources of income?"

"Not yet, and that's troubling. If he's mixed up in something illegal, he knows how to cover his tracks."

"I'll keep digging for more on Gailworth. Now it's your turn. You said you had some news."

As I expected, Harry had already told him about the plan to sneak into Quinn's office during the fire drill. Reluctant to tell Nick about the mugging, I stalled. Instead, I reminded him about my phone conversation with Rita Lowe, and how she had tossed out the idea that one of his mistresses might have committed the murder. I also brought up the exchange between Sybil Snyder and Glen Capshaw in the hospital stairwell. Capshaw's jealousy seemed worth considering if it turned out Snyder was seeing Lowe on the side.

"That's about it," I said. "It's conjecture at best. Nothing specific."

"What about taking your suspicions to the police? I don't like what happens when you start poking at hornet's nests."

"I'm not keen on contacting the police on my own. Cleo says they're not giving Sanjay or the home office any updates on their investigation."

"Probably standard procedure."

"I guess, but I still get the creeps when I think about Detective Kass interviewing me in the TMC library. If I go to him suggesting alternative suspects, he might think I'm doing it to take the focus off myself and Quinn. What if that backfires? I'd rather not take that chance unless we come up with evidence too convincing to be ignored."

"You may be right, but I'm not sure what you expect to find by prowling around in Quinn's office tomorrow night. You're better schooled in forensics than the general public, but the police department's crime scene people do it every day, hands on. If there was something to be found in there, they've already found it."

I couldn't argue with his logic. "My schooling in forensics was related to cataloging and disseminating forensic research materials and resources. That's very different from being a crime scene investigator. It was Harry's idea to have a look at the crime scene. He hasn't told me what he hopes to find, but he must have his reasons. Did he say anything to you?"

Nick took a long pull from his beer then put the bottle down. "Just that there's only an outside chance he's right. He didn't want to elaborate."

Nick suddenly reached out and brushed his fingers across my cheek, sending tingles down my arms to my fingertips.

"That's better," he said. "You had an eyelash on your cheek."

"Oh, thanks." I had been wondering how to bring up the subject of Harry and Rella. Nick's intimate gesture was the opening I needed.

"Nick, remember when I asked if you knew who Harry's dating? You said I'd have to ask him."

"I remember." He leaned back in his chair. "So did you?"

"I did. We talked last night."

"How did that go?"

"I'm not sure. He suggested I should get to know Rella better."

"Probably a good idea. Is there anything more you want to tell me about this?"

"No. Just thought you should know and that I'm okay with whatever makes Harry happy."

"Then we should probably call it a night. It's getting late."

"Not yet," I said. The parking lot incident couldn't be avoided any longer. "There's something else I have to tell you, but you're not going to like it. Just hear me out before you say anything, okay?"

I told him the whole story, starting with the flash drive Rita Lowe left behind, and ending with the assault in the parking lot. I filled him in on my conversation with Cleo about Lowe's informal notes related to Natasha's custody.

"Son of a…were you hurt?" Nick reached for me, touched my face.

"No, I'm fine. Except for my knees."

"You're thinking the mugger was after the flash drive?"

"It's possible. What do you think?"

"Sweetheart, you don't want to hear what I'm thinking. If I ever get my hands on the guy who did this to you—"

"Nick, I'm fine. That's not what's important now. We need to find out if the Gailworths knew that Lowe was going to recommend leaving Natasha with them."

"You mean, did they know about it before he was killed?"

"Right. Even if they didn't like the idea of having her diet monitored, at least they would have retained custody. Gailworth would still have his golden goose."

"And their motive for doing away with Lowe would be watered down considerably. What about now? Is Lowe's note going to be considered during the custody hearing?"

"We don't know. We're not even sure the note is still in the chart, or whether Dr. Snyder has seen it. Cleo is going to follow up and let me know."

"Did either of you keep a copy of that note?"

"I didn't, because I thought I'd have the flash drive, but I'm sure Cleo did. She's obsessive about keeping copies of everything."

"Sounds like we've covered everything, then." Nick stood and put his notebook in his pocket. "Will you be able to sleep?"

"I'd better. I won't be getting much sleep tomorrow night."

He took my hands, pulled me up from my chair and drew me close. I felt my core melting as he rocked me gently in his arms. He took my face in his hands, kissed my forehead, both cheeks, and then moved to my lips, gently at first, then with a surge of passion that left both of us trembling.

The moon, bringing in the tide.

"Do you want me to stay?" he whispered.

"I wish you could," I answered, "but my knees are killing me."

FIFTEEN

WEDNESDAY MORNING I was ready for work when I realized I needed a purse. I didn't have a spare and I couldn't borrow from Amah without some explaining. In a box of hiking gear, I found a black canvas fanny pack. Since all I had to put in it was my phone and car keys, it would do until I could afford something else.

At eight o'clock Sanjay D'Costa walked into the library unannounced. The curly lock of his jet black hair that stood up in a corkscrew at the back of his head was my first clue that his role as acting administrator was taking its toll. The usually well-groomed man must have slept poorly. He blinked behind his dark-framed glasses as if he were clearing sand from his eyes.

"Hello, Miss Machado, may we speak?"

"Of course." I gestured toward one of my visitors' chairs. "And please call me Aimee."

I wondered if this visit had anything to do with the fire drill scheduled for the middle of the night. Sanjay got right to the point, speaking in his lilting accent.

"I have spoken with Cleo Cominoli about our fire drill that will take place tonight in the emergency room. She tells me that our home office has made a special request, to which I have agreed."

"I see." Little did he know that he had approved a clandestine snooping session in Quinn's office. I waited for Sanjay to elaborate.

"Also I have agreed that it is good for Ms. Cominoli to have a set of keys to the administrative suite for the duration of Mr. Quinn's absence. Very wise in the event of trouble."

While he talked, I realized there was a photo of Harry and me sitting on the corner of my desk. It faced in my direction, so Sanjay could see only the back of the frame. I raced through my memory, reassuring myself that I had never shown him the photo. It wouldn't do for him to see it today, just hours before Harry was fixed to masquerade as an employee of TMC's fire alarm company.

"Is there anything else?" I asked.

"Just one thing." He leaned an elbow on my desk, his face hovering over the picture frame. I struggled to keep eye contact, praying he wouldn't take a sudden interest in the photo.

"What's that?" I began fiddling with the few folders and papers in front of me, hoping to feign an act of compulsive neatness so I could casually pick up the photo and tuck it into a drawer.

"I'm hearing from the police regarding the data on our security cameras. They are still unconvinced that there has been no tampering." Sanjay seemed affronted. "It is as if they do not trust me. Can you imagine how that makes one feel?"

Of course I can. The police don't trust me either.

"I'm sorry," I said. "I don't understand why you're telling me about this."

"Because tonight when you and Cleo take the fire company man into Quinn's office, you will, of course, be recorded on the cameras as they show you going into the administrative suite. The police will want to see that footage. They will have someone from their forensics team to look at it as soon as the fire drill has ended. They will see that the cameras work as they should during the nighttime hours as well as during the day. They will have to take my word that there was no tampering of the cameras the night of Dr. Lowe's death. You see?"

It seemed to me there were holes in his theory, but I didn't want to prolong our conversation. Harry's photo was still on my desk.

"I see, but I don't understand what this has to do with me."

"As I told Cleo, I'm sure you will both act professionally at all times while you are being recorded, but I wanted you to be aware that you will be seen by the cameras. Of course you see how it is important that we show our hospital's administrative personnel in a good light, so you will want to comport yourselves accordingly." He leaned in again, his chin nearly resting on the photo.

"Of course," I said. "If that's all, I really should get back to my work. I have a lot to do." In desperation, I pulled out the can of furniture polish and clean dust cloth I kept in my bottom desk drawer.

"Excuse me if I am impeding your work." Sanjay leaned back to give me more leeway for my tidying.

"Thank you." I gave him my best smile, scooped up the photo along with a pad of sticky notes and a stapler, and dropped them in a drawer. Then I shot a squirt of polish at the corner where the photo had been and started buffing.

Sneezing twice, Sanjay finally took the hint. At the exit door he paused. "So, Aimee, will I see you tonight at the fire drill?"

"I don't think so. I expect Cleo and I will head up to

the fourth floor as soon as the employee from the fire alarm company arrives."

As soon as the door closed behind Sanjay, I dropped into my chair and dialed Cleo. I asked what she thought of Sanjay's news about the security cameras.

"I don't like it. I'm sorry I didn't have a chance to call and warn you. Someone else came in right after he left. Do you think we should abort?"

"No. We might never have another opportunity to get Harry in there." Then a new wrinkle in our plan came to me. If video of our entry and exit from the administrative suite was going to be scrutinized right away, we wouldn't want to have to explain going in too soon. We would have to wait until just before the drill started and get out right after it ended. I'd never timed a fire drill, but they didn't seem to last very long.

"Cleo, do you know how much time we'll have once we get inside Quinn's office?"

"The drills usually take about ten minutes. Maybe a little longer in the emergency room. It depends what's going on. At one in the morning it should be fairly slow, unless some drunk driver leaves a bar with one too many for the road."

"God forbid. But I was hoping we'd have more time. Now that our cover story is going to be recorded on camera, we can't count on more than fifteen minutes. We'll get Harry inside a couple of minutes early. When the alarm sounds we'll have ten minutes until the all clear and maybe another two or three to get back out into the corridor where the cameras will pick us up again."

"Sounds about right. Are you going to ask Harry if that's enough time?"

"I'll tell him, but it'll have to be."

"Okay, instead of midnight, let's meet in the TMC parking garage at twelve thirty. We'll review our plan there, then take the elevator to the fourth floor. I'll have the keys with me. The drill starts at one o'clock, so we won't have an excuse to unlock Quinn's office much earlier. We can justify at least five minutes' lead time."

"Every minute helps. I'd better hang up now and get to work."

"Wait," Cleo said. "I have news about Natasha Korba. As of this morning she's out of Pediatric ICU and in a private room in the Pediatric Unit on the second floor."

"That's great. Have you heard how long before she'll be discharged?"

"No idea, but Sybil Snyder isn't going to take any chances on discharging that little girl too soon."

"Not with Hector Korba circling like a tornado about to touch down. He'll be incensed if Natasha goes home with the Gailworths and has a relapse."

I asked if she had talked to Jerrylu Stanley in the Health Information Office.

"I did. She said Sybil Snyder has seen the printout of Lowe's note about Natasha's custody. She told Jerrylu that technically, Lowe's informal note wasn't part of the medical record. She asked her to remove it from the chart, but to keep it safe."

"You made a copy for yourself, right?"

"Of course. You know me. It's under lock and key."

"I wonder if Snyder will use Lowe's recommendations in the custody hearing."

"Up to her, I guess. Let's keep our fingers crossed for Natasha." I heard worry in Cleo's voice. "So far, the courts have decided in favor of the mother and stepfather every time Korba has tried for custody."

"I guess there's nothing we can do to help that situation. It's frightening to think the little girl's life could be at stake."

"Back to the fire drill," Cleo said. "One more detail. Be sure to get Harry out of the hospital pronto. I told Sanjay I'd give him a written report about that panel in Quinn's office, but we can't take any chances that he'll decide to seek out our fire alarm guy to compare notes man to man."

"Oh, cripes. That cannot happen. I'll take care of it."

After talking to Cleo, I took a few minutes to mull over Sanjay's concern that the police might suspect him. I had told Harry that Sanjay was as innocent as a newborn lamb. Now I wasn't so sure. People sometimes joke that they would kill for a coveted job. What kind of person would actually go that far? And how well did any of us really know Sanjay?

Lola Rampley arrived at nine o'clock, dropped her purse in the bottom drawer of the volunteers' desk and acknowledged me with her usual cheerful greeting.

"Good morning, Aimee. Do we have any special tasks today?" She ran a finger over the smooth, shiny surface of her desk and looked up at me with a puzzled expression.

"Is something wrong?" I asked.

"I'm not sure. My desk seems rearranged. The pencil holder is usually closer to the phone."

"Oh, that. Bernie Kluckert was cleaning yesterday. He must have polished the desk. The two of you have to share it, and it seems he's sensitive to dust. Is there a problem?"

Red dots appeared on her powdered pink cheeks. "No, of course not. We mustn't let him become ill."

I couldn't read her reaction to my mention of Bernie. Was she pleased or annoyed that he had become co-owner of the desk? If I discovered that Bernie's interest in Lola was distressing her, he'd have to go. She was the most valuable volunteer I could ever hope for and I wasn't about to risk losing her.

"Lola, I have a few requests for printed articles from our forensic database. Do you want to start with those?"

"Of course, my favorite task." She rewarded me with a happy smile. "When they're ready I'll have you check them before they go out by messenger." As a retired librarian, she relished being trusted with chores beyond the capacity of the other volunteers. The few patrons who dropped in asking for help requested an interesting variety of information, most of it easily found once Lola or I explained how to search our collection and other outside sources.

With Lola's work lined out, my mind turned to Harry and the fire drill. Would fifteen minutes give him enough time for whatever he was hoping to find in Quinn's office? Another nagging consideration was Natasha Korba's medical condition. Her surgery had been eleven days ago, and she had improved enough to leave the intensive care unit. How much longer before she went home?

As soon as Lola's shift ended at noon, I called Harry to tell him what Cleo had said about the timing of the fire drill.

"Will fifteen minutes give you enough time?"

"What I'm looking for won't take long to find," Harry said. "It'll be there or it won't."

"Are you going to give me a hint?"

"Sure. Think invisibility cloak." He laughed. "I have

to go. There's a building inspector here who has no respect for my lunch hour. I'll get back to you tonight around ten o'clock."

Just like my brother to joke around when I'm trying to keep my boss and maybe myself out of jail. He'd been just as cavalier a few months earlier when *he* was a murder suspect. Our parents must have used up all their worry genes when I was conceived. Harry seemed to meet every setback in life with the belief that all's well that ends well. I met mine with the suspicion that catastrophe was just around the corner.

With half of my lunch hour already gone, I hurried over to the main tower to see if I could get a peek at Natasha Korba. The news that she was out of intensive care was the one bright spot in a week and a half of turbulence. With luck, Dr. Snyder could convince the Gailworths they should at least let TMC's nutritionist set them up with proper dietary guidelines for a vegan child.

As I approached Natasha's room in the second floor Peds Unit, I heard low voices.

"This is an abomination," Abel Gailworth said. "They want our child to eat flesh." He stood next to Natasha's bed with his wife at his side. Melissa's face was pale and drawn. Natasha was staring down at the meatloaf on her meal tray, sobbing.

SIXTEEN

THE GAILWORTHS SPOTTED me frozen in the doorway like Lot's wife turned to salt.

"Excuse me, wrong room," I said.

As I backed away out of the parents' line of sight, I still had a view of Natasha lying on the bed. I spotted an IV line for medications and fluids taped to the back of her hand, which was to be expected. She would still be on antibiotics and probably supplemental iron to encourage red blood cell production.

Dr. Snyder's instructions to the dietary department obviously had not been compatible with veganism. The meatloaf on Natasha's lunch tray had set Gailworth off. I'd researched enough cases like Natasha's to know she had been receiving nourishment through a feeding tube during her entire stay in the Pediatric ICU. In a regular room in the Peds Unit, she would be observed to make sure she could eat and drink on her own. The meatloaf was likely part of the first solid meal Natasha's parents had seen.

Abel Gailworth walked out of the room and down the corridor toward the nurses' station. I peeked in and saw Melissa, a thin, thirty-something woman wearing a blue gingham dress. She was devoid of makeup, with dark blond hair in a braid down her back. She held her thin, fragile-looking daughter in her arms, crooning to her and kissing the top of her pale blond head. I couldn't make out what she was saying, but Natasha was nodding and wiping tears off her cheeks. They both looked so vulnerable and desperate that I wondered what it was like for them, being forced to follow Gailworth's dangerously unorthodox religious dogma. Were they disciples or captives?

How could Melissa not know she was living with a fraud or worse? How could she put her child at the mercy of that man? I felt a rush of sympathy and understanding for Hector Korba. He had to know at least as much as Nick and I knew about Gailworth's shady past. If Korba had tried to convince Melissa that her husband was an opportunist and a con man, he had obviously failed. As long as Melissa Korba Gailworth stood by her man, Hector had little to use in court to challenge custody.

As soon as that thought crossed my mind, I realized it was wrong. Korba's best hope was to build his custody case by proving that Natasha's severe iron deficiency at the time of her surgery constituted child endangerment. That would explain his intense interest in the outcome of the Ethics Committee meeting. He had seen the minutes and knew they were useless. He needed the backing of the doctors involved in Natasha's care. Lowe's death had constituted a severe setback to Korba's game plan. Now there was only Sybil Snyder to testify on his behalf. Could he count on her? Or would she follow Lowe's lead, recommending Natasha remain with her parents?

From my vantage point in the corridor I watched Gailworth use his charm on the pretty young woman working at the nurses' station. He leaned toward her, spoke too softly for me to hear, and reached out his hand to touch her arm. Whatever he said caused her to laugh, obviously pleased by his remark. He laughed, too, then dipped his head deferentially, as if bashful in her presence. *What a crock*. But she fell for it and picked up her phone, no doubt calling the Dietary Department. He stood listening until she hung up. She apparently reported that the diet issue had been addressed. He reached out and took her hand in his, then covered it with his other hand. Even from the distance where I stood, I saw the rosy blush that tinted her cheeks.

As Gailworth turned away from the nurses' station and started back toward Natasha's room, I caught the self-satisfied smirk on his face. I slipped out of sight into the empty patient room next to Natasha's. From there I could still hear what was being said.

"Melissa, we've got to get her out of this unholy place." The urgency in Gailworth's words might have been concern for his stepdaughter, but I had my doubts. The hospital setting was chipping away at his control over Natasha. Whether he was overzealous about his beliefs or just determined to protect his investment, he wouldn't tolerate Natasha being out of his sphere of influence much longer.

I headed for Cleo's office to describe what I had witnessed. She gasped when I repeated what Gailworth had said about getting Natasha out of the hospital. My lunch hour was long gone, so I headed back to the library, leaving Cleo to follow up on Natasha and the Gailworths.

The rest of my workday was routine until an urgent call was transferred to me by a switchboard operator who heard the word *forensics*. A road construction flagman had been struck by a hit-and-run driver in a sparsely populated town in the northeastern corner of the county. The TMC helicopter pilot who was transporting the patient said the CHP officers at the scene wanted to know if our ER staff was experienced in collecting forensic evidence. I confirmed that they had been trained, but I assured the pilot that I would contact our sheriff's office so one of their forensic people would be on hand when the patient arrived.

Just before closing, I called the ER and heard that the hit-and-run patient was out of surgery and was going to make it. With that satisfying ending to my workday, I headed to Coyote Creek to prepare for the post-midnight invasion of Quinn's office.

SEVENTEEN

THE ALARM ON my cell phone woke me from a two-hour nap at eleven o'clock Wednesday night, giving me plenty of time to enjoy fresh coffee and a yogurt snack before meeting Harry at his condo at midnight. I had to dress in office clothes for the cameras, but I wanted maximum comfort, so I stayed away from dresses and high heels and opted for gray slacks and a navy blazer over a white shirt.

When I got to Harry's place, he opened the door and said, "What do you think?"

He spun around, showing off his phony fire agency duds. Khaki pants, white shirt, and a black jacket with a patch on the shoulder embroidered with a red flame. Under the flame were the initials FFG.

"Where'd you get the patch?" I asked. "And what does FFG stand for? I hope it's not real, or we could be in trouble if the cameras pick it up."

"Don't worry, it's not real. I ordered it online. Overnight shipping. You'd be surprised how easy it was."

"So what's FFG?"

"Fake Fire Guy." Harry grinned. "I checked, there's no real agency with those initials. At least not anywhere near Timbergate."

We were still standing in Harry's entry area when his doorbell rang. *Bad timing.* Why would he have company at midnight? The answer became obvious as soon as Harry opened his door.

Nick.

Before I could ask why he was there, he smiled and turned his left shoulder toward me. Another FFG. He was dressed just like Harry, and I had to admit they looked convincing.

"Wait a minute, Cleo and I can't sneak both of you into Quinn's office."

"No problem," Harry said. "Nick's not going up to the fourth floor with us. I might need him if I find what I'm looking for. If anyone spots Nick, all you and Cleo have to do is tell your acting administrator he's with me. We'll take care of the rest."

I sighed. "I'm beginning to think this was a terrible idea."

"Why?" Harry asked. "Afraid Quinn will find out and can you?"

"Of course. I've avoided speaking to him since he went ballistic about keeping you out of his office. But that's not all that's bothering me. What if the police have already come up with some solid leads? Maybe what we're doing is a risk without a reason."

Nick spoke up. "Aimee, it's been almost ten days since the doctor was killed in your boss's office. Have you heard anything about their having new leads?"

"No, but I wouldn't expect them to keep me informed."

"What about Quinn's stand-in? They must be communicating with him."

"If they're disclosing anything to Sanjay about the case, he's keeping it to himself." And probably enjoying his newfound status as TMC's top dog. "Besides, I get the feeling the police are considering anyone who works at TMC as a potential suspect. Maybe Sanjay's in the dark along with the rest of us."

In spite of my growing doubts, it was too late to turn back. Sanjay had already been told that the annunciator panel in Quinn's office needed to be inspected. If the fire guys didn't show up, he might start asking questions. Our acting administrator was wielding authority with a zeal that became more excessive and intrusive every day. The sooner Quinn was cleared and back to work, the better for everyone at TMC.

Harry and I rode to the hospital in Nick's SUV. On the way, I told them about the scene in Natasha's room on the peds ward and about Gailworth wanting to take Natasha out of the hospital.

"He's already put that little girl's life at risk once," I said. "I hate to think what might happen when she's sent home. His wife is either as submissive and dutiful as she seems, or she's so cowed by her husband that she's powerless."

"Do you think she's afraid of him?" Harry asked.

"If she suspects he killed Lowe, she must be."

"I thought the prevailing theory about frauds and cons was that they aren't killers," Nick said.

"Depends how desperate they are," Harry said. "I hear all kinds of stories from the cops in my classes at the dojo."

Nick pulled into the TMC parking garage and Cleo pulled in behind us. We checked the time. Twelve thirty. Right on schedule. I warned Harry and Nick that camera coverage of our foray would be scrutinized right away, although I still wasn't clear what Nick's role was, since Harry hadn't explained that. We reviewed our plan to get in and out as quickly as possible and to avoid making contact with any hospital staff, especially Sanjay D'Costa.

"One last thing," Harry said. "That alarm is going to be loud. You'll need these."

He handed each of us a set of earplugs, then we headed toward the main tower to take up our positions. Harry and Nick walked toward the building ahead of Cleo and me. Both men wore black caps with the bills pulled low on their foreheads. We entered through the little-used access at the back of the hospital that was primarily for transferring bodies from the hospital morgue to the coroner or to various mortuaries in the area.

We reached the elevators and the adjacent stairwell halfway down the corridor.

"Which do we take?" I asked. "Should the cameras see us coming off the elevator?"

"We'll use the stairs," Harry the FFG said. "Never use elevators during a fire—even a drill."

"Okay, but what are we going to do with Nick? He can't be seen on the fourth floor with us. We told Sanjay there would only be one fire guy."

"He's only going as far as the third floor," Harry said.

Cleo gave me a nervous, inquisitive look.

"Harry knows what he's doing," I assured her.

We made our way up the stairwell, leaving Nick behind on the third-floor landing. We had five minutes to spare when we stepped out into the fourth floor corridor and approached the door to the administrative suite. Knowing the security cameras were trained on us gave me a tingling sensation, as if someone with a powerful rifle had used the red dot of a laser beam to pinpoint me as a target. I glanced at Harry. Between the upturned collar of his FFG jacket and the ball cap pulled down low, very little of his face showed.

Cleo did the honors with her keys. We stepped inside Varsha's reception area and stood still for a moment to make sure no light or sound was coming through Sanjay's closed door to the right of Varsha's desk. He was required to be down on the first floor before, during, and after the ten-minute drill, but there was no guarantee he wouldn't need to make a quick trip up to his office.

Quinn's office door was on the opposite side of the reception area. Cleo quickly unlocked it. Just as we stepped inside, we heard the fire alarm go off. Harry walked over to the annunciator panel on the wall near Quinn's bathroom.

He smiled at Cleo. "You can tell your acting boss that the panel is working fine."

Cleo turned to me. "Does he really know, or is he making that up?"

"He knows," I said. "Maybe one of us should go back to the reception area and stand guard. Did you lock the door behind us when we came in?"

"I did. I'll go and wait out there. You can stay here in Quinn's office, but tell your brother to hurry. I'm prone to hyperventilating when I'm stressed."

The alarm continued in sharp bursts of three, then a pause, then three more bursts. I hadn't counted on how painfully loud the blasts would be. Harry pointed to his ears, reminding Cleo and me to use our earplugs. He put his in his ears, then went into Quinn's bathroom. I followed him, curious to see what he was looking for.

The toilet was seated to the right of the door at the back wall. A small sink stood next to it. He inspected the floor and walked to the other end of the small room

opposite the sink and toilet. The top half of that wall
housed a small medicine cabinet. Below that, there were
two narrow shelves and at the bottom was a cupboard
for supplies.

Harry opened the medicine cabinet, ran his hands
over every surface inside, then did the same with the
shallow cupboard below.

I checked my watch. We'd used three minutes. Harry
turned back from the wall, looked around the room, and
then focused on an elaborate light fixture hanging from
the ceiling by a chain.

"Step out of the way," he said. I backed up but
watched him through the bathroom door. He gave the
chain a firm pull, and the wall with the medicine cabinet swung toward him, revealing a dark space behind
it. I stood staring at it with my mouth open.

"We've used five minutes," I said, between alarm
blasts.

"I know," Harry said. "Stay right here." He pulled out
his cell phone, punched in a number and slipped behind
the false wall into the dark opening. "Don't let this panel
close. I'll be right back."

"Wait," I said, but he was already out of sight. I stood
there gripping the panel, afraid it would close, locking
him inside. What if I couldn't make it open again to let
him out?

I checked the time again. We had already used seven
of our ten minutes. I hadn't counted on being stuck inside the bathroom waiting for Harry. From her post in
the reception room, watching through the small safety
window in the entrance door, Cleo would spot anyone
approaching from out in the corridor. I couldn't see her
from where I stood, and with the blasting alarm only

partially muffled by earplugs, I wouldn't hear her if she called out a warning.

As the blasts continued and the minutes ticked away, my earplugs came loose and fell out. I couldn't retrieve them while I stood, bathed in sweat, holding the heavy wall in place. I wondered how long the secret door had been there. I remembered telling Harry about a private bathroom that had been added to the administrator's office when Quinn was first hired.

Obviously that job had involved more than installing a bathroom. Considering Quinn's past brush with death in the Middle East at the hands of armed assassins, and his concern for the safety of TMC's patients and employees, the secret passage made all kinds of sense. He wasn't about to be trapped with no way out if a shooter came looking for him. No wonder he didn't want Harry inspecting his office. This secret belonged only to Quinn and to someone who had been paid well to build it and keep quiet about its existence.

I suddenly realized the alarm was quiet. I looked at the time. Sixteen minutes. Where was Harry? Where was Cleo? Where was Nick? We had to get out.

After the steady blasting from the alarm, the profound silence in Quinn's office was unnerving. My ears buzzed and my head felt hollow. I strained to hear any trace of sound coming from behind the false wall, unable to trust my ears and praying Harry would reappear before it was too late.

"*Pssst,* Aimee," Cleo whispered from the doorway between Quinn's office and the reception room. "What's the holdup?"

I could barely hear her, and I didn't want to let go of the false wall.

"Can you come in here?" I whispered.

She tiptoed to the bathroom door and looked in, wide-eyed. "Oh, my god. What did you do to Quinn's bathroom?"

"Nothing. It's a false door."

"Where's Harry? We have to get out of here. Now that the drill's over, Sanjay could appear any minute."

I nodded to the space where Harry had gone. "He's in there. He said he'd be right back. Something must have gone wrong."

"What shall we do?" Cleo's breath was coming in short bursts. She wasn't kidding about hyperventilating.

"I'll wait here for Harry. You go out into the corridor. If you see Sanjay coming, think of something to distract him."

"Like what?" Cleo's breathing was so rapid that I expected her to pass out any minute.

"I don't know." I suggested the obvious. "Can you pretend to faint?"

"Not in a hospital. I'd end up in the ER."

Just then Harry reappeared from behind the false wall with a big grin on his face. Every tense muscle in my body relaxed at the same time and I almost collapsed with relief.

He stepped back inside the wall and told me to push it toward him.

"Really?" I was afraid he'd be trapped if it closed all the way.

"Really, Sis. I want to check something. Give it a shove." I did, and it closed with a solid snap. I looked up at the light fixture hanging from the ceiling by a chain. Harry had pulled it to open the wall. I was about to give it a yank when the wall opened again.

"Mission accomplished," Harry said, slipping around the open wall into the bathroom. "There's a release on the inside that's simple to operate. Let's get out of here."

EIGHTEEN

AFTER HARRY MADE sure the false door was seated back in its proper position, the three of us left the administrative suite and made our getaway down the stairwell and out to the parking garage. Cleo's breathing was nearly normal by the time we met up with Nick, who waited next to his SUV. He and Harry grinned and slapped high-fives.

"Enough celebrating," I said. "Tell us what you found."

"Let's go to my place where it'll be easier to explain." Harry glanced at Cleo. "Unless you need to get home? It's almost two o'clock."

"I want to hear this," she said. "I'll be right behind you."

At Harry's condo we gathered around his computer while he pulled up the blueprint he and I had made illustrating the floor plan of the fourth floor and the administrative suite. He used his drafting program to draw in the space he'd found behind the false wall; then he added a spiral staircase leading down to the third floor.

"How in the world did you think to look for that?" Cleo asked.

"I've designed a few false doors and safe rooms," he said. "One was a hidden entrance to a wine cellar, and another was a safe room in an attorney's office. They're more common than most people realize."

I asked the next question. "Where does the staircase lead?"

Harry and Nick exchanged smiles. "That's where Nick came in. I'd already shown him this floor plan. Remember this alcove?" He pointed to the recessed space in the corridor near the entrance door to the administrative suite's reception area. Cleo and I nodded. We'd both seen it countless times.

Nick spoke up. "Harry told me to look on the third floor for a similar alcove directly below that one. I spotted it right away and waited for Harry to text me. The alcove is recessed deep enough that the security cameras don't have a view of it. It's near the end of the corridor, and the doors to the public restrooms are in that alcove. No one paid any attention to me while I waited."

Harry picked up the thread. "So I went down the hidden staircase. I tapped on the interior side of the alcove wall Nick described, and he responded with an answering tap."

"Was there anything in that alcove?" I asked. "Chairs? Shelving for pamphlets?"

Nick shook his head. "No. Just the restroom doors on the east wall, and a locked steel door on the back wall with a sign in bold red lettering."

"What does it say?" Cleo asked.

"Have a look." Nick held out his phone. He had taken a photo of the door. The lettering read: HAZARD: NO ADMITTANCE. A graphic showed a man wearing a gas mask and a yellow hard-hat. Enough to discourage almost anyone from trying to open that door.

"I checked to see if it would open from the inside without a key," Harry said. "There was no way. Only someone with a key could open that door from either side. Once someone entered the alcove, they could disappear through that door and no one would notice."

"And remember," Nick said, "it's conveniently out of the line of sight of the security cameras."

Cleo's face went white. "Oh, I don't like this one bit. Now we know why Quinn didn't want Harry in his office."

"This doesn't mean Quinn's guilty," I said. "Lowe must have known about the secret passage. How else would he have gotten into Quinn's office that night?"

"True," Harry said. "If Lowe knew, then Quinn's efforts to keep his secret were already in vain. The cat was out of the bag."

"Not necessarily," Nick said, holding up his hands, palms out. "Maybe Quinn shared his secret only with Lowe, and only on the night of the murder."

"That doesn't make sense," Cleo said with a frown. "If Quinn wanted Lowe to meet with him, why wouldn't they both just use the normal entrance?"

"That's a question only Quinn can answer," Harry said.

"Not if he wasn't there." Cleo looked to me for backup.

I pointed out that Quinn insisted he wasn't in his office after hours the night of the murder. I asked Harry if there was any way to find out who had built the passage, and if so, whether that contractor would know how many people were aware of it.

"Doubtful. If Quinn wanted that passage kept a secret, and clearly he did, it had to be excluded from the permit and probably involved a hefty bribe. I'm betting Quinn hired someone from out of the area."

Cleo raised a hand. "Even so, someone in accounting

must have approved the expense for the bathroom. I was working at TMC when it was installed. It was obvious that work was being done in Quinn's office."

"Sure," Harry said, "but Quinn's signature was probably already on the paperwork for nothing more than removal of an elevator and construction of a private bathroom. It would have been rubber-stamped at that point."

"One more thing," I said. "Do you think we could be accused of some kind of conspiracy to withhold evidence if we don't tell the police what we discovered tonight?"

Harry and Nick exchanged glances. Cleo went white again.

"It isn't evidence; it's simply a theory that we're under no legal obligation to share," Nick said. "At this point, even Quinn has a right to keep it from becoming public knowledge."

"And consider this," Harry added. "The police investigators may have already discovered the secret access for themselves. If so, they would classify it as 'need to know' information and keep it quiet. I'm betting Quinn had the passageway installed as a safety precaution in the event of a hospital shooter or some other dire emergency." He looked to Nick, who nodded in agreement.

"My turn," I said, waving my raised hand. "Do we confront Quinn with this discovery?"

Nick replied, "There's a chance Quinn has already told the police about the secret passage, but if he hasn't, it won't look good if they find out later that he withheld that information."

"Should we ask him?" Cleo said.

"No." Harry and Nick spoke as a chorus.

"But maybe one of—"

"Cleo, they're right," I said. "You believe Quinn is innocent and so do I, but until we know that's true beyond a shadow of a doubt, we can't go to him about this." I waited for her reaction.

Cleo backed away from our huddle around Harry's computer and folded her arms across her chest.

"Cleo, trust us on this," Harry said. "If there's a chance Quinn pulled the trigger, we can't let him know what we've discovered."

"Tell you what," Nick added. "If you're willing to hold off on talking to Quinn, we'll reconsider after we know more."

"You're right, of course." Cleo raised her chin. "I would bet my life on his innocence, but I can't ask any of you to do the same."

"Then let's agree that for now, this secret remains among the four of us." Harry turned from his monitor and scanned our faces. We all agreed to keep what we knew to ourselves. Harry assured us he would try to identify the contractor Quinn had used and almost certainly paid under the table. If he succeeded, he might be able to convince the contractor to reveal if anyone else was in on Quinn's secret.

Our band of conspirators split up at three o'clock with everyone hoping to get some sleep before morning.

LYING IN BED in the pre-dawn hours, I had to admit things weren't looking good for Quinn. The idea that the police were looking at me as his possible accomplice kept me awake contemplating everyone who might have had a reason to want Lowe dead.

Natasha Korba's stepfather was at the top of the list. I didn't doubt that Abel Gailworth had Melissa under his thumb, but after seeing her distress in that hospital room and the way she had comforted her daughter, I had trouble imagining that she would go along with murder. If Gailworth had done it, I was almost certain he had kept Melissa in the dark. At least I hoped so. I wished I knew more about the submissive woman. How easily was she swayed? The trouble with suspecting Gailworth was that I couldn't imagine how he would have known about the hidden access to Quinn's office. Or why he would decide to commit the crime there. To frame Quinn? To what end?

Sybil Snyder's husband was a possibility, but equally hard to accept as a killer. Glen Capshaw suspected that Sybil had a lover, and he might have suspected it was Lowe, but Capshaw didn't seem like someone who would throw his life away over his wife's infidelity. He'd be more likely to sue for divorce and punish her in court than to come up with some devious way to commit a murder in Quinn's office. And it was highly unlikely that he knew about the secret access.

Who else? Rita Lowe's theory about her husband's affairs had to be considered. Maybe she was right. Had one of Lowe's mistresses decided that if she couldn't have him, no one could? The police might find it easier to believe that Mrs. Lowe had finally taken it upon herself to put an end to her husband's serial cheating.

None of this speculation explained why Lowe was shot in Quinn's office—assuming Quinn was telling the truth about being innocent. Lowe had sneaked in there for some compelling reason. Somehow, that reason got him killed.

Sanjay? I was almost asleep when his name popped into my head and brought me awake again. No. He didn't belong on my list of suspects. What possible reason

could he have for killing Lowe? That he would frame
Quinn, thus getting him out of the way so that Sanjay
could step into the administrator's position, seemed pre-
posterous. Then why had he come to mind? I grappled
for whatever thought had been in my subconscious. Then
it surfaced.

Opportunity. If anyone else knew about the secret
panel in Quinn's bathroom, it would be someone who
frequented the administrative suite. There were only two
possibilities: Varsha Singh and Sanjay D'Costa. Varsha
was a hardworking single mother of four young children—hardly the profile of a killer. In the hackneyed
world of television crime shows, however, she would be a
suspect. I refused to add her to my list, but I did wonder
if she knew about the secret passage. She had worked
with Quinn for several years. If there was a shooter on
the loose or a fire broke out on the fourth floor, surely
Quinn would have told Varsha how to escape. It would
be criminal of him not to. Wouldn't he have done the
same for Sanjay?

Giving up on sleep, I got up at five o'clock Thursday
morning and munched a bowl of granola while I made
notes to remind myself of the myriad thoughts that had
paraded through my restless mind. After several cups
of coffee and a cool wake-up shower, I thought I could
make it through the day, but I drove to work very carefully.

MY FIRST HOUR in the library passed while I sorted mail
and took care of routine tasks. By the time Bernie Kluckert arrived at nine o'clock, the coffee carafe in my tiny
break room was more than half empty. I was feeling jit-
tery and lightheaded.

"Reporting for duty, miss," Bernie said. His right arm twitched, but he managed to resist the impulse to salute.

"Good morning, Bernie."

He looked at me expectantly, but my sleepy mind drew a blank. Were there any plants that needed watering or surfaces he hadn't already dusted? If not, what would I do with him all morning? Then I remembered there was a carpet sweeper tucked away in the break room. He spoke up before I could mention it.

"Lola was complimentary about my cleaning," he said, displaying a beaming smile. "At our auxiliary meeting this morning, she thanked me right in front of Oslo Swanson." He winked. "I could tell Oslo was peeved, don't you know."

If I hadn't been so tired, I might have come up with a response. Instead I just nodded and asked if Bernie would mind running the carpet sweeper over the floors. I explained that Housekeeping only vacuumed the library once a week. He took me up on that suggestion with enthusiasm and went about his work, whistling under his breath.

Between helping walk-in patrons, responding to email requests, and preparing an agenda for the next Continuing Education Committee meeting, I found my thoughts kept turning to Varsha Singh and whether she knew about the emergency exit in Quinn's bathroom. I wanted to get Cleo's opinion before I asked Varsha about it. If she didn't know, I couldn't give it away.

I emailed Cleo to ask if she could do lunch at Margie's Bean Pot. She responded that she had to facilitate a luncheon meeting of the Credentials Committee. She suggested we take an afternoon break instead and meet in the hospital cafeteria at two thirty. By noon I had fin-

ished preparing the CME agenda. As I worked, Bernie
had traversed the library floor a dozen times with the
carpet sweeper, emptying its nose-tickling contents several times into the wastebasket next to my desk so he
could show me how much dust and dirt the Housekeeping Department's vacuum cleaner had missed. After putting the carpet sweeper away, he stopped by my desk.

"All clean now, miss," he said. "Young people don't
know how to do a job. They musta been givin' it a lick
and a promise, don't you see?" He flexed his gnarled
fingers and I suspected his hands were cramping from
gripping the sweeper's handle. I watched his irregu-
lar gait—he was favoring arthritic joints, no doubt—as
he walked toward the exit door. Three hours of carpet
sweeping had probably left him aching and tender, but
he did it for Lola.

The things we do for love. For a fleeting moment
Nick came to mind.

As soon as Bernie was gone, I locked up and spent
my lunch hour napping on the old chaise lounge in the
library restroom. Later, feeling refreshed, I managed
to keep my mind on my work until it was time to meet
Cleo. I caught up with her in the cafeteria, empty except
for a couple of dietary staffers doing their thing in the
kitchen. I bought a bag of pretzels and a bottle of water
from the vending machines. Cleo sat at the opposite end
of the room, out of earshot of the kitchen crew. I joined
her and asked about Varsha.

"Do you think she knows about the passageway?"

Cleo peeled open the wrapper of a Snickers bar.
"Good question. If she needed an emergency exit, she
would have to use Quinn's hidden passage. He must have
told her. He wouldn't let her perish to keep his secret."

"You're sure?"

"I'd trust him with my life, Aimee. Varsha would, too. Imagine a shooter approaching the door to her reception area. She'd be a sitting duck. There are so many shootings in the news these days; it may be only a matter of time before we have one here."

"All the more reason to believe Quinn had that emergency passage built not just for himself, but for Varsha and the assistant administrator who held that job before Sanjay came along."

"Yes, that was Karla Morgan. She left before you were hired. The position went vacant for a few months until Sanjay came on board."

"So back when Quinn was hired, he had two women to protect from potential disaster. Why the secrecy?" I asked.

Cleo swallowed a bite of her Snickers. "Because the more people who knew about it, the less likely it would serve its purpose in a crisis. Besides, no one else who works on the fourth floor needed it. They all have more than one exit into the main corridor."

"Nick said that door on the third floor—the one with the hazard sign—was locked. And Harry said it doesn't open from either side without a key. Anyone who could exit onto the third floor from that door with a key could also enter with the same key and go up the stairs to the fourth floor and into Quinn's office."

"Then what?" Cleo said. She did not look convinced. "Murder someone?"

"Maybe. Harry checked the false wall when he came back up from the third floor. He said it was easy to work the latch from inside to make the wall open into Quinn's bathroom."

"So Quinn *could* have been in his office the night of the murder if he entered from the third floor." Cleo looked sober and worried.

"Yes, but let's focus on other people who might have known how to get into Quinn's office. That woman you mentioned, Sanjay's predecessor... She had a key. Quinn must have asked her to turn it in when she left."

"Of course," Cleo said. "She had no further use for it, and Quinn wouldn't want it floating around."

"Then maybe Sanjay has that key. We need to find out."

"I know, Aimee, but how are we going to do that without tipping off Quinn that we know his secret? Or revealing it to Sanjay?"

"How solid is your relationship with Varsha?"

"We have a good rapport as colleagues, but we aren't close personal friends." Cleo massaged her temples, showing signs of strain and worry. "I haven't talked to her since Quinn was put on leave. I'm not quite sure how I'd approach her."

"Maybe you could express concern about her vulnerability in that reception area and see if she volunteers anything."

"Let me think about it." Cleo glanced at her watch. "I'd better get back to work."

"Me, too."

She touched my hand. "Before you go, did you decide who you're taking to the symphony?"

"I haven't asked my grandmother about it yet. I'll let you know tomorrow."

I saw the disappointment on her face and knew she hoped I'd show up with Nick.

As I started walking back to the library, I noticed my

right knee was giving me more pain than the left. I made an about face and dropped by the ER to see if one of the docs might have some advice. After X-rays, I was given a diagnosis of hairline fracture of the right patella and a prescription for pain pills.

NINETEEN

CLEO CALLED JUST before closing time with news. She'd checked the courthouse calendar and learned that Natasha's next custody hearing was set for the following Wednesday. Almost a week away. It wasn't yet clear whether the girl's condition would keep her hospitalized until then. If Korba put enough pressure on Dr. Snyder, my guess was Natasha would remain in-house for another week. I didn't envy Sybil Snyder, knowing she would bear the brunt of testimony at the hearing.

Knowing the date filled me with a new sense of urgency. I thought of Harry and Nick and wondered if they'd had any success with their respective inquiries. Nick was still checking up on Gailworth, and Harry was looking for Quinn's covert stairway builder. I texted both of them, saying we needed to meet.

At home, I stopped off at the main house to ask Amah about the symphony. When she opened the front door, the aroma that greeted me made saliva pool under my tongue. Their dinner was almost ready and my nose told me it was Jack's turkey enchiladas. She invited me to join them, saying Jack had already done the evening chores. I accepted and helped her set the table and chop veggies for a green salad. My stomach stopped growling after the first few bites of cheesy enchilada.

"Weather's supposed to be clear on Saturday," Jack said. "We're taking two of our newest llamas to the foothills for training. We could take three if you want to come along."

I wanted to help them out. I considered my knees and figured I could load up on pain pills.

"I'd like to," I said, "if we can be home in time. I have tickets for the symphony." That reminded me to ask Amah about the tickets. I'd been sidetracked by her dinner invitation.

"I would have loved to, sweetie, but since we're hiking that morning, I'd better take a rain check."

Amah wouldn't admit it, but a day hiking in the foothills with inexperienced llamas took a lot of energy. She would want to come home and relax instead of gearing up to go out to a concert. I told her I'd invite Nick.

She and Jack traded conspiratorial glances. "We'll make sure you're home in plenty of time," Jack said. I knew where they stood on the subject of my getting back together with Nick. Firmly on the plus side, and the sooner the better.

While we were doing dishes, I decided to get Amah's perspective on Harry and Rella. I reminded her that she had asked me if Harry was getting serious about a woman.

"Has he said something? Was I right?" Her excitement made me feel a little guilty.

"You were right, but it's kind of complicated."

"Oh." She dried her hands on a kitchen towel. "Shall we talk about it?"

"Maybe." I thought of Amah and Grandpa Machado's second wife, Tanya, and how well they got along. How had they managed that tricky situation?

Amah poured two glasses of white wine, and we settled on the couch in the family room. I filled her in on my talk with Harry. How long he'd been dating Rella, and why they hadn't come out in the open.

"No one seems to have a problem with it except me," I said.

The twist of Amah's lips told me she understood. "So you're uncomfortable with Rella's past relationship with Nick?"

"It just seems awkward—Harry dating Nick's ex-girlfriend. How did you and Tanya get to be so comfortable with each other?"

"We talked it out." She set her wine glass on the coffee table and took my hand. "I'm afraid you're speaking to the wrong person, sweetheart."

"You're suggesting I talk to Rella? How? I barely know her." That prospect was daunting. Rella seemed friendly enough toward me, but she had never encouraged chat or girl talk.

"You're a smart girl." Amah gave me a hug. "You'll figure it out."

Later in my apartment I shed work clothes for sweats and checked my phone. Harry and Nick had both sent texts. Harry's said, Still working on it. Nick's said, Call me. Good. I was going to do that anyway.

"Symphony?" he said. "Don't you usually go to those concerts with your grandmother?"

I told him she'd declined, and added that Hector Korba played bass clarinet with the orchestra. I told him about Natasha's new custody hearing date and Korba's insistence that Natasha stay in the hospital until then. I mentioned my suspicion that Snyder would recommend he have custody.

"What's that got to do with going to the symphony?"

"Nothing, really. It's just that I've had to say no to

Korba twice and he wasn't happy either time. I understand why he's so concerned about his granddaughter, and I feel bad about not being able to help him. I thought it might help to see him outside the hospital in a different setting."

"You have doubts about him parenting a ten-year-old girl?"

"He seems gruff, but I've never seen how he is with Natasha. He may be a big teddy bear. I'm sure he's hoping to guide her career, but I don't see him exploiting her in the self-serving way Abel Gailworth would."

"Speaking of Gailworth, let me give you the latest intel."

"The geeks found something?"

"They did. Remember our speculation about his income?"

"Sure. We know he isn't living entirely off the collection plate from his miniscule congregation."

"No way. He's been living off funds he managed to scam from several wealthy and gullible women."

"What kind of scam?"

"He sweet-talked them into donating to his most recent gig, the vegan church. Some of them coughed up as much as fifty thousand bucks a pop. Apparently he's adept at fleecing women with more money than sense. Lucky for us, there's a paper trail. Most of them reported their contributions so they could take the tax deduction. I'm guessing they took whatever else Gailworth was willing to give them."

"That sounds pretty sleazy." I switched my phone to my other ear. "Do you mean what I think you mean?"

"I wouldn't be surprised."

"Hard to understand why anyone would fall for his

phony pitch. I've always imagined vegans and vegetarians to be smart people."

"Most of them are smart enough to do their due diligence and follow proper guidelines."

"So Gailworth was using his vegan church as a way to con women? Do you think he stopped after he married Melissa?"

"He had to, didn't he? A wife would definitely cramp his style. That was almost three years ago."

"Do you think he still has money stashed away?"

"Only if it's well hidden, and I doubt he has much. His dwindling savings and his collection plate have kept him going. By now he's probably desperate to get a grip on Natasha's career."

"But why, if Natasha Korba is the pot of gold he thinks she is, would he put her health at risk the way he did?"

"Lack of common sense would be my guess," Nick said. "Gailworth has to keep up the vegan sham for the time being, but he and the girl's mother obviously hadn't done their research when it came to the nutritional needs of a growing child like Natasha."

"We have to protect that little girl." My jaw tensed with frustration. "I wish we knew more about her mother. I've tried a few searches and came up with nothing helpful. Not even her maiden name. Any chance of finding out more about her?"

"That's a work in progress, lady. Stay tuned." It had been a while since he'd called me *lady*. I liked the sound.

"What do you think we should do in the meantime?"

"What Korba wants. Keep the girl hospitalized until after the custody hearing and hope Korba and Natasha's doctor can convince the judge to place her with her grandfather."

"You know, Korba is single, and at least sixty. I doubt that's going to work in his favor."

"Does he date anyone?" Nick asked.

"If he does, I've never heard about it. You think a fiancée would help his case?"

"It wouldn't hurt. A wife would be even better, but I doubt he could get that done in the next few days."

I had to laugh. Nick didn't know Korba. I wouldn't put anything past him. But we had strayed off my reason for calling, so I pulled us back on topic.

"So are you available tomorrow night?"

"Symphony, huh? I'm tempted to play hard to get, but we both know I'm going to say yes. It sounds like you're a little intimidated by this Korba character. I'd like to have a look at him."

"I'm not alone. He probably intimidates a lot of people. I just want to make sure he doesn't intimidate Natasha."

"I get that. So what's the dress code?"

I thought about Nick's usually casual wardrobe. "A suit and tie would be nice."

"I can manage that. Shall we make a night of it and have dinner first?"

The thought of a romantic dinner with Nick filled me with visions of candlelight and a warm sense of hope for our future. "I'm going on a llama hike with Amah and Jack Saturday morning, but I should be home in time."

"Great. What time does the symphony start?"

"Seven o'clock."

"Then I'll make reservations for five thirty and pick you up at five."

TWENTY

My Friday morning emails consisted of the usual requests for articles. I printed some for the patrons who liked to read words printed on paper and arranged for a courier to deliver them. The rest I sent out as email attachments. My agenda for the noon meeting of the CME Committee was finished, and the related addendums were gathered.

With those chores out of the way, I mulled over the hidden passageway Harry had discovered in Quinn's bathroom and speculated about how many people knew it was there. Dr. Lowe, obviously. Cleo thought Quinn must have told Varsha and Sanjay. And anyone who knew about the false wall in Quinn's bathroom probably had a key to the secret door on the third floor. If Quinn hadn't killed Lowe, and Varsha hadn't killed Lowe, that left Sanjay. Impossible? No, but highly improbable.

I wondered if Cleo had found a chance to question Varsha. I sent her an email with just a question mark. She emailed back an exclamation point. I left Lola busy photocopying agendas and hiked over to Cleo's office. She looked up at me over her half-moons.

"Shut the door."

I shut the door and slid into the chair across from her. "What? Did you get her to talk?"

"It took some convincing, but I played up her vulnerability in light of the shooting in Quinn's office. I pretended to think that the only way the shooter could have gotten in there was through Varsha's work area. I told her she should insist on a safe exit from her work station. I even implied that I would raise the issue at our next Department Head meeting and get home office involved if need be. At that point she swore me to secrecy and finally told me about the passage."

I let out a breath. "What did she say? Does Sanjay know?"

"No. That's the weird thing. I was sure if Varsha knew, he would know. But she said Quinn didn't want to tell Sanjay until after his six-month probationary period, in case he didn't work out."

"Who else knows?"

"According to Varsha, just she and Quinn." Cleo's forehead was creased, a sure sign she was worried. She almost never did that. She believed it caused wrinkles.

"What about Sanjay's predecessor? Did she know?"

"Varsha wasn't sure. She said when Quinn gave her the key, he told her not to tell anyone, so she and the former assistant administrator never discussed it."

"Well, somehow Lowe got in there. And so did his killer. It's beyond belief to suspect that Varsha lured Gavin Lowe in there and killed him, and impossible to conclude that Sanjay's predecessor came from all the way across the continent to do the deed."

Cleo's eyes filled with tears. "Dear God, Aimee. This looks so bad for Jared."

"I know." I wanted to reassure her, but my heart was sinking, too. "There's got to be some other explanation. Harry's looking for whoever it was who did the construction work. Maybe that will give us a new lead."

We both had noon meetings to facilitate, so I hiked back to the library and we each went about our workday.

The CME Committee's luncheon meeting went smoothly with a new chair at the helm. The TMC library's forensic consortium, a major part of my job description, was still in its early stages and I had worried that it might flounder without Dr. Beardsley's influence. I was relieved when Quinn convinced Dr. Phyllis Poole to accept the chairmanship. She and I had been thrown together several months earlier in a precarious situation involving one of her patients. We weren't chums by any stretch, but that incident had created a bond of mutual respect. Poole believed in the forensic project, and with her reputation for toughness, she could wield the necessary clout to win over the rest of the committee.

Quinn was conspicuously absent from the meeting, but the physician members were tactful enough to avoid asking about him. The entire medical community knew that Quinn was a murder suspect, and they were all aware that home office had placed him on administrative leave while the investigation was ongoing. Sanjay D'Costa sat in as the ex-officio representative of administration, but he spent most of the time texting on his phone and paid scant attention to the business going on in the room.

The committee approved my budget items: two new print journals and the newest edition of a pricey book titled *Disposition of Toxic Drugs and Chemicals in Man* that was considered to be toxicology's bible.

At quitting time Cleo called, sounding frustrated. "We need to get Quinn back to work as soon as possible. I'm getting complaints from the medical staff and from ancillary services. They're not happy about Sanjay's knee-jerk management style. I know he's trying his best, but he's no Jared Quinn."

I commiserated until she'd finished letting off steam, and then tried to lighten the moment before ending our call.

"It's Valentine's Day and Sig is a romantic guy. Are you doing something special tonight?"

"Sig's rehearsing with the symphony, but he'll be home in time to go out for dessert later. I hope you haven't forgotten about tomorrow night's concert. Who did you end up inviting?"

"I haven't forgotten. Nick's coming with me."

I heard her whisper, "Yes!" Then she said, "Speaking of Valentine's Day, are you celebrating with Nick tonight?"

"Not tonight, but we're going to dinner tomorrow night before the symphony."

"Good. About time you two got back on the road to romance." I knew she was smiling. I let her think it was a belated Valentine's Day date. The truth was, both Nick and I had skirted any mention of the holiday for lovers. Maybe we weren't quite there yet.

At home I checked with Jack and Amah about what to pack for the morning llama hike, then locked myself in and settled down with the TV remote and a turkey pot pie. And more pain pills. Amah called at eight thirty on the old landline phone Jack insisted I keep in my apartment.

"Sweetie, are you busy?" she asked.

"Not really, why?"

"Jack and I are going out to the Feed Bag for dessert and coffee and we thought you might like to join us."

The Feed Bag was the best restaurant in Coyote Creek

and boasted a great dessert menu, but Amah and Jack
didn't need a third wheel tagging along on Valentine's
Day. I declined with thanks.

Ten minutes later my landline rang again. I considered ignoring it, thinking Amah would try to persuade
me to change my mind. After four rings, the answering
machine came on.

"Aimee, this is Jared Quinn. If you're home, pick up
your damn phone."

TWENTY-ONE

NOT GOOD. I could think of only one explanation for the anger in Quinn's voice. He knew about our invasion of his office. Should I pick up? Or should I call Cleo first to see what she knew. *Definitely call Cleo first.*

She didn't answer. Of course not. She and Sig were going out for dessert after the symphony rehearsal. I tried her cell phone, but it went to voicemail. I asked her to call me. That left me with several difficult choices. I could ignore Quinn's call and hope and pray he wouldn't decide to come out to Coyote Creek and throttle me, or I could call him back and play dumb. The other option was to wait to hear from Cleo. I opted to wait, but that only worked for about twenty minutes, until Quinn's next call. I let the machine pick up.

"Me again," he said. "If I don't hear from you by ten o'clock, I'm going to pay you a visit."

I checked the time. Almost nine o'clock. The last thing I needed was an irate Quinn on my doorstep. If he was angry enough to cause a commotion, Jack might decide to shoot him. But Jack wasn't home.

Minutes crawled by while I paced my small studio and glanced out my kitchen window watching for Jack and Amah to pull into their driveway, or for headlights to make their way down the lane to my home above the barn. Every call to Cleo went to voicemail. I needed to talk to someone. At ten minutes to ten, I called Nick, hoping he would answer but expecting to get his voicemail.

"Hey, lady, I'm glad you called. I thought you'd be all tucked in and resting up for tomorrow's big llama hike."

"There's a problem." I filled him in on Quinn's calls and my attempts to reach Cleo.

"I'm on my way. Call me if he shows up before I get there."

"No, wait. We can't have a scene at my grandparents' place. I'm going to call Quinn and get it over with. He doesn't have the authority to fire me while he's suspended. All he can do is read me the riot act."

"He can do worse than that if he's backed into a corner, especially if he really did kill that doctor." I heard Nick's quickened breathing. "Aimee, make your call, but do it from your cell phone, in your car, on your way here."

"What about my grandparents? I told them I'd hike with them tomorrow."

"Leave them a message. Tell them I talked you into spending the night with me. They'll be thrilled. And you can go home tomorrow in time for the hike, unless you think Quinn's a threat to your grandparents if he goes out there and finds you gone. If that's the case, we need to get the police involved."

"I can't believe he'd try to intimidate my grandparents." The thought took my breath away.

"I hope you're right, but you'd better hurry up and make that call, just in case. It's almost ten o'clock."

I dialed the number Quinn had left for me. He answered on the first ring, sounding surprisingly calm.

"You cut it pretty close, Machado. One more minute

and I'd have been on my way to Coyote Creek." Something in his voice made me suspect he was bluffing.

"I don't believe you, Quinn. You wouldn't dare trespass on my grandparents' property. One word from me and Jack would fill you with buckshot."

Quinn surprised me with a laugh. "Hell, I forgot about him. Your call probably saved my life."

"You could be right. No one messes with Jack." I let that sink in for a moment, then asked Quinn why he'd demanded that I call.

"Don't play dumb with me, Aimee. Cleo filled me in on your visit to my office during the fire drill at TMC. I want you to explain yourself, since I have no doubt you're the one who came up with the plan."

"Cleo said what? When?" I couldn't believe she'd done that without alerting me.

"As soon as Varsha told me about her conversation with Cleo, I made it my business to find out what was really going on. It took some persuading, but Cleo finally caved and told me about your brother's discovery. She said I'd have to get the rest of the details from you."

There was no point holding back, so I confessed how Harry and I had worked out the floor plan of his office and how Harry had suspected a false wall and a secret exit. I swore none of us would give away his secret, that we had all agreed not to tell the police what we knew.

"So Cleo said, but she did emphasize I should do that myself."

"Then you haven't told them yet?"

"No. I was hoping I wouldn't have to. How would their knowing about the passage help to prove my innocence? It's more likely to imply that I'm guilty."

"Still, if they find out later and think you were withholding information that could help them with the case, it would look bad for you."

"I'll take my chances. That passage is there to protect TMC's patients and employees from shooters and other crazies. The whole point is that it's a secret."

"But if the police found out someone else knew about it, that would be a plus for you, wouldn't it?"

"That's the hell of it," Quinn said. "No one knew except Varsha and me, and you'll never convince me that she told anyone. Don't you think I'd have come clean to the police if I thought there was some plausible explanation for how Lowe and his killer got in there?"

"What about the woman who was assistant administrator before Sanjay? What if she told someone? Maybe she let it slip accidentally and never mentioned it to you."

"I've already been in touch with her. She insists she didn't and I believe her."

"Have you been in touch with the contractor who did the work? Maybe he talked."

"He was paid well to keep quiet, so I doubt it. Don't even ask me how I found him in the first place. I figured if I could find him again, and he could shed light on how anyone else might know about the work he did, then I'd take it to the police."

"Then tell them that, if you decide to talk to them. It might help to explain why you didn't mention it right away. Are you having any luck finding the guy?"

"No. I'm still trying to track him down. I'm not even sure he gave me a real name. He said his name was Bob Smith and called his business Portico Construction Company. The work he did was top-notch, but the stairwell portion wasn't included in the plans when the job was permitted, so it wasn't strictly legal."

"Did he file a permit?"

"He did, but only for the bathroom portion. That's why he won't want to hear from me. He's a boomer who travels under the radar and keeps a pretty low profile. I may never find him."

Boomer. I was familiar with the construction workers' term because of Harry. A transient worker who travels from job to job. Indeed, he would be hard to track down, especially if he had done the secret passage portion of the job under the table. If he had used a phony tax ID or social security number, maybe even a phony business name, we might never find him. After all the trouble we'd gone to, it looked like a dead end.

"So how mad are you?" I asked. "Will I be fired when you get back to work?"

"I'm still deciding. Don't tip the scales by giving me any more reasons."

After talking to Quinn, I remembered I was supposed to be on my way to Nick's place. I called him back, assuring him that I was fine, then told him about my conversation with Quinn.

"You believed him?" Nick asked. "You really think he's innocent?"

"Nick, if you don't trust my judgment about Quinn, at least trust Cleo and Varsha. They've both known him for five years, and neither of them thinks he's capable of cold-blooded murder."

"I'll take your word for it, for now. Earlier when you called you said he sounded pissed at you. If he does anything again that makes you feel the least bit threatened, he's dead meat. And you can tell him I said so."

"Okay, but you'll probably have to get in line behind Jack and Harry."

"Speaking of Harry, have you talked to him since Rella got home?"

"No. Why?"

"He has some news, but I'll let him tell you. And I'll see you tomorrow evening. Don't forget to rinse off the llama dust."

News about Harry and Rella? I wondered while I got ready for bed. Were they engaged? Had they broken up? Should I call Harry and satisfy my curiosity? I decided to mind my own business, which at the moment was to get some sleep. I needed to store up enough energy to get through Saturday's llama training hike and still be alert enough in the evening to observe Hector Korba at the symphony.

THE NEXT MORNING, I did a couple of knee bends to test my pain level. I was still at the maximum dose of pills, so I made sure to take extra in my fanny pack. I hadn't mentioned the parking lot mugging to my grandparents, and by the time it occurred to me that hiking might exacerbate my injuries, it was too late to back out.

While Jack hooked up the trailer and loaded the tack in the back of his pickup, Amah packed our lunches. I was in charge of luring the llamas into the catch pen with cob, their favorite treat. They couldn't resist the combination of corn, oats, and barley. Once I had isolated the three novices we were taking on the hike, I enticed them with Amah's homemade llama cookies and got them haltered.

Loading them into the trailer was the first phase of their training. Again, bribing them was the way to go. Jack got the first two in without a fuss, but the third planted his feet in a stubborn stance. He was pretty green, and it took patience, but Jack gave him time to calm down, and eventually he succumbed to the lure of grain rattling in a can and hopped aboard with his pasture mates.

Soon we were on our way up the highway and into the eastern foothills. Jack had friends in the timber industry who allowed him to use their property for hiking. We put the trio through all the sorts of obstacles they might face on a pack trail. They were saddled, loaded with panniers carrying a minimal amount of weight, and led single file until we reached a small stream—their first obstacle. One of them balked at crossing water, and another stopped midstream to urinate as soon as he had all four hooves in the water. Neither behavior is acceptable, so we spent some time crossing and re-crossing the stream until they got it right.

Next, Jack took us off the trail where we could encounter downed trees and observe how the llamas reacted to the challenge of a barrier in their path. Would they balk, hurdle wildly over the barrier, or would they do what a well-trained animal should do—use the minimum amount of energy to clear the obstacle? Often, simply stepping carefully over the barrier is all that is necessary. And it prevents upsetting the carefully arranged burden the animal is carrying.

The obstacle training took the most effort, and with three novice animals, it was the most time-consuming. When we reached a clearing, Jack finally announced it was time for lunch. We tied the llamas where they could graze. Amah had packed smoked salmon and crackers in one of the panniers. She topped off our meal with Jack's favorite trekker's dessert—homemade oatmeal cookies loaded with raisins and walnuts. The hike had exacerbated my pain, especially in my right knee, so I sneaked more pain pills with lunch.

On the drive home, sitting between Jack and Amah in the cab of the pickup, I wondered whether to bring up the subject of Harry and Rella. Nick had asked me if I'd heard from Harry since Rella got home from New York. Why? Nick said he'd let Harry tell me. But tell me what? Neither Jack nor Amah brought up Harry's name in conversation, so I decided to let it go until I heard from Harry. As soon as we were back in cell phone range, I checked for texts or voicemails but found nothing. Jack teased me about being addicted to my phone like a teenager, so I put it away.

HOME AGAIN, AMAH and I turned out the llamas while Jack unhitched the trailer. We stowed the saddles, halters, and panniers in the tack room below my apartment in the barn. I gave Jack and Amah hugs and went upstairs while they drove up the lane to the main house.

I checked my phone and spotted a text from Harry. Have news, come by if u have time.

It was only two o'clock. Sure, I had time. Nick wouldn't be picking me up for dinner until five. I also had news for Harry. I wanted to tell him what Quinn had said about the contractor who put in that false wall and secret passage.

I did a sniff test, decided not to take time to change my hiking clothes, and headed to Harry's condo. When I rang his bell, Rella opened the door.

"Aimee. Hi." Rella looked very much at home in sweats and sneakers. "Harry just walked over to the workout room. He said you might drop by. Do you want to come in and wait?"

Interesting that she was answering Harry's door. Then the light dawned, and I guessed what Harry's news might be. She had moved in with him.

"Sure." I stepped inside. "How long do you think he'll be?"

"He said half an hour, but you know Harry." Rella smiled like an indulgent parent. "He'll get caught up in his workout and lose track of time. We could have a drink while you wait. Would you like coffee? Or wine? I just opened a nice Riesling."

Here was my perfect opportunity to take Amah's advice. Wine would help me get through an awkward conversation with Rella, but I had to drive back home, so I asked for coffee.

We sat in Harry's living room looking out at the view of the Sacramento River. I was still working out how to bring up the subject when Rella broke the silence.

"Now that you know Harry and I are dating, there's something I've been wanting to ask you, Aimee. This seems like a good time, and I hope it won't make you uncomfortable."

Her, too? I hadn't expected that. "I have something on my mind too, but you go first."

Rella put her cup on a side table, picked up a pillow and held it against her chest. I'd done that myself a time or two. Protective body language. *Not a good sign.*

"Here goes." She turned to face me. "Do you think I'm too old for your brother?"

It took a moment to register what she'd said. It had nothing to do with Nick? Rella's agenda was different from mine.

I shook off my confusion. "What do you mean? *Are* you older?"

"About four years, but Harry knows, and it doesn't bother him. I thought you knew. I assumed he'd told you."

"No. Something like that wouldn't be important enough for Harry to mention."

"If it isn't about my age, is there something else? You said you had something on your mind."

It was my turn to hold a pillow to my chest. "It's about the week you and Nick were in Paris. You had flown Buck there for a series of meetings."

A trace of frown creased Rella's forehead. "That was almost six months ago, right?"

"About that," I said.

A sudden blush tinted her cheeks. "Is this about the hotel mix-up and my sharing Nick's room that last night?" She had jumped to the crux of the matter and we couldn't turn back.

"That's part of it."

"What did Nick tell you?" She pulled the pillow, which had dropped to her lap, against her chest again.

"Pretty much all of it," I said. *If Nick's version of that night was true.*

"And you're thinking I'm not the right woman for Harry because of that?" Rella got up and went out of the room. She came back with her purse open. She pulled out her wallet. "Here's a photo of Remy, the man I was with in Nick's room that night. We met a few years ago when I was flying for United. He's a friend…okay, a friend with benefits, I suppose. We met for drinks that night and things just happened. I wasn't with Harry back then. I wasn't seeing anyone, so I called Remy."

"And Buck had a card game going," I said, "so Nick had to sit up at the bar until your friend left."

"I'm afraid so. I didn't know Nick had come back to the room until the phone rang late into the night. That's when I saw him in the other bed."

"Why didn't you let me talk to him?"

"I didn't know it was you until Nick told me weeks later. Some woman calling in the middle of the night asking for him? It could have been one of the women who'd been trying to cozy up to him in the bar. You know how he attracts…" She stopped herself. "I mean, you have to admit Nick's hot. Remember what I told you when I first came to work for Buck?"

"That you weren't still hot for Nick."

"Right. I figured he'd told you we had a bit of history. I wanted to clear the air about that."

"He hadn't told me before I heard it from you. I still don't know much about the time you were dating."

Rella surprised me by laughing. "It's a stretch to call it 'dating.' We went to a gun range together a few times. That's about the only thing we had in common, besides flying. He likes classic movies and reads a lot of fiction. Stuff that bores me. But that was only part of the problem." Rella visibly relaxed. "I have a cousin named Nicky. We're close, and he looks a lot like Nick. *Your* Nick. I couldn't even think of Nick as a kissin' cousin. It was just too weird."

At that point Harry came through the front door. "Hey, my favorite sister and my favorite pilot. What's going on?"

"Nothing much," I said, too quickly. "I've just been telling Rella what a bratty little brother you were."

Rella stood. Harry walked over, put an arm around her waist, and gave her a quick kiss on the lips. They looked equally smitten and I felt happier than I had in a long time.

Rella had just poured coffee for Harry when her phone rang. She took her call in the kitchen and came back to the living room saying, "It's Buck. I have to go to the airport."

Harry walked out with her, then came back inside and settled across from me in one of his overstuffed chairs. He took a sip from his cup. "Ah, she makes a good cup of coffee."

"So what's up?" I asked. "You said you have news."

"Why don't you catch me up first? Any progress on your end?"

"Some. But I'm not sure how useful the info is."

I gave him the highlights of my conversation with Quinn, including the fact that Quinn had already struck out trying to track down the guy who did the secret work. I asked if there was a way to find out who might have been doing covert construction work in the Sawyer County area back when Quinn came to town.

"How far back?" he asked.

"I don't know exactly when Quinn started at TMC, but it had to be about five years ago."

"That's quite a while," Harry said. "I was still an apprentice architect working in San Francisco back then, but who knows where the guy came from? I doubt he was a Sawyer County local if he was doing unpermitted work. At least that confirms what I suspected. He must have been a boomer from out of the area. I'll put some feelers out."

I waited an anxious moment for Harry to tell me his news, but he seemed content to sip his coffee in silence. I picked up my empty cup, put it back down, and prompted him a second time.

"Your turn. You've got me curious. Since Rella opened your door when I got here, I thought your news must have something to do with her being at your place."

Harry laughed. "So you thought what? That we'd eloped or something?"

I forced a laugh in return, feeling awkward. "Nothing that drastic. I just wondered if you two were taking things to another level."

He leaned forward in his chair. "Sis, it's nothing like that. Rella came over to work out with me in the weight room. She finished first and came back here to the apartment ahead of me. She's still living in her temporary home in Nick's apartment."

"That reminds me." I sat back, more relaxed now. "Nick said he sublet to her so she'd have room when her nephews visit. Are the boys still with her?"

Harry seemed to relax as well. "No, they're back home in Maryland with their father."

"Any word on her escrow closing?"

"They're telling her it could be any day now." Harry was silent for a moment. "Why? Did Nick say something about wanting his place back?"

I hurried to reassure him. "Good heavens, no, you know how easygoing he is about things like that, but it's been a few months now."

"It shouldn't be much longer. If Nick's okay with bunking in Buck's pool house, why are you asking?"

I hadn't meant to come off as irritated with Rella for taking over Nick's place. Now that I better understood their past "relationship," there was really nothing to object to. "Just wondering if it has anything to do with your news."

He smiled and shook his head. "My news is going to sound anticlimactic after what you've been imagining. I've been nominated for an Architect of the Year award for the mall project."

Puzzled, I said, "I was given the impression that it had something to do with Rella. What was that about?"

"That's because the nominations haven't been announced. Rella heard about it back in New York. She ran into a woman at the hotel where she and Buck were staying and they got to talking over drinks. The woman mentioned that she was on the nominating committee and let it slip that I was a candidate, but she told Rella I wasn't supposed to know about it yet."

"When will you find out if you've won?"

"It won't be announced for quite a while."

"So have you told Amah and Jack? Or Mom and Dad?"

"Not yet. I thought I'd wait. I don't want them to spend a lot of time with their hopes up and then have them disappointed."

I gave him a playful slap on the knee. "I'm proud of you, Bro. That's wonderful news."

"Thanks. Now will you stop making assumptions about my personal life?"

My smile was rueful this time. "I'll try."

TWENTY-TWO

I GOT HOME from Harry's with an hour to spare and headed for the shower. There were few occasions for formal wear in Timbergate, so I decided to go for it. I dressed in my most elegant outfit: a flowing red gown with a skirt that nearly touched the ground, topped off by a black brocade jacket borrowed from Amah.

When I opened the door for Nick, I caught my breath. In a gray suit, light gray shirt, and a necktie patterned in shades of gray, he looked like a million bucks.

"Hi, lady." He pulled me in close for a hug. "You look fantastic."

"So do you."

I was still in his arms, and before I knew it, we were locked in a kiss that left both of us disoriented. Nick recovered first.

"Are you hungry?" The question made us both laugh.

"Not really," I said, "but we'd better go. You made reservations."

WHILE WE FOLLOWED the hostess to our table at the restaurant, every woman in sight seemed to be sneaking glances at Nick. After we ordered, I caught him up on my visit to Harry's condo. I didn't bring up my talk with Rella. With luck, that conversation would remain between the two of us women. I mentioned that Harry had told me about the Architect of the Year nomination and then told him I'd filled Harry in on the latest concerning Quinn's secret passage.

"Quinn said he's had no luck tracking down the contractor who built the false wall and the secret passage to the third floor, but he gave me the name of the man and his business."

"Did you give that to Harry?" Nick asked.

"I did. Harry wasn't optimistic about finding the guy, but he's going to see what he can do."

"He must hear about guys like that through his work. It's the only lead we have so far. I'll pass it on to Buck's cyber sleuths, too."

Our dinners were delicious, but slow in arriving, which left us with little time to linger over a romantic meal. We barely made it to the civic center in time.

THE PARKING LOT was almost full when we pulled in. I didn't know what size of crowd to expect, but it looked as if the Sawyer County Symphony was sold out. I handed our tickets to Nick. "Shall we go in and find Cleo?"

We settled in, with Cleo on my left and Nick on my right. While Nick's attention was focused on his program, Cleo gave me a nudge with her elbow and raised her eyebrows. I got the message: *Nick looks gorgeous.*

I spotted a special note in the program mentioning that the orchestra would be playing a piece composed for piano by ten-year-old Natasha Korba, granddaughter of the symphony's bass clarinetist, Hector Korba.

"Cleo, look." I pointed to the program. Natasha's composition was titled *Peaceful Picnic.* I recalled the scene in Natasha's hospital room back on Wednesday. It had been no picnic and anything but peaceful. Abel Gailworth had refused to let Natasha eat her meatloaf, going to the nurses' station to complain while Melissa held her daughter in her arms, trying to comfort her.

The piece triggered visions of childhood excursions with my family to mountain meadows, gently rippling lakes, and whispering mountain streams. Our picnics always involved hot dogs or fried chicken—special treats Natasha was denied. As *Peaceful Picnic* ended, the audience rose in a standing ovation.

The conductor announced that Hector Korba would take a bow for his composer granddaughter, who was still recuperating in the hospital after an appendectomy. He nodded to Korba, who walked to the front of the stage, executed a regal bow, and thanked the crowd on behalf of Natasha. With moist eyes, he announced that his granddaughter would soon be home from the hospital and would play a solo at the symphony's next performance. That brought another round of applause from the sympathetic audience.

I wondered if Natasha's mother and stepfather were attending to hear their daughter's composition played by the orchestra. There was no sign of them.

After the final number, Cleo invited Nick and me to go backstage with her to give Sig our compliments. We found him in the greenroom putting his tuba in its case, while across the room, Hector Korba was taking his bass clarinet apart, cleaning each of the components and storing them in a case lined in royal-blue velvet.

I noticed Korba loosening the ligature that held the reed in place on his mouthpiece. He removed the used reed and inspected it, frowning before tossing it into a wastebasket. Watching him reminded me of my seventh grade attempt to play the clarinet in my middle school band. No one had mentioned that I would have to blow through it with a damp, slimy reed in my mouth, and that after every performance I would have to clean spittle out of the instrument. I decided back then that if I were to get serious about a musical career, I would choose an instrument that didn't involve saliva.

After arranging to meet Cleo and Sig at a nearby dessert place called The Creamery, Nick and I started toward the backstage exit. I hoped to leave without encountering Hector Korba. Our last conversation at work had been awkward, and I didn't relish the prospect of making strained small talk with him backstage.

Nick and I had almost made it outside when we saw that our getaway was blocked. Korba stood in the doorway, talking to the pianist who had played Natasha's composition. I recognized him as Dr. Leroy Droz, a dermatologist on TMC's medical staff. Droz was inspecting the back of Korba's neck.

"It looks like cellulitis," Droz said. "I'll call something in for you. Call my office in a week for an appointment. We'll see how you're doing."

I heard Droz ask Korba for the name of his pharmacy as Nick and I excused ourselves, made our way past them, and went out the door.

"Sounds like your bigwig board president is kind of a cheapskate," Nick said. "Couldn't he afford an office visit?"

"Of course he could, but if he has some inflammatory process going on, he's right to take the opportunity to ask about it rather than waiting all weekend for an office diagnosis."

"Ah, I hadn't thought of that." Nick took my hand and gave it a gentle squeeze as he walked me to his car in the parking lot. "This was fun. I'm glad I came."

"So am I." My hand tingled when he let it go. "What did you think of Korba? Did you see how he teared up when he took that bow for Natasha?"

"Looked like he was feeling some pretty intense emotions."

"I thought so, too. He's obviously a doting grandfather, and I don't believe his feelings are only about her potential as a money-maker. He genuinely loves that little girl."

When Cleo and Sig arrived at the Creamery, we all ordered cheesecake and coffee and then spent a few minutes rehashing the concert before the conversation turned to Korba and Natasha.

"Sig, tell them what you heard," Cleo said.

Sig frowned. "It was nothing, really, honey. Just Korba's usual bluster."

"I'm not sure. It might be more than that. Go ahead, tell them what you told me."

Looking uncomfortable, Sig put his fork down. "Hector's counting on getting custody after the hearing next week. He made a comment that it's a sure thing now. He has the testimony of her doctor to back him up."

I looked at Cleo. "Sybil Snyder must have led Korba to believe she'll recommend in his favor."

"That's no surprise," Cleo said. "It's no secret that Dr. Snyder thinks Gailworth is a creep."

"Even so," Nick said, "Gailworth is only half of the problem. The judge would need a mighty convincing reason to take the girl away from her mother. I gather the only thing Melissa Gailworth is guilty of is standing by her man."

"What a dilemma," Cleo said. "If Natasha is left in the custody of her mother and stepfather, let's pray the

judge orders mandatory counseling by a nutritionist."
She and I knew that was Gavin Lowe's recommendation, but we both hesitated to bring up the subject of his
flash drive in case the notes on it became part of Natasha's medical record.

"And she should have mandatory medical checkups
at regular intervals," I added. "I keep thinking about
the title of her composition: *Peaceful Picnic*. Maybe I'm
placing too much meaning on it, but I'm worried for that
child. Both Korba and Gailworth seem determined to
exploit her. I'm afraid both those men would demand
more than they should from a child her age, especially
one whose health is as fragile as Natasha's."

"I agree," Sig said. "Practicing, rehearsing, and performing can sap the energy of an adult musician, and
be even more exhausting for a child." He leveled a serious look at Cleo. "Are you going to tell them your
other news?"

"I was waiting for the right moment." Cleo aimed a
rare frown in Sig's direction, a sure sign she was feeling anxious.

Sig patted her hand. "I think now's the time, hon.
They need to know."

"Cleo, what is it? You know I'll hound you until you
spill it." I reached out and pulled her plate of cheesecake
out of her reach. "Make it quick or I'm going to finish
your dessert." I dug into her cheesecake with my fork.

"Okay, stop." Cleo leaned in, lowering her voice.
"Loren Davidson called me this afternoon with a new
development."

"On a Saturday?" It had to be something big for him
to be contacting Cleo on a weekend. And something he
felt he couldn't trust to Sanjay.

"Yes. He had just finished talking to Jared Quinn. It seems the police asked Quinn to volunteer a DNA specimen."

"Wow. That means—"

"They think they have the killer's DNA," Nick said. "Helluva new development. But why would he call Cleo instead of the guy who's filling in for Quinn at the hospital?"

"I think I know the answer," I said. "Sanjay's new, green, and could even be a suspect himself. The home office legal department has a long, comfortable history of working on medical staff legal issues with Cleo."

"She's right," Cleo said. "I suppose Sanjay might be asked to volunteer DNA, too, but he's not the only one." She sent an apprehensive glance my way. "Loren thinks the police will ask Aimee to volunteer a sample."

Considering my part in the altercation between Quinn and Lowe at the Ethics Committee meeting, I wasn't surprised, but I wasn't happy about it, either. I quickly lost interest in the cheesecake.

"Any idea what kind of DNA specimen they have?" I asked.

Cleo looked puzzled. "What do you mean?"

"Is it blood? Skin cells? Saliva? A strand of hair?" My mind raced through several possibilities.

"Oh, that. No. Loren didn't mention it, so I doubt if Quinn was told."

I got to my feet. "I guess it's time to be getting home." Nick stood and laid a steadying hand on my arm.

"Are you okay? You look a little shaky."

"I'll be fine. This news just caught me by surprise."

"Aimee, don't let this spook you. They'll be asking

any number of people for samples. It's actually a good thing. It'll work in your favor."

"Nick's right," Sig said. "Your DNA won't do anything but rule you out."

I thought back to the morning when I held Gavin Lowe in a wristlock in the conference room. Had I somehow mingled my DNA with his? Had he scraped skin cells off my hand with his fingernails while trying to loosen my grip? I didn't think so. He had given up struggling for fear of damaging his wrist.

I turned to Cleo. "You remember, don't you? Lowe had a surgery the afternoon of that Ethics Committee meeting. Quinn told him to get his wrist checked out first, in case I'd injured it. I assumed he did that, but we know he scrubbed in, then claimed his wrist was bothering him. He left the operating room before finishing the case."

"Right," she said. "And he threatened to go to Korba to get you and Quinn fired. But what's that got to do with…" She paused. "Oh, of course. He scrubbed in, so any DNA on his hands and forearms and under his nails would have been scrubbed away preoperatively."

"And he probably would have showered before getting back into his street clothes. The only DNA of mine they might have found would be a strand of my hair clinging to his clothes or possibly caught in his watch."

"I get what you're thinking," Cleo said. "After his surgery, he would have been wearing the same clothes he had on at the morning meeting. I'll see if I can find out what kind of DNA they have."

"I have a question," Nick said. "Did your legal counsel, this Davidson, say who else had been asked to submit a specimen?"

"No. I doubt if he would have been told. He only knows about Quinn because they talked, and he's only speculating about Aimee, but he thinks it's likely because she was questioned about taking Lowe down in the conference room."

"So you don't know if anyone else at Timbergate is going to be asked to volunteer DNA?" Nick asked.

Cleo held up a finger while she swallowed a bite of cheesecake. "I only know about Quinn. But remember, there are probably other persons of interest, not necessarily affiliated with the hospital."

"True," I said. "Rita Lowe comes to mind. I plan on getting in touch with her as soon as possible to ask if she's been contacted about a DNA sample."

"Too bad she didn't know the names of any of her husband's mistresses," Cleo said. "Seems like they should also be on the police department's DNA list."

LATER, BACK IN my apartment, Nick tilted my chin and studied my face. "Is this DNA business going to keep you awake worrying?"

"Probably, at least for a while. I can't help wondering if there's any possible way my hair or skin cells could have transferred to Lowe's clothing the morning I took him down during the meeting."

"It's possible, but think of the odds. It's more likely the DNA specimen the medical examiner found is from the actual killer. And even if they do find something of yours, you have a roomful of witnesses who saw your altercation with Lowe. That alone explains how you might have transferred something to him."

I laid a hand on his arm. "Only if the police believe me when I say I never went near Lowe again after that meeting. Or after he scrubbed in for his surgery that day."

"You're getting way ahead of yourself, but I know you," Nick said. "You'll keep chewing on this."

He pulled me against him and wrapped his arms around me in what was intended to be a reassuring hug. It was, at first, but then it became more. He touched his lips to my forehead, then to my ear, and finally to my lips. Just as my last stitch of willpower dissolved, my tender knees bumped against Nick's legs and I cried out in pain.

Nick stepped back. "What is it?"

"My knees. The hike this morning... They're still so sore."

"Damn, I should have remembered, but holding you felt so good, my autopilot switched on for a moment."

"So did mine, but I don't think I should—"

"I know. I'd better go and let you try to sleep. Don't worry about the DNA. And have someone take a look at your knees. Find out why you're still having so much pain."

"I already did. There's a hairline fracture of my right patella. The orthopedist said it would probably hurt like hell for another two weeks, and to be careful not to bump the knee for a couple of months."

"Oh." Nick thought for a moment. "Does that mean...?"

"We'll have to wait and see how it goes."

After he left I pondered the DNA question while I changed the bandages on my knees. Did I want to refuse and give the appearance of guilt, or volunteer a sample and possibly give tangible evidence of guilt?

Eleven thirty was too late on a Saturday night to call

Rita Lowe, but I made up my mind to call her at the earliest decent hour on Sunday morning. I'd beat around the bush a bit, asking if she had any new thoughts about her husband's murder and whether she might have learned the names of any of her husband's former mistresses. If the police had asked Rita for her DNA, maybe she would mention it.

TWENTY-THREE

Sᴜɴᴅᴀʏ ᴍᴏʀɴɪɴɢ ᴄᴀᴍᴇ too soon. After lying awake until two o'clock, I woke at six to the clatter of rain falling on the metal barn roof over my head. Too early to call Rita Lowe. I started coffee and killed time by listing a few things I could accomplish if I weren't distracted by the Lowe mystery. Laundry, food shopping, and paying bills were the top three, so I stopped there. No heavy cleaning or vacuuming. Doctor's orders.

Before tackling my mundane chores, I booted up my laptop and started an outline to organize my thoughts about Gavin Lowe's death and what had been accomplished so far in sorting out how it had happened and who was responsible.

Right away I realized there were too many suspects. Especially if I added everyone I had doubts about to the people the police seemed most interested in. I felt guilty for leaving Quinn on my list—he might have attacked Lowe in retaliation for being sucker-punched in the conference room—but I moved him to the bottom as least likely to be guilty.

Rita Lowe might have killed her husband to put a stop to his affairs. Or a jealous mistress might have done it, as Mrs. Lowe had suggested. The jealousy angle led me to consider Glen Capshaw, but only if it turned out that his wife, Sybil Snyder, was one of Lowe's sexual conquests. Sanjay D'Costa still seemed like a long shot. I stopped to count suspects. I was already up to five. Abel Gailworth and Melissa, six and seven, seemed to have the strongest motives.

Which suspect had the means to sneak into Quinn's office through the secret passageway? Quinn, of course, with Sanjay a close second. In spite of Varsha's conviction that he didn't know about the passage, he was in and out of Quinn's office more than anyone else except Quinn and Varsha. The Gailworths were outsiders. They wouldn't have known about the layout of the hospital and the secret entrance to Quinn's office. Dr. Glen Capshaw was familiar with the hospital, but I suspected he rarely visited Quinn's office. And Rita Lowe certainly wouldn't have known about the access.

I set my notes aside and turned my attention to breakfast. After I poured a bowl of granola, I realized I was out of milk, so I mixed in some yogurt-covered raisins and told myself it was trail mix. A cup of coffee washed it down just fine, along with my prescribed dose of pain pills. Next I dressed in jeans and a flannel shirt, pulled a rain slicker over my head, and went downstairs to fill the manger with hay for the llamas' breakfast. They were already huddled in the shelter of the barn to keep their wool dry. Rain had topped off the watering troughs, and there was no way I could rake out the catch pen or shovel llama dung. I was finished with Sunday morning chores in record time.

Back upstairs, I considered how to approach Rita Lowe. She had been the one to initiate contact with me about her husband's death. She had given me her phone number and invited me to stay in touch. Since it was still too early to call, I hand-washed some lingerie. Finally, at ten o'clock, I called Rita's number on my cell phone. When she answered right away, I said I hoped it wasn't too early.

"Not at all, Miss Machado, to what do I owe this call?"

"Please call me Aimee, Mrs. Lowe. I thought we might compare notes. See if either of us had any new developments to share."

"Oh, by all means. And you may call me Rita. Do you have something to tell me?"

"Nothing concrete, but I've given a lot of thought to your theory that a jealous mistress might be connected to the case. I'm sorry to bring up a painful subject, but I wondered if there was any possible way we might identify even one of the women Gavin was involved with."

I waited for a long moment, listening while she cleared her throat several times.

"Miss Machado, did you know that Gavin's body has not been released for burial yet?"

"No, I'm so sorry. I *am* being insensitive. I probably shouldn't have called, but you did say to keep in touch."

"Yes, you're right. I did."

"Were you told why the—his—body is being held?"

"They were circumspect, but I was asked to volunteer specimens of my DNA, so I suppose it's a forensics issue."

Good. Just the opening I had hoped for.

"Was there any mention of what the forensics crew might have found?"

"They didn't say, but I volunteered a cheek swab and allowed them to take samples of my hair. Seems silly to me. He's—was—my husband, so finding my DNA on his body or his clothing is to be expected."

"Yes. Of course it is." But depending on what the

medical examiner found, or where it was found, Rita Lowe might still have trouble explaining it. I guided her back to the subject of her husband's other women.

"Mrs. Lowe, it might help if you could think of any woman your husband may have been seeing."

Her heavy sigh signaled reluctance to continue. I gave her a moment, which paid off.

"Someone he worked with," she said. "As I told you, I made an effort *not* to know about his women, but there were signs."

My antennae started tingling. "What kind of signs?"

"The way he behaved around certain female colleagues, one in particular. When he was around her, and I was with him, he was exceedingly attentive toward me, almost absurdly so. In gambling I believe that's what they call a 'tell,' isn't it?"

Was it a tell? A way to cover up an affair? Or just a man concerned for his wife's feelings? "Are you implying that you have a specific woman in mind?"

"I'm afraid so, but you must understand that I could be wrong. I have no proof, and I certainly don't want to falsely accuse anyone of killing Gavin." She sounded sincere, but then again, what else would a respectable woman say?

"I understand, Rita. I would feel the same. It's just that you and I know we're innocent. Maybe the police should know about this other woman."

"It's not the kind of thing I could take to the police. They would only hear the sordid details of an unfaithful husband. They'd either pity me or worse—joke about it behind my back."

I'd almost given up on coaxing a name out of her when she startled me by spitting it out.

"Sybil Snyder," she said. "Gavin used to go all nervous if she was around us when we were together."

Jackpot.

I ended my conversation with Rita Lowe as soon as possible, after assuring her I would keep confidential what she had told me. I wondered if she really meant it, or if she hoped I'd find a way to cast suspicion on Sybil Snyder. Anything was possible, but I was more inclined to take a closer look at Snyder's husband, Glen Capshaw. I did not tell Rita about the conversation between Snyder and an angry and jealous Capshaw that Harry and I had overheard in the stairwell at TMC a week earlier. I wanted to keep that to myself and brainstorm this new wrinkle about Dr. Snyder with Cleo, Harry, and Nick.

The morning was gone and the rain had stopped, so I decided to drive to Timbergate and see what I could find out about Natasha Korba's medical status. I was torn between wishing her a quick, complete recovery and hoping she could be kept hospitalized until after the custody hearing on Wednesday afternoon, just three days away. I would feel a lot better about the little girl's future if before she was discharged, Lowe's killer was caught and Abel and Melissa Gailworth were cleared.

I TOOK THE elevator to Natasha's room in the Pediatric Unit on the second floor. A glance at my watch told me it was one thirty. Lunch would be over, so Abel Gailworth wouldn't be making a fuss about Natasha's food.

I walked toward the little girl's private room until I was close enough to see that her door was closed. Muffled voices from inside, at least one of them male, told me she had visitors. Not good. My looking in on Natasha—a child celebrity in a private room—would seem odd to her family, even inappropriate. I could think of no way to justify my interest in her medical progress. Simple curiosity would not do.

As I stood outside the door to her room considering what to do, the volume of the voices inside escalated until I heard that of a woman—Melissa Gailworth.

"Abel… Hector, can't you see you're upsetting Natasha? If you must argue, please go somewhere else, or I'll ring for the nurse."

Good for her, I thought. Maybe Natasha's mother has a spine after all.

The door burst open and both men stormed out and strode down the corridor, too angry with each other to notice me. I watched Korba stalk toward the elevators, Gailworth following after, saying, "You'll never get her away from us." As the elevator closed on Korba, it cut off part of his answering volley. "I'll see you in hell—"

Gailworth stood glaring at the elevator door, apparently undecided about whether to go back to his wife and stepdaughter or to give himself time to calm down. To avoid being noticed, I turned away and walked toward the nurses' station. I spotted Sybil Snyder coming toward me from the other direction. She wasn't a pediatrician, and it was only at Korba's request that she had taken over Natasha's care. I assumed that the only patient she could be visiting in the Peds Unit was Natasha. I had managed to avoid being seen by Korba or Gailworth, but there was no hiding from Dr. Snyder. She reached the nurses' station just as I did.

"Aimee, what brings you here?" she asked. "Do you have a relative in the unit?"

It surprised me how quickly I came up with a lie. "No, I'm not here to visit a patient. I'm working on a project for the library. I hoped to interview the Pediatric Unit nurses to see if there's a way to provide children's books for our young patients while they're hospitalized." After I said it, I realized it was only a lie if I didn't actually follow up on the idea.

"On a Sunday afternoon?" Snyder asked. "You're certainly dedicated to your job."

I bristled. "But you're here on a Sunday afternoon, too, Dr. Snyder."

"Touché, Aimee. I didn't mean to imply that your job is workaday."

"I'm sure you didn't, Dr. Snyder. No offense taken."

Snyder nodded, then asked the nurse at the desk for Natasha's chart and walked toward the girl's room. I turned to the nurse and began ad-libbing about my project involving reading material for the Peds Unit. Sometimes great ideas are born of desperation.

When that conversation came to a standstill, I asked how Natasha was doing. "I know you can't tell me anything specific, but someone told me Natasha might go home soon."

"Sorry, I can't say." The nurse leaned toward me then, in a confidential posture. "That's up to Dr. Snyder, but between you and me, I don't envy that kid, no matter who she goes home with."

As I was about to leave, Sybil Snyder returned with Natasha's chart. I loitered for a moment, hoping to overhear something she might say about her patient, but her comments were unrevealing.

"Let's keep the same protocol going for now," she said. "I'll dictate my notes right away."

No help there. Except it did tell me that Natasha was

no worse, and that whatever treatment regimen she was on was working.

Rita Lowe's suspicion that Sybil Snyder was one of Gavin Lowe's lovers prompted me to follow Snyder down the corridor to the elevator, as if I just happened to be going her way.

TWENTY-FOUR

SNYDER AND I stepped into the empty elevator. I waited to see if she was headed up or down. She pushed the button for the third floor. I nodded, as if that's where I was headed.

"Business on three?" she asked.

Another lie came too easily. "Since I'm here, I thought I'd remind the nurses about our in-house library service. They're so busy with patient care, they tend to forget that we can deliver reading material to patient rooms."

As the elevator doors opened, Snyder tossed off a perfunctory, "Good luck, then."

She stepped out, heading toward the nurses' station. I looked past her, all the way to the east end of the corridor, remembering what Nick and Harry had said about the alcove with the locked door marked HAZARD: NO ADMITTANCE. That door opened into a passage with the staircase up to Quinn's private bathroom. Curiosity led me in that direction. Since there were public restrooms at the end of the corridor accessed from that same alcove, I wouldn't need to explain why I was headed that way.

As I entered the alcove, I took a good look at the phony hazard door with the warning words and the graphic of a man in a hard-hat and gas mask. No doubt it was seen a hundred times a day by employees or visitors using the restrooms. It was one of those things that's so familiar it eventually disappears from the consciousness. No doubt everyone who worked on that floor assumed whatever was behind that door was someone else's responsibility.

Committed to my course, I entered the women's room and decided I might as well use the facility. I was about to step out of the stall when I heard someone else enter the restroom, obviously talking on a cell phone. The voice was Sybil Snyder's.

"Of course," she said, "I'll be there. Wednesday at ten o'clock." There was a pause, then, "Calm down, for heaven's sake. Remember your blood pressure."

I hesitated, torn with indecision. Wednesday at ten was the time and day of Natasha's custody hearing. Who could Snyder be talking to but Hector Korba?

I didn't want her to think I was eavesdropping on her private conversation, but I dreaded popping out of the bathroom stall and revealing myself. I listened as she continued, "Did you hear the police are requesting DNA samples?"

I wondered how she knew that, unless she had been asked to volunteer a sample herself. "Yes, I've already given mine." *There was my answer.*

Now I was stuck. I'd already heard too much, and I wanted to hear more. I kept quiet and hoped she wouldn't think to check for feet under the stall doors.

"No," Snyder said. "I don't suppose they would feel the need to ask you. The police explained that they only asked me to rule me out because I was present when Gavin Lowe flew off the handle during the Ethics Committee meeting. If you ask me, they should get a sample from Aimee Machado, too." That gave me a chill.

I prayed she would either finish her call and leave or enter a stall and tend to business so I could sneak out.

"Yes. I just looked in on her. Your darling girl is doing well." Another hesitation. "Don't be silly, Hector, of course I'm still—" Snyder paused. "I can't tonight. Glen has us booked for dinner with his parents. I'll try to come up with something for tomorrow night."

Wow, was I hearing what I thought I was hearing? Was Snyder making an adulterous date with Korba? Or was I leaping to the wrong conclusion? I wished to hell I wasn't stuck in a bathroom stall a mere three feet from her.

"I have to go now, but don't worry, I won't be discharging Natasha before Wednesday." Snyder paused, then said, "Tomorrow night, but we should find another place to meet. I'll think of something and get back to you."

Finally finished with planning her rendezvous, Snyder entered a stall toward the far end of the bathroom. I eased my stall door open, careful not to make a sound, and tiptoed toward the exit, feeling guilty for skipping hand washing but more concerned about making a clean getaway.

Outside the restroom, I didn't wait for the elevator. I wanted to be out of sight before Snyder reappeared on the floor, so I headed for the stairwell. I made it down to the second floor, where I hesitated, resting my knee. It occurred to me that Melissa and her daughter might be alone together in Natasha's room. It wouldn't hurt to check. Korba and Gailworth had both appeared to be leaving, and Snyder had completed her hospital visit. This might be my only chance to get some sense of Melissa as a mother and of her relationship with her vulnerable daughter.

My phony story about starting a reading material program for pediatric patients was a perfect excuse for visiting Natasha's room. It was such a good idea, in fact, that I made a mental note to follow up on it and make it happen. I stepped out onto the second floor, which was nearly empty of foot traffic on a Sunday afternoon. Approaching Natasha's room, I slowed and listened for the sound of voices. I heard the television set on low volume, with dialog that sounded like a Disney Channel sitcom. I strolled by the partially open door and observed Natasha watching the screen and Melissa dozing in a chair. No sign of Gailworth or anyone else in the room.

I doubled back and knocked, pushing the door open a bit wider. Melissa's eyes opened. She and Natasha both turned toward the door with startled expressions, making me wonder if they had been expecting someone else. Would Gailworth's return spark that hyper-alert reaction? Or Korba's? I suspected both men. Their animosity toward each other would be enough to set this mother and daughter on edge.

"Hello," I said. "I'm Aimee Machado, the hospital librarian. I'm making a courtesy visit. May I come in?"

Natasha, with brighter eyes and more color in her cheeks, said, "Sure, if it's okay with Mom." She turned her attention back to her TV show.

Rising from her chair, Melissa invited me in and introduced herself and Natasha. I didn't let on that I knew exactly who they were, but got right to my partially true reason for being there.

"I'm hoping to add a collection of books to our library for young patients to read while they're hospitalized. I was hoping you and your daughter might have some suggestions."

Melissa glanced toward her daughter, who gave a little shrug. "I don't get to read very much," Natasha said. "I spend most of my spare time practicing. Abel says—"

"Never mind what he says," Melissa broke in, a flush coloring her face. "This nice woman is asking what sort of books you would read if you *did* have time." I waited while Natasha considered that question. What she came up with threw me.

"Books about cooking," she said, "but with pictures. I like to look at pictures of good things to eat."

Melissa tried to redirect her daughter. "Honey, what about music? Or animals? Those are things you like."

Natasha's eyes glistened. "Sometimes I get tired of music. And Abel says animals are dirty and have germs. He gave away the puppy my grandfather bought for me."

This wasn't going well, and I had heard enough to get a bad feeling about Natasha's dysfunctional little family. I handed Melissa my business card and suggested she contact me if she and Natasha came up with any suggestions for the pediatric collection.

"Thank you for stopping by." She put my card in her purse. "I'll let you know if we can help."

With that depressing experience weighing on my shoulders, I left the main tower and struck out across the hospital campus to the small employee parking lot near the library where I had left my car. Natasha's mention of her grandfather buying her a puppy brought my thoughts back around to Hector Korba. On the drive home I thought back to what I had overheard Sybil Snyder saying to him on the phone while I hid in that stall in the women's room.

I tried to memorize every word so I could repeat them to Cleo, Nick, and Harry. Now we knew that Snyder was seeing someone behind her husband's back, but it wasn't Gavin Lowe. It was Hector Korba. What did this revelation tell us about Lowe's murder?

As soon as I got to my apartment, I made three calls. Cleo and Nick both agreed to meet me at six o'clock at the Four Corners Pizza in Coyote Creek. I left a message for Harry, who I assumed was spending quality time with Rella, since she had to fly back to New York City on Monday morning.

When we had ordered and filled our bowls with salad, we took a table near the back of the pizza parlor. I made short work of relaying what I'd heard from inside Natasha's hospital room, and the angry exchange between Gailworth and Korba as they walked to the elevator. I ended with an almost verbatim recitation of Sybil Snyder's phone call in the women's room.

"So, what do you think?" I asked.

"I think Snyder's going to make sure Korba gets custody on Wednesday," Cleo said. "It may be a sneaky way to get it done, but it might be for the best. That stepfather is a noodlehead."

"I agree," Nick said. "Sounds like a slam-dunk. You should be happy."

I gave the table a little slap. "You're both probably right. If Snyder's in bed with Korba, she's going to make every effort to paint him as the proper guardian for the girl." I thought back to Melissa Gailworth's challenge in Natasha's hospital room to both her husband and her former father-in-law. And I recalled the sad little conversation I'd had with mother and daughter on the topic of reading material. "I can't help thinking the girl and her mother are the innocent victims in this mess. I finally saw a spark of backbone in Melissa in that room. I don't understand why she's been letting Gailworth take the lead where her daughter's concerned."

"I might have an answer for you," Nick said, raising his hand. "Buck's geeks dug up some background on her that you'll find interesting."

"Good, because so far, she's been a ghost figure, first in Korba's shadow, and now in Gailworth's."

"There's a reason for that. It's pretty interesting."

"Hard to imagine, from what I've seen."

"I suspect that's what she wants people to think. The woman has a past she's kept well hidden."

"What kind of past?"

"I'll give you the capsule version." He leaned forward, elbows on the table. "Melissa was raised in a string of foster homes. In the next to last one, she endured months of abuse by one of the boys in the house, and no one came to her rescue."

"What about the foster parents?"

"Apparently they wouldn't act in her defense because the abuser was their biological son. Either they were in denial, or they were protecting him and their license."

"So what happened?"

"Melissa finally took matters into her own hands. She fought the guy off with a baseball bat. Apparently she hit a home run. The bastard went into a coma and died a few days later."

"What happened to Melissa?"

"The foster parents denied their son had attacked Melissa and claimed she was an incorrigible troublemaker who had graduated to murder. She was fifteen at the time. When the case went to court, the ruling was involuntary manslaughter, and the judge ordered the case expunged from Melissa's record."

I pushed my half-finished salad aside. "Hard to imagine Melissa with a past like that. How did you learn all of this?"

"It took some digging, but we were able to track down one of the other girls from that foster home. When we said Melissa might be in trouble, she wanted to help as a way to repay Melissa for protecting her from the same would-be rapist. She agreed to talk on the condition that we keep her identity concealed."

"Does Hector know about Melissa's past?"

"Apparently not. The woman we talked to said the boy's parents are long gone. Left the state, maybe even the country. Melissa never even told Darius Korba, her first husband, so it's pretty certain Hector Korba never knew. Anyway, after that ordeal, Melissa lucked out and spent the rest of her youth living with a decent foster family. She finished high school and spent a couple of years in college in San Francisco, where she met Darius. You could say the rest is history."

"So they married and had a daughter. Happy ending," I said, "until Darius died in Afghanistan."

"Right." Nick nodded toward Cleo and me. "Hector became protector and provider for Melissa and Natasha until Abel Gailworth came along. By then Hector had discovered and nurtured Natasha's musical talent."

Cleo sat up straight, alert to the significance of Nick's information. "It must have torn him up when Gailworth took control away from him. I wonder if Gailworth knows the truth about Melissa's past. If she didn't tell her first husband, do you think she would have told him?"

Nick tilted his head, mulling over that possibility.

"Darius apparently believed in his wife and had no reason to dig into her past. Gailworth's a different breed—a con man and a charmer. He could have coaxed it out of her. We're fairly certain he married Melissa to get custody of Natasha—a little Golden Goose. If he's holding Melissa's past over her head, he has her just where he wants her."

"Oh, no." I felt a sinking sensation. "Poor Melissa! If that's the case, she'll do whatever it takes to keep Gailworth from revealing all. Think of the leverage it would give Hector Korba in a custody hearing."

"Wait," Cleo said. "If the conviction has been expunged, Gailworth would be unable to prove it ever happened."

"Maybe, but just the threat of his going to Korba with it or taking it to the tabloids would be enough to keep Melissa in line."

A young server with rosy cheeks and a ponytail brought our pizza to the table. We each pulled a couple of slices onto our plates.

"I wish we could shed some light on Gailworth's past," I said, "in case Korba's lawyers haven't dug deep enough."

"I hear you," Cleo said, "but someone like Korba would have a dozen lawyers lined up to testify to everything you've uncovered about Gailworth, and more."

Nick glanced at me. "She has a point."

I wasn't going to give up so easily. "Still, we can't be sure of that. Maybe we should find out which judge is going to preside over the hearing. I'm pretty sure that's public record."

"And then what?" Cleo asked.

"I don't know. I'm not that familiar with courtroom

proceedings. Could we ask that judge's clerk if there's a way to submit information pertinent to the custody case?"

"No way." Cleo shook her head. "That's not going to work. The clerk isn't going to pass on third-hand information from an outsider. Judges don't want to hear off-the-record comments about a case."

I shrugged in exasperation. "Then what other options do we have?"

"You both know Korba," Nick said. "Why don't one of you arrange a private meeting with him? Ask how much he knows about Gailworth?"

"That man's as arrogant as it gets," Cleo said. "He won't take it well if he thinks we're meddling in something as sensitive as the custody hearing of his grand-daughter. Aimee? What do you think?"

I shuddered. "I'm not going there. Two weeks ago I told him to ask Sybil Snyder's permission before I'd let him see the Ethics Committee minutes. Knowing what I know now, I'm sure he was livid."

"No kidding." Cleo laughed. "Going to his mistress to say, 'Mother, may I?' isn't his style. Let me see what I can do."

"Good," Nick said. "We want that little girl to end up in the right hands."

"We also want to know why the doctor who saved her life is dead," Cleo said. "We have to find the guy who installed that secret passage in Quinn's office."

"We're working on that. Anything else?" Nick asked.

"Not me." Cleo looked at me. "You?"

"Afraid not. I got so caught up in worrying about Natasha and the custody battle that Lowe's murder took a back seat. It's too late to save him, but we need to do everything we can for Natasha. Lowe would have been devastated if her health was endangered again."

"I understand," Nick said. "Both of you knew the victim, and you want justice for him, so your incentive for finding his killer is different from mine. I don't know Quinn well enough to get involved, but as long as there's any chance Aimee's a person of interest, the two of you are going to keep me updated. Agreed?"

"Of course," Cleo said. "I just wish we knew more about what the police are doing."

"We all do," I said. "Maybe they're way ahead of us."

"I hope so." Cleo opened her purse and put a few bills on the table. "If I manage to meet with Korba without getting my head bitten off, I'll let both of you know."

"I'll get back to Rita Lowe," I said. "I'll assure her that her husband was not involved with Sybil Snyder. Maybe she'll think of someone else who might have wanted Lowe dead." I dug around in my purse and came up with a crumpled one-dollar bill and two dimes. Embarrassing, but both Cleo and Nick understood that I was strapped with grad school debt.

Nick stood, adding a five to the tip. "And I'll get in touch with Harry to see if we can do anything to advance his search for the boomer who installed Quinn's secret passage."

"Tell him time is critical," I said. "That custody hearing is only three days away."

TWENTY-FIVE

MONDAY MORNING PASSED in a blur of mundane paper-work. Lola went about her tasks while I ruminated on Sybil Snyder's phone conversation with Hector Korba. I watched the clock ticking toward noon. As soon as Lola left and the library was empty, I called Rita Lowe. She answered right away and I forged ahead, telling her I was certain that her husband was not Dr. Snyder's lover, since I had every reason to believe Snyder was involved with someone else. I said I'd rather not disclose who it was.

"That's impossible," Rita declared. "I was going to call you about the same thing…only my message to you is the opposite. I have just confirmed that Gavin *was* involved with Sybil Snyder."

I took a baffled moment to digest what she said. "I don't understand. How did you come to that conclusion?"

"One of my well-meaning friends decided to tell me about seeing Gavin and Snyder in a compromising embrace a month ago at a hotel in Sacramento. They were both there for a medical conference. Apparently Snyder's husband had stayed home to cover their office practice. My informant was torn at the time about whether to tell me, but yesterday she decided that since Gavin is dead, I'd want to know he was a 'louse and good riddance,' is how she put it."

I heard the pain in her voice and remembered that

she had loved the man in spite of his weakness for other women. *Save us from well-meaning friends*, I thought.

"Rita, are you sure your friend was right? Is there any doubt in your mind?"

She breathed a weary sigh. "I'm afraid not, but what I don't understand is why you thought Snyder was seeing someone other than Gavin. Can't you tell me who it is?"

"I'd rather not. Now I'm wondering if maybe I'm wrong. Let me think about it."

"As you wish," Rita said.

We ended the call agreeing to keep in touch. After hearing about Rita Lowe's husband and Dr. Snyder, my doubts grew. I ran Snyder's phone call with Korba over in my mind, searching my memory for a chance that I had misinterpreted its meaning. Was it possible she had been arranging to meet with Korba for some legitimate reason, nothing to do with an affair? Maybe they simply wanted to discuss the custody hearing.

I made a run to the cafeteria to pick up a sandwich and then swung by Cleo's office to ask whether she had contacted Hector Korba. I also wanted to relate what Rita Lowe had told me. I heard a voice from inside her closed office door and instantly recognized it as Korba's.

"I appreciate your concern," he said, "but remember, the road to hell is paved with good intentions." Before I could move away, Korba came out, nearly plowing into me.

"Miss Machado, you've escaped the library." Korba loomed above me, his solid build and massive head so intimidating, I couldn't imagine him in a lover's embrace with Snyder or any other woman. Nor could I imagine him in the role of doting grandfather to a fragile little girl.

"Excuse me." I held up my sandwich. "I was just meeting Cleo to have a bite of lunch."

"Then I'll leave you to it." Korba strode away and I dashed into Cleo's office, closing the door behind me.

"Sounds like that didn't go over too well," I said. "What happened?"

"Oh, man!" She held her arms out to her sides. "I'll never get the sweat stains out of this dress."

"That bad, huh? Give me the details."

"I approached it by telling him that some facts about Gailworth had come to my attention from a source I couldn't name, and that I thought it was important to pass them on."

"How did he react?"

She rocked her hand in a *so-so* gesture. "With mixed results. He seemed to appreciate hearing what we'd unearthed about the women Gailworth had bilked, but at the same time, he was peeved that we were taking an interest in his custody hearing. As if it was none of our business, which in his mind it isn't."

"So he hadn't already found out what we knew about Gailworth?"

"I don't think so. He made some notes, asked a few questions, but then he pretty much warned me to stay out of it and to tell my source to do the same."

"Do you still think he's the best choice for custody of Natasha?"

"So far, I do," Cleo said. "We know her stepfather is a fraud and her mother is a wimp. And there's that phony church with the half-assed vegan diet thing that almost killed the child."

I raked my fingers through my hair. "You're right. I

guess we're still in Korba's corner on this. I just wish I knew more about his relationship with Sybil Snyder."

"Why? He's a grown man. As long as he keeps his love life from affecting Natasha, it probably won't stop him from getting custody. And you're not even positive he and Snyder are an item, are you?" She waggled her pen at me. "That phone call you overheard could have been completely innocent."

"I have to admit it's possible. I'm not as sure as I was, especially since I just talked to Rita Lowe." I filled Cleo in on the news that Sybil Snyder had been observed sharing an amorous moment with Gavin Lowe as recently as a month ago.

"You're kidding." Cleo dropped her pen and pushed back in her chair. "Well, that trumps your suspicion about Korba, doesn't it?"

"It looks that way. My concern now is that Rita's so-called friend could have been wrong about what she observed at that conference in Sacramento, just as I could be wrong about what I heard Snyder saying to Korba on the phone."

"Good point. Otherwise, Snyder has tangled her personal life in a messy knot with her professional life. I would expect her to be smarter than that." Cleo picked up her pen and started doodling on a scratch pad. A habit I'd noticed that seemed to help her concentrate. "Besides, where would she find the time for an affair with either man, much less both of them? And how would she manage to keep those affairs a secret with a jealous husband like Glen Capshaw?"

"Don't ask me. I can't imagine it." She'd left me more confused than ever. "But I'm glad you brought up Capshaw. Now that we're aware someone is spreading rumors that his wife was sneaking around with Lowe, I'd like to know more about him."

"Like, is he capable of murder?" Cleo asked.

"Right. The day Harry and I heard him accusing his wife of cheating, he sounded pretty vindictive."

"I can't give you much help there. Capshaw is a member of the TMC medical staff, but he rarely admits patients here. He seems to limit himself almost exclusively to seeing patients in the office practice he shares with Snyder."

"What about Snyder's hospitalized patients? Doesn't Capshaw see them if Snyder isn't available?"

"Not very often. They have other physicians in their group who cover for Snyder." Putting her pen down again, Cleo steepled her polished red fingertips. "I don't see how any of this relates to Gavin Lowe's murder."

"Unless the DNA the police have turns out to match Capshaw's. Think about this. Someone claiming she saw Snyder and Lowe in a compromising situation reported it to Lowe's wife. Who's to say that same person didn't also report it to Snyder's husband? We know he's jealous and suspicious. I think we have to find out more about him. Like exactly where he was the night Lowe was shot."

Cleo threw up her hands. "How are we supposed to do that?"

I rose to my feet. "You're the one with the inside track to members of the medical staff. Let me know if you come up with any ideas."

As I headed for the door, Cleo stopped me. "Wait, I almost forgot to tell you. The symphony is scheduling an encore concert. This one's a fundraiser for the TMC Foundation and all proceeds will be used for upgrades to the Pediatric Unit. They came up with the idea because of Natasha's hospitalization."

"What a great idea." I thought about my plans for a children's collection for the library. "When is it?"

"This coming Saturday."

"I wonder if Natasha will be released in time to attend."

"Me, too," Cleo said. "Remember what Hector announced last weekend?"

"You mean about her performing a solo? You think he'd want her to do it that soon?"

"I wasn't about to ask him."

"Do you think she'd have the strength for that?"

"From what I hear, she's almost good as new. I think the only reason she's still in-house is that Korba and Snyder are delaying her discharge until after the custody hearing on Wednesday."

"From what Snyder said to him yesterday, I'm sure you're right. If Korba wins custody, it would be less traumatic if he took her home directly from the hospital than it would be to take her away from her parents' home."

I promised Cleo I would buy at least one ticket to the symphony's fundraiser. Two tickets, if I could convince Nick or Amah to come along.

Back in the library, I passed the rest of the day quickly. The forensic collection and the consortium were coming together nicely. Now that requests for forensic resources were increasing, I rarely had the kind of slow days I had experienced when I was first hired.

By quitting time I began to wonder how soon I might hear from Nick or Harry. Harry would be busy at the mall construction site, so Nick was the only one of us who had time on his hands for sleuthing. Thanks to

Buck Sawyer's billions and his personal vendetta against drug traffickers, Nick had access to some very talented geeks. If Buck's team of cyber spies could hack into chatter about illicit drug deals, they shouldn't have too much trouble picking up the trail of a shady contractor in the business of installing safe rooms and secret passageways. Those extras sounded like exactly what every drug kingpin needed.

My phone rang just as I was taking a last stroll through the empty library, turning off computers and checking for books or journals my patrons might have left lying around. I hurried to my desk and caught the call on the fourth ring. As soon as Detective Kass identified himself, I knew why he was calling and what he wanted. *My DNA*.

"I wondered if you might like to volunteer a sample," he said. "It'll only take a minute. We're asking a number of folks, so don't feel you're being singled out."

"I understand," I said. "Where do I go to do this?"

"I'm calling from the road now, and I'm not far from your workplace. Would you like to meet me somewhere private?"

"You mean right now?" I had been warned by Cleo that this might happen, and I had made up my mind to volunteer my DNA if I was asked, but I thought I'd have more notice.

"That would be great, if it's convenient," Kass said. He sounded so polite and friendly, he might have been inviting me for coffee instead of asking me to rule myself out as a murder suspect. I glanced around the empty library.

"Can we do it here, in the library? I'm just closing, but I could wait for you."

"I'll be there right away."

His call reminded me of my stolen purse and my fractured knee. After several days, I'd heard nothing from the sheriff's office. My mugging was under county jurisdiction, so I decided not to mix apples and oranges by mentioning it to Kass.

He arrived in less than five minutes, reassuring me that since he drove an unmarked car and wore street clothes instead of a uniform, no one would realize I was being visited by an investigator. As promised, the cheek swab took less than a minute. He thanked me for volunteering the sample and went on his way. The experience left me with an eerie feeling, as if I'd just surrendered the most essential component of my personal privacy.

I worried about the DNA sample as I closed the library. Heading to my car, I punched in Nick's number on my phone, forcing my thoughts back to the problem of finding the worker who did the job in Quinn's office. All we needed to know was whether the guy had given away Quinn's secret, accidentally or otherwise.

"Hey, lady. What's up?" Funny about voices. Some are annoying, some are just voices, and some are nice to hear. Nick had one of the nice ones. No matter what he was saying, I enjoyed the sound; I wondered if he felt the same when he heard my voice.

"I'm just leaving work. Have you talked to Harry today?"

"Saw him at lunchtime. We have some news, but we didn't think it was urgent enough to bother you and Cleo at work."

"I have news, too. Where are you?"

"Headed for the dojo. Do you want to meet us there?"

"I'm on my way." I turned on my wipers to clear away a light mist.

TWENTY-SIX

NICK AND HARRY were already on the mat when I arrived at the dojo at five fifteen. Last Monday had been the peewee class, but on alternate Mondays, Harry taught a special self-defense system called Arnis, which originated in the Philippines and involved stick fighting.

We had forty-five minutes before Harry's six o'clock students arrived.

"Nick told me about your knee," Harry said, filling a paper cup from the water cooler. "Hope they catch that sucker." He drained the cup and tossed it in the wastebasket.

"Thanks." I didn't want to blurt out the news about my visit from Detective Kass right away. I watched while the guys engaged in a few more minutes of randori.

They soon bowed off, giving us a chance to compare notes on what I'd begun to think of as "the case of the secret passageway." If we could discover who knew about it other than Quinn, we'd have a pretty good idea who had killed Gavin Lowe. The only flaw in that thinking was the possibility that Quinn had committed the crime himself.

The three of us gathered in a corner space that had been set aside as the sensei's office. Harry gestured me toward the most comfortable chair, out of consideration for my injured knee.

"Aimee, did you invite Cleo to this party?" he asked.

"No, she's not a martial arts kind of gal. She wouldn't appreciate the locker room smell in here. Besides, she has a life and a husband to go home to. I'll fill you in on what she told me and call her later tonight with anything she should hear."

"Good enough." Nick rolled his shoulders and flexed his neck, still in post-workout mode. "Why don't you go first?"

I started with Detective Kass and the DNA sample.

"You knew that was coming," Harry said. "Are you okay with it?"

"I'd be more okay if I knew what kind of DNA evidence they have."

Nick reached out and touched my arm. "You didn't shoot the doctor. No matter what they have, it'll be all right."

I heaved a sigh. "I hope so. It felt pretty weird at first, but I'm getting over it."

I went on, giving the pertinent facts about my meeting with Cleo and hers with Korba. Then I relayed what I'd learned from Rita Lowe, the important bit of news being that Mrs. Lowe had been told her late husband was having an affair with Sybil Snyder. "It's my feeling that Snyder's husband, Glen Capshaw, seems capable of exacting revenge if he knew about it."

"Hold it." Harry straightened up from a forward bend, finally ready to sit down. "According to my last update from Nick, you thought Snyder and Korba were an item. What happened to that theory?"

"As Cleo so aptly put it, a sighting of Snyder and Lowe together trumps my eavesdropping of Snyder on the phone with Korba. We decided that without proof,

Snyder deserves the benefit of the doubt where both men are concerned."

Harry's mouth formed a skeptical twist. "Where there's smoke, there's fire."

"Not necessarily," Nick said, giving me a pointed look. "Take my word for it. It's possible to be completely innocent and look guilty as hell."

Harry realized immediately that Nick was referring to Rella and the infamous *Paris incident*. "Oh, hell, man, you're right. I'm an idiot. Go on, Aimee."

I continued, "No one at work is even hinting at when Natasha might be discharged. I'm guessing Snyder and Korba will stall to keep her hospitalized until after the custody hearing on Wednesday."

"How do they do that?" Nick asked, exchanging a look of disgust with Harry. "Wouldn't someone notice that the kid is well enough to go home?"

"Her nurses might, but it doesn't work that way. As long as Snyder is the primary physician, she gets to say when Natasha is ready to go home. If Quinn were on the job, he might be paying close attention to Natasha's case, but since he's out on suspension, it would be up to Sanjay D'Costa to question Snyder's decision."

Nick raised his eyebrows. "And from what you've told us about him, he may not have enough backbone to challenge her."

"You're probably right, but to be fair, he would probably only intervene if it was a question of utilization of hospital resources. If Natasha's bed was desperately needed for another pediatric patient, Sanjay might ask Snyder to justify why she hasn't discharged Natasha. Apparently that hasn't become an issue."

Harry raised a hand. "So we're still thinking of the

custody issue as a motive? Abel Gailworth killed Lowe to keep him from testifying in favor of Korba?"

I decided to tell them about Lowe's informal note, leaning toward the opposite recommendation. "It doesn't square with Gailworth's primary motive at this point."

"You're referring to his potential loss of custody," Nick said.

"That's right." I struggled to make sure I was being clear. "But keep in mind we're not sure whether Gailworth knew what Lowe intended to recommend."

"Consider this," Harry said. "Even if Gailworth *did* know that Lowe recommended he and Melissa keep custody of the girl, the terms Lowe laid out would have pissed him off. Gailworth would have resented the hell out of having Natasha's diet scrutinized on a regular basis."

"So Gailworth is still a possibility," Nick cut in. "But here's another… What if custody of the little girl had nothing to do with the murder? What if Snyder's husband killed Lowe in a fit of jealous rage?"

I stood to work out the stiffness in my knee. "Okay, boys, you see the problem. We have at least two suspects with strong motives. We need to know how either Capshaw or Gailworth could have ended up in Quinn's office with Gavin Lowe. That's where you come in, Harry. What have you found out about the contractor who created the secret passage?"

"As it turns out, we have a lead," Harry said. "Thanks to Rella."

"You told Rella about that passage and what we're doing?" I looked at Nick, concerned. "Did you know about this?"

"Let Harry finish. You'll want to hear it."

"Here's the thing," Harry said. "I was doing an on-line search the other night for companies that build safe rooms and secret passageways. Rella peered over my shoulder and got interested. She told me that when she was in the military, she dated a guy who did that kind of confidential work in particularly sensitive government buildings. You've heard about the White House safe room?"

"Of course. Go on."

"It turns out some of the guys she knew in that specialty who have left the military are doing similar work now for civilians."

"And you think there's a chance the contractor who did Quinn's job might be one of them? That Rella might come up with a lead to help us find Quinn's contractor?"

"It's possible," Harry said with a shrug. "Rella knows about a couple of guys based on the East Coast who went off the radar. They're strictly word-of-mouth. No advertising. When I asked her if she knew how to contact them, she got curious."

"What did you tell her?"

"I said I couldn't explain unless I cleared it with you."

"How much do we have to tell her?"

"She needs to know about the passageway we found at TMC. Without that, she won't be able to identify the guy we're looking for."

"And you both trust her to keep it to herself?"

"She's ex-military, Aimee," Nick said. "She understands *need to know*. We have to give this a chance."

"Okay. If she's willing, let her do some checking, but let's not include her any more than necessary. I have my job to think about. I've already put it in jeopardy by involving the two of you."

Harry picked up his phone, walked a few feet away from us, and started texting.

I threw Nick a glance. "He's contacting her now?"

"She's only back east until she flies Buck home on Friday."

"That's not much time."

"True. But at least there's a chance she'll pick up a lead. Safe rooms and secret passageways are specialized work, limited to a small population. The guys willing to fudge on permits are an even more exclusive club, known only to each other."

Harry came back, smiling. "She said she'll hop a train down to D.C. while Buck's tied up in New York. She told him she wants to catch up with some of her military chums, which is true, but with any luck, she might turn up something for us while she's there."

"And she doesn't mind not having all the details?"

"Not at all. She said looking into this mystery beats hanging around in the city reading or going to movies and plays."

That described an ideal week for me, but Harry and Nick exchanged knowing glances, as if the idea of Rella taking in a Broadway show was ludicrous. If so, she definitely had that in common with Harry. I couldn't understand how someone as kindhearted as my brother could enjoy watching boxing matches and even cage fights, but he claimed he learned techniques from them that he could pass on to help keep his jujitsu students safe. If Rella enjoyed those events with Harry, maybe he had found his ideal woman after all.

"Okay, guys, I'm convinced, but there's something I don't understand. Harry could have done that job of Quinn's without a lot of special training and expertise.

So could a lot of other contractors right here in our area, and some of them are pretty hungry. Why did Quinn need to dig up this mysterious outsider?"

"Because he wanted secrecy and quality work," Harry said, "but he also needed someone willing to leave the secret passageway off the plans and the permit. The legit contractors around here make a living by doing honest work without bending the rules. I sure as hell wouldn't have put my license at risk. All the state inspector had to do was ask to see the empty elevator shaft under Quinn's bathroom and he would have realized that stairway wasn't in the blueprints when the permit was issued."

"And your pal Quinn was shrewd enough to figure out how to put the word out. He found the guy he needed."

I didn't like the implication that Quinn was shrewd. It implied cunning and sounded like the trait of a sociopath. *A man capable of murder.*

"One last question," I said. "When are we going to let Quinn in on this hunt of Rella's?"

Nick and Harry both hesitated, glancing at each other. Harry answered. "Let's wait and see what she comes up with."

"I get it," I said. "You both think there's a chance Quinn is guilty, don't you?"

This time Nick responded. "We don't know him as well as you and Cleo do. You have to give us some latitude to play devil's advocate."

I spotted some of Harry's students pulling into the parking lot. "It's almost six, so I guess we've finished our debriefing. I'll fill Cleo in on Rella's mission. I just wish we could know something sooner than Friday. One way or another, Natasha's custody is to be decided on

Wednesday morning. I'm afraid she'll be leaving the hospital the same afternoon."

Harry switched into sensei mode, greeting his students as Nick and I went into separate changing rooms. The Arnis class was starting when we emerged. We waved goodnight to Harry and walked out to our cars together. The sun had set while we were inside, chilling the evening air.

"Do you have anything planned for later tonight?" Nick asked, reaching for my hand.

Sensing an invitation, I regretted my reply. "I promised I'd get home in time to go with Amah to the nursing home where she volunteers. She's been asking me to read to some of the patients. Why?"

"I thought I might take you to dinner. How about tomorrow night?"

"That would be nice," I said, surprised, since we'd just gone to dinner and the symphony two nights before. "Is there someplace new you want to try?"

"No special place." When we reached my car, Nick released my hand and took me by the shoulders to face him. "We went out Saturday night to observe the little piano prodigy's grandfather. I'm talking about a date that doesn't involve a mystery." He pulled me toward him, and added in a low, husky voice, "More like a belated Valentine's Day celebration, since we didn't get to spend last Friday together."

I was relieved. So Valentine's Day wasn't off-limits after all. "I like the sound of that," I said. "And while we're on the subject of dates, Cleo just told me about an encore performance of the symphony concert we saw last weekend. It's on Saturday, a fundraiser for the TMC Pediatric Unit, and I promised to go."

"Ah, sorry." Nick put a hand over his heart. "I'm afraid I won't be available. I'm flying this coming weekend."

"I thought you were taking the month off. Isn't Rella still taking the extra shifts?"

"Not this weekend. She and Harry are going skiing at Mt. Bachelor and I'm flying Buck to Portland for the weekend to meet with some investors. Buck agreed we could drop Harry and Rella off at the airport in Redmond on our way."

I didn't let my disappointment show. "No problem. I'll check with Amah." I kept my voice light. "If she doesn't want to go, I'll go alone and hang out with Cleo. She and I are wondering if Natasha might do a solo."

"Is there a chance of that?"

"Maybe." I rubbed my hands together, to warm them. "This is only Monday, so the concert is still five days away. It would depend on when Snyder discharges her and whether she thinks Natasha is well enough to perform. No matter how custody is decided, Natasha still has a promising musical career ahead of her. The sooner the Gailworths and Korba come to terms, the better for everyone."

The night had grown colder as we stood outside, and Nick saw me shiver. "You're cold. I need to let you go home. So we're on for dinner tomorrow night?"

"We are," I said.

"Good. I'll pick you up at seven." He gave me a soft farewell kiss, which lingered just enough to make me want more.

At home I called Cleo. She didn't answer, so I left a message asking if we could get together in the morning.

Cleo stopped by the library at eight o'clock Tuesday morning after her breakfast meeting. I filled her in on what I'd learned from the guys.

"Rella, huh?" Cleo gave me a pointed look. "Are you okay with her being involved?"

"I wasn't at first, but if there's a chance she can dig up the name of the guy who did Quinn's remodel job, more power to her."

"Hmm." Cleo pulled down her half-moons and squinted at me. "Do I sense a change in attitude where the blond bomber is concerned?"

"I'm working on it." I was surprised how good it felt to say that.

"Glad to hear it." She patted the palm of her hand as if applauding my efforts.

The library's overhead pager suddenly came on with an urgent announcement. I recognized Varsha Singh's voice.

"*Cleo Cominoli, please report to Administration immediately. Report immediately to Administration.*"

Cleo's eyes widened. "What the heck? This is a first. Sanjay must have screwed up royally if Varsha's panicking."

"Use my phone." I punched in the direct line to Varsha and handed Cleo the receiver.

"Varsha?" she said. "What's going on?" Cleo listened for what seemed much too long, nodding, shaking her head, nodding again. "How long ago?" She glanced at her watch. "Damn, damn! Okay, I'm in the library with Aimee. I'll be right over." She handed me the receiver. "Cripes, you won't believe this!"

"You look like you've been hit with a brick. What's going on?"

"Natasha's gone. Her parents checked her out of the Peds Unit against medical advice at six o'clock this morning."

"They took her home? That's their right, isn't it? She's still in their custody."

"They didn't take her home," Cleo moaned, rubbing her temples. "They've left town and no one knows where they've gone."

"How? I mean, who says they've left town? Who would know that?"

"Their neighbor across the street is a baker who gets up before dawn. He looked out at five thirty and saw Gailworth loading several suitcases into his SUV. The neighbor's daughter and Natasha are friends, so he walked across the street and offered to take in mail and watch the house for the Gailworths while they were gone. He casually asked if they were going somewhere warm and sunny. Gailworth acted put out and told the guy to mind his own business, so the neighbor went back into his house, but he watched out his window until they pulled away. He thought it was odd that Abel and Melissa packed pillows and blankets into the car."

I was still in denial. "But that's not proof that the Gailworths are on the run with Natasha. They still have until tomorrow at ten to show up for the custody hearing. Maybe they have a legitimate reason to be gone overnight."

Cleo hovered at the door, nerves thrumming and poised to go. She spoke more rapidly than usual. "Maybe, but Korba and Snyder are in Sanjay's office right now, raising the roof. Snyder came in early to check on Natasha, and when she heard the girl was gone, she called Korba. He went directly to the Gailworths' house and no one was there. That's when he got the neighbor's story." Cleo picked up her briefcase. "I need to get over to Admin and get a conference call set up with Loren Davidson at home office."

"Why? If the Gailworths signed Natasha out AMA and they have legal custody, what can home office legal do?"

"They can reinstate Jared Quinn as administrator, even if it's just long enough to do damage control," Cleo said, halfway out the door. "Korba is pulling rank, forcing Sanjay to take a back seat on this. Going as far as calling it a temporary suspension. When the Gailworths started packing up Natasha's things in her hospital room, the nurse in charge was uneasy. Gailworth refused to wait for Snyder's signature on the AMA form, and he refused to wait until someone could come with a wheelchair to deliver Natasha to the parking lot."

"So what happened?" I asked.

"The stepfather scooped the girl up in his arms and headed to the exit, with Melissa Gailworth bringing up the rear. The nurse called Sanjay, who approved the child's release, pretty much after the fact. He now regrets that decision, of course, since Snyder and Korba are both ready to trounce him."

"Why is Varsha getting you involved? Can't she handle the conference call?"

"It's a chain of command thing. If Quinn and Sanjay are both unavailable, the chief financial officer is supposed to take charge, but he's out sick with the flu. I've been asked to step in, but only until we can arrange for Quinn to take the reins." She glanced at her watch. "I've got to go. They're waiting for me." She headed out the door at a brisk pace.

Cleo running TMC? Who would have thought it? Even if it was temporary and sort of a fluke, I was impressed. She had morphed into a willing and able leader right before my eyes. Moments after she left, my Tuesday volunteer came through the door.

"Morning to ya, Miss Machado." Bernie Kluckert stood at attention in front of my desk, waiting for orders. Still reeling from the news about the Gailworths and Natasha, I had trouble focusing my attention.

"Good morning, Bernie. I haven't had a chance to line out any chores for you. Would you like to start with watering plants?"

"Sure enough. My favorite job. And I have a surprise for you, but I left it outside." He held up a crooked index finger. "Wait just a moment. I'll be right back." He hurried toward the exit, his swaying antalgic gait a sure sign of discomfort in timeworn and arthritic joints. A moment later he came back, beaming and holding a potted plant in both hands.

"You brought a new plant?" I tried to sound pleased but hoped he wouldn't be encouraged to bring more.

"Not just any plant," he said. "An orchid from my own greenhouse. It's for Lola. A winter bloomer."

For Lola. I hoped to heaven she would appreciate it. Bernie's infatuation with her was sweet, but I worried that he'd end up disappointed if she didn't return his feelings. As I watched him arrange the orchid on the desk they shared, I knew it wasn't the day to hand out advice to the lovelorn. I had a more pressing concern.

Where was Natasha Korba? Had her mother and stepfather really fled with no intention of showing up in court on Wednesday morning? While Bernie went about applying his green thumb to our potted vegetation, I texted Nick and Harry about the situation with Natasha, asking them to check in with me ASAP. I was at a loss as to what to do about the Gailworths.

TWENTY-SEVEN

CLEO EMAILED AN update half an hour later. Loren Davidson had convinced home office to put Quinn back on the job, lifting his temporary suspension. *Temporarily.* Any sign that the police were ready to arrest him and charge him with Lowe's murder would put Cleo back in charge. Sanjay had been asked to take a leave of undetermined duration. I couldn't help but feel sorry for him. In his first job, fresh out of school, he'd already dealt with a murder in the administrative suite and the suspected abduction of a celebrity child prodigy.

Even worse, word had leaked out about what the media were calling Natasha's "disappearance." Local newspaper and television reporters had taken up positions outside all of the entrances, shouting questions at employees who entered or left the building and blinding them with the flash of cameras. As usual, our security personnel were pretty much impotent against the media, unless they felt justified using Tasers. That wasn't likely.

Nick and Harry both responded to my texts. Harry was up to his armpits in alligators at his mall job site. Rella was en route to D.C. He'd let me know if her contacts there came up with any leads as to Quinn's unknown construction worker. Nick was hanging out with Buck Sawyer's cyber geeks. Still on the same quest, they'd had no luck so far. I texted both guys back, saying I'd keep them posted on the Gailworth situation.

With no further word from Cleo, I turned to my latest library project. I wanted to make good on my spur-of-the-moment idea to read materials for the Pediatric Unit. The New York Public Library's site listed 100 Great Children's Books. More than enough titles to choose from.

Working on the list helped keep my mind off worst-case scenarios involving the Gailworths and Natasha. I kept at it until I looked up and saw Bernie standing at my desk.

"Miss, might I have a word?" I didn't like the look of him. From his somber expression, he appeared troubled. I hedged, hoping he wouldn't try to pull me into another conversation about Lola.

"Only if it's something brief. I'm afraid I'm awfully busy right now."

"I'll try to be quick." He squirmed and stared at the toes of his boots, then sent me a look so imploring I couldn't ignore it.

"Is it something urgent, Bernie?"

"That's the question, Miss Aimee. I don't know, but it might be. That's why I talked it over with Lola." He glanced at the orchid on their shared desk. "We're getting along, you see."

It *was* about Lola. I should have known. "That's nice, but I really don't have any relationship advice for you."

"No, no, that's not it. I'm doing fine in that department, now that Lola knows Oslo Swanson is a womanizer. In my day we used to call a fellow like him a two-timing louse."

"Then I don't understand. What did you want to ask me? And what does it have to do with Lola?"

"Something happened in here the day you left me

alone. I mentioned it to Lola, and she said the same thing had happened to her. We thought you might ought to know."

He had my attention.

"Do you remember what day that was?"

"I do. It was Tuesday a week ago. My first day on the job, don't you know."

I remembered. "Go on."

"Well, a couple of things came up that day. I talked them over with Lola, and she advised me that you might want to be informed."

"What happened, Bernie? Something you forgot to mention?" My sense of urgency about Natasha Korba made it difficult to hold my patience.

"Didn't forget. Just didn't know it was important until Lola clued me in. Her being your right-hand man and all, she knows what's what, don't you see?" Right hand *woman*, I mentally corrected.

"Yes, she's very sharp," I agreed. "What was it that she thought you should tell me?"

Bernie's focus seemed to drift for a moment. "She put me on to a new kind of denture adhesive, don't you know. Stopped that infernal clicking."

Cripes, was all this buildup really about Bernie's dentures? My patience was wearing thinner than a strip of off-market dental floss.

"Good for you." Though the clicking got old fast, his slippery dentures were not first and foremost on my mind. "Is that what Lola wanted you to tell me?"

His eyes widened. "Oh, no. Sorry. Lola said I should tell you about the man who came into the library while you were gone last Tuesday morning."

"Why? Was there a problem with the patron?"

"That's the sixty-four-dollar question." *Sixty-four?*

"Do you mean sixty-four thousand?"

"No, that copy-cat TV show came later. I mean sixty-four, from the radio show my folks listened to back in the forties. It was the most important question, don't you know."

I had to put a stop to his asides and get to the point, or this would take forever.

"Bernie, what *is* the sixty-four-dollar question?"

"Here it is. That morning a man stopped in and walked to your desk. I was dusting back in the stacks, but I heard him, so I looked through a space between some of the books and saw him opening your desk drawers. Well, I was new, it being my first day, but I wasn't liking the look of someone snooping in your desk, so I showed myself and asked what his business was."

"Did he identify himself?"

"Not by name. He said he was a regular in the library. Said he was looking for a pen and paper to leave you a note. Sounded kinda suspicious to me, so I told him I'd take a message. He told me to never mind, he'd just make contact with you later. Said he wanted you to look something up for him and it was kinda complicated. He spouted some medical jargon, and I had to admit he was right about the complicated part."

"And then he left?"

"Yep. I didn't think any more about it 'til Lola and I got to talking about our duties here in the library, trading war stories, so to speak. When I told her that one, she sat up and took notice, so here's my sixty-four-dollar question: did I do wrong by not reporting that fella to you right away?"

"Of course not, but I'm glad you decided to let me know. Do you remember what the man looked like?"

"In his fifties, I'd say. Average looking, except for the red hair and moustache."

Glen Capshaw.

I hoped I sounded calm and professional. "Thank you, Bernie. I believe I know who he was. I'll follow up with him and take care of the matter."

Looking relieved, Bernie went back to tending the library's potted plant collection.

A tingling sensation thrilled through me. I knew why Lola had advised Bernie to tell me his story. It sounded a lot like what had happened to her, except she hadn't been able to get a good enough visual to identify her intruder. Searching my memory, I realized Lowe's murder had happened two weeks ago, sometime late Monday night. On Friday of that same week, Lola's intruder had come into the library. Bernie was saying that another intruder, or possibly the same one, had shown up in the library a week ago, on the Tuesday following Lola's incident. The only doctor I knew with red hair and a moustache was Glen Capshaw. What had he wanted from my desk?

MY CURIOUS CONVERSATION with Bernie took a backseat to the news about Abel Gailworth taking Natasha from her hospital room. A glance at the time on my computer screen surprised me. I could swear I'd been at work for hours, yet it was only ten o'clock. An hour had passed since Cleo had been called to the administrative suite.

I was itching to hear an update on Natasha's where-abouts. Knowing Hector Korba, there would be hell to pay if anything happened to his granddaughter. He would start by suing Timbergate Medical Center out of existence.

It was impossible to get back to work on my list of potential acquisitions for the Pediatric Unit. Instead, I placed a call to Rita Lowe to see if she could give me a sense of the kind of man Glen Capshaw was. I asked her what she knew about Sybil Snyder's husband. She sounded glad to hear from me, saying she was getting almost no input from the police into the investigation of her husband's death.

"Capshaw is jealous and possessive, if you believe the gossips," Rita said. "I suppose it doesn't help that Sybil Snyder chose not to take his name when they married. I only met him a few times on social occasions, and our longest conversations were no more than an exchange of perfunctory greetings."

"What about the woman who told you she had seen Sybil Snyder with your husband? Is there any chance she might have done the same favor for Dr. Capshaw?"

"It wouldn't surprise me," Rita said.

"But she didn't imply she'd told Capshaw, or come right out and say so?"

"No, sorry, and I'm certainly not inclined to ask her, if that's where you're going with this."

"Of course not." I ended the call, promising to get in touch again if I had any further news. Rita did the same.

Cleo called a few minutes later. She was back in her office, relieved at having turned TMC's helm over to Quinn. She asked if I could get away for a face-to-face update. I readily agreed and left Bernie with explicit instructions: keep eyes on my desk area at all times. I gave him permission to lock the library if he felt uncomfortable and promised to be back in half an hour or less.

"No problem, Miss Aimee. You can count on a Kluck-ert. That's the family motto made up by my Grandpa. I carry it on down the line."

With eagerness to hear from Cleo outweighing my misgivings, I left Bernie in charge, hurrying toward the main tower through a sudden rain shower. Cleo had coffee poured for both of us, and the rich aroma filled her office. I plopped in a chair next to her desk—damp, chilly, and grateful for the hot beverage.

"What's the latest on the Gailworths and Natasha?" I asked.

"Not much is happening, except Hector Korba is going to have a stroke if the police don't think of some way to justify going after Natasha and her parents."

"Has Quinn thought of anything?"

"He's grilling Sybil Snyder about Natasha's medical condition, hoping she'll find a legitimate medical reason to convince the police the child is in imminent danger. That's the only way they can put out an Amber Alert. And the judge in charge of the custody hearing can't issue a bench warrant unless the Gailworths fail to appear at ten o'clock tomorrow as scheduled. As far as the letter of the law is concerned, Natasha is on a legal outing with her mother and stepfather."

I couldn't believe my ears. I certainly couldn't contain my exasperation as I said, "They've been gone since six o'clock this morning. It's after ten now. They could be in Oregon or Nevada by this time. Or on their way to Mexico."

Cleo was definitely on the same page. "That's what Quinn's thinking," she said. "He's inclined to think they went north just because that's the quickest way to leave

California. Korba agrees. He's convinced that Gailworth is headed for Canada."

"Why not Mexico?" I asked.

Cleo replied without hesitation. "Language, for one thing. According to Hector, Gailworth has always been prejudiced against Mexicans, and Hispanics in general. He wouldn't even allow Natasha to study Spanish in school. Hector thinks there's almost no chance they'd be headed in that direction. He's guessing if Gailworth can get them across the border into Canada, he'll book a flight to Europe."

She was confirming my worst fears. "So there's nothing anyone can do to track them down and bring Natasha home before they reach Canada?"

"It doesn't look like it. The Amber Alert would be the best bet."

"What are the criteria for the Amber Alert?"

"I just looked it up." Cleo read from a notepad on her desk. "Law enforcement has to confirm that an abduction has taken place. They need a description of the child and the captor, or at least the captor's vehicle. And they need to verify that the child is at risk of serious injury or death."

Her words sent chills down my arms. "Can Quinn get a description of the vehicle from our outside security cameras?"

"Already done. And Natasha's nurse has written up an incident report about Gailworth physically carrying Natasha out of her room and leaving without filling out the AMA form. Not quite an abduction, but he definitely removed her by force."

"What about Natasha being at risk of injury or death?"

"That's a tough one," Cleo said, "unless Snyder

swears Natasha's health is in danger. Hector is trying to bully her into coming up with any convincing medical reason, no matter how flimsy. So far, she hasn't caved, and I don't blame her."

"Right," I said. "She'd have a hard time proving that in court, since she admitted to Quinn that Natasha's been well enough to go home for at least a couple of days."

Cleo dropped her glasses on her desk and massaged her temples with her fingers. "The thing that's bothering me most about this is that Melissa Gailworth is going along with it. Is she really so loyal to Gailworth that she'd flee the country with him and take her daughter along?"

I stood and paced her office. "She might…if Gailworth is holding her past over her head. She and Natasha have been caught in the middle between Gailworth and Korba for a long time. Being torn between the two of them must have taken an excruciating emotional toll. Maybe she just wants it to end, and running away is her best hope."

"I wonder if they've left the country already. What's to stop them from catching a plane at an airport somewhere in Oregon?"

"I can think of one thing," I said. "Gailworth might have to use a credit card to buy airplane tickets. He wouldn't want to leave a paper trail proving he's fleeing the country. At least not this early on. For all he knows, law enforcement is already on the lookout for him and checking airports."

"I see what you mean," Cleo said, looking a little more optimistic. "Purchasing three one-way tickets to anywhere outside the U.S. on the day before the custody hearing would be hard to explain."

"Right," I said. My words were still tumbling out, as if speaking quickly would lead to a faster solution. I concentrated on slowing down as I continued, "So, if I were him, I'd try to get across the border into Canada, then wait until the last minute to buy tickets on an international flight." As I spoke, I had an idea. I walked around her desk and stood looking over her shoulder. "Cleo, go online and look for an airport located in Canada but close to the Washington State border."

Cleo put her glasses on and started tapping her keyboard. "Vancouver International."

"Good. Now look up the U.S. town nearest the border crossing from Washington to Canada."

Her fingers flew across the keyboard. "Blaine. It sits on the border and has a crossing called the Peace Arch."

"Does it have an airport?"

She tapped again. "No. It closed in 2008. Looks like Bellingham International Airport is close, though. According to this site, it's only about thirty minutes from Vancouver."

"Thanks. I'm going back to the library. Call me if you hear anything."

"I will. You do the same."

TWENTY-EIGHT

BACK IN THE LIBRARY, I asked Bernie if any patrons had dropped in while I was gone.

"Matter of fact, some did, but I took care of their needs." He seemed pleased with himself, so I waited for him to elaborate. He didn't, so I gave him a nudge.

"Bernie, do you want to tell me how you helped our patrons while I was gone?"

"One doctor fella wanted to make a copy of some pages from a magazine. Lola told me you don't charge for photocopying, so I told him to go ahead."

"That's right. Anything else?"

"Just a phone call asking you to call back. Somebody named Dick, or Rick or—"

"Or maybe Nick?" I asked.

"Coulda been. I don't hear as clear on the phone as I used to."

I went to my desk and looked at the number written in Bernie's spidery hand. It was Nick's cell phone.

"You did just fine, Bernie. It's almost noon, so you're free to go."

"Roger that. I'll see if I can catch Lola in the cafeteria." He whistled softly as he made his way to the exit.

As soon as the door closed behind Bernie, I called Nick's cell. He picked up immediately with his "Hi, lady" greeting.

"What's up?" I asked.

"That's my line. I'm checking in to hear the latest about the missing girl."

"We're still in the guesswork stage, but my best guess is still that Gailworth is headed north, hoping to cross into Canada and from there, who knows?"

"He could fly just about anywhere he wants from the Vancouver B.C. airport," Nick said. "If he does that, they'll have a hell of a time catching up with him."

"That's what I'm afraid of."

"So you're fairly sure Gailworth is taking I-5 north, but you can't come up with a legit reason for law enforcement to stop him?"

"No. We can't be sure he's taking that route."

"What would you want to do if you knew they were headed that way?"

"Good question. What would you do?"

"Head him off at the pass."

He sounded like a B-movie cowboy. Losing patience, I asked, "How? I'm praying they won't make it across the border, but I don't see how anyone can stop them. So far, we have no leverage. We can't claim Natasha's been abducted, because she's with her mother, and we can't claim they've skipped out on the custody hearing because it isn't scheduled to take place until tomorrow morning."

"Maybe there is a way," Nick said. "I just heard about it from Rella."

"Rella? Isn't she back east?"

"She is, but she checked in a while ago, and I told her about the unfolding drama with the little piano girl. Rella told me a story about getting hung up crossing the Canadian border with her nephews a couple of years ago when she wanted to take them up to B.C. on vacation."

"What happened?" I asked, eager for good news.

"When the folks at the border crossing saw kids in her car, she was told to pull over and wait while they did some checking."

"You mean checking their passports?"

"Turns out kids don't need passports to cross, but they do need birth certificates. And because they weren't Rella's, she had to produce a letter from their father saying Rella had permission to take them across the border. It turns out the officials at the border pay extra attention to children crossing into Canada, and it can take time to sort that out, especially if there's an active custody issue."

I suddenly felt light enough to float a few inches above the ground. "Oh, that's fantastic news. Thank God we finally have something working in our favor."

I heard Nick's quiet laugh, then he said, "When you're finished thanking God, you might want to thank Rella."

"I will, and you can thank her for me next time you talk to her."

Next I dialed Quinn's office with the news about the border crossing and the custody issue. He said he'd see if he could convince the police to follow up with the Canadian and Mexican borders.

"I'm betting on Canada," I said.

"So am I," he agreed, "and I'm betting Gailworth is not aware of what it's going to take to get Natasha across that border."

"I hope you're right."

"We need to think about timing," Quinn went on. "How long would it take for Gailworth to drive straight through to the Canadian border?"

"I've already looked that up. It's an eleven-hour drive

from Timbergate to Blaine, Washington. That's right on the border. It's a little past noon now. If Gailworth left at six thirty this morning, he's probably only made it about halfway, but there's really nothing we can do to stop him until he reaches the Canadian border."

"I'm still working on Sybil Snyder," Quinn said. "And Hector's still bellowing at her. She's trying to come up with some medical thing that would hold up in court, but Natasha is two weeks post-op and her hospital care has been flawless. She's in no physical danger from the road trip itself."

"What about danger from her stepfather?"

"That's the problem. Natasha's mother appears to be in favor of this 'getaway,' if that's what it is. If she doesn't see her husband as a threat, why should anyone else? There is no law against what they're doing. Not until ten o'clock tomorrow morning, when they fail to appear in court here in Timbergate." I heard Quinn sigh in frustration. "You know what scares the hell out of me about this?"

I was pretty sure I did. The same thing was alarming me. "You're thinking this is an act of desperation out of proportion to a custody hearing." I took a breath. "Quinn, do you think Abel Gailworth killed Gavin Lowe?"

"I hope not. But if he did, things aren't looking good for Melissa and Natasha."

"Then you don't think Melissa's in on it?"

"I doubt it," Quinn said. "If she was unconditionally in love with Gailworth, she was probably willing to go along with his nonsense until Natasha got sick. I suspect at that point Melissa began having second thoughts about him. Cleo told me what you found on Lowe's flash drive. If Gavin Lowe had lived, he'd have testified at the custody hearing. Suppose Lowe had already told Natasha's parents what he planned to recommend. Maybe Gailworth balked at the prospect of strict oversight of Natasha's health as a condition for retaining custody…"

"And decided to silence Lowe before his recommended conditions became known?"

"It might have worked if you hadn't found that flash drive in Lowe's briefcase. Now Lowe's requirements may be considered by the judge, no matter what Sybil Snyder recommends. Melissa and Gailworth probably know that with or without Lowe's testimony at the hearing, there will very likely be strings attached if they win continued custody."

"You're right," I said. "Child Protective Services would be breathing down their necks indefinitely."

"And if Hector Korba isn't granted custody, he'll be doing the same. One health checkup or lab test that isn't up to par, and he'll drag them back into court."

"At that point, Melissa might decide to walk away from Gailworth and the whole vegan routine if it means she can keep her daughter."

"Which would infuriate Gailworth," Quinn continued, "since their marriage is his only possible hope of controlling Natasha's career."

"Not to mention her income," I said. "But why take off with Natasha? It's illogical for Gailworth to think he can simply leave the U.S. and continue to exploit Natasha's career in another country. Do you suppose he's never heard of extradition? Hector Korba would jump on that in a nanosecond."

"True," Quinn said. "If that's his plan, he'd have a hell of a time finding a foreign country that would serve his purpose. I think he's skipping out for a different reason. He's acting like a desperate man."

"Then you *do* think he killed Gavin Lowe?" Aware that I sounded agitated, I made an effort to calm down, "But how would Gailworth gain access to your office, much less lure Lowe in there?"

"That's what has me puzzled. I can't imagine how either of them got in. Neither would have known about the third-floor passageway. Neither had keys to my office, and neither was seen on the fourth-floor security cameras that night."

"What about the third-floor cameras?" I asked.

"Now that you mention it, that footage was only checked to see if anyone was spotted near the laundry cart where the gun was hidden. Apparently, they came up with nothing suspicious. I wasn't given a chance to view any of the camera footage before I was placed on leave."

"And you couldn't ask Sanjay or the police to focus on the area near the alcove and the door with the hazard sign without giving them a convincing reason."

"They have one now." Quinn was silent, giving me time for his last revelation to sink in.

His words had the desired effect. "Are you saying you've told the police about the passage?"

"I did that when I was put back in charge. Hoping it would build trust. They seemed to accept my reasons for withholding the information, but I'm sure they haven't ruled me out as a suspect."

"So have they taken a closer look at the third-floor camera footage?"

"That's what I've been told, but I wasn't invited to the viewing. It isn't likely to single out any suspects right away, since everyone who works day or night shifts on that floor has to enter that alcove to get to the restrooms."

"Do you think the police told Sanjay about the passageway?"

"What I told Detective Kass is that, as far as I know, Sanjay isn't aware of it and I'd like to keep it that way. He agreed and said that for now, he'll put the passage on a need-to-know basis."

"Suddenly I'm feeling better about Detective Kass." My relief produced a nervous little laugh. "Do you suppose Sanjay is on his suspect list?"

"Could be," he said. "Kass seems good at his job, so he probably hasn't ruled out anyone just yet."

"Then as far as the police know, it's just you and Varsha who know about the passage. You didn't tell them about Cleo and me or Harry and Nick?"

"No." The response was abrupt, and he continued in the same vein, "You'd better see that your brother and your boyfriend understand that. I've already made it clear to Cleo that her continued employment depends on keeping it to herself. The same goes for you."

No more nervous laughter. I was a good soldier. "Understood. Are you going to ask the police what they saw on that third floor footage?"

"No. I want to see it for myself. Now that I'm back, that's going to be my first priority."

My cell phone buzzed—a text from Nick.

Quinn and I agreed to keep each other informed.

TWENTY-NINE

NICK'S TEXT WAS a request to call him ASAP. I did, even though it was almost one o'clock and I'd had a phone to my ear for most of the day.

"We have a sighting," he said.

"Where?" I switched the phone to my other hand and grabbed for a pen and notepad.

"I gave Buck's computer posse a description of Gailworth's vehicle and the license plate number and asked them to monitor traffic cameras in every direction. They just picked up a camera shot of Gailworth's car on I-5, headed north out of Oregon and into Washington on the Interstate Bridge."

"When?"

"About five minutes ago."

Energy surged through me. "Then we were right. He must be headed toward Canada."

"Looks likely. Has the lady doctor come up with a legit reason to issue the Amber Alert?"

"No, but let me get this information to Quinn and Dr. Snyder."

"You think this will light a fire under the doctor?"

"I don't know." I suppressed a groan. "There's nothing she can do unless she decides to knuckle under to Hector Korba and simply lie about Natasha's health being endangered."

"Talk to your boss and let me know what happens.

Gailworth is only four and a half hours' driving time from the Washington/Canada border."

I locked the library and headed across the complex to Quinn's office, eager to share my news.

Varsha knew the score and all the players, so she waved me through to Quinn's office. I expected to see Hector Korba and Sybil Snyder, but Quinn stood alone, staring out his window at the dormant snow-covered volcano that dominated the mountain range east of Timbergate. Maybe he found it symbolic of Lowe's murder—a violent eruption resulting in a chain of destructive consequences.

He turned when I closed his door behind me. "You have news?"

"Yes. Finally, something concrete." I told him what Nick had said about the image of Gailworth's car on the traffic camera confirming that he was headed north and had already crossed from Oregon into Washington.

He moved to his desk and sat. "Good to have that confirmed, but it doesn't give us legal cause to have them apprehended, and it doesn't fit the criteria for an Amber Alert." He looked up at me. "Have a seat, Aimee."

I plopped down across from him. "There must be something we can do, now that we know where they are. Doesn't leaving the country the day before a custody hearing prove they're on the run? Wouldn't the border guards stop them?"

"Unfortunately, no," Quinn said. "It's not likely the guards would know about the custody hearing."

We both sat for a frustrated moment of silence, aware that time was running out and puzzling over our next step. I felt a vibration next to my thigh and realized it was my cell phone buzzing an incoming text message.

I pulled the phone out of my pocket and glanced at the screen. The caller's number was unfamiliar, but the message was clear.

SOS

An electric current started at the back of my neck and raced all the way down to my tailbone. I read the message.

Help abel is being mean and mom is crying.

"Oh, my God, Quinn. I think this text is coming from Natasha!" I held out the phone so he could see the screen.

"Damnation!" He spoke to Varsha on his intercom, "Get the police on the line. Detective Kass, if you can reach him."

While Quinn talked to Kass, I sent a text back to Natasha asking where she was. She responded, Backseat with moms phone.

I replied, Does your mom know you're texting?

She answered, No she thiks im playing games

I told her help was on the way and to keep the phone on.

She responded, K pls hurry

Quinn hung up from talking to Kass just as I read Natasha's final plea.

"Kass is on it," he said. "He's looking for anything in Gailworth's past that might prevent him crossing the Canadian border."

"Like what?"

"He mentioned a criminal record—either misdemeanor or felony. The problem is time. He wasn't sure how long that would take."

"I told Natasha to leave her cell phone on. I'm not sure, but maybe they can use it to track Gailworth's progress toward the border."

"Good idea." He pressed a button on his intercom and asked Varsha to summon Korba and Dr. Snyder to his office *STAT*. While he did that, I called Nick, who answered on the first ring.

"What's the latest?"

I caught him up on Natasha's text and what Quinn and I were doing and asked Nick if he had any other suggestions.

"I can think of one. I'll get permission to use one of Buck's planes in case this results in the girl and her mother needing a ride home from wherever the police catch up with them. If the timing works out, we could have them back in time for that custody hearing tomorrow morning."

"I hadn't thought of that. Good idea."

"If I do fly up there, you'd better plan to ride along. The mother and daughter don't know me, but they obviously trust you. At least the little girl does."

Nick's last words filled me with apprehension. Natasha Korba was counting on me as a lifeline for herself and her mother. I couldn't bear the thought of failing them. I waffled between doubt and determination while Quinn and I waited for Korba and Snyder to show up.

Korba arrived first, bursting into Quinn's office like a mad bull, nearly knocking the door off its hinges.

"Where is my Natasha?" he bellowed. "What is this new development?"

Quinn stood and held his hands out, hoping to placate

the desperate grandfather. "Hector, try to stay calm. This is good news. We know they're all right and the police are doing all they can to—"

"Jared, what's happening?" Sybil Snyder rushed into Quinn's office and stopped in her tracks when she saw Korba turn and glare at her.

"You! You traitor," Korba barked at her. "A word from you could have started an Amber Alert hours ago. Now God knows if I will ever see my baby girl again."

Sybil turned to Quinn, who explained the events of the past half hour, starting with Natasha's text to me.

Korba shot a glare at me. "She texted you? Why not me? What have you done to turn her from me?"

I was shocked at his accusation. "Nothing. I barely know her or her mother. I have no idea why she thought I could help. Maybe because she knows I work at the hospital."

Quinn tried again to gain control over the chaos erupting in his office. "Hector, please, give us a chance to do everything we can to help your granddaughter and her mother."

Korba drew in a deep breath, shook his head, and said, "All right. Tell me everything you are doing to rescue my Natasha."

Again, as always, he referred to the girl as his property. Maybe that was why Natasha had chosen not to contact him for help. At ten years of age, she may have already realized his love for her was controlling and possessive—that he had been molding her into the image of his choice since she was a toddler, rather than encouraging her to explore options beyond the piano keyboard.

Quinn's phone rang. He picked up immediately, listened, made quick notes, and then told his caller about

Natasha's text. He listened again, then hung up and looked at the three of us who stood waiting.

"Okay, here's the good news. Kass has checked the IAFIS database and determined that Gailworth has criminal misdemeanors in his past back in Arkansas. A couple of speeding tickets and one DUI twelve years ago. That should be enough to alert the border guards. Whether those charges will keep him from crossing into Canada is up to them."

"What did he say about Natasha's text?" I asked.

"He said you should call him direct if you hear from her again." He handed me a sheet from his notepad. "Here's the number." He glanced at his watch. "That's the good news. The bad news is that Gailworth could reach the Canadian border in three hours."

"But we're not even positive that's where he's heading," I said. "He could take off in another direction. Maybe cross over into Idaho."

"Then Sybil must tell the police we need an Amber Alert." Korba looked at Dr. Snyder as if he'd gladly throw her professional career and medical license under a bus, along with Snyder herself, if she refused again.

"I think the situation has changed enough to warrant an alert." Snyder, who would not look at Korba, maintained eye contact with Quinn. "Under the circumstances, the child could be considered too medically fragile for extended travel. She was discharged with the understanding that she would continue to recuperate at her home with the opportunity for immediate readmission in the event of a relapse."

"There!" Korba pounded his fist on Quinn's desk. "You see? Call your police detective and get this done."

Quinn threw Snyder a grateful look and picked up his

phone. I glanced at the time on my cell phone while he spoke again with Detective Kass. Almost two o'clock. Most of an hour had passed since Nick called about sighting Gailworth's vehicle. Depending on traffic, Abel and his reluctant passengers could be less than three hours from Canada. How long to get the alert up? And what would Gailworth do if he happened to see it? Would it make him more desperate? The thought made me queasy. It also made me hope Natasha's stepfather hadn't caught on to what the girl was doing with her mother's phone.

I left the tense atmosphere of Quinn's office and took an elevator down to the relative calm of Cleo's first floor office to fill her in on the latest developments.

"Quinn promised to keep us updated," I said, after finishing my blow-by-blow account.

"Natasha texted you?" Cleo shook her head in amazement. "That's remarkable. I hope to God her mother has half that little gal's spunk."

"So do I, but look what Melissa is dealing with… She has no job or profession of her own. Until she married that slick-tongued con artist of a husband, she and her daughter depended on Natasha's intimidating and controlling grandfather. Now both men are pressuring her for control of Natasha's future."

My phone vibrated and I half expected another message from Natasha, but it was Nick saying the plane was available and to keep him advised. I texted back an okay and told Cleo about his offer to use Buck's plane to bring Melissa and Natasha home.

"Let's hope this ends well enough for that to happen," Cleo said. "I don't have a good feeling about that Gailworth creep."

"Neither do I, but we're not alone. He'll be dead meat if Korba and Snyder get their hands on him." We sat mute for a few minutes, alternately watching the clock and waiting for our phones to ring, until Cleo broke the silence.

"Speaking of Snyder," she said, "what kind of vibe did you get with both of them there in Quinn's office? Do you still think there's a chance they're lovers?"

It was a valid question, and I didn't have an answer. "Hard to tell under the circumstances. It was all about Natasha, and Quinn's office was like a pressure cooker. That's why I broke away and came here."

"So maybe Rita Lowe had it right. Maybe Snyder was noodling with Gavin Lowe and not with Korba."

Cleo's comment reminded me of Bernie Kluckert's story about a man matching Glen Capshaw's description who seemed to be looking for something in my desk. I dropped that bit of news about Sybil Snyder's husband.

"What the heck?" Cleo said. "Snyder's husband nosing around like that is more than a little strange."

"Even more strange considering that a week earlier, Lola saw someone doing the same thing. It could have been the same man. I would have mentioned it sooner, but with all that's been going on, it kept slipping my mind."

"I remember you telling me about Capshaw's jealous accusations. Maybe it had something to do with that."

"Maybe. Both Gavin Lowe and Hector Korba are members of his wife's committee, but what's that got to do with Capshaw rifling through my desk in the library?"

"Why don't you ask him?" Cleo said.

"You're kidding. How would I go about doing that?"

"I don't know, but you can probably think of something."

I couldn't believe what she was asking me to do. "You're forgetting he has a temper and suspects his wife of cheating. According to Rita Lowe's sources, he's even been informed that his wife was cheating with Gavin Lowe. I might as well come right out and ask him if he's a murderer."

She nodded. "Ah, good point. Maybe confronting Capshaw isn't such a good idea. Besides, now that Abel Gailworth is on the run, the odds seem to be in his favor as Lowe's killer."

Just then I felt my phone vibrate. Another text.

Help ru still there

THIRTY

I TEXTED BACK, Still here. RU OK?

She replied, K for now can u help us

I answered, We're getting help. Are you headed to Canadian border?

Thik so gotta go

I filled Cleo in, and then called Quinn from Cleo's phone to let him know I'd heard from Natasha and to see if he had any news.

"We're making progress," he said. "The police haven't made a decision yet on the Amber Alert, but they have contacted the Canadian border to be on the lookout for Gailworth's vehicle. Canada is pretty picky about letting people with a DUI on their record into their country, so that might be enough to keep him from crossing the border. We checked with the Canadian Border Services Agency, and they say if there's only a single DUI, and it's been more than ten years, there's something called Deemed Rehabilitation. Gailworth might qualify, but it would be up to the immigration authorities to decide whether to let him pass through. It's not certain to stop him, but it could work in our favor. At least it should slow him down."

"What about the pending custody hearing? Did the police tell the border people about that?"

"They did, but the Gailworths haven't yet missed their court date. They still have nineteen hours to get back to Timbergate for the hearing. Gailworth might argue that he plans to return home in time for the hearing, but I suspect the officials at the border will detain him, at least until they can do some extensive checking."

"Quinn, I'm worried that if Gailworth gets turned away at the border, he might head off in some other direction. If he does show up at the border crossing, we have to make sure he's held there somehow. Could the police say he's a suspect in a murder case?"

"They may be considering that, but I'll check with Kass just to make sure. Don't forget to call him about Natasha's latest text."

Cleo looked up from her computer as Quinn and I ended our call. "Here's something interesting. Take a look." She had pulled up criteria for entering Canada with a child, and it matched what Rella had told Nick. The Gailworths wouldn't need a passport for Natasha, but they would need a birth certificate.

I sent a text to Natasha's phone, praying that because she was sitting in the backseat, her mother and Gailworth wouldn't notice the phone vibrating.

Do you have a passport?

No

Did your mom bring your birth certificate?

In moms purse why

You cannot cross border without it

Gotta go mom crying

    Again, she was gone abruptly.

    Cleo gave me a look. "What?"

    I told Cleo the Gailworths had Natasha's birth certificate with them.

    "Darn," she said. "I was hoping Gailworth hadn't thought of taking it along."

    "Me too, but Natasha says it's in her mother's purse."

    "Too bad." Cleo glanced up at her wall clock. I did the same. It read three fifteen. Gailworth could reach the Canadian border in less than two hours. Would he try to cross, or would he check into a motel on the Washington State side and wait until morning? I considered a more frightening scenario. If he was more than a fraud and a con artist and if he had somehow found his way into Quinn's office and killed Gavin Lowe, was Gailworth capable of doing something far more desperate? Would he use Natasha and her mother as hostages?

    Cleo said, "Do you realize you've been in my office for an hour and you've been standing or pacing the whole time?"

    "I can't stop hoping we'll get her back and she'll be okay. I don't know what else to do."

    Cleo gently grasped my shoulders and aimed me at the door. "Go back to the library and take a breather. The police are on this. They have all kinds of reasons now to catch up with Gailworth, not least of which is that he's a murder suspect. He's not only left town, he's left the state and might very well try to leave the country. Hardly the behavior of an innocent man."

    Back in the library, I called Detective Kass and gave him verbatim reports of my texts with Natasha.

"Good job, but our first priority is to keep her safe. We don't want her stepfather finding out what she's doing."

"I know. I'm scared to death she's going to put herself in harm's way."

"If she texts again, tell her to turn off the phone and put it back in her mother's purse. It's too dangerous for her to be using it."

"I will. I told her to leave it on because her parents think she's using it to play games. I thought you could use it to locate them. I'm not sure how that works. I've only seen it on television crime shows."

"In some cases that would be a good idea, but we don't want to put the child or her mother in peril. Better have her turn it off and put it away. The Amber Alert is going to be activated any time now, and the Canadian Border Services Agency will be watching for Gailworth. We're going to catch up with him one way or another."

Relief washed over me at hearing what the police had in place, but it was chased by a bolus of pessimistic fear that a lot of things could still go wrong.

"Miss Machado?" Kass said. "Are you still there?"

"Yes, what?"

"I understood Mr. Quinn to say you have someone available to fly the girl and her mother home. Is that true?"

"Yes, my friend, Nick Alexander. He's a licensed pilot with an instrument rating. Would that be all right? I plan to go with him."

"I think we can arrange that. Tell him to stand by. I'll keep in touch. And please contact me right away if the girl sends another text."

"I will. Thank you." I hung up, feeling as if this day

had already lasted for a month. I glanced at my wall clock, amazed that it was only four in the afternoon. I did the math again and realized Gailworth could be a scant hour away from the Canadian border. I wondered how soon the Amber Alert would activate, dreading what might happen if Gailworth spotted it.

Minutes dragged by while I made a halfhearted attempt to turn my mind to anything that could be considered library tasks. As I opened my desk drawer to reach for the keys to the locked file cabinet where I stored committee minutes, I flashed on Bernie's description of the man he observed nosing around in my desk drawers. *Bright red hair and moustache.* It could only have been Dr. Snyder's husband, Glen Capshaw. What possible reason would he have for looking around in my desk? I came up with zero. Should I call him, using the pretext that I wondered if he needed library assistance? Say one of my volunteers had recognized him in the library?

I decided to wait until the Gailworth drama had run its course. Capshaw had told Bernie he was looking for a pen and paper to leave me a note. Then he said he'd get back to me later. That was exactly one week ago, and I hadn't heard from him. His failure to follow up seemed to contradict what he had told Bernie, but maybe Capshaw had found what he needed elsewhere.

I found myself comparing Capshaw and Gailworth as suspects. Gailworth had a lot at stake financially, so the motive there was money. He thought Lowe had to be prevented from testifying. On the other hand, Capshaw's only motive that made sense was a crime of passion incited by Lowe's alleged affair with Capshaw's wife. Love or money. Which was it?

As I sat there watching the clock approach five and

wondering what to do with myself after closing the library, my cell phone came to life.

Ru there

Yes but you need to stop using phone dangerous

Abel says we are close to bordr

Border guards will help you. They know what to do

K but I maybe did somethig bad

What did you do?

Threw my birth certif out window mom and Abel dont know

Why?

You said they wont let me in canada without it am I in trouble

My eyes filled with tears for that child. She had done the one thing she could think of that might stop Abel in his tracks. I hoped she was right.

You're not in trouble. Turn off your phone and put it back in your mother's purse, K?

K thak u

I locked the library and raced across the complex to

Quinn's office with my phone to my ear, telling him about Natasha's text and asking where things stood with the police. He told me they were in touch with the Canadian officials and that Gailworth had been apprehended moments ago just as he pulled in line at the border crossing. Melissa and Natasha were emotionally exhausted but physically fine. The wave of relief that passed through me was so strong that it turned my legs to rubber.

We called Detective Kass from Quinn's office, where Korba and Dr. Snyder seemed to have taken up permanent residence. Quinn put me on the line and I reported on my final text conversation with Natasha, while Korba glared at me with loathing instead of gratitude. Kass said he'd let me know if and when Nick and I might be allowed to bring Melissa and Natasha home. I didn't relay that part of the conversation in front of Korba for fear he would either object or demand to come along with us.

After I left Quinn's office, I called Nick right away to give him a heads-up. He suggested we meet at the Timbergate Municipal Airport coffee shop to wait for further notice about the flight to pick up mother and daughter. They were now being termed Gailworth's hostages and were being routed through the red tape necessary to turn them over to the jurisdiction of the Timbergate Police Department. After a couple of hours of formalities involving various law enforcement agencies, Kass called with the okay to bring Melissa and Natasha home.

TWO HOURS LATER Nick and I touched down at Bellingham International Airport in Buck Sawyer's six-passenger Eclipse 500. It was a smooth night flight through clear skies in the light jet that Buck used primarily for small groups and short trips. Our return trip would have us back in Timbergate before midnight.

When we walked into the terminal, we spotted mother and daughter seated in a waiting area. A female officer who looked to be in her fifties and wore the uniform of the Bellingham Police Department acted as their chaperon. When Natasha spotted us, she jumped up and ran to me with a bright-eyed smile.

"You saved us," she cried.

"You saved yourself, Natasha. You were very brave." I glanced over her head and saw her mother give me a wan smile and wipe a tear from her face.

We signed the woman officer's required paperwork and were soon on our way home. It was Natasha's first time in an airplane, and she was giddy with excitement, looking down through the clear night at the sparkling city lights spread out like spilled diamonds on black velvet.

"I want to learn to fly," she called out from her seat behind Nick.

Nick glanced at me. "Something tells me she'll do it."

I thought of the girl's musical talent and her spirit, and had no doubt she would learn to fly and do anything else that commanded her interest. I sent a silent thank you to Gavin Lowe, the doctor who had saved her life and lost his own.

In the seat behind me, Melissa remained quiet, and I had to wonder where her thoughts were taking her. She would face some soul-searching and difficult days, not the least of which was appearing before a judge at ten o'clock in the morning to decide the fate of her daughter. I wondered whom she feared most: the judge or Hector Korba. I also wondered if she knew whether her husband had killed Gavin Lowe. I was surprised that the authorities had allowed her to fly home with us, but Nick and Detective Kass had worked out an arrangement that seemed to satisfy everyone.

Kass was waiting for us in the terminal when we touched down at the Timbergate Municipal Airport near midnight. From there it would be up to the TPD to decide the next step for Melissa Korba Gailworth and her daughter. I wondered if the custody hearing would go on in spite of what had happened during the past fifteen hours.

Natasha should have been stressed and exhausted after all she had been through, but she was wide awake and seemed invigorated by her adventure. As Kass escorted her and Melissa toward his vehicle, Natasha broke away and ran back to throw her slender arms around me.

"I'll never forget our secret messages," she said. "I was really scared Abel might do something bad until you told me it would be okay."

"It was okay because you were smart and brave," I said. "If I'm ever in trouble, I hope I'll be just like you."

"You will." She gave me another hug and ran back to her mother.

As Detective Kass helped Melissa and Natasha into his vehicle, I glanced at Nick and was surprised to see the emotions of both sympathy and relief revealed there.

"Great kid," he said. Then he abruptly changed the subject, quickly regaining his customary unflappable air. "Are you hungry?"

"It's kind of hard to tell, but I think so."

He took my hand in his. "You know, we were supposed to be on a dinner date tonight. I made reservations. Even got a haircut. I still owe you that belated Valentine's Day dinner."

I gave his hand a squeeze. "What do you have in mind?"

"Whatever's still open."

We ended up at Burger King, feasting on Whoppers and french fries and rehashing our flight and the events that led up to it. When the food was gone, exhaustion began catching up with us and we sat in our booth trading yawns.

I asked Nick one last question, "Do you think Abel Gailworth would have hurt Melissa or Natasha if he hadn't been stopped?"

"Hard to say. He doesn't appear to have committed any violent crimes in his past, unless it turns out he killed the doctor."

"I wonder how long it will take for the police to figure that out."

"Not long to rule him out, if he has a good alibi, but otherwise, the stunt he just pulled has definitely backfired. He's going to be under a lot of scrutiny."

"True, but I can't imagine how Gailworth could have ended up in Quinn's office with Dr. Lowe."

He grasped my arm and gave me an affectionate little shake. "You don't have to figure that out, Aimee. It's not your job to solve the murder."

I flinched a little, thinking I had a right to my curiosity in this case. "I know, but it's never far from my mind, especially after being asked to volunteer my DNA."

"The police have asked lots of people."

"You know, there's still Glen Capshaw to consider. I keep hoping the police will take a good look at him. So far, I have the feeling he's escaped their attention."

"That's the lady doctor's husband, right? What's her name again?"

"Sybil Snyder. She took over Natasha's case after Gavin Lowe died."

"Don't be too sure her husband is being overlooked. Detective Kass seems very invested in solving Lowe's murder." He stifled another yawn and said, "It's late and you have to work tomorrow. I'd better let you get home."

"You're right, but I'm afraid I'm too wired to fall asleep."

"I could help with that." The smile that accompanied his offer sent a little thrill through my body. Still, I knew that tonight of all nights I needed my rest.

"Thanks for the offer, but I'd better settle for warm milk and pain pills."

"Your knee still hurting?"

"Only when I'm awake."

As I opened my car door, Nick said, "Wait, you're not escaping that easily."

"What? I thought we'd covered everything."

"This is the end of our official Valentine's date. Tradition says I go in for the goodnight kiss. I won't hurt your knees, I promise."

He put his hand behind my neck, easing my face toward his while tingles raced through my scalp. I melted into the heady pleasure of a kiss tasting of hope, desire, and just a trace of catsup. *Nobody does it better than Nick*, I thought. *Not even James Bond.*

THIRTY-ONE

I woke Wednesday morning with the remnants of a dream slipping away. Natasha had been sitting cross-legged on the closed top board of a baby grand with an iPhone in her hands. She was texting as the piano carried her across a star-filled night sky like a magic carpet. Not hard to interpret that dream after the events of the previous day. With Abel Gailworth in jail in Washington, I wondered how the judge would handle the morning's custody hearing. It did not look good for Melissa; I suspected Hector Korba might win this time.

At work I watched the clock inching toward ten. To take my mind off the impending hearing, I walked into the stacks to check on Lola, who had been uncharacteristically subdued ever since she arrived. I found her thumbing through an issue of the *Journal of the American Geriatrics Society*.

"How's your morning, going, Lola? Anything I can help with?"

"Oh, I don't think so, Miss Machado." She closed the magazine, but not before I noticed that the title of the article she had been reading had to do with intimacy and the elderly. Definitely not my area of expertise. Lola knew almost as much as I did about researching credible sources, so I decided to take her at her word and mind my own business.

The hour between ten and eleven o'clock dragged

while I sat at my desk trying to imagine what was going on at the courthouse where Natasha's immediate future was being decided. Having heard no word that the hearing had been canceled or postponed, I imagined Hector Korba and Melissa Gailworth were both there with their lawyers—and Natasha, of course.

I distracted myself by pulling up the latest draft of my budget. The monies earmarked for the forensic component of the library were insufficient to fulfill its mission. Dr. Beardsley, who had provided the seed money, had underestimated how popular it would become, and how quickly the budget would be depleted. Now that Beardsley had retired, he couldn't be counted on to fund the project indefinitely, so in addition to my other duties, I would either have to convince home office to chip in with a hefty subsidy, or I would reluctantly add "grant writer" to my job description.

I was reworking the numbers, hoping to come up with a better result, when my phone rang. It was close to noon. Most routine communication at work relied on email, so phone calls suggested the matter was more urgent. As it was in this case. The caller was Quinn, with an update on Natasha's hearing.

"She's going with Child Protective Services," he said.

"Oh, I hadn't thought of that. I expected the judge to postpone and let her stay with Melissa. How did you hear?"

"Korba just left my office. He took it better than I expected, since both he and Melissa are under the same restrictions. Neither of them can be alone with Natasha until custody is settled."

"Did he have any idea how long that would take?"

"No. Gailworth's arrest has complicated the issue.

Melissa has no job and no savings, apparently. Korba mentioned that she received the standard death benefit of a hundred thousand dollars when his son was killed in action. Korba had insisted she invest it and let it grow. Melissa had no formal education and no job skills, so he supported her, allowing her to be a full-time mother until she married Gailworth. Less than a year later, Gailworth had established his church in Timbergate and Melissa's investment portfolio was gone."

"So she has no means of supporting her daughter?" I spotted Lola working her way toward me and lowered my voice. "That's not going to work in her favor."

"It gets worse. Apparently the judge frowned on the idea of exploiting Natasha's musical gift as a source of income."

"Since Korba's loaded, he must be guessing he has the upper hand. No wonder he's willing to wait it out." As Lola approached my desk, I told Quinn I had to go.

"Miss Machado, I'm finished for the day." Lola stood there, hesitant, as if she had something more to say.

"Is something on your mind, Lola?"

"I'd like to check out a journal, but I'm not sure I'm eligible. Our collection is for medical staff and employees. I'm just a volunteer."

"Not a problem. We'll create a guest account for you, so you can check out whatever you like. I'll set it up so you'll be able to go online and use it from home as well. I'm sorry I didn't think of this sooner."

Lola brightened. "That's lovely. Do you have time to do it now?"

"I do. It'll just take a minute." I suspected which journal she had in mind, but I didn't invade her privacy by asking. Lola was soon on her way out with her reading material tucked discreetly under her arm.

I wasn't able to touch base with Cleo about the outcome of the custody hearing until later in the afternoon, when she found a moment to give me a call. Her reaction was similar to mine. We both felt sorry that Natasha and her mother couldn't be together, but we were glad the judge was not rushing a decision.

At closing time I bundled my budget projections into a tote bag, along with some templates I'd downloaded from various philanthropic websites detailing what they required in their letters of intent. A dreary way to spend an evening, but necessary, if it would help keep the forensic consortium alive.

When I called Nick from home to tell him Natasha was referred to Child Protective Services, he agreed it was the best temporary solution. He said he would pass the news on to Harry, since they were going to be working out at the dojo.

"Did Harry tell you we're flying tomorrow?" Nick asked.

"No, I haven't talked to him today. Where are you going?"

"Harry has a late afternoon meeting in Sacramento with the council of instructors from the dojos in our region, so we're taking Buck's little Cessna 206. It hasn't been out of the hangar in a while and needs some air time. We're going down early so we can visit the state building inspector's office. Maybe we can dig deeper into the identity of Quinn's under-the-table freelancer. We know he filed a permit for Quinn's bathroom, and the permit is public record. Even if he used a phony name, we might find a way to trace him."

"Then Rella hasn't had any luck back east?"

"No. Harry says she's still trying, but nothing so far. We'll see if the permit might help her."

"When will you and Harry be back?"

"We're staying down there tomorrow night and most of Friday for the first day of a black belt tournament. It'll be a chance to catch up with friends and sharpen our skills."

"As if you two need sharpening… I envy you. I haven't been to a tournament since I started working at the hospital."

"You'll get back to it. Things at the hospital are bound to quiet down eventually."

"I hope so. The troops are restless with Quinn's status as administrator still in doubt."

"Keep your fingers crossed that Harry and I come back Friday night with good news on that front."

GLEN CAPSHAW CAUGHT me by surprise Thursday morning by strolling into the library shortly after I unlocked the doors at seven thirty. We knew each other on sight but had never been formally introduced. He walked to where I sat at my desk and held out his hand.

"Good morning, Miss Machado. I'm Glen Capshaw." His handshake was warm and his smile seemed genuine. His benign demeanor did not fit with the angry, accusatory voice Harry and I had heard in the hospital stairwell. Nevertheless, I was wary. He *was* vying for first place as a murder suspect. After the formalities, I asked what brought him to the library.

"This is my third visit, actually. Your helpers may have mentioned that I've dropped in twice before." At least he was being honest about that. I didn't mention that he had been observed twice rummaging in my desk.

"They did," I said. "As I recall, on your second visit you told my volunteer you wanted my help with something. That was more than a week ago. Is that why you're back?"

"That's the gist of it, but I'm afraid it's rather complicated and sensitive. I hope you'll allow me to explain."

Uh-oh. I felt a flicker of apprehension. I hoped we weren't going to wade into the quagmire of his personal life.

"I'm afraid I can assist you only with library-related issues, Dr. Capshaw. Is there some medical procedure or treatment you'd like me to research for you?"

"No, but I can't think that my question would raise any issue of confidentiality. I simply want to know the dates of the Ethics Committee meetings that have been held over the past six months or so. If you'll pardon the pun, would divulging that information constitute a breach of ethics on your part?"

"Of course not. TMC's medical staff committee calendar is posted online for any of the doctors to see. You should have the password."

"I do, and I've checked the calendar, but those dates don't seem to include the *ad hoc* committee meetings my wife has been attending in the evenings."

Oops. Sybil Snyder's *ad hoc* committee meetings sounded more than a little suspicious. If they were legitimate, I would have been aware of them. No wonder her husband was checking up on her.

"Is this the reason you've made three trips to the library in less than three weeks?"

"I'm afraid so. On my first visit, I found no one to

ask, so I had a peek at your desk calendar until I was deterred from that approach by your vivacious woman volunteer. Then again, when you were absent, an elderly gentleman with the demeanor of a bar bouncer sent me packing." He smiled, remembering. "Rest assured, I got the message."

"I'm not sure why you're asking, since you say your wife has already given you the dates."

"She felt she may have some of them wrong. It's just our way of reconstructing our personal calendar over the past few months. Now please tell me how many Ethics Committee meetings have taken place in the past six months, including *ad hoc* meetings. I'm confident that you possess that information. I'm most interested in the dinner meetings."

I wasn't eager to tell him I had facilitated only the one Ethics Committee meeting since being put in charge, and that no previous meeting had taken place during the past six months. I definitely was unaware of any *ad hoc* evening meetings. Apparently, Sybil Snyder had given him the impression those meetings happened on a regular basis. What had she been doing on those nights when Capshaw thought she was fulfilling her service to the medical staff? Had she been fulfilling the desires of Dr. Gavin Lowe?

"I'm not aware of any *ad hoc* meetings of the committee, but that's not unusual, Dr. Capshaw. Your wife may have called a few members together on the spur of the moment without asking me to assist. If that's the case, she'll report the outcome by calling for another meeting of the full committee."

Capshaw stood. "One would think so." His effort to smile resulted in a wince of embarrassment. "Thank you for your efforts at diplomacy. I've asked you an awkward question, and you've managed to neither confirm nor deny that my wife is having an affair. Your explanation would stand if we were talking about one very recent spur-of-the moment meeting. I'm asking about a series of meetings over a period of several months. If those meetings were legitimate, a record of them would be in your files. Isn't that right?"

The gloves were off. The Capshaw who had reproached his wife in the hospital stairwell was back. I had no choice but to tell him what he wanted to know. I pulled up the medical staff committee calendar on my computer screen.

"I have facilitated only one Ethics Committee meeting, and that was a Monday morning breakfast meeting two and a half weeks ago. Before that, the most recent previous meeting was six months ago, facilitated by Cleo Cominoli. That was before I was asked to add this committee to my job duties. It was also a breakfast meeting. I have no record of any other Ethics Committee meetings this year. Do you want me to look at the previous year?"

Capshaw stood, pushing back his chair. "No, that won't be necessary." I suspected his blood pressure was skyrocketing; his usually ruddy complexion had taken on a purple hue. He managed to utter a choked "Thank you" before striding out of the building.

I called Cleo, who answered immediately.

"Cominoli, how may I help you?"

"I don't know," I said. "I think I just got Sybil Snyder killed."

THIRTY-TWO

I EXPLAINED MY remark to Cleo, who agreed that I had no legitimate reason for withholding the information about dates of the Ethics Committee meetings. She convinced me that Glen Capshaw was likely to opt for divorce over homicide. That prompted me to ask if she had made any headway determining Capshaw's whereabouts on the night Lowe was killed.

"I have one lead," Cleo said, "but I haven't had a chance to follow up on it. I'm tied up in back-to-back meetings all day today. If I find out anything before quitting time, I'll let you know."

"What's the lead? Maybe I can follow up myself."

"Trust me. That wouldn't work. Gotta go."

With Cleo unavailable and Nick and Harry out of town, I sorely needed someone to talk to. Rita Lowe? Jared Quinn? Both of them shared space with me on Detective Kass's suspect list, but Abel Gailworth's recent outrageous behavior and arrest might have bumped him up to first place. He had certainly proven to be a loose cannon.

When Bernie Kluckert arrived at nine, he acted subdued. After offering a polite greeting, he went about his chores without initiating conversation. I recalled the journal Lola had checked out the day before and wondered if that had something to do with Bernie's mood. I hoped he wouldn't ask for advice in that area. I could research the challenges that physical intimacy presented for seniors, but I couldn't presume to speak from personal knowledge on the subject for another forty years yet. At least I hoped it would be that long.

After Bernie left at noon, I locked up and walked across the street to Margie's Bean Pot, where I was surprised to find Jared Quinn and Varsha Singh sharing a table. When they spotted me, they waved me over. I filled a bowl with the day's special, Hoppin' John—a famous dish that combined black-eyed peas, rice, and diced salt pork—and carried it with me to their table.

Quinn stood, pulling out a chair for me. "We're brainstorming here. Maybe you can help, but I won't insist if you were looking forward to a relaxing lunch hour."

To Varsha, I said, "Are you sure I'm not interrupting?" Now that I knew she was single, it occurred to me that she and Quinn might be inching toward something more than a working relationship. Her exotic beauty and her loyalty to her boss would make most men take notice, although her four young children might be an obstacle. It was hard to imagine someone so close to my own age already having a brood like hers. At least she didn't have to worry about her biological clock ticking away.

"Please do join us," Varsha said. "Jared was asking me how much I recall about the time when the remodel was done in his office. I'm afraid I haven't been much help."

"I'm still hoping we can come up with a scenario that would explain how Lowe and his killer knew about the passage," Quinn said, again taking his seat. "That has to be the key to solving this damned thing."

Varsha smiled and held her palm out to Quinn. He fished a quarter out of his pocket and dropped it into her hand. I had to laugh. She had obviously put her swear jar into practice while I was still hesitating. I held out my palm and Quinn fished out another quarter for me.

"All right, you two," he said, "quit picking on my vocabulary and let's get back to the subject at hand."

I filled them in on Nick and Harry's excursion to Sacramento and their hope of getting some kind of clue from the construction permit that had been issued for Quinn's bathroom. I went on to explain about Rella's connections in D.C. and the chance that she might turn up something there.

"I've already scrutinized my copy of that permit," Quinn said. "I can't think how that could help, but I appreciate their efforts on my behalf." I didn't remind him that their efforts were primarily on *my* behalf. As far as I knew, I had not been ruled out as a suspect.

Varsha asked, "Aimee, what about the woman you mentioned? Rella, is it? If she manages to identify the person who did the work, what are the chances he can be found?"

I conceded that it was unlikely.

Quinn agreed. "It was a catch-22 for me. I wanted someone who would bend the rules to keep the passage a secret. Now, when I need the guy, he's nowhere to be found."

"You're sure he's the answer?" I asked. "You think he let it slip to someone about the passage? Maybe that's not what happened. Can you think of any other way it could have been discovered?"

"I've stayed awake nights trying to think of another way, but nothing comes to mind. I had three keys made. One for myself, one for Varsha, and one for Sanjay's predecessor. That one was returned to me. I keep one with me and the other as a backup in my home safe. I still have both of them." He nodded at Varsha. "I gave Varsha a key in case she needed an emergency exit if there was a catastrophic event at the hospital. She still has her key, so there's only one explanation. Someone else has a key."

"Maybe more than one someone else," I said. "Lowe was in there and so was his killer. That could mean two more keys. I heard a saying just the other day. 'If more than one person knows, it isn't a secret.' We don't know how many keys were made once the cat was out of the bag."

"Hell and damnation," Quinn said. "That's all I need. It's bad enough I had to tell the police about it. I hope their *need to know* policy is as secure as they claim."

Varsha and I both held out our palms while Quinn fished for more change.

I dropped two more quarters in my purse. "Do you know what the police are doing to track down other people who might know about the secret access?"

Quinn shook his head. "I'd like to think they're working on it, but now that Natasha Korba's stepfather is in custody, they seem to be concentrating on him. At least for the moment."

"Is Abel Gailworth back in Timbergate?" Varsha asked.

Quinn nodded. "He's back and in jail. Melissa's willing to press any charges the district attorney's office can come up with, and Hector Korba is loaded for bear. He has an army of lawyers already in place. He won't stop until he has custody of Natasha, and Gailworth is in prison. Gailworth can't afford bail or a lawyer, so he'll be assigned a public defender. Maybe that's already been done."

"So he's in jail for trying to flee the country with his family against his wife's wishes, but he hasn't been charged with Lowe's murder?" I wanted to be sure where things stood.

"That's what I've been told by Korba." Quinn folded his napkin and placed it on the table. "Apparently I'm still a suspect myself, since I'm getting scant information from Detective Kass about the status of the murder investigation."

I watched Quinn and Varsha leave Margie's together, chatting comfortably. They would make a striking couple, if that's where their relationship was headed. I wondered if Varsha shared my qualms about dating the boss. I turned my attention away from romance and quickly finished my bowl of Margie's Hoppin' John. Lukewarm, but still delicious.

BACK AT MY DESK, I wondered if Nick and Harry's excursion to the building permit office in Sacramento had turned up any new leads. Nick had said they would be home Friday night. They had promised to update me, but neither of them had checked in by phone or text. I envied them the opportunity to spend time at the jujitsu tournament with people from the other dojos in the region. I promised myself I would find a way to get on the mat more often as soon as my knee was healed.

The remains of Thursday afternoon slogged by as I labored over one of several grant proposals, in between filling requests for articles from online medical journals.

Necessary tasks, but hardly exciting. And no word from Nick or Harry. By quitting time I could hardly keep my eyes open.

I DROVE HOME through drizzling rain, tossed hay to the llamas, then raided my fridge for leftovers. The choices were dodgy. The cottage cheese failed my sniff test. The fresh salad mix was anything but fresh and the bread was turning green. I was out of cereal and milk, so I settled for a snack of pretzels dipped in honey mustard while I made a grocery list. With nothing better to do on a Thursday night, I decided to run errands. I filled my car with gas, shopped for groceries, and even did a load of laundry at Amah's.

Later I surfed channels, but nothing caught my eye, so I settled in with a new C. J. Box novel I'd borrowed from Amah and Jack. The drizzle had turned into light rainfall that sprinkled the roof over my head in a gently hypnotic pattern.

An hour and several chapters later, my cell phone rang. *Nick or Harry?* Neither. It was Rita Lowe.

"Aimee, I hope it isn't too late. I have a bit of information for you." I assured her that it wasn't too late and asked why she had called.

"Do you recall our conversation about my well-meaning friend who spotted Gavin and Sybil Snyder together at a medical conference in Sacramento a little more than a month ago?"

"Yes. We both wondered if she had reported that sighting to Sybil's husband, but you were reluctant to ask."

"Indeed. That's why I'm calling. I just got off the phone with her. Apparently she shares her nose for scandal with several cohorts. She was sure I'd be interested in a new snippet and felt compelled to deliver it to me before someone beat her to it." I heard the disdain in her voice.

"What did she say? Did Capshaw know about his wife and your husband?"

"Apparently so. I always imagine her circle of gossips standing around a cauldron and stirring rumors like the three witches in Macbeth. It seems one of them took it upon herself to 'put a bug in Capshaw's ear,' is how she put it."

"Did she say when this happened?"

"Oh, early on. At about the same time I was told. But there's more."

"Really?" I said. "What else did she say?"

"Sybil was seeing a second man on the side. Someone other than my husband."

Double, double toil and trouble. I was rapidly developing a soft spot for the well-meaning gossips of the world.

"Did she say who it was?" I flashed back on Sybil Snyder's phone conversation with Hector Korba, but I didn't want to feed his name to Rita.

"I'm afraid I didn't get that information. But my source, whom I shall call Witch Number One, is positive that *her* source, Witch Number Two, is reliable."

"Is there any way you can get the man's name?"

"Unlikely. Apparently Witch Number Two wasn't willing to go on record with that. Sorry."

"Don't apologize. If the word about this second man is out there, chances are we'll hear about him eventually."

"I hope it won't be too late," Rita said.

"What do you mean?"

"If Capshaw's jealousy led him to kill my husband, what's to stop him from doing the same thing if he finds out about Sybil Snyder's other lover?"

Her comment set my thoughts spinning. It hadn't occurred to me that Hector Korba's life might be in danger. If he were gone, who would see to the welfare of Natasha Korba and her mother? Rita and I agreed to stay in touch, especially if either of us could confirm the identity of the other man in Sybil Snyder's convoluted sex life.

THIRTY-THREE

"ANY WORD?" CLEO checked in by phone Friday morning at work. She was as anxious as I was to know if Nick and Harry had come up with any leads.

"Nothing from the guys, and nothing from Rella, but I did have an interesting call last night. Want to do lunch?" The doctors who served on medical staff committees steadfastly refused to meet on Friday, so it was the one day that Cleo was usually free at lunchtime.

"Sounds good. I'll drop by the library at noon. We can walk to Margie's together."

When Lola appeared for her morning shift at nine o'clock, she looked particularly perky. I wondered if her romance with Bernie Kluckert had something to do with the twinkle in her eye. Then I recalled how subdued Bernie had been the day before. Lola never hesitated to ask about my love life, but I stifled my impulse to ask about hers. I already had plenty to think about.

The morning was busy enough to pass quickly and keep me from obsessing about when I might hear from Nick and Harry, or when they would be home from Sacramento. I was replacing the toner cartridge in our copy machine when Lola approached.

"Miss Machado, may I have a word?"

"Of course, Lola. What is it?" I glanced at the wall clock. Eleven thirty. Ample time to hear Lola out before noon.

"I'm afraid it's rather personal. Nevertheless, I'd like your opinion." Her cheeks flushed, and I caught a faint scent of lilacs. "That is, unless I'm imposing. I don't want to make you uncomfortable."

I clicked the toner cartridge in place and invited Lola to sit with me in the library's reading alcove.

"Now, why don't you tell me what's on your mind and we'll take it from there?"

"I've been offered a proposition," she said. "It's rather sudden, but I'm considering accepting, yet I don't want to act rashly."

"What sort of proposition?" I hoped she wasn't going to leave her position in the library in favor of another department.

"An engagement, actually." Lola's lips pressed together in a shy smile. "Bernie has asked me to be his fiancée." Not what I was expecting, but I kept a straight face in spite of my surprise.

"Then you're planning to marry him?"

"Oh, no. Marriage at our age is far too complicated. We each have trusts leaving our assets to our grown children, and our individual incomes allow us to get by nicely without depending on each other. Bernie just felt I would be more comfortable with a formal acknowledgment of our commitment, so he suggested we be engaged until…well, until…you understand."

"Yes, I think so." *Until death do you part.* "But you and Bernie have been seeing each other for such a short time. Are you sure this commitment is what you want?"

"Bernie and I are not strangers to each other. His late wife and I were friends a number of years ago. She always spoke warmly of him and how thoughtful he was. And now that we're reacquainted, I'm finding him to be wonderful company. We enjoy many of the same things. And we don't have the luxury of a long future together. Bernie is almost ninety, you know. We want to share quality time while we can."

"It sounds as if you've given this a lot of thought. How do your children feel about it?"

"They're quite happy, actually. They've been hoping I would find a nice companion. They check up on anyone I date. They weren't too impressed with Oslo Swanson, but they know Bernie's a straight arrow and they like him."

I glanced at the time. Cleo would be stopping by any minute. "Lola, your practical approach to romance in the golden years makes a lot of sense. I think you and Bernie are going to have a lovely engagement."

"So do I, Miss Machado. I hope one day soon it will be your turn to wear an engagement ring." I caught the unspoken implication. *You're not getting any younger, either.*

Cleo entered the library, saving me from the need to respond. Lola wished us a good lunch and went on her way.

Cleo and I walked the short distance to Margie's Bean Pot, where we were greeted by the fragrant aroma of lentil soup with lamb sausage. We each filled a bowl at the self-serve bar and headed for our usual table in the back corner.

I quickly filled Cleo in on Rita Lowe's news that Sybil Snyder had been juggling two lovers while trying to keep her husband in the dark.

"No idea who the second man is?" Cleo said.

"Rita had no idea, but I still suspect it's Korba."

"Hmm. Gavin Lowe I could almost understand.

He was still kind of hot, in a middle-aged sort of way. But Korba? That would be like making love to a steam roller."

"There's no accounting for Sybil Snyder's taste," I said. "We can't be sure he's the other man, but if he is, Rita Lowe suggested he could be Capshaw's next victim."

"You're implying that Capshaw killed Lowe out of jealousy?"

"That's Rita's take. She thinks Snyder's other lover might be in Capshaw's sights."

"There's a flaw in that theory," Cleo said. "Capshaw can't be the killer. He was nowhere near TMC the night Lowe was shot."

"What?" I dropped my spoon and nearly spilled soup on my lap. "How do you know that?"

"The checking I've been doing has paid off. Capshaw volunteers at a free clinic on an Indian reservation two counties away. He volunteers there every Monday night. He was on duty the night Lowe was killed."

"Are you sure?"

"Trust me. I'm sure. He may not be great husband material, but I've heard that he's extremely dedicated when it comes to donating his time and medical skills. He's also been involved in Doctors Without Borders for several years."

"I suppose it's implausible to think he hired someone else to dispatch Gavin Lowe."

Cleo sighed. "Anything's possible, but I'm guessing the only thing Capshaw's guilty of is thinking his marriage to Sybil Snyder is worth salvaging."

"Then the only suspect with a motive that makes

sense is Abel Gailworth. I hope the police are following up on that angle."

"Sorry, but I got the latest from Quinn on that score just before I met you in the library."

"Really?" My left trapezius muscle seized up in a cramp. "Don't tell me Gailworth has an alibi."

"He has an alibi. A pretty good one."

"I suppose he was doing God's work in some homeless shelter that night." The cramp tightened, working its way up the back of my neck.

"Nope. He's still a sleaze. He was in San Francisco that night, but if he was doing God's work, he was trying to save the soul of a hooker with a heart of gold."

"Beautiful. Saved by debauchery. Did Quinn tell you about this, too?" The cramp reached the top of my head. *Ouch.*

"He did. It seems the police did a pretty thorough job of investigating the preacher man after he pulled his *let's flee the country* stunt with Melissa and Natasha."

"So Detective Kass is suddenly sharing that kind of information with Quinn? Why?"

"Because Gailworth's abduction case began at TMC. For now, Quinn's back in charge and not accused of any crime. As administrator, he has a right to be kept informed." Cleo smiled. "Looks like Kass is kind of stuck with that, but you can imagine he's not thrilled."

I put down my spoon and took a long sip of water. "Okay...so the police have eliminated Gailworth as a suspect, and we know Capshaw couldn't have done it, but we still have a few improbables to consider."

Cleo shrugged. "Like who?"

"Varsha knew about the secret passage. She had a key."

"Forget Varsha," Cleo said with a dismissive gesture. "You might as well accuse me."

"Okay, then. Sanjay?"

Cleo shook her head. "What motive?"

"I get the impression he'd like to have Quinn's job."

"Murder Lowe and frame Quinn? Risk death row in the hope of a promotion? Sanjay might be ambitious, but he isn't stupid."

"Then consider Rita Lowe's motive," I said. "Years of putting up with her husband's cheating. Maybe she reached a breaking point."

"You're going with the scorned woman theory?"

Her question spun me in another direction. "Possibly, but if not Rita, then let's apply that theory to someone else. If Macbeth's tale-telling witches are to be believed, Sybil Snyder and Lowe were lovers. Maybe *Snyder* was the woman scorned. What if Lowe had dumped her for a new flavor of the month? What if taking Korba as a lover on the rebound hadn't quelled her anger?"

Cleo looked skeptical. "It's a stretch to imagine Hector Korba as anyone's lover, even on the rebound."

"Well let's think about that."

"Ick." Cleo's nose wrinkled. "Why?"

"Not about his qualifications as a lover. About where he fits into this mystery. Remember, until we saw what was on Lowe's flash drive, we thought it was a given that Lowe would testify in Korba's favor at the custody hearing."

"But don't forget, Lowe's note showing that he was leaning in the other direction didn't surface until at least a week after his death."

"True. And when it did, the note still wasn't a slam

dunk for Natasha's parents. There were conditions attached."

Cleo nodded. "That's right. Korba would have used that to his advantage. I've known him a long time, Aimee. He's as cunning as a Mafia don and he's already demonstrated amazing patience and tenacity where Natasha's concerned. I don't see him blowing his chances by gunning down Lowe. He'd use other forms of persuasion."

"Could you see him killing Lowe in a jealous rage over Sybil Snyder?"

At that, Cleo laughed out loud. "Sorry, no. Not in a million years."

I sighed. "Then we're almost back to where we started. With Gailworth and Capshaw off the list, that leaves Quinn as the prime suspect."

Cleo gave me a somber look. "Not quite, Aimee. It leaves Quinn and you."

With that, the cramp dialed up another notch, but I managed to exit the restaurant without moaning in pain and making a scene.

LATER THAT AFTERNOON I was feeling much better, thanks to a stop in the ER and a prescription for muscle relaxers. My cell phone signaled an incoming text from Harry. He and Nick were leaving the dojo in Sacramento, stopping for a bite to eat, and then heading to the airport. They would be back in Timbergate at six o'clock. He ended with a brief comment: "Might have a lead."

Six o'clock. Two hours to wait for an explanation.

THIRTY-FOUR

FRIDAY EVENING NICK, Cleo, and I huddled with Harry in the dining room of his condo to compare notes over coffee and chocolate-dipped biscotti. Nick reported that he and Harry had copied the permit for Quinn's bathroom and forwarded it to Rella. While she was in D.C., she asked around, but came up with nothing.

Then, just as she arrived back in New York Friday morning to fly Buck Sawyer home, she heard from a former pilot buddy who had left the military and joined the Secret Service. Her buddy had done some checking on Quinn's contractor, whose name was on record as Bob Smith, owner of Portico Construction. According to the buddy, Bob Smith—not his real name—was no longer a boomer doing safe rooms and secret passageways. He was no longer, period. Ironically, the man who protected folks from home invasions and terrorists had choked to death in D.C. on a hot dog from a street vendor's cart.

"But you said we might have a lead." I fixed a look at Harry.

"I got that in a text from Rella this morning. She didn't have time to go into detail."

"Where is she?" Cleo asked. "Shouldn't she be here?"

"She's probably touching down at Timbergate Muni right about now." Nick checked his phone. "I was right. She and Buck are at the hangar."

Harry read aloud from his screen. "No word yet. Maybe tomorrow."

"That's a big fat disappointment," Cleo said. "I was hoping she had news that we could take to the police." She tapped Harry's phone. "You guys need to let us know the minute you hear anything useful from her. Then maybe we should all get together again tomorrow."

"Not going to happen," Nick said. "Tomorrow's Saturday. I'm flying Buck to weekend investment meetings in Portland. On the way I'm dropping Harry and Rella off at the airport in Redmond so they can do some skiing on Mt. Bachelor. We'll all be back home late Sunday afternoon."

"Can Rella call us from the ski resort if she hears anything?" I asked.

"If not, we'll make it work," Harry said. "We're staying overnight in Bend. We can check messages and call you from there when we get down from the slopes."

"That'll work. Cleo and I will be at the symphony tomorrow night, but I'll keep my phone on and set it to vibrate."

Since we had nothing further to discuss, Harry kicked us out, locked up, and headed off to catch up with Rella. Cleo went home to Sig, which left Nick and me walking together toward our cars in the condo's visitor-parking spaces.

Nick draped an arm over my shoulders. "I don't know about you, but biscotti and coffee isn't what I consider dinner. Want to go somewhere for a quick bite?"

I smiled. "All that sugar and caffeine will keep me awake if I don't counteract it with something. I'll race you to the nearest pizza."

He leaned in and planted a kiss on my temple. "You're on."

We pulled into the pizza place in what we agreed was a tie. The cheesy slices worked their soporific magic. Within twenty minutes, we were both yawning.

In the parking lot, Nick walked me to my car.

"If I weren't flying tomorrow, I'd try for another of your mind-blowing good night kisses, but I've barely recovered my powers of concentration since that last one three days ago. I hear we might run into a little weather tomorrow, so I need to be sharp."

"Then a hug would be safer for both of us," I said. "My kneecap is still pretty vulnerable."

Nick laughed. "A hug, then. But we'd better do it like porcupines. I've been taking a lot of cold showers lately."

What started as a platonic hug soon had us wrapped in each other's arms, bodies pressed together as if we were slow dancing to an evocative love song.

"Too bad we're in separate cars," Nick murmured. "I'd really like us to go home together."

I stepped back reluctantly. "Define *home*. I live in a barn and you live in Buck Sawyer's pool house."

"Good point. But I'll get my apartment back as soon as Rella's escrow closes. What about you? Do you have a timetable for moving out of the llama barn?"

"I'm afraid it won't be soon. I either pay down my school loans, or pay rent, but I can't do both." The conversation was drifting toward an unspoken question that hung between us. Would we ever be sharing a home again?

We agreed to call or text while Nick was in Oregon if we had any new developments to share in the Gavin Lowe murder case or Natasha's custody situation.

THIRTY-FIVE

I PASSED MOST of a quiet Saturday catching up on back issues of the Journal of the Medical Library Association. After a short nap and a quick bowl of soup, I showered and dressed in a straight black skirt and silver lamé blouse. I anchored my hair in an artfully messy do and chose small silver hoop earrings. Comfy black suede boots were the finishing touch to my symphony attire—they allowed me to walk comfortably without putting stress on my knee. Cleo, fashion maven that she was, would approve. I grabbed a sweater and headed to Timbergate.

The civic center crowd was pouring into the building when I arrived at quarter to seven. I found Cleo inside, milling around and exchanging greetings with her fellow symphony supporters. We made our way to our seats with five minutes to spare. Several members of the orchestra were already warming up on stage. Strains from woodwinds and violins wafted through the auditorium. I spotted Hector Korba running notes on his bass clarinet. Cleo's husband, Sig, worked the valves on his tuba.

"Look. Here it is." Cleo pointed to a page in her program. "Natasha *is* going to do a solo. Debussy's '*Clair De Lune.*'"

"Looks like they've saved her for last. I hope she won't be too tired."

"She'll be fine. It's only seven o'clock, and it's a short

program. Just a little over an hour, plus a ten-minute intermission. Sig said Korba asked the conductor to arrange it this way in order to get the judge's permission for Natasha to perform."

The lights in the auditorium flashed, signaling the last of the patrons in the lobby to take their seats. Cleo asked if I'd heard from Nick. I said the only message was a text sent from Portland saying the flight was uneventful and that Rella had not heard from her contacts.

"Sounds like she struck out." Cleo closed her program. "It isn't looking too good for Quinn, is it?"

"There's still time," I said. "Keep your fingers crossed." I checked my phone for new messages. There were none. I assured myself that it was set on vibrate.

The remaining musicians entered from the wings, settling into their positions. As a guest soloist, Natasha would remain backstage until it was time for her to perform. Next came the first violinist, who dipped a slight curtsy to acknowledge respectful applause for the concert mistress. She took her chair and signaled the principal oboe to play a pitch while the various sections of the orchestra tuned their instruments.

The audience hushed then clapped at the entrance of the conductor. He turned to face the orchestra, and with the raising of his baton, the concert began.

Fifteen minutes into the program, I felt my purse vibrate on my lap. The vibrating went unnoticed by Cleo on my left and the elderly man on my right, both enthralled by the music. Our center orchestra seats were smack in the middle of the third row. No way could I disrupt the auditorium by scooching past a dozen people, especially the bigger ones who would have to stand to let me by. To excuse my racing up the aisle and into the lobby, I'd have to be having a coronary. Still, the timing almost guaranteed the call was from Harry and Rella, who had planned to have dinner in Bend after their day of skiing. Harry had said they'd call from there if they had news.

I folded my sweater and placed it over my purse so no one would notice if the phone vibrated again. Five minutes later, it did. I nudged Cleo with my elbow. She turned to me, frowning at my breach of etiquette. I pointed to my purse. She shook her head and shrugged. I mouthed, *phone,* and the light dawned. Her eyes widened. She illuminated the dial on her watch. Another ten minutes until intermission. While we sat through Chopin, Debussy, and Liszt, my phone vibrated twice more. Finally the conductor turned and bowed to enthusiastic applause, ending the first half of the program.

After inching up the aisle and into the lobby, Cleo and I stepped outside under the shelter of the civic center's covered entryway. One message was from Harry. The last three were from Nick. I read the first message. *Korba signed p.o. for piano hinge call me.* I showed it to Cleo.

"Any idea what this means?"

"No, but his granddaughter plays piano, so I assume he has a piano and that it has hinges."

I read through the messages from Nick. They all said the same thing. *Call me.*

I punched in Harry's cell number first, just as the warning bell sounded from inside the lobby. I followed Cleo back inside, where the crowd was filing back into the auditorium.

"Is he answering?" Cleo fanned herself with her program.

"No. Damn. I can't get through."

"Did you try Nick?"

I was punching in his number as she asked. He answered immediately.

"Did you get Harry's message?"

"Yes, but I didn't understand it. I tried to call back and couldn't reach him. What's this about Korba ordering a piano hinge?"

"Damn, Harry can explain it better, but there's a snowstorm screwing up cell service and land lines in Bend. The roads are closed so he and Rella couldn't drive down the mountain to their hotel. He was afraid you wouldn't call back until after the concert, so he called me from the ski lodge up on Mt. Bachelor. I got the crux of his call before we lost our connection."

"What did he say?"

"Just before the storm hit, Rella finally heard from her source. It turns out the contractor had an employee working with him. He needed something called a piano hinge in order to install the false door in Quinn's bathroom and went to Varsha to get a signature on a rush purchase order. I guess it was pricy, and the guy wanted to make sure it was authorized so it wouldn't come out of his own paycheck. Quinn was out for a few days, and Varsha assumed it was something needed for the bathroom job, so she referred the request to the accounting department. Someone there forwarded it to Hector Korba for a signature."

"So Quinn and Varsha never knew Korba signed the purchase order, but what's that got to do… Oh, I get it. You think Korba knew something unusual was being installed in the bathroom because of that hinge?"

"That's what Harry thought. That makes it likely that

Korba knew there was more to the job than installing a bathroom. From what you've said, he seems like the kind of guy who might get curious. If I hear anything else, I'll be in touch."

The final bell rang in the lobby. The warning lights flashed. We needed to get to our seats or we'd miss the second half of the program.

"Nick, I have to go."

"Wait. Is Korba performing?"

"Yes. And Natasha has the final number on the program. Her piano solo."

"Don't tangle with Korba. We don't know if this means anything, but you and Cleo need to keep your distance, just in case."

"Okay, we won't let on if we come across him."

"Is the little girl's mother there?"

"If she is, she's backstage. We haven't spotted her in the audience."

"Call me back as soon as that concert ends. And steer clear of Korba."

I filled Cleo in as we hurried back into the auditorium. Everyone in our row was already seated, so we made a series of awkward apologies as we scooted to our mid-row seats.

I couldn't keep my eyes off Korba during the remainder of the program. Did he know about the secret passageway to Quinn's office? On the last day of his life, Lowe had mouthed off about going to Korba to get Quinn and me fired. If he did, had the subject of Natasha's custody come up? Was it a case of *you scratch my back and I'll scratch yours*? But Quinn and I weren't fired and Lowe had not sided with Korba in the custody case. What had taken place during that meeting? Or had it even happened?

Puzzling questions and conflicting thoughts about Korba kept me distracted throughout the remainder of the symphony until it came time for Natasha's solo performance of Debussy's *Clair De Lune*, the final piece on the program. The conductor announced her as guest artist of the evening but did not mention the relationship between Natasha and Hector Korba. I noticed Korba's frown and suspected that he felt slighted by the omission.

Natasha made her entrance in a pink satin dress decorated with lace and ribbons. It shimmered in the glow of a spotlight. Her blond curls were tied back with a matching pink ribbon. She walked to center stage, executed a solemn but graceful curtsy, and then walked to the baby grand and took her place.

I glanced at Korba throughout Natasha's performance. He sat there beaming, then wiping his eyes several times, obviously overcome with pride and love. The sight of him was at odds with Nick's warnings about Korba as a suspect in Lowe's death. Thinking him capable of murder seemed completely out of the question.

Natasha played her piece elegantly, with a sensitivity beyond her years. Her little fingers seemed to caress the keyboard with a mystical quality, evoking tender images of lovers embracing in a flowering garden on a still, moonlit evening. As the last note died away, the audience erupted in a standing ovation. When the conductor motioned for her to take a bow, Korba left his chair and walked to her side to take her hand and share her spotlight. Cleo glanced at me with raised eyebrows. I wondered if that moment was rehearsed, or whether

Korba was unable to resist the urge to lay claim to his granddaughter in her moment of triumph.

Natasha exited the stage and Korba returned to his chair. Although the fervent applause was for the soloist, which would usually result in an encore from her, the orchestra would finish out the evening because of Natasha's still delicate health.

Seeing Korba close his lips around the mouthpiece of his bass clarinet, I wondered if he had been asked to volunteer a sample of his DNA. I recalled being in the greenroom the week before when he discarded his reed into a wastebasket. I knew that any evidence I collected could not be used to convict Korba, but it could be used to compare his DNA with whatever the police had taken from Lowe's body. Based on that comparison, Detective Kass might be motivated to ask Korba to volunteer a cheek swab.

Nick had said to steer clear of Korba, but picking up a discarded reed, once the man had left the greenroom, was virtually risk-free.

THIRTY-SIX

"Want to come backstage with me?" Cleo asked.

"Definitely." I told Cleo what I had in mind as we made our way to the greenroom.

Sig was packing his tuba into its case while he and the other musicians chatted among themselves in easy camaraderie. I caught a glimpse of Natasha leaving with her mother and her temporary guardian from CPS. I noticed Korba watching them go from where he sat, off to himself. He looked pensive, then seemed to mentally shake himself and began tending to his instrument. Would he discard his reed this time? And if he did, would it end up in a wastebasket, indistinguishable from a dozen others?

While feigning interest in the chat involving Cleo, Sig, and other nearby members of the orchestra, I kept my eye on Korba, watching as he broke down his instrument. Just as he detached the reed from the mouthpiece, Dr. Leroy Droz approached him. Korba set the mouthpiece and reed on a small table next to his chair. Droz was the pianist who had played Natasha's composition at the symphony's performance the previous week. I recalled Korba asking him for a curbside consult about some kind of rash on his neck. Curious, I strained to hear their conversation.

"How's that ointment working, Hector?"

"Good. The rash is almost gone." Korba reached his

hand up to his neck in a gesture I'd noticed several times before.

"Well, continue with it for another week, just to be sure. Since you don't remember how you got the scratch, we want to make sure we have the problem under control. Cellulitis can become worrisome if it gets away from us."

Korba uttered a clipped reply. "Thank you, Leroy." He looked uncomfortable with the topic, and I thought I knew why.

Cellulitis can begin with something as simple as a fingernail scratch. Connecting the dots, I knew that forensic techs bagged the hands of murder victims to keep them from being contaminated before their fingernails could be examined for evidence. For a breathless moment, I imagined a scene in Quinn's office: Lowe and Korba in a physical altercation that resulted in Korba's neck being scratched by Lowe's fingernails. Were Sybil Snyder's secret lovers having it out? Coming to blows over a woman? That might explain part of it, but why would they be in Quinn's office? And how would one of them end up being fatally shot?

Dr. Droz went on his way, along with most of the musicians. Sig and Cleo were almost ready to leave. Cleo knew what I was up to, but she tossed me a glance that told me she couldn't stall much longer. I had no excuse for staying in the greenroom once they were gone. Did I dare approach Korba and try to sneak away with the reed? Nick's warning held me back. *Steer clear of Korba*.

I watched Korba pack away his bass clarinet, seemingly distracted and acting on autopilot. The mouthpiece and reed were still on the table next to him. *Think, think*. I hadn't seen any of the other musicians toss reeds in the wastebasket near Korba, but the only way to be sure was to take a look. To get close enough, I decided to chance saying a polite *Hello*. It was the courteous thing to do, since Korba and I were colleagues in the broad sense of the word.

I closed the few feet between us, glancing at the wastebasket as I reached Korba. Candy wrappers and makeup sponges, crumpled facial tissues, but no reeds. Korba reached toward the table, picked up his mouthpiece and placed it in his instrument case. While his back was turned, I scooped the reed off the table into the wastebasket. As he closed his case, he turned back to glance at the table top. A slight frown crossed his face. Then he noticed me.

"Miss Machado, did you enjoy the program?"

"Very much. I wanted to tell you how happy I am to see Natasha playing again. Her performance tonight was beautiful."

"Of course." He stood and lifted his instrument case, apparently forgetting about the reed. "She will go on to great things. It's in her blood." He nodded toward Cleo and Sig, saying "Good evening" on his way out of the greenroom. As soon as the door closed behind him, I scrambled to pick the reed out of the wastebasket, holding it by its edges as I wrapped it in a tissue.

"Got it," I said. "Let's go."

We made our way to the stage door exit, the last people to leave except for the auditorium staff, who were still inside cleaning up and handling other details that needed post-performance attention. I parted company with Cleo and Sig in the parking lot. They had been able to park close to the building, but my car was on the far end of the large and nearly vacant lot. The lighting had already dimmed, apparently in energy-saving mode. I hadn't been able to park directly under a light standard, but I managed to spot the dark outline of my old Buick in the distance.

I hovered near the building exit for a moment to check my phone for messages. One text from Nick, nothing from Harry. I read Nick's message:

Concert over? Pls ck in. No contact with Harry. Home tomorrow 5 pm weather permitting

I texted back, saying the concert was over and I was heading home. The deserted parking lot brought to mind my purse snatcher. I wouldn't let that happen again. Rain began to fall as I crossed the asphalt. I picked up my pace, but kept it at a brisk walk, keys in my hand, ready to use as a weapon.

I had almost reached my car when I heard the roar of a motorcycle engine. *Not again.* I ran the last few feet, glancing at my tires, making sure the air pressure looked normal. I slid in, locked my doors and started my engine. The motorcycle passed by my car on the driver's side but kept going. In black leather and a helmet, the rider was unrecognizable, but the body looked masculine. He kept going, exiting the parking lot and heading for the street. Apparently, he had nothing to do with me. I turned out of the parking lot, and in minutes I was on the highway, headed home.

Then my cell phone rang. I glanced at the screen. The caller was Sybil Snyder. Odd…why would she be calling me at ten o'clock at night? I pulled off at the next exit and wound my way back to a well-lit street where I could park in front of a Starbuck's. I opted for caution

in spite of feeling silly about my over-the-top reaction
to the motorcycle back at the civic center. I couldn't
freak out every time one appeared. As if to prove my
point, another motorcycle pulled in behind me at Star-
bucks. The rider walked inside, focused on his phone.
I went in and read Snyder's text. Urgent meet me TMC
re Natasha STAT.

That was too compelling to ignore. I texted back:
Where?

3rd floor visitors' lounge.

Pre- and post-op rooms were on the third floor. Hin-
dered by the sudden onset of heavy rain and gusty wind,
I drove to TMC. I was alarmed for Natasha. How could
she have looked so healthy just an hour ago and now be
back in the hospital? And why would Sybil Snyder be
calling me?

I was a block away from the hospital when I noticed
a light in my rearview mirror. At first I thought it was a
car with a missing headlight, but when I slowed to turn
in, a motorcycle shot past me and continued on its way,
spraying rainwater in its wake. Three of them in one
night tested my tolerance for coincidence, but I hadn't
been mugged and I still had my fanny pack. I parked
and shot off a quick text to Cleo, alerting her to what
was going on with Dr. Snyder. I said I'd fill her in ASAP.

Chilling rain pelted me, soaking my sweater as I hurried from the parking lot to the main entrance. Inside,
I shed the sweater, folding it over my arm as I rode the
elevator to the third floor.

The visitors' lounge was located near the center of
the main corridor. I found Sybil Snyder there, perched

on the edge of a faux leather club chair that had seen better days. When I walked in, she looked up from the screen on her smartphone.

"Aimee, thank you for coming."

"What is it, Dr. Snyder? Is Natasha all right? Has she been admitted?"

"Oh, no. I'm sorry if I worried you. She's fine."

"Then where is she? Why is she here?"

Snyder slipped her phone into the back pocket of her formfitting designer jeans. "I'm afraid my message wasn't clear. Natasha isn't here. She's with her CPS guardian. I asked to meet with you because I believe we very much need to talk about her future."

"But why me? I'm sure there are people more qualified to help sort that out. The judge who presided over the recent custody hearing is still withholding a final opinion, isn't he?"

"There's more to this situation than he knows. Come with me. There's something I want to show you."

Leading me down the deserted corridor to the east end of the third floor, she turned into the recessed alcove with the locked door marked by a hazard warning—the door that gave access to the hidden staircase leading to Quinn's office on the fourth floor. I followed her into the alcove. My breath caught for a moment when Snyder slipped her hand into the front pocket of her jeans and took out a single key. She fitted it into the lock, pushed the door open, and stepped inside. She turned to where I stood immobilized by surprise and indecision.

"Hurry, come with me," she whispered. "I know who killed Gavin Lowe."

THIRTY-SEVEN

WHAT WAS GOING ON? Why did Sybil Snyder have a key to the secret staircase?

"Step inside, please," she urged. "I have to shut this door before someone sees us."

I hesitated, calculating the odds. Would I be taking a risk to follow her? She carried no purse, wore no coat. There was no room in the pockets of her jeans for a gun or any other weapon with more bulk than her ultra-slim cell phone. There was no place on her person to hide a weapon, and I had no doubt I could easily take her down if she attacked me hand to hand. On the plus side, she wanted to tell me who had killed Gavin Lowe—something I desperately wanted to know.

I asked again. "Why me?"

"You're the only person I'm sure I can trust with the truth."

The risk seemed worth the reward. I stepped inside. She locked the door and we were pitched into darkness. Before I could reach in my fanny pack for my penlight, the space lit up in a pale blue glow just bright enough for us to maneuver up the spiral staircase. A motion sensor light, no doubt.

"Follow me," she said.

We wound our way up the stairs, and when we reached the top, she activated the mechanism that opened the false wall into Quinn's bathroom. We went through into his dark office, where Sybil switched on a single small lamp on his desk.

"Let's sit over here," she said, walking across the dimly lit room to a table flanked by straight chairs. I followed and sat across from her.

"Dr. Snyder, please explain yourself. Why is it necessary for us to talk in here? And how do you know we won't be interrupted? Suppose Jared Quinn has reason to be called in tonight?"

"I doubt that," she said. "I've been led to believe he's out of town. A funeral, I think."

"Then who's on duty in case of emergency?"

"Apparently Sanjay D'Costa is acting as backup."

"Really? Then home office must be easing up on him. But how do you know?"

"One of the charge nurses mentioned it as I was doing rounds."

An adrenaline rush sent numbness coursing across my shoulders. Impatient for her to get to the point, I said, "Dr. Snyder, if you know who killed Dr. Lowe, and you feel it's important to explain yourself to me, please get on with it."

In the shadowy room, I couldn't read her expression, but her body language told me she was struggling for control. She stopped wringing her hands long enough to run them through her hair.

With a shudder, she began, "First, I brought you here so you would believe me when I explained the whole story. How else could I convince you of something as unusual as a secret staircase?"

How else, indeed? I didn't let on that I already knew about it.

"A good point," I said. "But how do *you* happen to know about it?"

"I learned of it from a man I've been meeting here." I waited for her to say his name, but she didn't offer it.

"Was it Jared Quinn?" I asked, although I was almost certain it wasn't.

Snyder looked up, startled. "No, he has no idea that we…that I know."

"Who, then? Gavin Lowe?"

"No, Gavin didn't know until I had a key made for him."

"I'm sorry, Dr. Snyder, but let me be sure I understand. Were you meeting both Gavin Lowe and this other man in Quinn's office?"

"Don't judge me without knowing what my life is like." Snyder crossed her arms, hugging herself, her head bowed—a posture out of character for the woman I thought I knew. She looked up at me. "Take my advice, Miss Machado: never marry for the wrong reason. I found it difficult to be unmarried and lonely, but to be *married* and lonely was far worse. It soon became unbearable."

I was trying not to panic. "I'm in no position to judge you, but please, tell me what you want from me. I'll go with you to the police. If you know how Dr. Lowe was killed, that's where you need to tell your story." I was beginning to wonder if she was about to confess that she killed Lowe herself.

"I can't tell the police that I witnessed the murder," she said. "I wasn't in this room when it happened, but I have reason to know who *was* here. Once that reason comes out, my marriage will shatter, and I'll be dragged through hell."

"But you must be prepared for that. Otherwise, why are you willing to tell me?"

"I hoped you could use the information somehow, without my having to reveal my part in it."

I didn't want to tell her how unlikely that was. *Absolutely impossible.* "Why don't you finish your story? Then we'll decide what we can do. Maybe you should start by telling me about the other man you were seeing? The one who gave you a key."

A shiver ran through her. When it passed, she spoke barely above a whisper, "It was Hector Korba. That's why I brought you here. We mustn't let him gain custody of Natasha."

Snyder went on to tell me she and Korba had begun their affair almost a year earlier. That was when he told her about the secret passageway to Quinn's office. He told her he had known about it from the time it was constructed, but kept it to himself.

Back then he took the opportunity, the first time Quinn was out of town on business, to have a key made for himself. Because Korba was chairman of the board, the locksmith did not question the need for any further authorization before making the extra key to the hazard door. Korba never let on to Quinn that he knew about the passageway.

"But why did he want a key?"

"You know the man. His life is about power and control. He enjoyed being in on Quinn's secret. He thought it might come in handy someday, and it did."

When her flirtation with Korba became an affair, he had a duplicate key made for her. The empty office—with its secret entrance, private bathroom, and comfy couch—became an ideal place for late-night trysts. No sneaking off to motels or worrying about being spotted in places she would have to explain to her husband. As far as Glen Capshaw knew, his wife was either in meetings or tending to sick hospital patients.

"That doesn't explain how Gavin Lowe got in here the night he was shot," I said.

"That's the rest of the story." She was interrupted when a Life Support Unit siren announced its arrival at the emergency room entrance four floors below. Snyder stood and walked to the window, where windblown raindrops peppered the glass. She looked down, then turned back to me. "God. I can't believe what kind of fool I've been."

"Dr. Snyder, are you sure you want to go on with this? Maybe we should go to the police now. You should be talking to them instead of me."

"I suppose you're right, but first, I need to talk this through, see if it makes sense. Then we'll see."

My nerves were ragged, but I imagined hers were far worse, so I feigned calmness, hoping she would get to the heart of the matter quickly.

"You were saying there's more to your story. About how Dr. Lowe came to be in here the night he died?"

Snyder came back to the table with a gait like a sleepwalker's and sat across from me.

"Hector Korba was a surprise as a lover," she said. "Gentle, tender, and generous—everything my husband was not. At first I enjoyed our times together, although they weren't often. There was always some risk of our being found out by Quinn." She shook her head. "I suppose that risk added to the excitement, but we were careful not to leave any sign that we'd been here. Quinn never caught on."

"What about your husband?" I was reluctant to tell her that Glen Capshaw had questioned me about Sybil's bogus meetings. *Not yet.*

"Glen has always been jealous and suspicious, long before he had any reason to be. I suspect that's a large part of what drove me away from him. He complained when any man looked at me or spoke to me. He claimed I should be flattered by his jealousy, but instead, I was made to feel guilty for something I hadn't done. It's almost impossible to prove a negative."

"That sounds terrible. Did you try to work it out, maybe with counseling?"

Sybil laughed softly. "Tell a physician with a colossal ego that he needs counseling? No, and asking for a divorce seemed out of the question. Even before I began the affair with Korba, Glen would have accused me of adultery. We were partners in our medical practice. I knew Glen's vindictiveness was too terrible to contemplate. He would have destroyed both of us financially and professionally in order to punish me for wanting out of our marriage."

Remembering Capshaw's vitriolic rant in the stairwell, I could easily believe Dr. Snyder's fears on that issue.

"Dr. Snyder, tell me about Gavin Lowe. That's why you brought me here, isn't it? How is his death related to Natasha? I don't see the connection with what you've said so far." I glanced at Quinn's ornate wall clock, amazed that only twenty minutes had passed; it seemed we had been there for hours.

"I'll try to make the rest brief," Snyder said. "A few months ago, Hector became more demanding, more possessive. He wanted us to marry. He began pressuring me to ask Glen for a divorce. I knew what was behind it. Hector wanted custody of Natasha. He believed being married would increase his chances. I tried to tell him what hell it would be to divorce Glen, but he continued to insist until I finally broke off our affair. He demanded that I return my key to the passageway. I gave it back to him, but he didn't know I'd had a spare made. I'm compulsive about that sort of thing. I tend to have duplicates of everything."

Even lovers, I thought.

"Is that when you started seeing Gavin Lowe?"

"Gavin and I were at a conference in Sacramento just over a month ago. We went for drinks one evening, and one thing led to another. After that, I had a key to this room made for him. Since Hector and I were no longer seeing each other, I foolishly decided I could meet Gavin here. We thought we were being discreet, but somehow his wife and my husband both found out about our affair."

I knew how. *Macbeth's witches.*

"Then what happened?" I asked.

"The first time we met here there was no problem. The second time was the night he was killed. I had been called to respond to an emergency with a patient, so I texted Gavin that I probably wouldn't be able to meet him. That was around nine o'clock. He texted back that he would wait."

"So he was up here alone, waiting for you to show up?"

"Yes. I managed to take care of the emergency by ten thirty or so. I checked my messages and saw that Gavin was still waiting for me. I hurried to the hazard door on the third floor. No one was around so I slipped inside and started up the staircase. Halfway up, I heard voices. Two men arguing." Snyder doubled over, clutching her stomach. "God help me… I froze, terrified. At first I thought Glen had somehow found his way here to confront Gavin and me, even though it seemed impossible."

"Couldn't you make out the voices?"

"After a moment, I recognized them—Gavin and Hector. It was a bad dream. I didn't know whether to join them and try to reason with Hector, or to run away."

"I understand why Lowe was in here that night. He was waiting for you. But why Korba?"

"An embarrassing miscalculation on my part. Hector had been visiting Natasha and someone told him I had just checked on her. Apparently, he had the notion that he could persuade me to meet him here in Quinn's office. Perhaps to reconcile. I imagine he was surprised to find Gavin already here waiting for me."

"And Lowe must have been surprised when Hector showed up instead of you. Was their argument about you?"

"Not at first." She hesitated for a moment, remembering. "Their dispute was about how Gavin would testify at the custody hearing. It turned out Gavin wasn't going to offer the testimony Hector expected from him. Hector wanted sole legal and physical custody. I heard Gavin say that he believed Natasha's mother deserved another chance. That he intended to make that recommendation in Natasha's medical record."

I remembered the day I'd found the flash drive in Lowe's briefcase. Korba had been standing there when I put it in my purse. That was the day my purse was snatched in the grocery store parking lot. *By a man on a motorcycle. Had the same man just followed me here?*

"So Hector knew Lowe's intentions right from the start?"

"Yes, and when he saw you put that flash drive in your purse, he suspected it might contain Lowe's notes documenting his decision about Natasha's custody. He didn't want that to end up in Natasha's medical record."

Panic had begun to creep into my voice. Were we in danger in this place? I began to speak more rapidly. "Is that why my purse was snatched that night? In the hope that I hadn't looked at the contents of the flash drive?"

"Of course. Hector hired a thug to do that bit of dirty work. He couldn't count on you returning the flash drive to Rita Lowe without checking its contents. But as we now know, it was too late. Both Hector and the Gailworths had already seen it before I had it removed from Natasha's chart. As the primary physician, I was the one to decide whether to disregard Lowe's recommendation and make my own."

"Then why snatch the flash drive with Lowe's notes?" I was halfway out of my seat, listening for danger, certain that Hector's hired thug had followed me to the hospital and then reported my whereabouts to his boss.

"Hector feared those notes would be interpreted as a motive for murder. He had hoped to remove all trace of them," Snyder said.

She didn't share my sense of urgency, of course. I was standing now. Korba would enter through the passage, so as to remain undetected by the cameras. That meant we should flee through the reception area and out the front door, but that would set off a motion-sensor alarm, when what we wanted was to escape unnoticed. Did we risk leaving through the secret passage?

"But I had seen the notes," I continued. "So had Cleo and the director of the Health Information Office."

"That might be contested as hearsay, but the flash drive was tangible. It couldn't be easily refuted."

"This isn't helping me to understand why Dr. Lowe was killed. Surely not over the custody battle."

Front door or secret passage?

"Of course not," Snyder said. "That could have been managed. But you must recall that Gavin had recently become quick to anger. When he realized Hector and I had been lovers, he vowed that he would never under any circumstances recommend that Hector have custody of Natasha. He became insulting, accusing Hector of using me as a tool in his custody fight."

That sounded right to me, but I didn't say so. I thought I could see where this was going. But now my panic had taken a new turn. Perhaps Korba wasn't my main worry at this moment.

"Dr. Snyder, did either of them know Quinn kept a gun in his office?"

Snyder glanced toward the desk. "I suppose both of them knew it was in that unlocked drawer. Waiting around in this office, anyone would be tempted to do a bit of exploring."

A chill went through me. How did she know the gun was kept in his desk drawer? Unlocked?

Sucker. She had almost convinced me that Hector was the killer and that he had acted alone. *This wasn't the time to show my hand.*

"Dr. Snyder, it sounds as if the two men quarreled, one of them took the gun out of Quinn's desk and during the scuffle, it went off, killing Gavin Lowe. Is that what you think happened?"

Snyder dropped her head into her hands. "Yes, but I wasn't here in the room—I only heard it while I stood on the staircase just outside the false wall. I *believe* that's what happened."

"Why didn't you go to the police?" There was more to this story than she was telling, and I couldn't figure out how to leave safely until I'd gotten to the bottom of it. I'd let her keep talking just a moment longer.

"I was afraid of Hector. I didn't want him to know I'd overheard his quarrel with Gavin. If I accused him of murder and the police decided not to arrest him, he would have come after me. I didn't know what to do, so I pretended I still cared for him and that the fling with Gavin was a mistake. He went along with that, because Natasha was still critical and in the PICU. Without Gavin to supervise her care, Hector needed me to take over."

I tried again to persuade her, urgency in my voice. "Then that's what you need to tell the police. We should go. Right now." If I could just get her to the police station, the truth of her story could be sorted out there.

"Yes, we need to go." She rose and walked toward the bathroom. I followed her, turning off the desk lamp on the way. When she stepped inside the bathroom, I heard her gasp.

"Quite a yarn you've spun, my darling. Some of it is even true." It was the unmistakable voice of Hector Korba. I felt a thud in my chest—my heart trying to leap out of my ribcage.

Snyder backed up as Korba advanced on her. "Now let's see if I can convince Miss Machado to believe my version." He turned on the desk lamp and motioned toward the table and chairs. "Please ladies, let's sit and chat."

THIRTY-EIGHT

IT SEEMED I was destined to spend all night in Quinn's office, perhaps ending my life there. Snyder and Korba might not be on the same page, but they had more in common with each other than either of them had with me. It also was clear that both of them were involved in Gavin Lowe's death.

I saw no sign of a weapon in Korba's hands, but he was wearing a sport jacket with pockets that would easily accommodate a variety of handguns. I had a fanny pack holding nothing but car keys, my pen light, and my phone. I had a gimpy knee and I was wearing a long, straight skirt. Not ideal for using my legs in a combat situation. At least my boots had low heels. It wasn't much, but it was something. I weighed my options while I waited to see where Korba was going with his monologue. He spoke as if he were presiding over a board meeting.

"I shall assume that I have the floor, and I will make this brief." His left hand rested on the table. I was acutely aware that his right hand was out of sight. "Before we begin, I will ask that you turn off your phones and place them on the table."

We both complied. Korba nodded in my direction. "Miss Machado, I regret that you have been dragged into this unfortunate situation; however, since you are here, you are entitled to the whole truth. Then we must decide how to proceed." I didn't like the sound of that.

Korba began his rebuttal. "I overheard Dr. Snyder's creative version of the events that led to Gavin Lowe's death, but I must correct several important details, the first being that she *was* present in this room when he was shot."

I looked at Sybil for her reaction. She sat rigid and silent, her hands folded on the table, while Hector continued.

"It is significant that she failed to mention that she alone knew about the gun in Quinn's drawer. It seems she had been unable to resist the temptation to 'explore,' as she put it."

"That's not true. They both knew it was there." Snyder's voice vibrated with tension.

Korba held up a finger. "Please, Sybil, I still have the floor. Let me finish." He turned to me, his eyes hooded, his large face a study in shadows. "It was Sybil who upped the ante by producing the gun. Until then, Gavin and I were merely venting our anger."

In spite of my apprehension, I raised my hand. "I have a question."

"Yes, of course," he said.

"How did you know I came here after the concert? Did you have me followed?"

"Of course. As soon I realized how meddlesome you are, I began keeping track of you."

"The man on the motorcycle, right?"

Korba waved my question away. "Never mind about that." Easy for him to say. It wasn't his kneecap that was fractured.

"Then tell me this," I said. "Is it true that you wanted

Dr. Snyder to file for a divorce so you and she could marry and eventually obtain custody of Natasha?"

"It's true that we had discussed that arrangement, but in fact, it was Sybil's idea. She was in a childless and loveless marriage. She saw me as her escape from that situation. I confess I would have gone along with it gladly, but she muddied the water by sleeping with the one man who could stand in the way of our plan."

Sybil remained mute. He patted her folded hands. "You see, dear, unlike your husband, I do not suffer from the tyranny of a jealous nature. But I was severely disappointed with your lapse in judgment. Any man but Lowe, my dear."

I broke in, "So you would have gone on with the plan if Lowe had been willing to help you gain custody of Natasha?"

"Of course. Natasha is my blood and my destiny. Music is *her* destiny. She can fulfill that destiny only if I am her guardian and mentor." Pity Natasha if Korba gained complete control of her life. Snyder glanced at me. Whose side was I on? Which one of them did I believe? *Neither.*

"How did Dr. Lowe end up being shot?"

Hector bared his teeth in a ghastly smile. He turned to Snyder. "Why don't you answer Miss Machado, my dear?"

"He was strangling you, Hector. I had no choice." She turned to me. "You saw Gavin at the meeting that morning, how he attacked Jared Quinn. This was worse. He swore he would not testify on Hector's behalf. In return, Hector threatened to destroy Gavin, to see that he lost his medical license. Gavin became irate and jumped Hector, tightening his hands around his neck. He was rabid, like a madman. I had to do something or Hector would have been killed."

Mother of God. Snyder and Korba's tangle of conflicting stories and motives made it impossible to sort out the truth. Now they both had admitted being involved in Lowe's death, but they were claiming…what? Justifiable homicide? I could pretend that I believed them, but if I failed, what were the odds I would survive? At that point I simply wanted to get out of there alive.

Could I distract both of them just long enough to take Korba down? Or was Snyder the more dangerous foe? As I grappled with possible plans of attack, the fire alarm suddenly burst out in deafening shrieks, causing both Korba and Snyder to cup their hands over their ears.

Seizing the opportunity, I gave the table a mighty shove, catching Korba at gut level and knocking him over backward. While he floundered, I upturned the table and slammed it down on top of him. The crack I heard had to be the wooden tabletop connecting with his skull.

Snyder jumped up and tried to bolt, but I grabbed the swanky infinity scarf that was wound in two unbroken circles around her neck and gave it a merciless jerk. She landed on her butt.

Like a rodeo calf roper, I used her scarf to bind her hands and feet together behind her back while she screamed bloody murder. I lifted the table off Korba and knelt down to check on him. His face was a mess and he was out cold, but his pulse and respirations were strong.

Snyder writhed and swore, demanding to be untied. "There's a fire, you idiot! We need to get out of here."

Just as I realized there might actually be a real fire in the hospital, the door between Quinn's office and Varsha's reception area opened. Cleo stepped into the room and took in the scene.

"Holy freakin' cannoli, Machado, what have you done?"

Seconds later Sanjay stepped in behind her. His eyes went wide when he spotted Korba on the floor, unconscious and bloody.

"Miss Machado, this is most distressing. I hereby place you on suspension pending an investigation into this…this…calamity."

"Never mind that," I said. "Help me get them out of here. Is the fire on this floor?"

"No fire," Cleo said. "When you wouldn't answer your phone, I came looking for you. I sneaked into Varsha's reception area, and when I overheard what was going on, I pulled the alarm to distract these two and give you a chance to do your Wonder Woman thing."

"She wisely called me in to assist," Sanjay said. "I have summoned the police. They should be arriving shortly."

While we waited, Korba's cell phone began vibrating on the floor near his hand. I picked it up and read the message he had just received. It was from Natasha.

Goodnight Pappo I love you

THIRTY-NINE

AFTER A TWO-HOUR interview with Detective Kass at the police station, I was finally turned loose. It was around midnight. Hector Korba was in TMC's emergency room under police guard, being observed for signs of a concussion. Sybil Snyder was still being questioned by the police.

Cleo had been interviewed too, but her story took less time. She was waiting for me in the TPD lobby with Sig at her side.

They invited me to their condo, where Sig served hot tea and banana bread while Cleo filled me in on the details that led her to come to my rescue. She had started to worry when she hadn't heard from me more than an hour after I'd texted her about my meeting with Dr. Snyder. She called Nick in Portland, but he hadn't heard from me, either. He insisted she get someone to check on me, suggesting Jared Quinn. But Quinn was out of town.

As far as Cleo knew, I was still at the hospital, meeting with Dr. Snyder. She didn't want to worry Sig, so she told him she'd been called in to process a visiting doctor's temporary privileges. Too smart to walk into trouble alone, she called Sanjay, telling him a situation at the hospital required his intervention.

"You weren't in the library," Cleo said, "or in the doctors' lounge, so I asked at every nurses' station until finally someone remembered seeing you on the third floor with Dr. Snyder."

"That's when you guessed where we were?"

"It seemed like a good bet. I figured whatever was going on with Snyder had something to do with Dr. Lowe and the secret passage."

Sig sat next to Cleo, his arm around her shoulders. "My wife is not just a pretty face, you know. My little Italian macaroon is one smart cookie." He shook a finger at me. "But I'm putting my foot down. No more of this crime solving business with you. It took five years to get her down the aisle. Now that I've got her, I want to keep her."

BUCK SAWYER'S WIFE and I sat together Sunday afternoon exchanging small talk in the waiting area of Timbergate Municipal Airport. Delta Sawyer kept up a running dialogue about redecorating their mansion on a hill west of Timbergate. I was too tired and sleep-deprived to do more than nod approvingly and pretend to know the difference between a finial and a mullion. But I was a librarian, so when I found time, I would be compelled to look them up.

Nick finally touched down with his three passengers. Buck and Delta went on their way, while the rest of us headed for Harry's condo. I filled Harry, Nick, and Rella in on everything they'd missed, but a lot of questions went unanswered because it was too soon to know how the police would sort it all out.

FORTY

QUINN HAD INSISTED I take a couple of weeks off, so I did a lot of sleeping in and reading at first. That was the week that Rella's escrow closed and she moved out of Nick's apartment. It was also the week that work started on remodeling of my apartment over the barn.

Jack and Amah had talked to Harry about expanding the space, and he had agreed it could be done. With his fine architect's eye, he had figured out how to use the existing deck on two sides of the apartment as the space for the expansion. By the end of the second week of my vacation, my little home had grown from a studio to a fairly spacious two-bedroom apartment.

During the remodel I had been camping out in Amah's guest room, so on the second weekend, Nick helped me move back into my barn-top home. We spent most of the weekend together, rearranging furniture and painting walls and ceilings.

By Sunday afternoon we were tired, but happy with the outcome of our paint job and maybe a tiny bit high on fumes. While we sat discussing whether to eat in or go out, my cell phone rang. *Cleo.* She never called on weekends. I had to answer.

"What's up?"

"I just heard from Jared Quinn. Thought you'd want to know the latest on the Korba situation."

"Of course. I can't stop thinking about Natasha and

the text she left for Hector on that awful night in Quinn's office. It nearly broke my heart."

"Mine, too, but I'll get to that. First, it appears Korba and Sybil Snyder finally got their stories straight. His version was closer to the truth than hers. She finally admitted that she pulled the trigger, but they both swear that Lowe was trying to kill Hector. Hector's skin cells were found under Lowe's fingernails during the autopsy, but the police didn't have DNA to make a match until you gave them Korba's clarinet reed that you found in the greenroom. That helped support Hector's claim that Lowe was trying to strangle him. The police took a sample from Korba, and got a match they could legally use."

I recalled Dr. Droz consulting with Korba about the outbreak of cellulitis on his neck, and how often I had seen Korba rubbing his neck in what I thought was an unconscious reflex.

"I've been wondering if either of them were arrested for killing Gavin Lowe."

"Not yet, but that case is far from over. In the meantime, Snyder is suspended from the medical staff, and Korba has resigned from the board." Cleo was quiet for a moment, then continued, "I'm still puzzled about Gavin Lowe's violent outbursts. They were so out of character for the man I thought I knew."

"I might be able to shed some light on that," I said. "Rita Lowe and I met for lunch last week and had an interesting talk. It seems Lowe had been showing signs of a personality change for quite a while. She suggested he see someone about it. He did, reluctantly, and was diagnosed with intermittent explosive disorder."

"That's a real diagnosis? Don't we all have a tendency to blow our tops on occasion?"

"Most of us let off steam once in a while, but this condition is more severe. I found it on the Mayo Clinic website, and it fits Lowe perfectly. It describes people who react grossly out of proportion to situations."

"Sort of a grownup version of a temper tantrum?"

"More serious than that. Think of things like road rage and domestic abuse. Behaviors that cause bodily injury or property damage. Lowe's attack on Quinn during the committee meeting would definitely qualify."

"Did Rita say what brought it on?" Cleo asked.

"No, and I didn't feel I should push her for details. I did some research that indicates it can be biological, emotional, or psychological. Or maybe a combination. Apparently Lowe hadn't been in therapy long enough to get to the bottom of his root causes."

"How's Rita doing? She's been through a lot these past weeks."

"She sounded as good as could be expected. She said she's relieved to finally know what happened to her husband. She's been under a lot of stress for a long time because of his infidelity, then his explosive disorder outbursts became more frequent and violent. I imagine she'll eventually find some peace after she's grieved and accepted her loss."

"I hope you're right. She deserves it."

I asked Cleo about Jared Quinn. "Have you heard whether he's been cleared?"

"Looks like it. He sounded like his old self tonight on the phone."

"What about Hector Korba siccing that purse snatcher on me? And holding Snyder and me against our will that night in Lowe's office?"

"Quinn says Korba will definitely put in some jail time for that, even if he's cleared of a murder charge."

"I hope he's out of all of our lives for a long time," I said, a catch in my voice. "Especially Melissa's. She finally has an opportunity to build a new life for herself and Natasha."

"It's looking good for Melissa. Her lawyer has petitioned for sole legal and physical custody. And the best part is that Korba has set up a trust for them, now that Abel Gailworth is out of the picture."

"It's good to hear that the man still cares for what's left of his family. Maybe there's hope for their future. And it's good to hear from you. I'll be happy to get back to work tomorrow."

"I'm looking forward to it, too. It's been a dull two weeks without you, but don't tell Sig I said so."

I filled Nick in while we sat on my new couch eating Chinese take-out and watching an episode of *Dr. Who*. When we finished our dinner, Nick paused the TV.

"What do you suppose prompted your grandparents to do the remodel?"

"I don't know, but I'm going to be pretty happy with all the extra space. They claim it's a good investment. The truth is, they like having me nearby. Now that they see us back together, they might be worried I'll be moving out."

"So they remodeled as an incentive to keep you here?"

"Maybe," I said. "What do you think?"

"You might be right. Your place is nicer than my apartment, now. I wouldn't blame you if you wanted to stay."

"It's not just that. I feel like they need me. They've done so much for me, I want to be here for them as long as I can."

Nick reached for my hand. "Aimee, I want you to be here for me, too, for as long as you can. You must know how much I want you back in my life."

"And I want you in mine." I took a breath and said what was on my mind. "You know, there's plenty of room here, if you don't mind nodding off to the howling of coyotes and waking up to the gobbling of turkeys."

"I like the sound of that." He draped an arm around my shoulders and we sat back to watch the rest of our *Dr. Who* episode. When it ended, Nick turned off the TV. "Do you think any of the doctors at TMC has a TARDIS I could borrow?"

I laughed. "Since Dr. Who doesn't work there, probably not. Why?"

"A vehicle that moves around in time and space looks like more fun than the planes in Buck's fleet." Nick rubbed his knuckles along my cheek. "I wouldn't mind going back in time."

"Why go back? Wouldn't the future be more interesting?"

"It might, but first, I'd like to go back and redo that bungled night in Paris. With a few minor changes in how it unfolded, we wouldn't have lost six months together."

"Not a good idea. I wouldn't want to change anything that's happened between us. It turns out I had a lot to learn."

"About Rella and me?"

"No. About myself."

"Care to explain?"

I stood up and took his hand. "I'd rather show you."
"What about your knee?"
"It's feeling much better."

* * * * *

ABOUT THE AUTHOR

SHARON ST. GEORGE had the good fortune to spend an idyllic childhood in a small Northern California town, riding horseback and camping with her family in the nearby mountains. One of her favorite pastimes was reading fiction, and a trip to the library was always an occasion of great joy. She's traded horses for llamas, but she still treks to the high mountain lakes near her home—always with a mystery novel in her backpack.

Sharon's writing credits include three plays, several years writing advertising copy, a book on NASA's space food project, and feature stories too numerous to count. She holds dual degrees in English and Theatre Arts, and occasionally acts in, or directs, one of her local community theater productions. *Breach of Ethics* is her third novel and the third book in the Aimee Machado mystery series, which began with *Due for Discard* and continued with *Checked Out*. Book 4, *Spine Damage*, was released in 2017.

Sharon is a member of Sisters in Crime and Mystery Writers of America, and she serves as program director for Writers Forum, a nonprofit organization for writers in Northern California.

For more information, go to www.sharonstgeorge.com.

Get 4 FREE REWARDS!

We'll send you 2 FREE Books
plus 2 FREE Mystery Gifts.

Harlequin Intrigue® books feature heroes and heroines that confront and survive danger while finding themselves irresistibly drawn to one another.

FREE
Value Over
$20

YES! Please send me 2 FREE Harlequin Intrigue® novels and my 2 FREE gifts (gifts are worth about $10 retail). After receiving them, if I don't wish to receive any more books, I can return the shipping statement marked "cancel." If I don't cancel, I will receive 6 brand-new novels every month and be billed just $4.99 each for the regular-print edition or $5.74 each for the larger-print edition in the U.S., or $5.74 each for the regular-print edition or $6.49 each for the larger-print edition in Canada. That's a savings of at least 12% off the cover price! It's quite a bargain! Shipping and handling is just 50¢ per book in the U.S. and 75¢ per book in Canada.* I understand that accepting the 2 free books and gifts places me under no obligation to buy anything. I can always return a shipment and cancel at any time. The free books and gifts are mine to keep no matter what I decide.

Choose one: ☐ **Harlequin Intrigue®**   ☐ **Harlequin Intrigue®**
　　　　　　　Regular-Print　　　　　　　　Larger-Print
　　　　　　　(182/382 HDN GMYW)　　　　(199/399 HDN GMYW)

Name (please print)

Address　　　　　　　　　　　　　　　　　　　　　　　　　　　　Apt. #

City　　　　　　　　　　State/Province　　　　　　　　　Zip/Postal Code

Mail to the **Reader Service:**
IN U.S.A.: P.O. Box 1341, Buffalo, NY 14240-8531
IN CANADA: P.O. Box 603, Fort Erie, Ontario L2A 5X3

Want to try 2 free books from another series? Call 1-800-873-8635 or visit www.ReaderService.com.

---

*Terms and prices subject to change without notice. Prices do not include sales taxes, which will be charged (if applicable) based on your state or country of residence. Canadian residents will be charged applicable taxes. Offer not valid in Quebec. This offer is limited to one order per household. Books received may not be as shown. Not valid for current subscribers to Harlequin Intrigue books. All orders subject to approval. Credit or debit balances in a customer's account(s) may be offset by any other outstanding balance owed by or to the customer. Please allow 4 to 6 weeks for delivery. Offer available while quantities last.

Your Privacy—The Reader Service is committed to protecting your privacy. Our Privacy Policy is available online at www.ReaderService.com or upon request from the Reader Service. We make a portion of our mailing list available to reputable third parties that offer products we believe may interest you. If you prefer that we not exchange your name with third parties, or if you wish to clarify or modify your communication preferences, please visit us at www.ReaderService.com/consumerschoice or write to us at Reader Service Preference Service, P.O. Box 9062, Buffalo, NY 14240-9062. Include your complete name and address.

HI19R

Get 4 FREE REWARDS!

We'll send you 2 FREE Books <u>plus</u> 2 FREE Mystery Gifts.

FREE Value Over **$20**

Both the **Romance** and **Suspense** collections feature compelling novels written by many of today's best-selling authors.

YES! Please send me 2 FREE novels from the Essential Romance or Essential Suspense Collection and my 2 FREE gifts (gifts are worth about $10 retail). After receiving them, if I don't wish to receive any more books, I can return the shipping statement marked "cancel." If I don't cancel, I will receive 4 brand-new novels every month and be billed just $6.74 each in the U.S. or $7.24 each in Canada. That's a savings of at least 16% off the cover price. It's quite a bargain! Shipping and handling is just 50¢ per book in the U.S. or 75¢ per book in Canada.* I understand that accepting the 2 free books and gifts places me under no obligation to buy anything. I can always return a shipment and cancel at any time. The free books and gifts are mine to keep no matter what I decide.

Choose one: ☐ **Essential Romance** ☐ **Essential Suspense**
              (194/394 MDN GMY7) (191/391 MDN GMY7)

Name (please print)

Address   Apt. #

City   State/Province   Zip/Postal Code

> **Mail to the Reader Service:**
> **IN U.S.A.:** P.O. Box 1341, Buffalo, NY 14240-8531
> **IN CANADA:** P.O. Box 603, Fort Erie, Ontario L2A 5X3

Want to try 2 free books from another series? Call 1-800-873-8635 or visit www.ReaderService.com.

*Terms and prices subject to change without notice. Prices do not include applicable taxes. Sales tax applicable in NY. Canadian residents will be charged applicable taxes. Offer not valid in Quebec. This offer is limited to one order per household. Books received may not be as shown. Not valid for current subscribers to the Essential Romance or Essential Suspense Collection. All orders subject to approval. Credit or debit balances in a customer's account(s) may be offset by any other outstanding balance owed by or to the customer. Please allow 4 to 6 weeks for delivery. Offer available while quantities last.

Your Privacy—The Reader Service is committed to protecting your privacy. Our Privacy Policy is available online at www.ReaderService.com or upon request from the Reader Service. We make a portion of our mailing list available to reputable third parties that offer products we believe may interest you. If you prefer that we not exchange your name with third parties, or if you wish to clarify or modify your communication preferences, please visit us at www.ReaderService.com/consumerschoice or write to us at Reader Service Preference Service, P.O. Box 9062, Buffalo, NY 14240-9062. Include your complete name and address.

STRS19

Get 4 FREE REWARDS!

We'll send you 2 FREE Books plus 2 FREE Mystery Gifts.

Love Inspired® Suspense books feature Christian characters facing challenges to their faith... and lives.

FREE
Value Over
$20